EMPIRE OF

GLASS

EMPIRE OF GLASS

A NOVEL

KAITLIN SOLIMINE

PUBLISHING

NEW YORK, NY

Printed in the United States
First Edition
10 9 8 7 6 5 4 3 2 1

Ig Publishing
Box 2547
New York, NY 10163
www.igpub.com

ISBN: 978-1-63246-055-4

*"Follow me. Don't follow me. I will
say such things, and mean both."*
—Steven Dunn, "Before We Leave"

"I call you a 'dream.' I am also a dream."
—Chuang Tzu

Translator's Note

You never enter Beijing the same way twice. For centuries this was a hidden, forbidden empire: nine gates through which to pass, each with a melliferous name (*Gate of Peace, Gate of Security, Gate Facing the Sun*), each moat, wall, guard tower knocked down then rebuilt. First the Mongols, the Manchus, then the Boxers and Brits. So many defenses needed to protect the Peaceful Capital that eventually it was renamed Northern Capital—Beijing— for fear of instilling a false sense of quiet.

In the twenty years I've lived here, I witnessed hutong alleyways paved over by four-lane highways, a landscape of construction cranes pocking the horizon with hungry, steel arms; my old neighborhood with its elderly inhabitants, once accustomed to shared squat toilets and courtyard kitchen fires, shipped to the suburbs to make way for a Holiday Inn and an office tower with iridescent windows reflecting an endlessly gray, heavy sky.

The world feels drenched in that same impenetrable gray as my taxicab from Beijing international airport reaches suburban Huairou Cemetery. The city around us begs for rain. Along the dirt alleyway to the cemetery gates, a pack of street dogs lazi- ly rise, sniffing their tails. A pair of eyes faces our approaching headlights, briefly golden, briefly human. *Hello, old friend*, I want to say, only I haven't met this dog before. There's just the feeling of having known him for quite some time.

Not far from Huairou Cemetery, the Gobi hovers, China's "endless sea" of golden sand dunes and failed reforestation: parched, exposed roots and nomadic tribes now cemented to rows of apartment blocks buttressing northern winds. In spring, these winds roll south, roiling the capital's streets, clogging alleyways with dust, narrowing eyes of bicyclists who tongue grains from their teeth, cursing the season's turn. In April, snow arrives: fallen catkin blossoms drifting to earth in a city overpopulated with poplars and willows, too many females of the species lending seeds, expectations unmet. And in late May, I land in the city, temperatures climbing past thirty centigrade, old men in tank tops on wooden benches fanning sagging breasts, the sky a dome of heat and haze, encapsulating one of the world's largest cities, once my favorite in the world.

In my pocket, Baba's missive from two weeks earlier pulses digital blue:

Come home for Mama's twentieth memorial.

The first and last text message he ever sent.

I'd replied in Mandarin: *You have a mobile phone? :-)*

He didn't answer. He never understood messaging to be a two-way conversation.

Beyond the gate announcing the cemetery's Peaceful Garden, parched willows rake thin soil. A concrete wall guards the dead inside: stone steles and a mausoleum for the poorer souls in sealed boxes. Ashes rise from a crematorium to a nondescript sky, quickly lost. I want to tip my head upwards to swallow it all, disappear.

"Menglian!" someone calls from behind the gates as I hand the driver my fare. The stranger uses my Chinese name, the one I give to acquaintances and write on China's never-ending bureaucratic forms. Baba named me Menglian during my earliest days living with his family, the Wangs: Menglian, or 'Dream of the Lotus,' similar to the Chinese name for Marilyn—as in Monroe. *I'm not blonde*, I said, but Baba laughed and said, "All Americans are blonde." Only later did he call me "Lao K" after his wife, Li-Ming, decided this was appropriate—"Old K," the girl named "K" who keeps returning—because it was expected from my teenage years onward I'd always return from my hometown in coastal

Maine to this city, one of the world's most populated, and to the strange Chinese family who first hosted me here.

"Menglian!" the voice repeats.

Rounding the corner, I see a woman wearing silver-rimmed glasses and waving a red glove. She looks vaguely familiar—a scent you pass on the street yielding a feeling but not a name.

"Nice to see you again, Menglian!" Her short hair, the same as Li-Ming's in her last days, is not a style befitting older women yet she and her friends sport the hairdo like it's required for Party pension. She's tall and thin to Li-Ming's short and squat. Her oblong face is mottled with sunspots. She squeezes my shoulder, inferring we once shared something deep and lasting. I can't pull the woman's name from my jetlagged memory; in her dying days, Li-Ming had so many friends, cheery-faced women drifting in and out of the apartment like ants attempting, unsuccessfully, to transport a rotting piece of fruit.

The woman introduces me to a laughing, happy crew of women. They wear blunt, dowdy heels dusty from the walk from bus station to cemetery, long skirts glancing socked ankles, bright colored cardigans (peacock, seafoam, lavender) buttoned to their necks, hair the requisite crop.

"This is Li Xiahua," she says, pulling me to a tall, pretty lady with plum-lined eyes.

"And Pang Huayang." Pang: stout with a humped back, dyed black hair, an elbow-shaped chin; someone you know your entire life and only in middle age realize is your best friend.

"Of course you know Mama's oldest friend, Kang-Lin." I'm led to a woman with large breasts peeking beneath a tight, too-sheer aqua blouse. The only name I've remembered from those early days is Kang-Lin's—and her face, from photographs—the uncharacteristic freckles dotting her cheeks and nose, the round, rimless glasses guarding a pair of well-kohled eyes. Kang-Lin was Li-Ming's friend decades earlier, a girl Li-Ming referred to as the "owner of the books"—it was Kang-Lin who gave Li-Ming her beloved Cold Mountain poetry when they were young. Li-Ming never spoke of what had happened to Kang-Lin, but the woman's re-appearance seems something of a celebration. After Li-Ming's death Kang-Lin sent my Chinese host mother's sarira to me in Maine—the Buddhist crystals that form in the cremated remains of only the most devout. Cold Mountain himself left behind sarira. Li-Ming did too, or so I hoped the afternoon Kang-Lin's package arrived, the envelope's gritty contents entrenching my finger as it dug deeper, as I wondered how a body so fleshy could turn granular and coarse.

"Nice to finally meet you, Kang-Lin," I say. She takes my hands in hers, priest-like. The chimney in the distance spews smoke—ashes of a body expired?

Baba, usually on time to pre-arranged meetings, isn't here to explain Kang-Lin's return; his tardiness feels like the hollow of an unrung bell. *Where is he?*

"Your Baba will be here soon," Kang-Lin says, insinuating she and Baba have recently been in touch.

The plain-faced woman perks up, waves into the distance. "There he is! There's Wang Guanmiao!"

I follow her finger's point as Kang-Lin also turns, dropping my hand. Crows bobbing between trash piles on the path to the cemetery look up too, staring down the road to where the sub-urbs hum and chatter, preoccupied with their forward-looking progress.

Ba, the crows bleat.

Ba, my heart beats.

Ba. Ba. Ba.

I once read crows have the ability to remember a face they saw years earlier. Are these the same crows Baba passes on his an-nual pilgrimage to his wife's grave? Do they recognize him? His hair, what's left of it, parted? His body in the Western-style suit I bought him five years earlier (he'd giggled when the tailor traced his armpits; I'd reveled in this childishness, my generosity)? His feet are crammed into loafers his daughter Xiaofei brought from Hong Kong, recently spiffed and shined. When dressed smartly, he looks like a boy in man's clothing, never quite grown into the adult he became. He strides, oblivious to the pines above his head, the curious crows bowing in unison. He waves. And waves... It's taking him too long to reach us.

"Yes! We're here!" We say.

Waiting. Waiting and waving.

Time takes on a curious rounded feel like the edge of an old coin.

Finally he places a hand on my arm. With the other, he pats down what remains of his hair. He's an injured bird attempting to fly: all heart, no hop.

"Here," he says, reaching that same hand into his knapsack and extending a book for us to see. "She told me you were looking for this."

He hands me a book wrapped in a tattered pink pashmina (the same pashmina I left in his apartment during my Beijing University year) and I don't need to unwrap the package to know—Li-Ming's Cold Mountain poems, the collection of eighth century Taoist-Buddhist poetry she wanted to read me during the last weeks of her life and yet we always found ourselves speaking of other things, distracted by a life waning into its final form—

What makes a young man grieve
He grieves to see his hair turn white...

"Now that we're all here, shall we go?" The short-haired woman gestures at the burial grounds hidden behind lazy willows.

"Quick, quick," Baba says, leaning so close I smell his lunch—garlicked and soyed—on old man's breath. He whispers, "Did she visit you today too?"

Before I can reply I haven't heard Li-Ming's voice in years, he forces a smile—stained teeth, suntanned cheeks, cracked lips—evidence of a life lived in this thirsty city. He grips my elbow as we follow Kang-Lin's knowing sashay, the woman's slender hips hidden beneath folds of a long, black skirt, heels clicking a consistent beat, all of us entering this walled city of bones together.

Confident there will be time for reading later, I tuck the book into my purse, its weight slapping my side, Beijing's sun shouldering the last touch of dusk.

*

But the book isn't what I thought. I learn this a few hours after I return to Baba's apartment in Deshengmen, the six-story building with brown walls scarred by Beijing's arid seasons, trash chutes with chunks of hardened zhou, dusty bikes rusting in entranceways, abandoned a decade earlier for Xiali sedans that crowd the courtyard.

"Where are Li-Ming's Cold Mountain poems?" I hold up the book to Baba's face, peel open the pages that aren't full of the ancient poems I hoped but of Li-Ming's scrawl—a journal or notebook. At the kitchen table in the living room where Baba sleeps nightly on a futon, he leans over a warmed bowl of soy milk from breakfast; in this apartment, no meal is too old to reheat, no room holds a single purpose. This is the China of old.

"That's the book," he says, nonchalant as a cat.

"No, Li-Ming had a book of Cold Mountain poems. She said one day it would be mine."

I hold open the spine of the Cold Mountain poetry book whose pages are bizarrely absent, ripped out and discarded, replaced by a blue-lined bijiben notebook—the kind Chinese high school students use for character study. Contained inside are rows of tight, careful calligraphy, penmanship I recognize as Li-Ming's. On the outer cover, a new title, "Empire of Glass," is repeatedly scrawled over the smiling hermit face of Cold Mountain—*EmpireofGlassEmpireofGlassEmpireofGlass*—like a schoolgirl obsessively penning her beloved's name.

"It has to be here somewhere," I say, ducking below the bed.

I want the poems she promised she'd leave me. I want to read the notes she wrote in the margins, the criticisms she said would one day make sense, the book I couldn't find after her death no matter how much I searched the apartment shelves full of Xiaofei's tattered textbooks and mothballed baby clothing.

"Don't bother," Baba says. "This is all that's left."

*

I first met *Empire of Glass*'s author, Huang Li-Ming, twenty years ago when I was sixteen and she was forty-four. I was an American high school exchange student living with her family in a cluttered apartment in the center of Beijing during an auspicious year according to Chinese superstitions, my 16th (16: one followed by six, 一六 also means "will go smoothly"), and a terribly inauspicious year for her, her 44th (the number four, 四, a homophone for the Chinese word for death). Beijing wasn't as gray then—yes, the populace wore tans, olives, and navies, and Tiananmen's bloody stains were only recently painted over, but there was an energy to the wide boulevards filled with bicyclists and yam vendors and smells you hated at first then yearned for decades later when they were replaced by car exhaust and factory run-off from the suburbs. That energy was humanity. Life. Limbs and elbows spurring rusted bikes to the most exciting of newly-formed ventures (black market currency exchanges outside China Construction Bank, stolen factory Patagonia fleeces in Silk Market alleyways, or hamburgers—and free ketchup!—at McDonalds).

There was no better time to be an American teenager in Beijing, bicycling wide willow-lined avenues, getting lost in endless mazes of hutong alleyways still clustered around the city's heart. When my Mandarin was advanced enough to hold a lengthy conversation, Li-Ming invited me to sit with her on the sundeck after school for what she called her "poetry lessons." We never actually talked about poetry.

"Do you remember the days you couldn't tell the difference between a baozi and jiaozi?" she once asked, then launched into a diatribe about the tastiest red bean baozi she discovered in a Tianjin back alley. "Like the Buddha's touch: the baozi was that good." She ran her tongue along the memory of sweet paste clinging to her gums.

Another afternoon: "Did you know there's a particle of physics so small it controls all the energy in the universe?" At the most cellular level as well as the most expansive, she said, science's knowledge breaks down. "Big and small, equally unknown." She peeled apart the fingers of Baba's beloved ficus plants, oblivious to her destruction.

"Fools," Baba called us every afternoon he returned home from his danwei where he grinded glass for telescopic lenses, carrying bags of wilting lettuce and flaccid carrots from WuMart and smelling like metal—cold and distant. 神经病.

"Did you know there's a hill in the center of the city so cursed only the bravest go there to die?" This she asked me the afternoon she also told me about the cancer crawling from her breasts to her brain. The same afternoon she told me about her plans on Coal Hill—how I'd help her get there in a few months' time. How everything would be different once we reached the mountain's crest, once we read the poems together, able to see everything and nothing.

Our minds are not the same
If they were the same
You would be here?

During each session, the book of Cold Mountain poetry sat on her lap, opened to a page she'd occasionally glimpse, running her fingers over the lines as if they had a shape, but never reading them aloud. She took comfort in the fact I sat with her, and I sat there because I took comfort in the fact she sat with me. Not until much later did I realize the greatest friendships are those with whom we have the easiest ability to sit still together, the people in our lives who don't question our intentions or why we find ourselves side-by-side on lazy Beijing afternoons with dust caught like a yawn between the sun's fingers, ficuses scratching our backs, pages open on laps lit so white by the final burst of light, we can't read the lines.

Li-Ming was impetuous, stubborn, fanciful, and at times, adrift as a spring aspen seed. Her daughter sought in her a distant, loving approval, and her husband, or so I thought at the time, saw her as a companion, that person you forget to question after so many years, a presence critical to your life, but never illuminated as such. Not until I read Li-Ming's book would the world of that year flip on its head, my involvement in her final days proving I was just one last spoke in a wheel rolling for a long time; despite how much I desired to be the central hub, for Li-Ming, the world was not so carefully defined—was she mentally unstable? A genius? A spiritual scribe? Who was she? I now wonder, lifting my pen from the page and glimpsing a city so full of silver skyscrapers the sky has been made irrelevant....

Had I known of *Empire of Glass*'s existence, I may never have returned to China after Li-Ming's death. I may have been too disillusioned to believe China could retain something of the old in the new, that the woman I knew may be there yet, waiting at the top of Coal Hill for me to join her beneath that sickly Scholar Tree, to hand her an ending, close the loop. But I'll explain more of that later.

For most of its existence, *Empire of Glass* was hidden beneath the living room's futon, discovered by Baba when sweeping away decades of dust. Had he still believed in poetry, still heard the beat of his own poetic heart, he may have studied the pages longer— but he merely kicked it under the bed the way he'd nudge a stray Deshengmen cat out of his path. Not until the days drew nearer to his wife's memorial, when his daughter moved to Hong Kong and I settled in the U.S., did he feel the oppressive loneliness that comes with age, with living too long in one place, the corners of his apartment edging closer, such that eventually he knelt on the concrete, dug deep beneath that futon he once shared with his wife, and cursed the heavens for smacking his head on the wooden frame. "Here you are, old friend," he said, rubbing the sore bump, but then again, so much of what I'm telling you is already reimagined, reconfigured so convex angles are made concave, mirrors reflecting other mirrors reflecting an uncertain, setting sun.

The ethical challenge of translating *Empire of Glass* is not lost on me: this strange, hodgepodge book was Li-Ming's last gift to me and my implication in its narrative makes me an unusual, if suspect, translator. Yet I expect this was carefully orchestrated—Li-Ming would've known of my return for her memorial, the agony on the stray dog's eyes, the lichen climbing the cemetery's front wall. She expected me to understand her language as well I could, and to one day provide this translation, which has become her last work, this novel. Li-Ming's *Empire of Glass* reflects the desires of poet Stephen Dunn: "Every day, if I could, I'd oppose history by altering one detail." Li-Ming took this directive one step further, altering enough of her life's details to completely rewrite the world we expected her to leave us.

For Li-Ming, the world we see with our eyes or touch with our fingers is but one dimension. There's another perspective, one read between letters and shuffled barefoot over the cold dirt of mountain caves while tempered pines shake off spring snow. And this is where we find a circular, ever-coiling link between beginning and end, that and this, other and self, form and formlessness that is the subject of Taoism, Buddhism, and of course, we'd be remiss not to mention here, Li-Ming's beloved Tang Dynasty poet, Han Shan—or "Cold Mountain."

If young men grieve growing old, what do old men grieve?

Li-Ming would've rewritten Cold Mountain's verse to assert that old men—and women!—grieve the beginning. Which is why in the end she returned to hers. And although we carried her there on her backs, the load is much lighter now.

"Lao K"
Beijing, China
2016

Empire of Glass

Kang-Lin

Autumn in Beijing falls like a knife slicing a pig ear—indecisively slippery. Still warm enough to wear skirts, but growing colder, threatening a long winter. That was the day I first heard his name: "Han Shan"—Cold Mountain. He was a person but also a place, a long shadow stretching across a valley, yellow rock faces the shape of bald men's foreheads. Something larger than you could measure with a bamboo meter-stick or an unspooled ball of yarn. How could a man be a mountain? How could a poet leave no trace except words? I was twelve. We were hunched together, shaking off the impending cold in the Nationalist-era Academy of Sciences with its brick walls and cavernous hallways, in a laboratory hovering over microscopes and examining the cells from a scrape of our cheek's inner skin. The class outing that day was meant to be the most exciting event of our early lives and, although leaving school for the afternoon was something few were permitted, we weren't convinced. Our classmate, Jiangwen, with his characteristic dullness, picked his nose in the back corner, incapable of examining anything more than his snot.

We were a strange crew of children, sons and daughters of military cadres and closer than anyone could be—revolution did that—but to us, we cared only whose tin lunch cup was shiniest, who could recite Mao's verse with the loudest, most sycophantic voice. *Simple pleasures, simple minds*, my mother would say, and although I didn't understand the chengyu's exact meaning, I knew this was an insult. She only used chengyu to embarrass or deride.

"Look!" My best friend Kang-Lin pinched my arm, causing me to lift my eye off the lens, momentarily blinded by the immensity of the world around us. She pushed my head onto her microscope.

Look: Kang-Lin's cells were beautifully alive, kaleidoscopic. Mine simply rested on the slide, dead and dull, as if never animate to begin with.

"They're beautiful," I admitted. This didn't surprise me. Everything about Kang-Lin sparkled. That's why we loved her.

"Can I see yours?" Kang-Lin asked, expecting my cells would be equally wondrous.

"I think there's something wrong with my eyepiece."

Kang-Lin pushed me aside, leaning over and straining to take a look.

"What's wrong, Li-Ming?" Teacher Liang interrupted from the front of the room. She had a white, moon-shaped face and hated my mother so made me feel second-rate by assigning me additional after-school cleanup duties or grading my tests extra harshly. I couldn't admit to Teacher Liang my cells looked less than vivacious, especially when compared to Kang-Lin's. This would only prove I was indeed the offspring of once-Nationalist scum, no matter how much my mother insisted she'd merely signed her name to the Nanjing Nationalist Youth League because her teacher threatened her with a beating if she didn't. Whenever I told Teacher Liang my mother's excuse, she said, "I could've taken the lashes of ten thousand whips before joining the loathsome enemy."

Her heels snipped the concrete as she approached. Everything in the building echoed and moaned, alive and yet on the verge of death, much like our city. Teacher Liang stood over me, her shadow dampening my spirit, even at the cellular level.

"I think I'm dead inside," I said. This was the truth.

Teacher Liang laughed. "Did you hear that class? Li-Ming thinks she's dead inside." She leaned over and her lily perfume failed to mask the fact she hadn't been to the communal showers in a week. As I held my breath, she lifted me by my shoulder, but

I was too heavy so my arms lay flack, feet firmly planted. Never had I been so good at staying put.

"Lift your arms," she nudged.

I relented, raising my arms above my head but when I did, my jacket buckled at my neck, pinching my spine.

"Now make a starburst with your palms."

I followed her instructions even though my jaw clenched, my teeth ached to bite her hand.

"You're moving, so you're alive," she said, smugly proving her point. Still holding my jacket and pinching my neck, she peered over the class's heads, chin pointed in defiant superiority, so many faces looking expectantly for guidance, faces and names I've forgotten even though we were everything to one another then, calling one another "Comrade" and believing together we'd prove the Motherland's might to the world. Little did we know how quickly and eagerly we'd turn against each other, like the wild dogs in Han Shan's poem who fight to the death over the rarest of bones.[1]

"Not everything that moves is alive and vice-versa. Cold Mountain says 'contemplate the void: this world exceeds stillness.'" Kang-Lin piped in.

"Your frivolous words have no place in protest," Teacher Liang dropped her grip and I felt gravity like a bed springing to catch me from a bad dream.

"My words do too have meaning," Kang-Lin insisted but Teacher Liang ignored her, reserving her hatred for the children of class scum like me. Kang-Lin's parents' roles in the Party

---

[1.] Here, Li-Ming is likely referring to this Han Shan poem (as translated by Red Pine):

> "I see hundreds of dogs
> and every one of them scruffy
> lying wherever they please
> rambling whenever the whim arises
> but throw them out a bone
> and watch them growl and fight
> as long as bones are rare
> a pack of dogs can't share"

protected her from Teacher Liang's scorn even though we all knew she was restraining herself from slapping Kang-Lin's dewy cheeks like our physics Professor Shi would to Fat Meng, the chubby boy in Form Five who always ran off with more than his student ration of lunch (an extra mantou, an ear of corn, bowl of tofu curd—all stuffed into the waist of his oversized pants, the curd dripping down his legs in slimy trails visible through the cotton fabric).

Teacher Liang returned to the chalkboard, apparently victorious.

Kang-Lin was unperturbed. As the class quieted and Teacher Liang twirled chalk between her fingers readying for the next lesson, my friend casually wiped her glass slides on the lapel of her checkered cotton shirt. I pictured her cells like squished jellyfish writhing between the plates. Her cells could not die, would always be dancing and bright. And she would always come to my rescue, my dearest friend Kang-Lin, for reasons I couldn't yet understand. Would I ever? What had I done to deserve her affection and protection?

We'd met when we were seven, both of us fascinated by the fishermen sitting on the moat encircling the Forbidden City every afternoon, how their bait squirmed beneath the murky surface, how only after many hours the line would jig, a fish reeled in on the hand-spooled rig, the fishermen smiling, triumphant as cats.[2] Such a small coup, but we loved playing witness. Loved watching the fishermen snap the fish heads in one terse twist, deboning the bodies on a cloth laid out for this purpose, pink-gray flesh and tiny bones stilled and silenced in such a quick, careless gesture. That's how I fell in love with Kang-Lin, if love is indeed the word. But that's how it always happens, doesn't it? We love a person because they love what we love, see the world how

---

[2] Did Li-Ming know fishing was seen as a political act in ancient China, the protest of an existing regime accomplished by the lazy, contemplative act of waiting on a rod to jig? Too late to ask; we must draw our own conclusions.

we see it. Then we're side-by-side for some time. Long enough to worry maybe we don't see the world the same way at all. But that's a part of the story I'll get to later. For now, suffice it to say, by the time I leave this world, Kang-Lin will have traveled to Rome, Paris, Istanbul, New York, Tokyo, Singapore, Berlin, and Nairobi. She'll know a universe outside China. Kang-Lin is fated for great things. She'll crumple many lovers with the strength of her thighs and fists, tossing their love notes into wastebaskets.

Me? I was a black-hearted girl, daughter of a black-hearted woman. I didn't yet know: We inherit the deaths created for us long before. Two months, the doctors pronounced, and inside my stomach, the sound of a sheep bleating over a long, shrewd sunset echoed between my bowels. Cancer is a fickle beast. Of course I would die first. Every story always finds its rightful ending—mine, yours, no different. The ending's always ugly. It's the beginning we cling to, for obvious reasons. Which is why I started this with the beginning. "Time can conquer all," I once read; someone famous must have written it. Time. If only we could comprehend time in a non-linear way, like Cold Mountain and Kang-Lin. This was why her cells pulsed with color and movement, why I was a dead person the moment I was declared "alive."

After Kang-Lin's outburst, I accidentally belched so loudly Teacher Liang dropped her beloved chalk to the ground where it chattered like winter teeth. She muttered something under her breath.

"What's that?" Kang-Lin shouted. The entire class turned to face her, heads tilted like shadow puppets behind the curtain. Where are you now, false friends?

"Kang-Lin, let it be known that Huang Li-Ming, the girl you think is your best friend, is crass as a Capitalist," Teacher Liang referred to me by my given name so that her words grew fangs.

Kang-Ling smiled, proudly exposing wide, straight teeth. On the windowsill beside us, an oblivious magpie rustled its feathers, plucked a fly from an invisible arch in the air, then took to the sky as if flight were a forgone conclusion. Birds: the lucky ones. If I hadn't been trying to distract myself, I never would've noticed the creature. *Form asks shadow where to....*

"Three black marks on your record today, Huang Li-Ming," Teacher Liang announced. "And four for you, Ms. Smart Mouth," she nodded at Kang-Lin who was still smiling as if she knew the secrets of the greatest Taoists ever to climb Tian T'ai. I should've known she'd lead me down paths with no ends. That to seek an ending is to fall into the beginning and start all over again. The circular madness of koans: the sound of one hand clapping.

"Teacher Liang is stupid," Kang-Lin said as we walked home that evening. She stopped, turned to face me. The full moon: my friend's head silkworm silver. "Don't let her make you stupid too."

I pulled moon strings from Kang-Lin's hair, dropped them into a pile at our feet. Our shadows expanded and contracted, obscuring the moon, hips joined and parting like sea to sand. We could be one, and then we could be separate. I missed her even though she wasn't yet gone. I thought: How is it always the case we remain stuck in moments we know are fleeting, imper-manent? Or maybe I'm thinking this now and remembering it such: We were already best friends for five years. We didn't know a tenth of what life would teach us but there was the sense this walk home was a critically important moment, that I was making a memory before I'd experienced enough of my life to understand it. We forget one day we'll turn into the person looking back at this one and think: I miss you.

"Why does Teacher Liang make fun of us?"

"She's jealous," Kang-Lin said, throwing her long hair over her shoulder. I could see why: Kang-Lin was young and beautiful where Teacher Liang was old and ugly.

"How do you do it?" I asked. I meant: how did she stay happy when everything around us was a wall in danger of crumbling? The outer edifices started first, the city wall's bricks chipped with pickaxes, ground into dust that would eventually form the cement undergirding the Second Ring Road with its endless pulse of traffic. By the time the city was like an old sweater to me, before I could intuit the sun cresting hutong alleyways, peering through the last turrets of the inner wall and pinpointing passing bicyclists—by that time, the city walls were being knocked down, large trucks scurrying boulders to outer provinces to prevent the inevitable autumn mudslides, an attempt to roll back the Gobi's lung-clogging spring sandstorms. The city of my childhood, once impervious to outsiders, was inhabited by mustached Mongols from the north, narrow-hipped beauties from Hunan, wide-eyed Uyghurs from the mountainous west. And Soviets with their fur-capped hats and screaming, pink-faced babies. But then the Soviets departed, taking with them the stench of good vodka and bad cologne, and the city huddled together, fearing the battle for which we always steeled ourselves. Our beloved official, Liang Sicheng, lost the city wall's last stand: he believed our city would be better off with greenery rather than concrete highways, but Party officials disagreed—what use was a public park circumnavigating the city when what we really needed was room for an underground metro, coal-burning factories, four-lane highways, and apartment blocks to shield the sun's view? *I'm sorry, Liang Sicheng. I'm sorry you believed in something the rest of us couldn't see. Does that mean that green oasis in the desert is not there still?*

"Making Teacher Liang jealous is simpler than you think," Kang-Lin said as she plucked a fallen catkin blossom from my shoulder. Her bangs fell over her double-fold eyelids and I knew she'd always be beautiful. I would've been jealous if she didn't love me so much; that's how it is with beautiful people.

"Meet me in three nights at midnight on Coal Hill beneath the scholar tree where Emperor Chongzhen hung himself. Don't tell your parents and don't make any noise when you leave the danwei. Bring only yourself and wear pants."

"Why pants?"

"Questions only lead to more questions." She smiled. I knew she was quoting something she'd read somewhere. Propaganda regularly blasted through the neighborhood's speakers; words not ours filtered through our lungs and lips, found their way into conversations where they weren't meant. She sensed my discomfort because she laughed and touched my arm as softly as a bird to the thinnest winter branch.

"Oh, I sound like a real Comrade now, don't I? What I meant was just trust me and meet me there."

"Okay," I assented, looking to our feet where our moon bodies intertwined, the necks of cranes.

"That's funny," Kang-Lin said, nodding at our shadows.

"What?"

"Cranes always visit me when I most need encouragement."

"Then that's a good sign," I said, but my tongue clutched my throat. Before I could ask why Kang-Lin would need encouragement now, what it was that awaited me at Coal Hill, my friend shifted her knapsack over her shoulder and walked to the entryway that was hers: Three. I lived one entryway down in Entry Four on the Fourth Floor. The rooming assignment was a perverse way of my mother's danwei insulting her for her black label, reminding us we'd forever be haunted by so many premonitions of death.

One step up her family's stairwell, Kang-Lin turned.

"See you in class tomorrow," she said. Her face was illuminated by a flickering bulb, cheeks glowing like orbs of moon on Nameless Lake where sad, desperate students drown themselves, and for a moment it felt as if it were already tomorrow and she was speaking of today.

*

The next three days I skipped class. I couldn't return to school to see Teacher Liang. Instead, pretending to go to school in morning then returning home and picking the lock with a hairpin, I made makeshift fishing lines out of safety fasteners and twine then walked to the city moat where I dipped my rig (to which I affixed a few cooked grains of rice) below the surface. A few nibbles but no bites. The final afternoon, bored of the unsuccessful fishing attempts, I found an old hairnet of my mother's and attached the netting to the hands of a tiny doll and threw the doll off the roof to parachute her to earth as if she had wings (the netting flattened; she plummeted like a stone). I walked through Tiananmen, all the way to Houhai where I waded, ankle-deep, in the lake's piney, autumnal waters. Mandarin ducks bobbed wooden-like on the surface. I egged them closer with an open hand but they weren't fooled by my lack of sweets so scurried off quickly, leaving a wake the shape of a valley—or maybe the cleft of a heart.

When I finally met Kang-Lin three nights later at midnight as she requested, beneath the scholar tree on the path up Coal Hill, the city finally felt like a blank landscape onto which I was meant to etch my story. How we managed to crawl out of our shared beds without disturbing our relatives, our footsteps silent down the echoing cement stairwells, doors not slamming behind us, I don't recall. But I'm confident we were there that night, as we'd promised one another.

As I walked up the hill, the moon escaped into a smaller wedge, waning into what would soon be a very black sky. Strange: I didn't think about the fact my parents hadn't returned from their posts in the western provinces, nor that one day they would—and what would I tell them I'd been doing?

Kang-Lin's head was barely visible but I saw her hunched body facing away from me. She was on hands and knees, silky white pajama pants a victory flag—or a flag of surrender? Her hands dug at a mound beneath a seemingly heavy rock. She must've rolled the rock aside because she can be as strong as I choose to remember her. She heaved dark objects from earth to sky, settling them beside her.

"Kang-Lin?"

She turned, hair stuck to her bottom lip. If I hadn't known she was a real human, I might have mistaken her for a ghost girl.

"You came!" She sat on her heels, toes curled, and I could now see books piled at her side. Her ready smile was a channel of light.

"Sit," she said, patting the ground.

Like the monks in Yonghegong, I folded my legs and lay my palms flat on my knees.

"You sit well," she chided.

We were beneath a tree as gnarled as my Third Uncle's hands (he'd thrown a grenade at the Japanese in Manchuria only to find the grenade was a dud and his hand was a stump). The ground beneath us was unstable, full of rocks and roots. In late autumn, dry, bristly grasses, desperate for a spring too far off, rubbed our thighs, an old man's kiss. What was I to do but listen? The fading moon percolated through the withered tree. *Hello, Moon. I see you seeing us.*

"This is the Scholar Tree," I realized aloud.

"You're smart, Li-Ming. That's why I brought you here."

I didn't dare tell Kang-Lin I'd run past the wooden gates of Jingshan Park to force my way to Coal Hill—the only guard was so asleep at his post that when he finally awoke to see the door swinging behind him, he thought he was dreaming so he closed his eyes again to enter the world of the living by falling asleep. I stepped over the raised stone at the park's entrance meant to keep out ghosts—but where did ghosts roam if not within these desolate urban forests?

Kang-Lin didn't care about ghosts. She shut her eyes, mouth pursed as if about to speak but unsure how to begin. Her body could levitate; in an instant, she'd gone from frantically digging into the earth to sitting peaceful and still. Perhaps that was the secret she intended to teach me: how to shape shift like the Taoist immortals who inhabit the clouds, cranes, trees.

"Sisters, we are gathered here today to learn the words of the masters," Kang-Lin started, chin tucked, knees folded beneath her small frame.

I didn't want to inform her we were only two sisters and her talk sounded grandiose, misplaced.

She continued: "We will read your works and memorize your words. We'll become like the letters of nüshu, passing knowledge through us, our pens and lips. We'll be vessels of a deeper knowledge."

In the distance, a gunshot sheared the silence, and although my stomach churned, Kang-Lin didn't open her eyes. I shut my eyes again, awaiting another pealing shot, a common occurrence those days—but nothing arrived. We were certain children living in an uncertain era. In a few months, everyone we knew would ask us to turn against one another, which had the unanticipated effect of bringing many of us closer together.

"I didn't come all this way and risk getting three lashes from my grandfather's belt in order to read. You know I hate homework."

Kang-Lin ignored me, reaching for the pile of books beside her and handing me a particularly heavy tome with a silky cover and flaking spine that opened almost too naturally in my lap.

"This isn't ta-ma-de homework," she said. She always cursed in ways both crass and provocative; I imagined this would make her into a famous poet many years later.

I held the first page to a strand of moonlight the tree couldn't catch. The words were difficult to read in the dark, but from what I could see, it was a book of poetry.

"These are my grandfather's. The one who didn't make it to Taiwan."

She'd already told me years earlier: her grandfather on her father's side was a Nationalist. During the revolution, he hid their silver cutlery and jade jewels in his village home's basement; once discovered for the crime, the local PLA unit dragged him into the streets. Luckily for him, he didn't make it to the firing squad—a heart attack, just outside his hometown's square. My mother knew Kang-Lin's family history, reprimanded me I shouldn't spend too much time with my friend—that her family was "blacker" than ours, so black their veins ran hei, or sometimes went the joke. What saved Kang-Lin's family from endless torture was her father's betrayal of his own father; when Kang-Lin's grandfather died, the junior Kang took his father's remaining possessions to the local party chief and turned in this legacy. He professed in a public letter never to have felt any affection for his traitorous father, stamping his family name with his own blood. For this unfilial act, Kang-Lin's father was sent to a post in Beijing within the gates of Zhongnanhai. For this, Kang-Lin and her inherited curiosity were protected. For the rest of us, there was something dangerously attractive in entitled, ennobled people bred of such devoted patriotism.

"I found these books in a box beneath my father's bed," Kang-Lin said. Her parents, both in the PLA, were on assignment in Dongbei where they reported on Mao's latest campaign, "huilin kaihuang," a ritualistic destroying of forest so crop yields of millet and corn would improve. Kang-Lin and her siblings were in the care of her grandmother—the one who lost her husband during the war of resistance. Her grandmother's brain was failing (rumors said she regularly wore her underwear on the outside of her pants in the middle of winter and was seen smuggling baijiu rations into her cleavage), but whatever the cause, her grandmother's negligence meant Kang-Lin could do a lot of things other kids couldn't—namely stay out late and rummage through her house after her grandmother went to the market. Kang-Lin found army-issued condoms and sanitary pads, beacons from a distant future, telling us what our lives would one day become without the requisite warnings we were better off staying who we were now. The books were one of Kang-Lin's scores that month, further evidence we may one day be as powerful and chesty as we dreamed—and she'd been waiting for the perfect night to show me.

The book on my lap appeared to have been printed many decades earlier; the characters in tight rows in the old, complicated script. There were also books in English, those boring, upright letters dotting the pages.

"These aren't just any books," Kang-Lin's eyes ran glassy. "These were my grandfather's. My father's father. The one…" she paused, stuck in a history without an end. She swallowed resolutely and continued: "And he loved them, hiding them to save for my grandmother, who then she gave them to my mother, and my mother planned to give them to me, once I was old enough to understand the English. I didn't know where she'd hidden them but then I found them. And recently, with all the book burning campaigns, I worried we'd lose them. So I brought them here. We have to protect them. Be very careful." She shot me an incriminating look as I ran my fingers over my book's spine.

"Shall we read them?" I wanted to know what words were worth dying for. Recently, language felt like a ticking time bomb—the language we knew we could speak and that we couldn't. Words were shoved under beds, behind pillows, tucked in the fleshy crevasses of folded tongues. We lived and died for language, or so Kang-Lin's grandfather's legacy taught us. We were young, but old enough to believe that without language we had nothing, wouldn't be able to tell a sycamore from a scholar tree.

"My mother said certain places are embedded with spirits," Kang-Lin ignored my question.

"By spirits you mean ghosts?"

She clucked. "No, something that isn't in human form. Like thought, or hope. And these spirits live in trees, and ponds, and rivers. Sometimes they even hop from a tree to a gecko."

"Or a cockroach?"

She slapped my wrist. "My mother said there are many cultures that believe places should be protected, that we shouldn't build on them or take too much from them."

"Not even grow corn and millet on them?"

Kang-Lin's father was overseeing the expansion of a millet farm in Heilongjiang along a river so cold, or so he wrote in a letter she read me one afternoon after school, that this inhospitable northern river flowed black as calligrapher's ink. I tried to imagine a river like that but all I saw was a shanshui painting so real I could stroke the grasses, dip my nose into the waters. I wondered what it would be like to step inside a work of art, to have one's existence and wanderings constrained by the frame.

"I don't know exactly," Kang-Lin admitted. "She told me this when we were in line for our rations so I worried someone would overhear and report us for bourgeois thought, but my mother can be in these moods where she doesn't care what anyone thinks— I suppose this was one of those. I don't know how she and my father get along but maybe its because he never listens to her; as long as she births sons, he keeps her. That and the fact her father died on the Long March." She repositioned her seat. "What I'm trying to say is I think this is one of those places, don't you? Every time we pass through this park on our walks from school to the danwei, I can't help but feel like this tree is talking to me."

"And what's it saying?"

"It's saying 'stop.'"

"'Stop'? Stop what?"

"Stop everything. Slow down. Take a seat. Watch the way the sun bats at my tree eyelashes."

"Trees don't have eyelashes."

"You know what I mean. In a poetic way."

But there wasn't any sun. Past midnight, the moon slipped behind a cloud. From where we sat on this outcropping in the middle of the city, we could see the entirety of the horizon spreading east, the last of the hutong courtyard fires squelched for the night, smoke rising, the few remaining danwei units skittering like cockroaches about a factory floor, street lamps twinkling in spokes from the city's heart. If we walked toward that far horizon's edge we would find industrial Tianjin with its cluttered, oil-slicked port, the Yellow Sea frothing white, the futile tip of Korea, the vast, enigmatic Pacific. And then what? What was beyond that? Our circular longing was contained by a linear endpoint: we knew we wanted to get beyond this realm, our ability to see only as far as the horizon, but how could we? We didn't know yet. We hadn't written life's inevitable story to its inevitable end.

A rustling in the bushes across the path startled us back into our bodies; a man in army fatigues and a woman with her skirt scrunched above her waist walked unsteadily from behind a shadow of trees rimming the hill, clinging to one another's waists and stumbling, as if drunk, or in love, or both.

"Duck," Kang-Lin whispered, pushing my head into her lap.

If the amorous couple saw us, they didn't mind. Such are the ways of people in love, I thought.

When they finally dipped out of view, I lifted my head and sat up, looking at Kang-Lin's face, which was turned to the distant edges of our city, her wide forehead faintly moon-spun.

"So this tree spirit, what else did it tell you?"

Kang-Lin's bottom lip did that trembling thing when she's about to say something important.

"It told me to pay attention."

"Pay attention. Like in school?"

"No, not in school, and not to wicked Teacher Liang. Pay attention to this tree. The moon. To you. To words we're not meant to speak. I'd never felt so outside of my body as I did the first night I came here with these books. Like I was looking down on the world from the heavens, like Xiannü in that myth, I'd sprung wings and flown above this all and could barely tell the difference between a steel smelter and an iron ore. I was outside earthly things; they meant nothing. Yet I had this intense feeling that everything earthly meant everything. These books, like the one on your lap, teach us there are roads that aren't roads and they lead to places that aren't places. You see, beginnings and endings are actually the same—it just depends on how you're approaching them."

"So up is down and down is up."

"Exactly," she said, only she wasn't joking. She was like one of those socialist rhetoric teachers who stood on wooden boxes outside our school now. "Cold Mountain isn't a mountain at all, you see: when you know that you're already in Cold Mountain then you'll realize there was no journey to get there."

"That sounds contradictory."

She sat up straighter, folding her legs and leaning forward, hands on knees, so I could see just the top of her face, mouth obscured in shadow. "My grandfather wrote me a note before he died: *It's only in living our futures that we sink into the unforgivable weight of our pasts.* Four days later, he was gone. My mother was never the same. My parents moved and left me with my grandmother. I meant to keep that note forever but somewhere along the way I lost it. I still remember the words. That's why language is important. It's a vessel."

Here was my friend whose summer feet smelled of vinegar, whose scalp puckered so dry in winter the dandruff puffed each time she removed her woolen hat when she walked into the front gate of Beijing PLA Children's Academy. When you held her hand, her fingers were cold and clammy and, if you hugged her, her bones were made of glass, joints of seashells. Yet she wasn't as fragile as she appeared. She believed things none of us had the capacity to believe and because of this, I had to tell her, so I started from the beginning—

"Can I tell you something?" I asked but didn't await an answer.

There was a time I hadn't told Kang-Lin about, or anyone for that matter. I'd been at my aunt's house in Guilin for the summer when my parents were in Guangxi for reeducation. My aunt left to get leeks at the market and although I was only eight, I'd been reading Tales of the Eight Immortals and wanted to know if I could fly off the apartment building, to test whether that crane would catch me as it did in the myths. Those months, I thought my parents had deserted me, that I'd always have to live with my aunt who smelled of mung beans and castor oil. She also beat my back with a broom whenever I talked back; it took decades for the switched scars to fade. Inspired by the Eight Immortals, I peeled open the window overlooking the roof and climbed barefoot onto the thin aluminum siding. The air was so hot I immediately burst into a sweat, salt cresting my tongue. My toes nestled the edge. I opened my arms like I imagined the beautiful He Xiangu would do. I thought: this is what it's like to grip one's fate in one's hands. I could do this—I had the only power we're given from birth, the power to control our destiny, our story's ending. The revelation was powerful and terrifying. This was when, without thinking, I tipped my head back and saw the sky. I'd never no-ticed the universe so big and empty. This acknowledgment filled me with an overwhelming sense that not enough people stop to look up at the nest of space surrounding us, to feel so small when most of our lives we feel so big. All along I'd been thinking my life was like everyone else's—large and real—but the sky proved me wrong. I tucked my arms into my sides and reclined against the rooftop, stunned, tracing the shape of my fingers, plucking the scabbed skin on my knees like a deranged erhu player. That was when my aunt screamed at me from the kitchen: 'What the turtle egg are you doing?' She never minced words. I climbed in, knees dusty and shaking, and she spanked me eight times, so hard my ass was sore for a week.

"Talk about a return to the heaviness of earth," I said, refer-encing He Xiangu's lightness of being.

Kang-Lin's eyes were half-closed. The moon shifted from view, entirely gone, and the world was a shadow so dark it didn't have a shadow itself.

Her voice startled me: "Everyone knows that feeling. Only some of us choose to live within it. Others push it away, like a street sweeper brushing dust into gutters, because…"

"Because what?"

"Because they're scared they'll never be able to live if they feel that way all the time."

"So that's why I wanted to jump?"

"No, not quite," Kang-Lin said. "You've always been a person who likes to straddle boundaries. Didn't you tell me your head was stuck in your mother's vagina for hours? That they thought you'd strangle yourself during the birth?"

I hadn't remembered telling Kang-Lin that story but we told one another everything. That's how it was.

"Yes, so what?"

"So you're a li-mi-na person," she said.

"Li-mi-na?" This sounded like a word in English our Teacher Pang hadn't yet taught us.

This time she spelled out the English letters: "L-I-M-I-N-A. My mother said it's the place we go when we're neither here nor there. Like how in our language, we say 'nie'—that place beyond this one but also within reach. Wait, give me that," she pulled the poetry from my hands, flipping through the pages looking for something. I don't know how she could see words in this intense blackness. Maybe in a past life she was an eagle or an owl. I liked to believe we were both birds. Birds who couldn't die. Birds who knew the earth and sky in a way humans never could.

Her finger slipped down the page with ease. "Here, Han Shan says:

Who takes the Cold Mountain Road
Takes a road that never ends
The rivers are long and piled with rocks
The streams are wide and choked with grass
It's not the rain that makes the moss slick
And it's not the wind that makes the pines moan
Who can get past the tangles of the world
And sit with me in the clouds?"

"Don't you see? You're a li-mi-na person too. We slip between the spaces where doorways meet, float over cities and swim below the ocean's waves. We should've been born as an owl or a tree. But too late for that; no use bemoaning heaven's decisions that weren't ours to make. Or were they? Look: the sleeping magpie dream-chirps on a tree. She's happy and free. Her bird fingers curl over the thinnest branch. Without a thought, she lifts her wings, floats on a passing breeze to some other tree beyond sight and I think, 'there you go again, showing off without knowing your greatest gifts.' We need to enter time. We need to let it envelop us and disappear. Do you think the magpie worries about the shift between today and tomorrow? Do you think the mandarin duck predicts the crossing of autumn to winter or that the crane envisions how much time has passed since her last mating?"

I guessed the answer she expected was 'no.' Only humans seemed capable of ruining everything with what we thought was our brilliant knowledge. But if we were so brilliant why were we always proving ourselves wrong?

Before I could ask, she reached to the pile beside her, plucked a book from the top: a translation of what Teacher Ming, our history and literature professor, called a Roman classic. Rome: None of us believed our Chinese ancestors once took Romans as our army's soldiers. Implausible to consider: rosy-cheeked, blonde, blue-eyed, double-metered men standing beside their shorter, darker-haired comrades. Teacher Ming, lecturing that rainy day in the classroom that smelled of pig's feet, was inordinately proud. As if he was once Roman himself. "Luo ma," we all repeated in the Chinese transliteration. The word didn't have as much punch as it did in Italian: "Roma." We tried that too: "Rrrrroma!" Rolling the rrrrrs. Feeling invincible. That's how we learned then: Loudly. Teacher Ming was sometimes ridiculed for his outlandish assumptions (for one: that the United States would reach the moon if the Chinese didn't get there first) so we thought this was another, but he spoke with such conviction we hoped he was right—those days, right and wrong were striated. You had to align yourself with right, but if right became wrong, you better jump left. If left was meant to be right. But what if you didn't jump quickly enough and the right had already shifted back? Feet planted on two ships at sea, legs peeling apart, your body split in two. Rome. A powerful place. We weren't sure if it was left or right. Or if left was right or right was…?

"Lucretius," Kang-Lin said. "He's Roman. He knows everything."

"Knew," I corrected. "He's dead."

"His words are alive."

I snuffed. I wanted to believe, like she did, there was something worth protecting in the breath passed between us, the moon winking through waving sycamore branches of a tree dead longer than we'd been alive, would never live again but would remain for thousands of years, a reminder its branches had once been strong enough to support the strangled death of one of the nation's last emperors. I'd never loved my city more than I did this night. *Wo ai Beijing Tiananmen*, we sang in our loudest voices, chasing each other like feral cats down the alleyways now paved into six-lane highways. *Wo ai Beijing Tiananmen*. How could a song chisel into your heart, become a rhythm you'd cling to years later if only to convince yourself there's a long, red string reaching from that moment in time to this one, that you're one and the same with the young girl carving out the center of your story?

Kang-Lin read a poem from the Roman book, her English lyrics clipped as a horse's gait:

From winter's grip, first birds of the air
Proclaim you,
Goddess divine, and herald your approach,
Pierced to the heart by your almighty power.
Next creatures of the wild and flocks and
herds

Bound across joyful pastures, swim swift
streams,
So captured by your charms they follow you,
Their hearts' desire, wherever you lead on.
And then through seas and mountains[3]—

In the distance, a foghorn moaned. The loudspeakers cleared their throats, one by one extending a cacophony of words: "All Comrades report to their danwei. Midnight sessions to commence immediately."

Kang-Lin stopped, eyes wide and white. She didn't often show fear on her face but tucked it into a tapping toe or jumping knee.

"Do you think they know about us?" I asked.

She quickly stowed the books in her knapsack, clipping it shut, then stood, wiping grass off her backside. My eyesight shifted—whereas I'd begun to see her clearly in the dark, now she was just the outline of a skinny, hunched body.

"They're going to know we're gone."

"We have to come up with a worthy excuse." I strummed my thoughts for something to convince my grandparents why I wasn't home.

She said: "Let's say Teacher Ming asked us to clean up our stations at school."

"At midnight? Why would we need to do that?"

"Rats."

"Rats?"

"Yeah, the rats only come out after dark. We had to kill the rats, like the Chairman says, so we had to go there after midnight

---

[3.] Li-Ming spoke of Rome just once during our afternoon sessions: "I never read that book on Rome. I should've read other books too. My singular pursuit ruined me." Her hair was a cuckoo's nest, lips a temporary palsy, and yes, she was beautiful, because she was close to an end. "You did the best you could," I said, knowing I sounded trite, the angle of sun available only to those who stop and cock a head to pay attention. But everything sounds trite when nearing completion or contained within the footnotes of a text.

to perform our patriotic duties."

"And why didn't we tell anyone we were going?"

"We didn't want to wake them. Or thought they'd be worried for our health. Rats carry diseases—isn't that where the plague started? And our families looked too peaceful in their sleep to bother them. Trust me, it will work."

"Rats," I repeated. The more the thought sunk in, the more I had to hand it to Kang-Lin: she was good at thinking on the fly. I, on the other hand, ruminated too long, exposing whatever it was I'd meant to protect. I worried Kang-Lin chose the wrong person with whom to share her grandfather's treasured books, but before I could examine that fear too closely, she tapped my shoulder and motioned for me to follow her down the hill.

That's when I noticed she'd left a book on the ground at my feet: Han Shan's *Cold Mountain*, the same poetry that was on my lap and must've slipped off when the loudspeakers startled us. I picked it up, the book's silk cover silvery cool, like offering bowls left outside a temple gate in winter.

"You forgot this!" I called to my friend, already descending downhill, shadow sliced in half at the hips.

"You coming?" Her chirpy voice willed me into action.

I shoved the book in my knapsack and adjusted the pack squarely over my shoulders: "I'm right behind you!"

But no matter how quickly I ran, I'd never catch her, never reach the girl who once seemed so close I could trace her shape as well my own, could share her head's form within a woolen hat, her hand's grip within a glove, her mouth's entombing a spoon lumped with sticky-sweet congee.

Over time, the city closed its shell around us and the moon crawled onwards in its endless journey across the arched curve of the sky's spine.

Hello, Moon.

Good-bye.

Baba

Summer: Beijing's hottest on record, star-palmed leaves dropping to the streets as readily as cicadas and my husband wiping
sweat off my forehead. Telling me to stop writing. To stop. To
stop what—breathing?

What was the name he called me before the Great Unraveling?[4]
Wife. Or mostly: Old Woman. An inside joke? Not exactly:
Old Woman is what everyone called their wives at a certain age,
in a certain era in which we played certain parts.

Where were we?

Home. The musty, spirited apartment we'd known for decades. And although it was the first time I knew him, it was also
the first time he knew me, wadding my temples, making sense
of the senseless in the most tender, incessant gesture. That's how
these events occurred: reciprocal, the two of us straddling the
cliffs of our lives, looking at each other as if we were meant to
love the face facing us, but how can you love something you only
know as a familar scent housed within an aging carapace of skin?

And so we forget who we are again. *Why am I telling this
story?*

*Year after year we move on—where we raise the dust today—
long ago was an endless sea.*

My husband's, your Baba's, story started well before he was

[4.] The unraveling: she refers to this "unraveling" here and several times throughout the text although a particular moment of the "Great Unraveling" cannot be
deciphered by your translator. "Where did we unravel?" she asked me on the
sun deck one evening, or I think I remember her asking as the moon crested,
buttering our heads. "I don't understand," I said. She simply smiled. Early, I
mistook her mischievousness for knowledge, her coy smiles for someone who
could answer the greatest questions. Later, I wasn't as naïve.

born, reaching full sprint the autumn his father called him and his brother *ye haizi—wild kids.* He was "Little Wang" then, to differentiate him from the older Wangs on the block. That wet season in the first year of the Communist Era, the Wang boys fashioned themselves wild beasts, cutting through Shanghai's shower-sodden streets, shouting curses at slouched men on stools, slapping posters glued to city walls: *Long Live the Chinese People's Volunteer Army! Oppose the Imperialists!*

Big-Eyed Sheng, their eldest cousin, laughed like he owned the city. The fastest in the family, he beat Chiang Kai-shek's son in a city track meet ten years earlier and never let anyone forget it.

"I'm the fastest man in China!" he shouted after they left the high school's morning classes, skipping the afternoon mathematics and physics lessons to run the alleyways to their daily assignment. This particular afternoon they'd sell the eyeglass lenses their fathers made in the Old Chinese Quarters apartment, the same work they conducted since before the War of Liberation. Glass making was a natural profession for men who spent their childhoods chopping hay in the fields of Zhejiang province—thick, calloused fingers invincible to sparks and slivers. In their rucksacks, lenses clinked, and to Little Wang, they sounded like shell buttons racking washing boards in his hometown. How many years since he'd been in the country? A city boy now. Their glass lenses: warped at the edges, useless, not worth a fen. The brothers swindled clients to purchase a pair then packed up and sold their damaged wares at a different street corner the next afternoon. They preyed on the fat cats from the Northern Capital with their Party pride and People's Currency freshly minted with the Chairman's round, happy face. Of course, they didn't tell the fat cats with their bulging waistlines the lenses they sold were riddled with imperfections—the glass curved ever-so-slightly so after a few days you'd see bright circles around street lights, rings around the sun.

Big-Eyed Sheng panted as he stopped beneath the fluttering

green awning of the Park Hotel, hands on knees, operatic sweat atop fat cheeks. "You'll never catch me," his breath heaved.

"Never," Little Wang agreed, side-eyeing his brother.

Although his brother wasn't slow, he always let Big-Eyed Sheng win their races; in the past year, Sheng's girlfriend Ling-Ling fed him pork jiaozi every afternoon to the point his slacks needed to be let out. He was their 'big' cousin in more ways than one; they didn't want to upset him in thinking he'd lost his speed—when he was upset, he didn't direct his furor toward the perpetrator, but also the perpetrator's friends, parents, distant relatives. He was an infinitely-tentacled octopus with hands everywhere, like their government. They were only beginning to understand what that meant, how their Middle Kingdom speared the world with its sharp edges and slick-tongued proclamations:

中

"We'll never catch you," Doufu, Little Wang's brother, said— "Doufu," a variant of his nickname, "Bofu," and reference to his brother's tofu-soft thighs.

Cousin Sheng straightened and helped them set up shop: a wooden Republican-era stool the boys carried with them everywhere and atop it, their dead mother's tattered indigo handkerchief she once used as a satchel to carry her meticulously-tailored cotton pants to market in Shangyu. Doufu laid out the latest collection of eyeglasses. The industrious smell of freshly-ground glass clung to their fingertips—part of the larger machinery of the world they could sense but didn't fully grasp.

That morning, as on every morning, their father set the prices. Along with Second, Third and Fourth Uncle, the elder Wang spent most nights grinding glass in the windowless back room of their two-room apartment where Doufu and Little Wang slept on the floor. In the mornings, their father and uncles departed for the Little World market outside Yuyuan Garden, bringing home sheet glass and sandpapers in bulk from the leftover goods at the

U.S. army supply store. The Party had claimed Little World after the Nationalists fled to Taiwan and the remnant goods were distributed at random, rationed to those who needed them. The boys and their uncles were grateful; the hand that feeds wins the heart.

Tink.

Tink.

Doufu tapped the lenses on the hotel wall to promote the product's durability. A woman in a tight red skirt, a fit more common in Hong Kong than the mainland, walked out of the hotel and grabbed a lens from Doufu's hands. She smacked him over the head with it.

"Don't do that!"

"Don't do what?" The brothers asked as her high heels clopped away.

"That!" she flung her hand dismissively, tossing them their lens, and they watched her melon-shaped ass sashay until she was lost to the lines of coolies on their rickshaws.

"Did you see that one?" Little Wang elbowed his brother.

"See what?" Of course his brother would pretend he hadn't seen the woman's finely-tuned shape. Doufu held a lens to his eye as if through it he could watch the Chairman leading the Long March.

"You didn't think that woman was attractive?"

"No."

"Not even a little sexy?"

"Little Wang, if you're only watching a woman walk away what's the point? The Fat Cats… those are men who really know women."

"Sure," Little Wang snatched the lens from his brother's hand and held it to his own eye. There wasn't a swimming Chairman. He directed the lens, and with it his gaze, back to the busy, wet street, searching for the beautiful woman.

New rain kissed the pavement, fat gifts from the cloud-pregnant, autumnal heavens. Farmers slapped donkey haunches, women opened floral umbrellas and tip-toed cautiously over ex-panding puddles. The green awning above the boys hiccupped and sighed. The lenses fogged, lost their translucence. Their thin cotton shirts clung to their backs; they shrugged off the coming cold. Behind them, their goods were stacked and tied together with cotton strings. At least the lenses were dry, they reassured one another, nodding like they'd seen their father and uncles do, wordless communication they assumed occurred naturally be-tween all adult men.

"All you care about are the fat cats." Little Wang reached for a lens and cut the edge into the Park Hotel's brick wall.

The truth: his brother was obsessed with the Party, avowed it his life goal to become a member. He'd work late nights on his school work—particularly drawn to physics and engineering—in the hopes of attending Shanghai's Shipbuilding School to some-day build ships for China's proud, new, People's Liberation Navy. Doufu was their father's son—obsessed with industry and the opportunity given when they moved from their backwater village of Cen Cang Yan to the city. To be *city folk*. They left everything in their hay-roofed pingfang atop Zhejiang's marshy coast—their mother's bones buried among the spiny shrubs of Xia Gai Moun-tain, their grandfather's plots of dehydrated tomato vines, his parched pumpkin patches besotted with desperate thorns. Little Wang's brother and father never looked back, not even when the boat escorted them down that ribbonous river toward neighbor-ing Shangyu City, slicing golden fields only country sunsets could set afire. Why did it seem only Little Wang remembered this?

Doufu grabbed the lens from his brother. "You don't get it. You're muddle-headed."

"Get what?"

"This." Lifting the same lens, his brother peered through the center then carelessly tossed the glass into the street where it landed in a puddle, losing its luminosity.

"See what we can waste with just one throw?" Doufu had a

47

way of making nonsense out of sense.

"You're not making sense," Little Wang said.

"Listen," his brother said, then spouted numbers and figures, profit calculations: *45 kuai a kilo! Two kuai a sale!* A bad lens wasn't useless, he laughed, it was a commodity! Little Wang half-listened, watched as a toddler squatted in front of their stoop to piss on the steps. The toddler's mother waited patiently, staring toward the old horse stables that now housed Party ammunitions. Pigeons cooed somewhere above them, hungry for sun. Doufu kept at it: *weren't our lenses, the profits they generated, translatable into rice, red beans, yams?* But Little Wang knew: His brother saw the world in angles, supported by the rational forces of engineering, all that girded the physical. He knew following well-traveled paths—school in the city, a party membership—would reward him. Little Wang didn't believe in such rewards. Ever since their mother's death the week after the Nationalists stormed their village, he avoided politics. He wanted to roam the streets alone at night, skipping rocks down Shanghai's wide boulevards and musing over the shapes of rooster women leaning in the doorways of the abandoned jazz halls, inviting him past the slanted doorways with clucks of plum-tinted lips.

"A product is only as good as its function. In other words," Doufu bent, plucked the lens from the puddle, wiping it on his pants, "a lens without an eye is not really a lens. Its just glass! An eye is what makes your belly full!" He slapped Little Wang's stomach.

"You're quite the philosopher."

"I'll make the next sale. Watch me."

If there is a next sale, Little Wang thought, reaching into his breast pocket to touch his mother's thimble—the only silver she saved from before the Nationalists swept through the village, the same silver she'd given to him the day she died. He always kept it in his pocket, played with it the way a coolie scratched the blisters on his thighs and shins; distraction—a cool drug.

A Party official stepped from a black car, feet sloshing winningly through puddles. His head dipped beneath an umbrella. When he reached their stand, he folded the umbrella to a crisp close and perused the boys, judging their clothing, their wet hair sticking up at birdlike angles. The official wore a dry Mao jacket and pleated khakis, his shoulders touched with rain. He picked up a pair of lenses with clammy fingers, examined the lobby's golden light seeping through the hotel's rotating doors. His chest was wide, the bronze buttons on his uniform in danger of popping off.

Wagging a fat finger in their faces, he said, "Shoddy... Terrible... Your goods are rubbish." He dropped the lenses to the ground, slapped open the umbrella, and stepped into the downpour, immune to the dampening effects of rain. As he strode away, their father's product easily discarded, Little Wang wondered if maybe his brother was right. Perhaps the only way to be anything in this world was to play by the rules of the Fat Cats—but what were those rules? We could be born into a certain position in life, he thought. Meet the right people, properly answer questions. We could do all this and still one day a fat foot could stamp its shape in our face. He'd seen this happen just weeks earlier outside a food rationing store near Xintiandi: a young party member wearing a Mao suit asked for an extra ration for his pregnant wife just as a passing official overheard the request. The official slapped the man and demanded, in front of a growing crowd, that the perpetrator show his party membership card, but the man hadn't carried it with him. Within minutes, this man was accused of being a Nationalist spy and dragged to a politburo office. The city's bicycle bells and vendor calls overwhelmed his cries. The crowd, moving to the next public spectacle, dispersed.

The lenses in a puddle again, this was the first time Little Wang saw all of the industry of their everyday existence so quickly made irrelevant: his father at that tortuous machine, slouched in a constant C, the moldy mats on the floor where they slept each night, the apartment smelling of garlic, sweat-stained sheets, rat droppings, an ever-present mix of exhaustion and spoiled peanut oil. How long could they live like this? They were tu baozi, the city folk reminded them as they spat globules of phlegm at their feet. *Country shits.*

Little Wang raised his fist, a finger extended, lips curdling: "There's a turtle shit posing as a Communist!" He shouted to the back of the Fat Cat.

The Fat Cat turned, face umbrella-shadowed. "What did you say, Tu baozi?"

"I said…"

Doufu's palm stamped Little Wang's lips. "He said 'have a nice day,'" Doufu said, his own lips purple. He was their father's son: weakened in the presence of the powerful. Their father, who instructed them to lower their heads when they passed a foreign face, and then, after the foreigners left along with the Nationalist pigs, the same gesture expected for party leaders who saved them from Japanese occupation.

The Fat Cat shook his head dismissively, ducking into the flooded warmth of a chauffeured car.

"You're the turtle shit now," Doufu said, bending to retrieve the damaged lenses. Irreparable. They knew—a cracked lens was worthless, displayed the world in kaleidoscope: broken trees, broken boulevards, broken faces, broken all the hours spent smoothing its sides. Little Wang wanted to push his brother, for him to land with a thud in that growing puddle over which the Fat Cat stepped. But he held his fist and watched as Doufu lifted the cracked lenses to his eye. How did he see Little Wang? Half his head this way, the other cut in two, nose and chin distorted. Little Wang hadn't seen himself like this in a long time: only when they snuck into the Big World arcades before the war. A mosquito laden summer, their mother waiting for them on the stoop, their limp, overpriced kites at her side. Hours were like water to the boys visiting the hahajin, the funny mirrors that made them shorter, stouter, longer, leaner. They could've stood there forever, watching themselves grow older in their various shapes and forms. *Haha*, they laughed. In their duplications they could be everything and anything.

Haha. Life wasn't broken yet.

Haha. Time, and with it the rest of their lives, remained theirs to shape.

Haha. Little Wang released his fist.

"Stay here," Doufu said. "I'm going to find Cousin Sheng. We should pack up now that our products are useless."

"Fine," Little Wang said. "Tell Ling-Ling I say 'hi.'"

Cousin Sheng was regularly running off with Ling-Ling, a classmate from the poorest region of Jiangxi, to the abandoned rooms at the Big World arcades. At night, he arrived home smelling like rotted sorghum; the same smell Little Wang knew from their private school's bathroom where boys leaned against wooden stalls, hands wrestling beneath pant zippers like catching a slippery fish, leaving glistening snail's trails on the walls.

"Ten yuan for a pair of lenses! Two for seventeen!" Little Wang shouted to the pedestrians and bicyclists as his brother's wide back disappeared into the gray streets. Cold water leaked through the awning, kissing his neck.

The coolies lined the curb, starlings on a wire, damp newspapers draped over their heads, arms limp as shadow puppets. They waited in front of the foreign Y.M.C.A. recently converted to Party offices, windows re-shined, doors repainted red. Little Wang mused at how quickly a city could belong to different owners, wear an entirely new mask.

"What you looking at?" he asked the lead coolie, a boy they called 'Sing-Song' because he lacked two front teeth and whistled when he spoke. The same boy teased prostitutes exiting the Park Hotel each morning, calling them to straighten their skirts and smooth their hair. But the 'rooster women' just winked and named him 'Little Friend' to which he beamed a wide, toothless smile, as if he actually had a chance.

Sing-Song exposed that gaping smile. "I'm looking at a boy about to be arrested!" he nodded up the street toward the corner of Central Tibet and Nanjing Roads. Bicycling bodies shrouded their view of anything other than gray-clothed limbs and arms. "Time to pack up, Glass Grinder!"

The coolies folded their rickshaws and departed quickly, pant legs slapping the ground, wet tongues to parched lips.

"What is it?" Little Wang could barely hear his own voice.

"Licenses!" Sing-Song's legs accelerated, his bicycle catching speed.

"What?" As Little Wang stepped from under the awning, the rain slicked his hair, stung his eyes. He scanned the length of the busy street for Doufu and Cousin Sheng but he couldn't see anything except his own sopping, startled eyelashes.

Little Wang quickly gathered the lenses into his mother's satchel, but the heaviness of his clothing slowed his movements. The coolies, pedaling off, laughed, shouted for him to hurry him *turtle feet*. But where was his brother? Of course he couldn't find him—his brother was always distracted by two things: one, selling enough lenses to appease their father and uncles; and two, a girl at school named Liu Li who Little Wang thought was homely but his brother loved. By now, Little Wang realized his brother's vanishings were a way of averting blame, like the morning of their mother's disappearance, how he'd been nowhere when Little Wang wrapped his arms around their mother's beloved soap tree so tightly Third Uncle had to pry him free. They'd lost her. But how could she be lost if he could still picture her face, hear her voice singing from behind the bamboo groves as she plucked sweet potatoes from pickled earth?

"Wang Guanfu!" Little Wang shouted his brother's proper name, the name their father called him but no one turned: not a bicyclist nor anyone among the hordes of street vendors who followed the call of the coolies—*Zou! Zou! Zou!* Little Wang didn't know from what he was running, but the urgency propelled him forward. The lenses cradled beneath his armpit slowly slipped away, joining the rain's wash like fallen, silver leaves.

"Wait!" he called to Sing-Song's disappearing back. But the coolies were gone. He could barely see to the other side of the old racetrack. Even the Park Hotel's glittering revolving doors were shrouded in gray. Several lenses caught on a grate. As he struggled to pry them loose, he saw his father and his uncles, slumped shoulders aching while they welded metal to glass, blinking feverishly to stay awake. *Keep your eyes trained on the machines...* What was the use? His fingers worked as quickly as they could, but the joke was on him. Maybe Cousin Sheng was the fastest after all. Maybe he was, as Doufu always suggested, the lesser of the Wang men.

As he pried loose a particularly stubborn lens, a heavy hand wrapped itself around his neck, gripping the collar of his shirt. The strong hold lifted him off the ground, legs spinning on the futility of industry and air.

The hand thrust him into the warm backseat of a car. A heavy door slammed shut.

"Wang Guanfu!" he shouted one last time, his voice pointlessly addled.

Little Wang immediately knew where he sat: a Shanghai City Police car, the dry navy leather sliding beneath his soaked behind. The officer started the engine then cursed, spit spraying the dashboard:

Illegal peddling.
Children.
Parents to blame.
Careless.
Capitalist.

Their car split the street in two, effortlessly parting lines of bicyclists from the damp bodies of yexiao vendors.

As the officer's words blasted the windshield, Little Wang

fixed his gaze on the buildings rolling by—his first time on wheels
and watching the world from behind the glass. Traffic conductors
stood on yellow and black pedestals, arms bending at sharp angles. Pedestrians melted into a mass of gray and black. Only the
occasional red dress flashed at him like a magpie's tail in flight.
He tried to catch a glimpse long enough to revel in the shape of
a woman. No such luck. Windshield wipers splashed aside rain
yet it was dry and hot inside the car. He folded his hands beneath
his bare legs. At an intersection beside People's Park, he saw his
brother huddled beside Cousin Sheng. Both shivered, invisible to
everyone but Little Wang. The car lurched forward as his brother's hand raised, their eyes meeting and Doufu's mouth opening,
stuck in an incredulous—

O.

Little Wang wanted to say his brother's name, but his tongue
couldn't form the syllables. From where he sat, Doufu was the
insignificant one now. A pane of glass separated them.

"Who you looking at?" The officer asked, eyes unblinking in
the rear view mirror.

"No one."

The car slid around a turn, his brother's reflection replaced by
crowded streets, the searching glare of rain-slick headlights. "Just
a kid on the street."

"You're the kid," the driver said. "And you'll call me Officer
Feng from now on."

Officer Feng with the big ears and shining bald head.

Officer Feng with the double chin.

*Officer Feng with the whiskered cheeks, a black mole the size of
Hangzhou City.*

Little Wang placed his palms on the window. His breath
clouded the glass, fingers outlined. In the fogged parts, he wrote
his milk name, the one his mother called him as a child—

王关零

—as the cab pulled to a stop.

What did his brother know?

Little Wang peeled open the door, but before he could start toward the street, a man as wide as a shikumen doorway jogged out of the station's swinging doors and yanked him by his elbow.

"Thought you'd run, eh?" He dragged Little Wang up the front stairs.

Officer Feng's car backed away, down the street to another call, another group of street kids selling goods, or maybe one of Big Eared Du's opium dens.

"I can run so fast, I'll run as fast as a car. In fact, I'll have my own car soon."

The fat man's smile spread almost as wide as his waist.

"And I'll have a driver. I'll call him Officer Big Ears Feng."

"Ah, just like the famous Big Eared Du," the man said.

"Exactly."

The officer laughed, his belly shaking against Little Wang's arm.

"Enjoy your stay," he said, escorting Little Wang into an unlit cell full of street kids lounging on benches and sprawled across the floor. The boys snickered and took up more space so Little Wang couldn't sit. Outside, the rain slowed to a patient drizzle. A strip of evening sunlight peeled cautiously through the bars of the cell's only window, highlighting the dust, making even the air between the bodies tired and spent.

The smell he knew well from his back alley home: urine and sweat. He avoided eye contact and found a corner beside two younger boys playing cards. Because of their matching cropped haircuts and stout Guangzhou noses, Little Wang assumed they were twins, a blessing in Old China—double the manpower, double the grandchildren. But these jailed twins clearly missed the mark.

"You want a turn?" The twin on the left asked. His brother elbowed him in the ribs and whispered something into his ear.

"Sorry," the first twin clarified. "Guess this is only a two person game."

"That's fine," Little Wang said, backing against the cold cement. He pulled his knees to his chest, clenched shut his eyes and tried to sleep, but all he could hear was the slap of cards, the lull of country accents. All he could see was that bright red ass and how it went *swish swish* through the streets as if owning them. *If I could dream, Doufu,* he wanted to tell his brother now—that mouth flash-frozen in a gaping 'O' outside the car window—*I'd dream only of this:*

O

*

Little Wang awoke to a ring of feet surrounding him, feet owned by tight-lipped smiles and clenched fists with purple-blanched knuckles. The boys spit slurs in Shanghainese, Hokkien, Hakka:

Country Bumpkin.

Nationalist.

Turtle Shit.

In the cell, they held his face to the ground, painting brush strokes with his saliva against the gray cement.

王八蛋

A pun that made "turtle shit" out of Little Wang's surname, turned a KING into EXCREMENT.

Dirt sandpapered his tongue and iron taste dripped into his throat, filling his chest with the unmistakable feeling of drowning—unmistakable despite the fact he'd never drowned, at least not to his memory.

"Say it, Chicken Face! Say 'Big Ears Officer Feng sticks it to me'!"

They fingered his pockets, digging deeper, fumbling past pieces of lint, finally finding his mother's thimble and tossing it to one another, laughing gui smiles as the silver flickered in the barred moonlight. Little Wang closed his eyes, trying to think of something wonderful, but everywhere was a mess of color like the wavering tarp on which he'd watched the Ba Jin film that August evening in Shangyu City, the sun setting over Xiagai Mountain, teaching him the lesson of impermanence. Gold and red, purple at the edges, transitioning to pink and navy. Even the sun could be desiccated by darkness. His stomach tightened. They kicked his chest and a voice he didn't recognize rose from the surface, desperate to be heard—

"Never!" That voice said. If it weren't for the hot, sticky syllable clinging to his lips, he would've thought someone larger, much more powerful, had spoken.

Instinctively, he kicked back, feet striking shins. Knees. Anything. But he couldn't kick them away. There were nearly a dozen of them. He tasted blood. He closed his eyes. He tasted the tart peach candies his mother bought after the Ba Jin film from a man with pockmarked cheeks and a mouth full of missing teeth. What night was it when he never fell asleep on the long walk home, his mouth busy with salivations of peach, the wonderings of ghostly images on screen? The first time you see a face on film you touch your own cheek to remind yourself how real you are. He'd reached up to feel his mother's cheek and she'd grimaced like his touch seared her skin. This was before she was in bed with the boils, tiny blisters climbing her legs the day she found a package from the Japanese on the road to Shangyu. She'd opened the box and slipped her fingers through the long, dry grains of rice before another villager snatched the parcel from her. Months passed after her death before they'd understand: 炭疽热. *Anthrax*. It didn't matter who got there first, who was first infected: they were all victims in one way or another. Their mother—the boils too painful to endure—at least she eventually chose her death, though they blamed her for not asking permission to slip into the river, bags of rice tied to her ankles, as if personal endings were a collective decision.

But Little Wang didn't know this yet—couldn't compile the details of a life that make a story, and vice versa. In this scene, his legs tired.[5] The boys tired of their taunting. Slipping through one of the prisoners' fingers, his mother's thimble clinked along the floor, rolling under the cell's bars and into the hallway where a fat hand clenched it, holding it to a flashlight's beam. All the boys could see, crawling toward that very same light like bats to the moon, was the half-crescent double chin, the whiskered cheeks, that mole with the long, black hair sprouting, a hungry weed.

"Wang," the lips moved, teeth yellow, flashlight blinding as it searched for his face. "Come with me, Wang Guanling." Little Wang's milk name. So he'd seen the foggy scribbling on the car window: *Wang Guanling*—the name Little Wang's mother spoke the night of Ba Jin's film, the night she smoothed her hands through his hair promising him the nightmares would end, the night before the boils scaled her body, firing a fever into her forehead, making her words unintelligible, the thimble she placed in the pocket of the pants she made for his ever-growing legs, the thimble he kept even after he outgrew the pants, even after the silver lost its purpose—a lens without an eye, a thimble without a needle.

Instinctively, he put his hands in his pockets, reaching for the thimble but only cold knuckles scraped his thigh. Gates unlocked, chains fell to the ground: the door opened just wide enough for him to slide through, ducking beneath the hot, sharp smell he knew from that afternoon, that hand heavy on his neck, its long pinky nail indenting his skin.

"Come to my office," Officer Feng's hairy mole pulled a shadow across his cheek to his salt-whiskered chin.

With only the flashlight's orb to guide his steps and boyish

[5.] "What's imagined and what's real?" Li-Ming passed me a telescopic lens, asked me to examine the cluttered hutongs beyond Houhai, mentioned a woman named Cao 'E whose name I wouldn't encounter again until reading this text decades later. I couldn't find my way to the hutong eaves, the lens focused only on the placid faces of colorful Mandarin ducks.

laugher echoing behind him, Little Wang shuffled past the cells of sleeping criminals, vagabonds, construction workers without city permits, rooster women with jasmine petalled hair and clicking high heels. Officer Feng's wet breath dampened his neck, a long fingernail tattooing Little Wang's skin with a crescent moon.

"I have a job for you," the officer said, thrusting Little Wang into a room where two men sat beneath a swinging yellow bulb, pushing mahjong tiles across a slab of cardboard. Cigarette smoke tendrils grayed the air. Officer Feng plopped onto a wooden stool, twirling a glinting object between his fingers. Little Wang's mother's thimble, he thought, but no—squinting, Little Wang realized it was one of the lenses his brother and he hawked earlier. Officer Feng's greasy fingers smeared the lens such that whatever clarity once seen through it was clouded.

Officer Feng reached into his pocket for Little Wang's mother's thimble, holding it opposite the lens.

"This silver could take you somewhere," he said, holding the thimble to the light. Silver in those days: a rarity, possessed only by the newest of Party members, the chosen few. "But this," he flicked the lens and the tinkling sound brought the mahjong players to a stop—damp lips pulled into frowns, fat brown hands paused atop the white tiles—"This is a skill that could take you to the wilds of Manchuria." Officer Feng kicked the lens across the cement to the boy's feet.

Little Wang bent to retrieve it, rubbing the rough edges, knowing this was his father's oversight at the grinding wheel. Officer Feng hadn't noticed the inconsistencies, only the perfection of a lens that could make objects at a distance appear near. Like all fat cats, he believed the unbelievable.

"I'll give you back your precious silver…" Officer Feng said, pausing, lips wet and hungry for what Little Wang imagined to be a thick piece of fatty pork, "if you agree to join the People's Volunteer Army tonight and leave for the War to Resist America and Aid Korea." He spun the thimble on the table: spinning and spinning—would the spinning ever stop? Gravity won and the thimble slowed, careening off-balance before settling to an unstable rest.

Little Wang raised the lens to his eye to peruse a warped room: Officer Feng's head bulging and narrowing like in the hahajin mirrors, his own hands stretching then fattening. That midnight moon over a decade earlier, when the Nationalists marched through their village lighting fires above the Xiagai Hills. Hadn't it been that way? He was still too young to question a childhood barely passed: his mother pushed to the ground and instructed to hand over everything she owned. Everything. But as the officers ransacked their home, she shoved the thimble beneath her tongue. He imagined the metallic taste flooding her mouth like a well-known song.

He reached across the table to snatch the thimble from Officer Feng's fat hands and popped the silver in his mouth, sucking on its serrated edges so hard his tongue bled.

"You're one wild child, Comrade Wang," Officer Feng said. "Crazy enough for the army. You think you can handle that?"

Officer Feng handed Little Wang a piece of paper with his milk name on it.

A pen.

A crimson stamp.

The date: October 15, 1950.

Opening his eyes wider, Little Wang saw his hands anew: larger, stronger, capable of great things. His mother's thick hands smoothing a stretch of fabric. His father's fingers blistered after a night grinding glass. *Cen Cang Yan Hands*, his father said, comparing the width to that of his brothers'—every man in the countryside possessed palms the size of crows. Little Wang imagined these hands scaling the pine-covered Changbai Mountains beside the Korean border, paddling across the black Yalu, while Officer Feng rambled on about the war soon raging at their borders.

Little Wang signed, using the characters his mother made

him practice every morning before school, the milk name—*Wang Guanling*—she called him at birth. He reveled in the title Officer Feng bestowed upon him: Comrade. Officer Feng called him *Comrade* Wang. Not even his brother was a Comrade.

"Shoulder-to-shoulder with Men of the Cities and Men of the Country," he said. "You could make lenses to see our nation's enemies from afar, Comrade." Officer Feng belted a somehow cheerless laugh.

Comrade Wang forced a laugh in response and marveled at his ability to fake camaraderie, his capacity to make smooth and spotless objects that had warped, faded. A lens without an eye is just a piece of glass. *True, Doufu. But it's our touching of objects that gives them a use, a name.*

Tucking the thimble into his pocket, he nodded his assent to the fat-faced officer. He'd join the People's Volunteer Army. He'd leave for the border the next day. Everything they said, he'd do. For once in his life, he reveled in the complacency of saying yes: 对对对.

Officer Feng snatched the lens from his hand, slapping it atop the mahjong board. Feng's colleagues glimpsed up to nod their ascent, before resuming the shuffling of tiles—white on brown, white on brown. *Click-tap. Click-tap. Click-tap.* Their hands slid with a feminine grace across the board.

"You'll leave tomorrow at sunrise," Officer Feng said, breaking Comrade Wang's reverie. "So hurry home."

*

Comrade Wang's unsteady breath fogged the midnight air as he stumbled, loose legged, down old Avenue Joffre with its autumn-heavy parasol trees toward the Chinese Quarter. On Chen Xiang-ge Road, his father waited for him in the arched shikumen doorway of their crowded apartment block, long body aslant, arms crossed in a flattened X, eyes lowering as Little Wang proudly, valiantly, stepped closer. Tomorrow *Comrade* Wang would leave for the border's war.

"Welcome home your very own Grandma Liu!" he shouted, mocking the idiom from *A Dream of Red Mansions* about the country bumpkin who felt like an outsider at the Jia Family home. It was the only story his mother, the sole literate member of their family, read him before bed. He smiled at the thought he'd finally made use of those hours his mother quizzed him on the story's details.

"*Son*," his father said, curtailing an attempt at humor. "*Son*, you will follow me."

Phlegm rose from Comrade Wang's lungs as he entered the damp apartment with its sleeping bodies lined in corners, an uneven chorus of snores. His father had never spoken to him this way; to his father, Comrade Wang was always Wang Guanmiao—or Wang Guanling when nostalgic. His father held a single candle, guiding his way. He cautiously stepped over his sleeping brothers toward the grinding room in the back. This was where Comrade Wang often found his father after midnight, shaping another set of lenses. His was a simple aim: to feed their growing guts. All he cared was that his boys were well-fed when really, Comrade Wang wanted to tell his father, theirs was a hunger extending well beyond their guts. Shouldn't he, of all men, understand this? It seemed unlikely a son could be so different from his father, but here it was—a lineage split like a branch spiraling downwards to the earth when it should be reaching up, seeking the sun.

Son. Son. Son. How could there be so many ways to speak just one word? *Erzi.*

儿子

The baby's legs taking their first step, Comrade Wang's primary school teacher said of the ideograph for 'son.' *Ready to run.* He wanted to run this very moment, but his legs followed his father to the grinding room where moonlight nicked the corners of his station and painted the old man's black hair silver-gray.

Comrade Wang begrudgingly shook his head as his father

gripped his arm and led him to the grinder. His father simply called him 'son.' He could've called him a useless fool. Could've said the boy's brain was hu-li hu-tu, filled with the confusion of a growing manhood, the wasted education squandered. He could've pointed to his own shoulders, orbs of bone bursting beneath thick, tanned skin—calcified knots from years carrying water buckets from the river in Shangyu to his family farm at the base of Xia Gai Hill, his body tattooed with the marks of hard labor. He could tell the boy he was spoiled. That he'd done nothing to live up to the image of his dead mother. He could say all this, but he didn't. He simply called the boy 'son' when he saw his lanky figure striding down the alleyway toward their home, a proud smile stretched across the boy's face and a long shadow reaching to the man who was now a widow, warning him Comrade Wang was the victor, returning home for the last time.

His father pulled a wooden stool across the cement, scratching like needle to glass. Comrade Wang's skin twitched.

"Sit," his father said. He rolled the grinding machine on its hesitant, rusted wheels, positioning it atop the boy's lap then walked to the front room, leaving him alone with his work.

Comrade Wang cleared his throat, swallowed. His breathing was near normal again yet everything felt different. In the darkness, he could barely see his knuckles, let alone the lenses he was supposed to grind into convex and concave shapes, the lenses now impossible to sell at the Park Hotel because his legs had been too slow. *Turtle's legs. Baby's legs.* First steps. How could he not run as fast as his brother? Why had Doufu left him behind, his shadow leering as if mocking Comrade Wang's inability to lift his feet and make a move?

"Turtle shit," he said loudly so his brother, asleep in the front room, would hear. Their father was already there, undressing for sleep, his shirtless chest a sunken, yellow cave.

His father unrolled his pants to his ankles, leaving them in a heap on the floor then slipped beneath the quilted beizi they'd shared for a decade, the one his wife made with her industrious, thick fingers. Not one sleeping body roused at the sound of Comrade Wang's voice, his uncles' bones clinging too deeply to the necessity of exhausted sleep.

His father blew out the candle and the wick fizzled from orange to red to purple to blue to black—how quickly time was lost in the span of a flame becoming smoke. He slept on the mattress the boys shared with him, its innards filled with discarded newspaper shreds. Every morning they awoke smelling like yesterday's news.

Comrade Wang worked intently, the sliding of glass to the grinder's tough sandpaper.

Sharply: the pulling of midnight moon lighting the backs of his hands.

Sharply: red-gold-blue sparks flecking the air as he worked to smooth the glass that would one day allow a man to see across a four-lane avenue, to the Huangpu River with its overstuffed junks floating listlessly, its brisk current dragging their Great Nation's farmland run-off to the East China Sea. Maybe his father was right—maybe this industry was important; after all, what are we without our vision?

"Are you going to turn around?" Doufu's voice startled him—the glass slipped beneath his distracted grip and chafed his knuckle so badly white fat showed through, pink blood meandering hand to wrist. "If you have something to say, you should be man enough to say it to my face."

Comrade Wang turned. His brother's dark shape greeted him, barely framed by moon: Wide-shouldered, bow-legged, flat-foreheaded. Although his brother inherited their father's hardened heart, his body was their mother's—sturdy, broad shouldered, thick limbed. Comrade Wang, on the other hand, was the perfect picture of their father's physicalities—long-limbed but not at all limber, as if he and his father hadn't grown into the bodies assigned at birth. His brother marched through the world, led by a tank-like chest. Everywhere he went, he demanded an audience. Comrade Wang simply leaned against walls, pulled a long shadow across floors like a dying, dehydrated tree.

"Fuck your mother's pussy," Comrade Wang said, not recognizing the tenor of his own voice. As he gripped his injured hand, the veins beneath his skin pulsed feebly.

His brother's face wavered, lips slinking into a frown—or did they rise into a grimacing smile?

"Go," his brother said.

"I'm already gone." Comrade Wang reached for the soft blue satchel their mother made from old handkerchiefs years before. In it, he packed what few belongings he'd need (underwear, socks, a comb, the silver thimble). He tore a swatch of cotton from an old work shirt and wrapped the cloth around his bleeding hand. His brother stood in the corner of the grinding room patiently witnessing his departure like a stray cat.

"You're really doing this," his brother said.

"Yeah."

"Were you going to say good-bye?"

"Good-bye." Comrade Wang slung the packed knapsack over his shoulders. Carrying a load suddenly felt more natural than ever, his body comforted by the burden. He was, after all, a countryman's Wang.

He turned and headed for the door, tiptoeing over the sleeping bulges in the front room. He counted each good-bye: Second Uncle with his calm, closed eyes; Third Uncle with his pregnant wife in Cen Cang Yan drinking the folk medicines meant to provide a son; Cousins Sheng, Ling, and Zhang, each taller than the next, their long Wang noses and flat-topped heads; and finally, his Father, the man usually awake after midnight now assuredly asleep. Comrade Wang had never witnessed his father asleep before—he always roused before them and worked well past their bedtime. As his foot lifted over his father's chest, he looked like he exhaled into this world from a distant place—his lips curled downward in a removed frown, eyes, closed, displaying their beloved double-flap eyelids, his chest more expansive than ever. Their father asleep: nothing like the man he knew in life—the man moving from one door to the next hawking shoddy goods, his Cen Cang Yan hands with the thickest fingers of any urbanite. *My father*, he thought, perhaps the last time he'd think those words in the man's presence. The shape of Comrade Wang's body still dented the mattress beside the old man, so many years this mattress buoyed them in sleep.

"I'm not the dreamer now," he whispered thinly, hoping his brother would hear. "You are." He waited under the shikumen frame for his brother's retort. Nothing came but the kiss of a passing breeze, the shuffling of unknown feet on nearby Yan'an Road. Finally, he closed the wooden door behind him. He observed his own shadow, how it pulled knowingly down the alleyway leading to the center of the city. If he took that first step across the threshold, he could never look back. He positioned his knapsack squarely on his shoulders, lifted his head to look forward and only ever forward, and sucked in his stomach. When he did, his abdomen recoiled—the earlier beating in the prison cell left his waistline bruised and sore. He doubled over, coughing up the remains of that day's lunch (week-old congee and a stale, bready mantou).

"Good-bye," he whispered, if only to himself, as he stepped into the quiet, empty path and over his spent, moonlit remains.

Amber street lamps traced his path, led him up snaking roads to wider avenues he'd never before traversed. Brick buildings entombed the moon, the sky the only witness of this farewell to the city of his teenage years. What did it matter what he could see beyond here? Today, said the constant drumroll of time. Again: Today. Today. Today.

Comrade Wang sang his reply: *North, north, north.*

Finally, the moon descended below the horizon of sloping brown roofs, showing only half its face between buildings; in the morning, the sun regained its rightful prominence in a boastful, post-storm sky. At dawn, Comrade Wang entered the volunteer army's station, slipped into his newly issued uniform (crisp at the wrists, cuffed at the ankles), and joined the others who looked just like him—suited in olive with brown belts cinched tightly around thin waists, hands clasped tightly, ever so sweatily, behind backs—boys becoming men. From a photograph on the wall of the dressing room, General Peng Dehuai looked over them with stern, paternal pride. They saluted him, sharing in the excitement that maybe one day they too could be generals, could survive their own long march northward over their nation's highest mountains and fastest running rivers.

In chorus now: *North, north,* they repeated, excited by the prospect of walking to their nation's borderlands. Our new nation, they said, pulling on the word that implied an empire turned into a homeland. Finally, they were a part of something larger than their own thin shapes, those timid shadows they wanted to abandon in the alleyways of this squat city. Surrounded by their comrades, they told themselves this direction was the right one. The only one. They believed if they squinted just so, they could see the end, a final destination bursting hot and bright from down the long tunnel of interminable marching days. Within a week, that scent of hot glass, so long embedded in Comrade Wang's skin, was gone. His knuckles healed, new skin eagerly closing in atop the old in a spider web of scars his wife would one day kiss over and over again trying to make them disappear.[6] At night, along unlit country paths, the moon directed the troops toward tomorrow's sunrise. The future never felt so within their grip and the past—well, they did not speak of wasted, foregone things....

---

[6] How many kisses erase a map of scars? Did she know their boundaries—their right angles and crisscrosses—as well as she could remember the decisive pull of dying sunlight on his head as he bounded the four flights of stairs in evening, carrot fronds waving from a canvas bag that once held a pig's head, its ear flapping just as assuredly and reminding her that silent creatures have their own manner of speaking?

They marched over purple hills swathed in evening sun and skipped into sloping, empty valleys, across dung-scented oxen-plowed fields of towns with new names like Rising Sun Village and People's Hope Fields and through clustered, smoky villages smelling of a childhood they'd once known but couldn't name anymore.

They called each another 'Brother' and forgot what cruel nicknames they once shouldered at home. They were family now. One Jia—家—sheltered beneath a shared roof. Their true fathers—Chairman Mao, Lin Biao, Deng Xiaoping, and Peng De-huai—once crossed mountains as high as these, survived winds that seared skin off cheeks; these brave men would lead them home. If they followed the paths of their comrades and generals, fell solidly into a confident, forward-facing line, they knew, like a flock of swallows racing to overtake a setting sun, they'd never fall behind.

Kang-Lin

Once outside Jingshan Park, we jogged down the hutongs, ducking below beizi hung to dry, feet too loud for our ears, fear gnawing at our shins as we left the city's spacious heart and entered the cluttered arteries clogged with coal fires rising from inner courtyards. This was the coldest autumn Beijing had known; our neighbors hoarded coal rations, fought over fallen summer twigs like wild dogs tearing apart chicken bones. Kang-Lin and I turned past the old city moat where months before we spent our Sundays fishing for trout. Behind fogged windows, human shapes shifted, bodies rising from bed, forearms wiping sleep from eyes, fingers sliding the fragile innards of eggshells into boiling water. Doors opened and closed, moons kissed mirrored reflections on frosted patches beneath gutters. Kang-Lin was quiet, which meant she wasn't sure our agreed-upon excuse for our whereabouts would save us. Methods of possible punishment strummed my thoughts: the lash of a leather belt slipping across my bare buttocks, the swat of a metal wok against hipbone, the slap of a wet-palmed hand to chilled cheek. My grandfather's bulging eyes, my grandmother's manipulative scowl: I was never the grandchild they expected. If only they had a grandson. I never asked anyone why I was an only child. The "Most Prideful Child," my parents called me behind closed doors. I jogged after Kang-Lin, lungs burning, my heavy pack slapping my back, surely leaving a bruise.

At the corner to our parents' danwei, she stopped. I'd never seen my friend so breathless.

"You… go… first…" she wheezed.

"No!" I wasn't going alone. We sinned together, we accepted guilt together. That's how friends were. "Why me?"

"You're a better liar. I saw it in your eyes in Teacher Liang's class when she had you by the neck."

Like a sewing needle pricking the softest thumb, Kang-Lin reached inside me and scooped out something resembling pride. What was left dangled in the cold air between us. I was ugly from this angle. Moonlight glinted off cracked windowpanes and somewhere a hungry tomcat meowed, shrill as an old tai-tai unhappy with life's meaningless lot.

"That's not true," I protested, but as soon as I spoke, a shadow approached from the corner of the danwei.

Kang-Lin pulled me to duck behind a pile of coal briquettes saved for the factory's fires.

The footsteps drew closer, our heartbeats pulsing, then the sound miraculously shifted farther away, toward the blare of the loudspeakers.

"Go," she nudged me.

"No." I still didn't understand why I had to be the brave one. Or was she insinuating she wasn't going home, that she had other plans not involving me tonight?

I turned to ask why she wouldn't walk home with me but then a shadow much larger than my own consumed the brick wall and wavered there, steady yet shifting, a foot tapping, hand on hip.

"Wang ba dan…" Kang-Lin's curse was fragile as a cuckoo's song in winter.

I turned from my friend to face the shadow's owner and there she was—Teacher Liang: her cool, tall figure, a cigarette between her fingers, her free hand brushing snow off her lapel. When had it started snowing? I tilted my head to the sky and the heavens descended toward me in patterns of impeccable light. The world didn't care about me at all right now, and for the first time I wondered if it ever had, yet here I was, standing face-to-face with the enemy, being called to say or do something brave beyond measure. I knew I wouldn't perform well.

"If it isn't my favorite student," Teacher Liang said. A laugh the size and shape of an apple formed a cloud between us. The apple took its time disappearing. "Out for a midnight stroll?"

"My grandmother needed soy milk for my grandfather who's sick with the flu," I lied. Kang-Lin was right. It felt good and right on me—the first in a long line of lies tasting as sweet as mung bean soup.

"Soy milk? At midnight?"

"For his stomach." I wasn't surprised at how easy these traitorous words spilled from my mouth. For once I felt I had something to protect—and that object was shrouded in my backpack, lying against my back like a stone. The moon itself as witness: we were tied inescapably to the words we loved, the idea of a language so beautiful and forbidden.

"I'm sure she'd rather you get home now that it's snowing." Teacher Liang pulled the cigarette to her mouth and sucked on it, horse-like in her devotion. I vowed I'd never love someone who smoked.

I nodded, stepping around her and shuffling my feet to avoid slipping on the slick path between buildings. Kang-Lin stepped out as well, standing beside me like a devoted sentry. She nudged me to walk forward and although my feet didn't know better, I followed her lead.

"You're lucky your father was a good friend of mine," Teacher Liang called to Kang-Lin as we walked away. "Your friend Li-Ming isn't as lucky with that cunt of a mother."

Something within me unraveled, a top snipped loose of its string, a planet released of gravity. My entire body went limber, knees separating from thighs, thighs stretching from hips, hips removed from waist, waist departing from—WAIT: to where had the balloon of my beating heart escaped?

Many years later I will look up from this blue-lined book hoping to see something of the girl I was that night outside the apartment complex's dusty windows but there's nothing. For millennia, winter promised spring. That, as we know, is the natural progression of things. Nature: something we could rely upon for consistency. But it was the night I learned we'd lost the natural way that I also lost myself.

I stood looking at Kang-Lin who was nodding at me to hurry home. Her face told a story I could read to its last page—we escaped more severe punishment and now were free to carry out our plan: To read these books cover-to-cover as many times as we could and to live by their words; to teach everyone we knew of their significance, or to carry this with us, the most sacred secret two young girls can carry? There was a glimmer of hope blanketed by urgency. I imagined us like the Bodhidharma, using words to rid the world of words as he traveled from India to Indonesia and all the way to the Shaolin Temple. That's the inescapable tragedy of youth: everything feels utterly important. Only with age, the inevitable passing of years, do we forget how much urgency there once was. How much power was contained in the necessity for everything we did to be filled with so much purpose and meaning.

"Hurry home before I call your Capitalist pig of a mother," Teacher Liang said. Her face glistened, a pork hind left too long on a banquet table. I half-expected houseflies to encircle her cheeks. She'd always be the ugliest woman I'd ever know even though the local cadres wrapped their meaty forearms around her hips at every danwei party.

Kang-Lin tugged on my sleeve and once again gestured it was time to go.

"Fine," I was sure I whispered even though there was nothing in me that wanted to return home.

As we jogged along the usual paths, past the second row of buildings just constructed in the Soviet style, their square, unembellished shapes, I could see my friend's shadow wavering through the alleyways, but not her form. She was five steps ahead, always a little faster, more eager to get where we were going; it didn't matter if it was the Wangfujing night market or the Fragrant Hills or the communal toilets outside school. Always, she got there first. Always, I followed. I wasn't yet old enough to understand I'd be following her forever, that I'd never catch her.

"Listen," she said, when she finally stopped at the bottom of her apartment's narrow entryway. In the new danwei complex, her parents were afforded a plum second floor spot—not on the undesirable ground floor, but high enough for a hearty cross-breeze in summer.

"What?" I was at the short end of a very long rope that started unraveling in class the week prior and now frayed to the point I wasn't sure which section was safe to hold.

"You have to promise me something. Are you listening?"

I nodded but she couldn't see me; the moon was on her shoulders, not mine.

"Promise?" Her head leaned closer.

"Yes," I said. "I promise. But tell me what I'm promising."

She cuffed her hand around my wrist.

"Promise me tomorrow you'll return to the Scholar Tree at midnight. I haven't finished reading everything I need to read to you. If we meet there, I can read to the end. Then I'll tell you what we need to do in this life and in all the lives we will one day become."

"Isn't there just this life?"

"It's not that simple."[7]

"Nothing with you ever is." This sounded more caustic than I'd intended and her eyes did that thing they'd done earlier where they grew both bright and damp.

"Just trust me. Can you promise you understand there's more than this?" *Zhe ge bi nei ge hai you duo.* A strange construction of duality, like no form in form; no shadow without shadow. She always talked in riddles and when she didn't sound pretentious,

---

[7.] As Cold Mountain writes, "If you were too dumb the life before, you won't be enlightened today."

she sounded like someone worth listening to.

"Okay," I said. "I promise."

"Good," she loosened her grip and walked to her stairwell. Earlier we said we'd each ascend separately so as not to make too much noise. Naturally, she would go first. But on the first step, she paused, only her feet to shins visible in the dark, the rest of her body cut by night. She said, "You must believe me." She didn't wait for me to confirm, instead leaving the weight of that mighty "must."

"Of course I believe you," I said, but it didn't matter—she was already on the second landing slipping her key into the lock and quietly sliding past the doorframe and into bed. I waited a few minutes, long enough for two homing pigeons to fly past the moon, their shrill whistles cutting the night in half, the moon soon enshrouded in a thick, impermeable cloud.

"Of course," I said again. Funny how words lose potency when spoken to no one in particular.

The cloud hung around the moon, satisfied.[8] I stood there, waiting, for what I wasn't exactly sure but already knew there are times in our lives we must sit and wait, stare at walls or into the spines of books, and if we don't patiently observe the passing of events we'll miss the point entirely, even if that point is beyond comprehension, cannot be pulled through the thin head of a needle or draped like a cloak over the entirety of the universe, a sheet blanketing a lampshade or shrouding a forgotten corpse.

Finally, I walked into the apartment where my grandparents stood in the doorway with a look on their faces of relief and anger. I swallowed so deeply I could hear my heart in my throat, feel the moon crash onto the city's rooftops, this roof above my head specifically, this home, now mine, where I vowed to sleep until I didn't wake up.

[8.] When had it stopped snowing? In the world of Li-Ming's making, the moon mocks us.

Baba

The chill of Changbai Mountain in November bites your heels. Fleas survive the frigid temperatures. You don't know how, but the critters ignore the cold, crawling up your legs and burrowing into the warmth of your sparse, downy leg hair.

Fat Wang instructed his colleague Skinny Wang, previously and occasionally known among certain circles as Comrade Wang, to bathe in vinegar to kill the fleas. Like a well-trained schoolboy, Skinny Wang dutifully did so every night alongside his comrades; in the morning, they'd gather in tight groups to lick the freezing yellowed tips off their fingers, huddled together under the cotton bedding with the winter-white sun above as frosted as their bones.

"Marching time!" Comrade Deng barked one morning, sliding his face under the front flap of their tent. Deng was their leader. He guided them to the 40th Battalion's station in Andong City, on the border of North Korea. He was also the son of a party member who participated in the Long March. Deng never let the troops forget this, repeatedly telling the story of how his father lost his toes to frostbite on Jiajin Mountain every time one of the boys complained about the cold in Liaoning.

Fat Wang snored, asleep on the ground beside Skinny Wang, oblivious to Deng's call.

"Fattie!" Deng barked, stamping Fat Wang's cheek with the butt of his cold gun. "Wake up. It's marching time."

Walking was bearable only by listening to the music of it: *beat beat* stomps your right heel; beat beat echoes your left. Rocks easily tumbled out of their way, mice scampered beneath the thick roots of tall pines. At Andong City, they set up camp just in sight of the Yalu River, the new nation's watery border with North Korea. Chunks of ice stoppered the river's flow, a wide expanse of silver-black set against small puffs of coal smoke rising sporadically from the villages surrounding the unassuming city. These boys stood at the edge of the empire. The Middle Kingdom. On their topographical maps, China was the center, Korea a tiny spigot grasping for the waves of the vast Pacific.

Skinny Wang sat at the scope, setting the focus on the yellow marshy banks across the Yalu, his Russian *pps* submachine gun strapped across his chest, the same gun the great Martyr Lei Feng would display in posters glued to walls all over the country. Skinny Wang only fired the weapon once—during his first day on the job when, skittishly, he mistook a deer grazing in the far bank's forests for an enemy advance. The deer dropped, twitching, as several North Korean villagers ran from behind the pines, knifing the animal's throat and fighting over the meatiest parts. Despite this mistake, it was his assignment to watch for abnormalities on the shore and to alert Deng of suspicious activity—American troops amassing over the hills, a plane's wings tipping above the horizon. He sat for weeks seeing nothing but dense winter clouds punctuated by large bodies of black geese in flight and flocked Vs of seagulls. One day, a pair of red-crowned cranes streaked across his view, nearly knocking him off his stool—so wide were their wings he thought he witnessed a fighter jet rising above the purple-fogged banks.

"See a ghost?" Fat Wang poked Skinny Wang's shoulder. Fat Wang stirred a tin of hot mung bean soup, a hungered look on his face. The thing about Fat Wang was that he wasn't actually fat—in fact, his body was quite toned, but his face was wide and his cheeks hadn't outgrown their childhood plumpness. Skinny Wang wondered if this annoyed his comrade, both the cheeks and the name. The nickname also tied him to Skinny Wang because the two were both Wangs, one fat, the other skinny, and they found themselves gravitating toward one another on the march, over the nightly campfires, in the tents, two planets drawn into orbit by the same sun. But neither understood why, nor found anything particularly compelling in the other. Fat Wang was from Beijing, as many of the troops were, and Skinny Wang kept his country boy beginnings to himself, only the occasional farmer's idiom popping out accidentally which he'd quickly gloss over with a mention of rooster women in Shanghai. Women were what kept the boys going (talk of them, fantasies at night, glimpses in the villages through which they'd marched)—all this time together, too many men without the accompaniment of the female sex, they became skeletons of their old selves. Their teeth like fangs ripping into their once-weekly allotment of pork belly, cheeks and chins swathed with stubble and grease—a warm bath was a luxury, a clean, sharp razor even more so. As Fat Wang stirred his soup, he hunched, shoulders shrugged as if matted with a coat of fur.

"I didn't see anything but a few birds," Skinny Wang said, readjusting the scope. He sat so long like this, a charcoal ring indented a halo around his right eye—the stronger side—and sometimes, when walking to camp, he'd cover his left with a hand in order to see properly. His left eye had grown so weak if he viewed the distant world with both eyes, his vision wavered, his mind incapable of making sense of the doubling of objects, the crossing of scenes.

He lowered the scope, scanned the banks with his naked, useless eyes. The white cranes had alit on a muddy patch, dipped their long necks into the river for a drink. White on brown. Two mirror images—but were there two? This was not the first time Skinny Wang's eyes deceived him: first, his mother's face below the husky river surface—and later, a face he didn't recognize in the dark, smudging clear in a photograph's reluctant ink. But now, behind the cranes, a white face was dressed in white—could it be? Most definitely a woman, her face smeared with dried mud, head thrashing, hair golden in the morning sun. He narrowed his focus, ignoring the cranes, even Fat Wang's didactic diatribe that began each morning with the sun's rise. Today's fixation:

"You know why they call this place *Andong*?" He thought he was the smartest of the soldiers because he'd read the Marxist heroes cover-to-cover. He even quoted Lenin's *Materialism and Empirio-Criticism* while they showered in the open-roofed bathhouses, one hand atop his groin to protect against the drafts bleeding in from above. They'd mock there was something quite material hidden beneath Fat Wang's palm to which their lesser-endowed comrade would simply smile and shake his head: his comrades would never understand Lenin.

"No, I don't know why Andong is Andong." Skinny Wang squinted deeper into the scope.

Fat Wang hammered on: "They called this city Andong—'pacifying the east'—because we once controlled all that land, all of Korea." We. Skinny Wang didn't ask his comrade if he meant *we* the Communists or we the Nationalists. We meant so many things those days, was a pronoun fought over by both the Party elite and the provincial farmer. Fat Wang's sweat, sweet as rotted sorghum, bombarded Skinny Wang's nose as his comrade raised his arm to show him how much our China once owned; of course, Skinny Wang saw none of what he pointed toward, his back to Fat Wang, eyes scanning a distant shore, still searching for that ghostly face he saw seconds earlier.

"Hold on," he said, interrupting the history lesson. *There it was*: that white face again. He magnified the golden head, dipped the scope lower: white hands tied behind a thin, bent back, knees deep in frosted mud. The woman nodded forward. A cluster of men kicked at her prostrate chest. Her body fell limp. Men in army uniforms dug their heels into her back, flicked still-burning cigarettes into her nested hair.

In the unfocused foreground, the cranes lifted their heads, swiveled their intertwining necks in a gleaming 8. Behind them, the woman hadn't moved in minutes. The tallest man lifted her in his arms, threw her easily over his shoulder. Skinny Wang blinked, making sure he was seeing what he thought he was—a foreign woman, probably an American, held captive by Chinese and North Korean soldiers.

"You have to see this," he told Fat Wang, but just as quickly regretted his mistake—he hadn't yet learned how we can inadvertently step into history's sweep with a word, a gesture.[9]

"See what?" A voice hovered above his shoulder. By the smell of cigarettes on the man's breath, he knew it was Deng, the only man in the troop allowed a smoking ration. Deng shoved Skinny Wang aside and placed his eye to the scope.

"Aiya," Deng said, his gloved hands caressing the tube. "Looks like I'll be making a trip across the river this afternoon." Although Skinny Wang couldn't see his commander's pancake-flat face, he could hear the man's smile rising like a schoolgirl falling in love. As afternoon sun blanketed the trees, the cranes on the distant Korean shoreline patiently flapped their wings, slowly lifting above the black river and into the golden-pink horizon. Their shapes grew larger as they flew toward the men, dampening the sky overhead and hurling shadows as big as jet planes on the winter-tough ground holding steady beneath their feet. Together, Fat and Skinny Wang glanced up long enough for the sun to be stamped out by birds in flight, their own shadows muted, lost. When their vision returned to earth, they saw Deng's boat ribbon-cutting the thinnest section of frozen river, already halfway to that distant shore, a trail of broken ice littering its path.

*

[9] "You have to be careful where you step," Li-Ming said. We circled manmade Rending Lake, only a few waltzing elderly clutching one another and dancing beneath the strange, metallic spires in the park's center. Synthesized music blast from a public speaker. I looked down, ensuring my footing was stable. Li-Ming laughed. "I don't mean literally," she said. "I mean, you could walk right into the pig shit of history if you're not careful." I didn't have a footing in history—being a teenaged American somehow made me feel exempt from history's course even though my kind has been rewriting the world's narratives for centuries.

They called the white woman 'Nurse' because when they first received her, she was dressed in a tight white cotton uniform like the other nurses attached to the unit.

They called her 'American' because when they asked her questions, she always answered the same way: 'No.'

They knew the English word for 'No' from the smuggled Western films they watched projected onto a pillowcase in the 40th battalion headquarters in Andong on Saturday evenings.

Deng said they should examine the films to study the behavior of the enemy. But they cared little for the frivolous story lines, couldn't tear their eyes from the milky necks of the actresses, black eyelashes batting, mouths parting seductively for a kiss, perfect 'O's calling to the boys. They nearly fell into the makeshift screen, that dark cavern behind soft tongues. Around the campfires, they traded playing cards displaying women like those actresses: women's full white breasts swelling toward the camera, legs spread to expose shaded triangles hidden beneath flared skirts. They joked this must've been American Nurse's profession—acting in American films—before she entered the war and became a pawn of the imperialists, before she was separated from her battalion and ended up in their hands, in Deng's.

American Nurse became their possession, the Party headquarters in Beijing told them, for only a week before Deng decided what to do with her—whether or not she could return to the Korean side of the border or if she'd stay in Andong. They wanted to know everything about her and they devised stories as they squatted over the putrid earthen holes in the latrine, in the canteen over meals of rice congee.

She must be a showgirl from New York City.

I bet the cavern between her legs smells like the underbelly of a cow.

Perhaps she's a spy sent by the Americans listening to everything we say.

"Maybe she's Russian," Fat Wang said one night as they

watched American Nurse's shadow falling asleep inside Deng's tent; for the third night since Skinny Wang first saw her along the Yalu, she sat alone there, tied with hemp rope to a chair beside a gas lamp lit for their leader to read his daily dispatches from the capital. Deng said that most of all, he liked to smell her whenever he walked into his bunk. She smelled different from Chinese women. More like a Manchurian whore, he said. Jasmine petals and cinnamon sticks.

Skinny Wang had never known Manchurian whores until he came to Andong—'Peaceful City.' This city felt foreign and not particularly at peace: the Yalu with its green-black depths said to swirl perilously high in spring and the brightly-painted women clustered like pigeons around parks, train stations, and public bathhouses with their whispers following you home, stinging your ears like winter air *(Shall we dance, Comrade? Two yuan for a kiss of this virginal neck...).*[10]

They watched American Nurse while Deng was out "on assignment," which really meant he was partaking in the local Manchurian fare, getting his fill of that smell—"untamed Dongbei pussy," he assured the boys. They sat around a fire fashioned from twigs and unused food ration boxes. Across from them, American Nurse's shadow hadn't moved in minutes. They assumed she was sleeping. Skinny Wang imagined those women from the movies, felt himself running his hand along their cheeks, down their long, white necks. Aside from the films and the one-time grope of a classmate's breast in his high school bathroom, he hadn't any

---

[10]. "A rustic living in a beam-and-thatch dwelling
has few horses or carriages at his gates,
but in deep woodlands the wild birds gather
and the broad valley streams are full of fish;
he takes his children to gather bramble-berries
and his wife to help him
husband his fields; back in his home
he has nothing to treasure
except the books piled high on his bed."
—Han Shan (trans. Peter Hobson)

physical contact with women. As soon as he got too close to one, he was overwhelmed by the difference in odor—a woman never smelled as animal as a man; the female scent was more complex, like soil and sky, elements we see every day but still don't understand inherently.

Fat Wang passed a cigarette to Liu Xiaodong, the oldest of the troop and the comedian among them; Liu had been a police officer under the Nationalist regime and joined the Communists when they took over his hometown of Jilin. Having served under two governments, he knew how to work a bureaucracy. Even though he had the look of a clean-cut soldier, as soon as the cigarette was lit and held to his mouth, he became someone else: rougher, looser, frayed. Skinny Wang envied the ease with which Liu transitioned from youth to manhood and back again. Wang himself always felt too young, his hairless cheeks giving away his youth among this group of elder soldiers. Still, they respected his expertise, renaming him "Hawk Eye" for his ability to perfect a telescope's view, for all the innate knowledge he had about glass grinding and lens shapes. Skinny Wang never told them about his father's legacy, the hours the boy spent mirroring him on the grinding machine, bodies slumped, fingers blistered—personal histories had no place in these ranks.

Comedian Liu elbowed Fat Wang. "Did you hear the one about the chickens in the north?"

Skinny Wang expected a joke, but Liu's eyes didn't smile.

Liu continued: "All over Zhen'an, the cocks are dropping to the ground like dead flies. Villagers say the Imperialists poisoned them, that the bastards are infiltrating our motherland's food supply." His shoulders raised with a fighting spirit as he flicked his cigarette into the fire, flames reaching to consume his discard. He waited for the sparks to disperse, for frowns to fade, then nodded toward the tent with a shrug and said: "I say we pay American Nurse a visit. She looks lonely."

Fat Wang didn't respond. He kicked his pack of Panda cigarettes across the circle to Peng Lihai, the troop's cartographer who left a pregnant wife at a grain farm in Shandong. Peng lit his cigarette, kicked the pack to Skinny Wang's feet. Skinny Wang took the cue, struck a match and inhaled the resinous tobacco, letting it seep into his tongue. Smoking was another habit he picked up in Andong, along with gambling for food rations and pornographic playing cards. In Shanghai, cigarettes were expensive, smoked only by the highest party cadres or the street boys who stole from the army surplus at Little World. Skinny Wang exhaled. Smoke: it cleared his thoughts in a way nothing before ever could, made him forget his brother, who'd enrolled in shipbuilding school in Shanghai, allowed him to set aside memories of his father and uncles, no longer selling their illegal lenses and now living in the Zhejiang countryside where they reclaimed plots of land from before Liberation. He exhaled through his nose, relishing the slow nostril burn.

As Skinny Wang pulled the cigarette to his mouth for another drag, Fat Wang stood over them, fists clenched but arms slack. "They killed our chickens, eh?" He nodded in Liu's direction. "Time for revenge, I say. Let's go, Hawk Eye." His sweaty palm squeezed Skinny Wang's shoulder. "Liu's right. American Nurse looks lonely."

Skinny Wang shook his head, nodding at his cigarette.

Liu kicked the butt out of his hand, squelched it with a toe. "Let's go," he said.

When Skinny Wang looked up, Liu's fat face was hungry. "Let's go," Liu repeated, using the plural 'we'—*zamen*—the 'we' that didn't allow retort, the 'we' Skinny Wang knew from a childhood in Shanghai, mindlessly following his brother's every command like a dandelion seed caught on spring wind. But what if he'd known that taking that first step toward Deng's tent would lead him down the slippery weasel's hole of his life, years clambering for roots along the dark, precipitous fall into a cave of his own making? Who was he in that moment that he'll never return to? Would he have stood there longer, head titled to an ambivalent moon, stars winking at him, all his ancestors up there watching—his mother too?—wishing for once he had the strength to stand in one place? But we don't write our lives in hindsight. We write them under each beleaguered breath, by raising an arm, loosening a syllable from serpentine tongues. We write ourselves into being with the pen of our actions, the ink of our thoughts.[11]

Skinny Wang sucked the remnant cigarette taste lingering in the air, made a tilted crack of his cervical spine, and, with Liu's *'zamen'* ringing in his ears, trailed his comrades into Deng's tent. The men moved slowly and quietly, careful not to startle their commander's possession. In the golden lamplight, American Nurse was a docile, sleeping goddess. Skinny Wang had never seen anything so beautiful and exotic; what surprised him most

---

11. "I have a favor to ask you," Li-Ming said. We sat on the sun deck enjoying the winter sun's early apricity, ficus plants prickling our backs with spiny, impetuous fingers. "What do you need?" I was eager to earn her affection, to become the most loved member in this strange tribe, the Wangs, a name once bestowed to kings now most common in the kingdom. But memory is a fickle test: her nose, waxen and freckled; her shirt, plaid flannel, soft when brushed; her eyes, loose in their sockets, unsteadily judging the world beyond the slanted, frosted windows of our perch. She was beautiful to those who knew her; to others, I don't know—she was average, commonplace? Where are you magpie who flicked my window each morning, thrice tapping the glass then flying off? Where are you baggy-faced yooo yooo egg vendor with your rusted bicycle and clanging bell? I'm making excuses for what happened next, diverting the eye's attention so the heart can't hear itself skip a beat. "I need you to help me to my ending," Li-Ming said. Sun pooled at our feet, climbing slowly to our ankles. Quickly, I thought of an excuse: "You're not that sick." But as soon as I spoke, I knew there was another explanation. "Someone sighed, said 'Cold Mountain sir your poems possess no sense'," she quoted her beloved, the same man I was eager to read. "No," I said. "Your ending isn't beginning yet." But four months later, I heard my pitched, catching voice say, "Yes, okay." *Yes, I will take you to the tallest mountain in the city. Yes, I will find a way to end this. Yes, you will be cloaked in white and we will mourn you for decades, until we ourselves are the ones being mourned.* But during the earliest question, the initial rebuttal, a housefly zipped between the ficuses, smelling for rot and decay. When it landed on Li-Ming's shoulder, I didn't brush it off. How has that become my life's greatest regret? Not the midnight in the dark room or the mid-morning on the hill or everything that followed—perhaps shame is a tattoo we can't erase.

was how her skin was golden-pink, not white like the actresses he'd seen on screen.

Fat Wang lifted American Nurse's head off her chest with the back of his hand. Her eyes flashed open, wide and white, irises the patina of winter sky. *Mo-gui*—the devil's eyes in Shanghai's Xiang Gong Temple, the evening his brother left him there alone, telling him it would grow hair on his chest, under his arms. Not so—Skinny Wang's underarms: ever bald as a baby's head.

American Nurse's *mo-gui* eyes blinked. Liu ripped a swatch of cotton from his shirtsleeve then slid it across her chin in a makeshift gag. She stomped her foot. He prodded beneath the fabric to touch her lips then reached into her mouth, tracing her gums and teeth like a cartographer to map.

"What you got down there?" he asked in mock adoration.

She clamped her jaw.

"Cunt!" he recoiled, blowing air onto his injured hand. The makeshift gag fell to the ground where American Nurse stomped on it. He pushed her over so her torso was still tied to the chair, legs free. She kicked his shins with a resilience Skinny Wang hadn't seen since his mother elbowed the Nationalists who knocked down their door.

"Be easy on her!" Peng said. He tried to help American Nurse back into the chair, but she slapped his hand and he flinched, stung by the refusal of assistance. The boys didn't understand why she didn't yield as easily as those actresses.

Skinny Wang stood in the corner. How could he react? He'd learned long before this night that interfering in another man's story only brings misery: like that midnight the Nationalists stormed through Cen Cang Yan carrying fire-lit sticks and breaking down the wooden doors as if they owned these homes. The young Wang cowered in the corner of his family's cluttered *pingfang*, a child unable to open his mouth, lips glued stubbornly, heartbeat rising into his throat, eyes clenched. A soldier with a gnarled hand smacked his mother to the floor. His brother rose to protect her and was just as summarily knocked off his feet; he fell so hard he broke his arm. That night, the Nationalists ransacked the home, taking with them every possession but an old stool, its leg broken in the melee, and the silver thimble his mother shoved into her mouth when she heard the jeeps approaching, the same thimble now tucked into the chest pocket of Skinny Wang's uniform.

Peng danced, shaking off the unexpected slap, his knuckles colored the underbellies of seabirds.

Fat Wang joined in: "You take her shoulders, Peng. Liu, peg her arms and I'll handle her legs."

Just like that, Peng, Liu and Fat Wang stifled American Nurse's movement like a fisherman strangling a freshly caught trout.

"Hawk Eye!" Peng wrapped his arms around American Nurse's upper body. "You grab her head."

Skinny Wang didn't know what his comrades meant for him to do, but American Nurse's hair was coiled at his feet like golden weeds, the curls sliding over the floor as she thrashed.

Fat Wang pinned her legs with his knees. With a free hand, he reached down and unlatched his belt buckle. With his other hand, he removed a knife from a sheath beneath his waist. "Just give me a minute, boys."

American Nurse didn't have a knife. Her legs, her best hope for running away, flopped limp.[12]

[12.] For as long as I knew her (shorter than a cicada's life span but longer than a cricket's), Li-Ming was fascinated with animate objects turned inanimate. The first month of my arrival, she accompanied me to the warehouse of a famous Beijing shadow puppeteer, telling me he was an old friend yet asking me not to tell Baba where we were going. On the outskirts of the city, near the Fragrant Hills that still smelled of jasmine and fresh-cut grass, the puppeteer converted a giant factory space into a storage room for his shadow puppets from decades of performances. They hung from the rafters, mismatched sizes, colors, and trans-lucencies, and when the sun hit them at a specific angle, they seemed to wave, like a fetus in utero reaching to her mother's touch. "Isn't this beautiful?" Li-Ming asked. I didn't know the word "creepy" in Chinese so I said, "Very strange. Like death." "No, not like death at all," she said. "Like immortality." I've since

From where Skinny Wang stood, even upside down, her face had an unkempt beauty like he'd never seen—long black eyelashes, pink cheeks, a round, smooth chin with a small dimple as if her mother pressed her thumb there when the girl was born and the indentation remained. Behind her ear was a scar, a thin, rosy sunrise. What accident caused this mark? Skinny Wang thought of the white-lit scenes of the Soviet movies they watched in the camp. Had she spilled from the door of an automobile on a wide highway? Been struck by a tree branch while horseback riding? Had her father beaten her with his ivory cane?

"You'll have your turn next," Fat Wang said, as if reading Skinny Wang's thoughts, only he'd misjudged the latter's intention. How easily love is mistaken among rivals. Fat Wang smiled up at his skinny friend as he stood over American Nurse's head, her mo-gui eyes shut. She didn't want to see anymore; Skinny Wang understood why.

Fat Wang's pants were at his knees, exposing tight white underwear worn through to the dark crack of his ass. Although five years Skinny Wang's elder, with pants like that, that grin on his face, he looked thirteen.

"Go already," Fat Wang said, nudging his comrade's shin with his shoulder.

Peng tugged on Skinny Wang's sleeve. "Don't worry, we'll share." His country boy's smile lit the dark.

Skinny Wang wanted nothing more than to run, but he couldn't. He wanted to shake himself free and rise like the eastern sun above Andong's purple hills, but instead, he sat outside the

---

wondered what happened to that puppeteer and his stock of immortal puppets. The autumn leaves, a red world lit from the inside, kicked up as we walked away from the lonely man and his puppets that afternoon, leaving a season or two in our wake. His warehouse was in a Beijing suburb that's now a technology park, rows of high-rise condominiums scooped up by eager millennials as investments, so new and empty with their cool granite countertops, stainless steel appliances. Who buries trees? Who memorializes stumps and roots? Where do the dead puppets lie now, forever entombed in a world without light?

tent and reached for one of Peng's last cigarettes. He wanted to race past the Manchurian factories with their smokestacks, leaving behind the black Yalu, the golden tents, American Nurse's perfect pink cheeks, the cigarette smell on his fingers, the telescopes and their long beige barrels steadily pointing toward a distant shore that could look, at times, like a foggy dreamscape, almost within an arm's reach, like its sands could be caressed with one's trembling hand.

But he sat outside the tent. He smoked the limp, tarry cigarettes. Waited for his turn in a game whose rules he'd only begun to understand.

Halfway through his second cigarette, after Fat Wang and Peng each, in sequence, emerged from the tent buckling their belts, a triumphant smile pulling at their lips, Liu did the same. When he returned, he walked with his chest puffed, lingering for only a moment to look at the darkened eastern sky, the Yalu's silver crust, the snow-swathed hills of Korea. His fellow comrades looked outward with him, aware, if only for a brief moment, they were part of something much, much larger.

"Your turn now," he said, nudging Skinny Wang's shin with his rubber-capped shoe. He gestured toward the cigarette but quickly nabbed the butt from Skinny Wang's fingers and tossed it into the dust. "No time for that," he said, his eyes shining a white hunger, breath visible. "A woman awaits."

Skinny Wang nodded, pressing into the cold earth to lift himself to standing. He shook blood into his legs, marveling at the body's ability to go numb at even the slightest suggestion of rest, before following Liu's path toward the tent, lifting the front flap just long enough for moonlight to swagger in, lighting his way.

Kang-Lin

We could sit a thousand years beneath a wan's worth of trees under the scope of millions of stars forming trillions of galaxies that
we simultaneously can and cannot see. We could sit there because
we've been asked to. Because someone we loved long enough to
matter to us asked us to return here. We could sit with our bones
growing cold, that same cold edging into our hips and down our
femurs to our knees and our tiny, frivolous toe joints. We could
remember this time—when we sat too long in the growing cold
of midnight—because we are now old enough to look back on
times like these and sigh.

Ahhh… Why did we do that again?

The answer is simple: love. No, it's much more complicated—
involves a tangled mix of: fear, love, disgust, envy, awe, stupidity,
genius, madness, and something so close to the inane we could
call it "meaning," but we cannot decipher exactly the right adjec-
tive nor human emotion. Needless to say, there we sat, freezing
to the point of exhaustion, not having worn thick enough socks
or our winter-weight school pants. The scarf that was once ours
had been handed down to our younger cousin who wore it like a
Russian babushka because she thought it was funny to make fun
of foreigners and our parents indulged her with hooting laughter
and the widening of their eyes with their fingers.

What else is there to say about a girl who wakes up one day
and wants to be more than who she is, who she'll never be?

I sat beneath the ambivalent leaves of that Scholar Tree in late
autumn. I didn't know it was the last season the tree would ever
bloom, so quickly it shrank and hardened like a peach in the sun.
I wish everything beautiful didn't eventually turn hard and ugly.

I sat long enough the cold made my feet numb, the tree drop-ping its last leaves on my shoulders.[13] I wanted to tell a story from the beginning so I could understand why we chased fishermen along moats and down willow-arched alleyways past the stench of an old man's piss and the mad woman who called for a daugh-ter named "Little Plum" and how this made us laugh and spit mouthfuls of peach teas we'd bought in glass bottles from the il-legal vendor in the third alleyway past the gated entrance to PLA Children's Middle School. Why was I studying alongside China's best and brightest? Why did anyone think I was anything like them—how they spouted Mao phrases with bitter ease, how they pledged allegiance to our new flag with its strident stars—how was that me? But it must have been. And I played the part so brilliantly. But then again, not brilliantly enough.

Because I was alone. Because the cells in my cheek were dead and Teacher Liang knew it. Because those who understood more than I knew I didn't believe enough. There's a fine line be-tween losing yourself to a cause and holding the smallest kernel of disbelief—it makes you shine differently than the other stars hunched over their metal desks in Classroom #5, Hallway #2. But we are only obvious to those who harbor the same pea-sized glowing kernels. That's why Kang-Lin led me to the tree, and why she abandoned me there. Because we can't learn anything in the presence of others. Because, like Han Shan says, loneliness is liberation.[14]

While I waited, I picked at a scab on my elbow and read

[13.] "Kang-Lin took me there. Where is Kang-Lin?" she asked one night as I wiped sweat off her brow. "Who is Kang-Lin?" I later asked Baba. "I don't know. One of Li-Ming's old colleagues?" But something told me he knew. Something told me he swept this name beneath the bed along with Li-Ming's hand-knit sweaters (too hot for summer, never worn again), her Fed Zorki camera (retired once it was too heavy for her to lift), and this book. For how many years was she chasing a ghost? For how many years will I?

[14.] A contemporary Chinese writer, Gao Xingjian, would one day echo Li-Ming's compulsion towards loneliness, writing:

the words I imagined Kang-Lin wanted me to read. How this old man somewhere on an unnamed mountain over a thousand years ago had written on walls, or on his hands, or on the carved wooden shaft of a broom, and someone thought these misshapen characters were pertinent enough to human life to memorize, to pass down to others, to eventually press woodblocks into thick, woolen pages, to butterfly sew with horsehair and distribute to the most learned, in every cardinal direction.

Listen, he says, in his most patient verse…

That chilled evening, as I sat counting the ways in which my best friend had wronged me, Kang-Lin was sent, by whom or what jurisdiction we'd never learn (although we had our suspicions), to live with her parents in Gansu, in a far-away village with a name like Left of Nowhere, or East of the Third Hill, or Big Cliff Above Valley. She didn't say good-bye, was transported by bicycle cart by her grandmother on a train before class, before I could ask her what she planned to do with these books, what

---

"You know that I am just talking to myself to alleviate my loneliness. You know that this loneliness of mine is incurable, that no-one can save me and that I can only talk with myself as the partner of my conversation.

In this lengthy soliloquy you are the object of what I relate, a myself who listens intently to me—you are simply my shadow.

As I listen to myself and you, I let you create a she, because you are like me and also cannot bear the loneliness and have to find a partner for your conversation.

So you talk with her, just like I talk with you.

She was born of you, yet is an affirmation of myself.

You are the partner of my conversation, transform my experiences and imagination into your relationship with her, and it is impossible to disentangle imagination from experience."

I met Gao Xingjian once at the Frankfurt Book Fair; we found ourselves sharing an elevator in the center's hall, just the two of us, miraculously, and although I spent several rushed seconds attempting to say something revelatory in Chinese, my lips clamped shut. "Thanks," I said in English, as he held his arm against the door for me to pass. I suppose when we are in the presence of those whose words we love, we lose all semblance for words; perhaps there's an allotment of well-put phrases in the world and if we're not one of the creators of those phrases, we best stay silent.

other magic we could perform beneath that ancient, cursed tree. What was I meant to do with Cold Mountain, a language cupped within seashells?

Since that night, I've wondered if because of the book she was sent west. I wondered if I too would be punished for my curiosity—"to read too many books is harmful." But I found strength in a language not my own, a realization that form is but one manifestation of reality—the physical: a farce. We love the physical but fear it too—if only we understood:

> Who takes the Cold Mountain Road
> Takes a road that never ends

I never heard the last lines of that famous Roman verse she began, the English-language tome in her bag and now in some distant village or perhaps buried beneath a rock or burned in the latest courtyard fire—she'd left only one piece of a puzzle whose size I couldn't gauge from where I sat.

The next night I sat at home alone, my grandmother at a struggle meeting near school, loudspeakers blaring:

> *Pig.*
> *Ten years.*
> *Four evils.*

I sat on the living room futon, leaning against the cold concrete wall, and pulled the book from my knapsack. I ripped one of the earliest pages from the book, sheared off a piece, placed the paper on my tongue. I let it melt, attempting to taste the words but all I sensed was birch, dust, and the tips of fingers, a muted, unforgivable salt. I chewed, swallowing the shred, and then another, fully consuming an entire page, the earliest of Cold Mountain's poems, or so said whoever chose to place them in this order, how words along a cave wall could become strokes of a printer's ink in a bound book—is this what he expected? I wanted to hate Kang-Lin. I suppose part of me did, but another part was dumbstruck by my aloneness in a world that once felt so vibrant and alive.

Kang-Lin, we were so stupid. Stupid to believe we are any-thing important or bigger than our stupid, small bodies. Then I remembered the moon rising above the Scholar Tree, how round and white and ebullient with its perpetual circling around the earth. Rising, setting, rising, setting. How consistent. The very same moon Cold Mountain once peered up at from his perch above the clouds. Things are different, but then also very much the same. There was a deep, abiding comfort in this revelation, that I was small but also large, important and meaningless, could be remembered—and just as easily forgotten.

I chewed the tough paper, hoping eventually this lost man's language would find its way to the pit of my stomach, a heavy boulder burrowing into the riverbed of my body's final shape.

People who meet Cold Mountain
they all say he's crazy
his face isn't worth a glance
his body is covered in rags
they don't understand my words
their words I won't speak
this is for those to come:
visit Cold Mountain sometime[15]

[15.] The night after Baba hands me this book, I dream of taking a long train ride and finding myself in a town with the air of a business hotel lobby: wide bou-levards, flashing traffic signals, empty high-rises reflecting an obscured sun. "Is this Cold Mountain?" I ask a man in a suit who picks his nose with a long pinky finger, looking equally as lost as I feel. He stares. *There is no Cold Mountain,* a voice says. *There is no Cold Mountain. There is no Cold Mountain. Give up.*

Dear Kang-Lin,
You'll ask me: Why write? You'd laugh at the sight of it.
Pen in hand. Paper on lap. Empty lines.
Anger: a cool stick, a bare ass.
Forgiveness: the ass's whip, stammering you into submission.
Friends forgive. Friends leave behind books.
In the dark the moon is bright and whole as the night we met.
You traced stars on the map above our heads and we reached up to poke our fingers through the canvas of a known world.
But we didn't.
And now you are gone.
No fish caught from Zhongnanhai's moat. No fishermen hauling an evening's meal. All dried out. The city walls crumbling, newly paved roads for bicycles, mianbao vans.
Old Bug Eyes in the library sniff-sniffs when I ask for the collection of poems in his name. *Good luck.*
This city smells as bad as Gan Ming's underarms.
Rats swarm the hills, carve underground aquifers, sludge concrete of earth and sky.
Wo de. Mine.
Ni de. Yours.
Ta de. Hers.
Teeth crowded with garlic and scallions: How can we trust their chattering?
In this poem, who is Pick-Up and who's Han Shan?
I laugh a wicked tone, wait for you to howl across the expanse of wasted land between us. *Motherland*, they say.
[A blackout—my ink invisible: *Damn the imperialists!*]

Yours,
Li-Ming

Baba

A lamp: flickering, sputtering, spitting dying light from buckling to bulging tent wall. Warm leg beneath his legs. Cool arm
around his waist. Stroking of cool, smooth cheek. Golden light.
Golden hair. Golden breasts. She pulls him closer. Devil's blue
eyes flash—Fat Wang's flashlight finds them in the dark, loving
shapes mocking the walls barely holding back the wind. Laughter outside. Cackling. Roosters pecking at frosted dirt. Closing
his eyes. Squinting. She pulls him onto Deng's mattress with the
integrity of a bull, dirty hair smell enveloping them, their bodies
no longer skin and bones but hair, hair everywhere. The world is
made of hair. And snail's trails crawling from pelvis to chest. A
warmth inside his belly—the resonance of a struck bell. She can't
know what she does to him. He held her by his knees, her knees.
She went limp. She did not speak his language. Who is she again?
    He tried: "I'm sorry."
    Wo dui bu qi.
    Her hand to his mouth, combing his hair like mother to child.
    Wo shi ni de haizi.
    The last time he was a child: in his mother's arms at the river, she
let him go first into the current then followed afterwards. Didn't he
know her ankles were tied with rope? That she'd sink like a briquette
to the bottom, the last oxygenated blood finding its way first to lungs,
then trachea, and finally lips, parted, for no one to see but herself, if
only eyes could still see under the dark, sun-streaked waters of the
Cao'E River,[16] that final belch reaching the surface, a seedling from

---

[16.] The Cao'E River of Shangyu is now a polluted waterway begrudgingly pulsing
north to Hangzhou Bay and named after a fourteen-year-old girl famous for dying
in its waters. Her father, Cao Xu, committed suicide here, and, the story goes, for seventeen days Cao'E searched for him, sitting patiently at the riverside for his return.
According to one account, she threw her clothes into the water, hoping he'd reach

soil or a bird's beak cracking its shelled womb. Did he see this bubble when it crested the river's skin? No. He was halfway to the city of Shangyu when his father found his body lying like a sunning muskrat on the riverbank, panting and starry-eyed, a four-year old who didn't know how to swim but somehow conjured enough strength, or rather, buoyancy, to float, to survive. The soap tree: he'd seen it from the river, those long arms reaching to lift him towards the sky, saving him with his mother's scent.

For a long time that's what he believed—floating was survival. And survival was life. So life was a contained buoyancy, the ability to stay afloat when all else threatened to drag you down, bring you to the depths of which he'd only once overheard (his uncle's palmed whispers in their Shanghai apartment, telling Third Cousin how Wang's mother succumbed at the bottom of a river bed, so traumatic for Little Wang he'd forgotten it all, turned rebellious, a side effect of never again being allowed near a body of water by a father who'd throw himself into a life of grinding glass, smoothing ragged edges). Little Wang who became Comrade Wang who became Skinny Wang who would soon become Hawk Eye. He was known by many names but he was still Little Wang when his father stood over the grinding machine and taught him the earliest lesson he'd know about beauty:

First you feel for the imperfection in the glass, rubbing a thumb here, like this.

Don't touch the glass with your grubby fingers.

Always wear gloves when you work the grinder.

You want to lose a thumb?

Here, feel that? That's a groove. The worst blunder...

American Nurse slid Skinny Wang's pants to his ankles in a simple clip, a groomer unbridling a horse's bit. She climbed atop him, straddling him such that she couldn't see what was within

---

for them but when he didn't, she jumped in the river and drowned herself in an act of filial piety. Myth or truth? Cao Xu himself drowned while officiating a ceremony to honor Wu Zixu, the Wu Clan's eldest ancestor, most famous for his filial piety.

her but only the shape that made her who she was: a silhouette hidden behind tent walls, a neck capable of being caressed, kissed. Without a thought or motion, he fumbled deeper inside a place he couldn't see but understood the way we think we understand a far away shore; her skin slipped against his, soft and damp. She wanted to be inside him too, so she leaned forward, tongue to teeth. Her loosened words stuck to his mouth, his dry, wind-chapped lips. Her hair was all he could see from there to the river, past the bridge, the mountainous backdrop the troops scanned every dawn. Everywhere he looked was hair.

"I'm really sorry."[17]

Wo zhen dui bu qi.

Her palm pressed like casket to mouth, lips against her hand so as to kiss her flesh to his.

His eyes worried shut. On the black screen of his memory: the night of Ba Jin's film, flickering black and white on a barrack bed sheet in Shangyu City, that stench of the drained river reaching their noses and stinging their eyes, his mother scratching the boils climbing her thighs like ivy. A full moon guided her to the river, her home for countless generations. His hand reached for hers beneath the glittering surface, her hair gripped his wrist. Too

---

17. I stood in the darkroom beneath Li-Ming's danwei, a hand to the radio, the other across my chest, atop Baba's. The pictures Li-Ming took of me smudged clear in ochre light, and, aside from the photographs, our faces were all we could see of one another. I asked Baba to join me here, thinking the darkness could make everything worth saving, childish enough to believe we could right a wrong by adding yet another. I wanted to be loved by the characters in this story. I wanted them to find me distantly fascinating and consumable. The smell of turpentine followed us home. The moon cast a cool, bitter light atop the snow-drifted aspens, our feet, and all this felt like the reason we were drawn together and why we could, so quickly, cleave apart. When we got home, she was gone but her mark was everywhere—the abandoned tea kettle on the stove, its cool, steel body still rimmed in steam, the crane beizi on the futon cocooned in her body's shape, the book, the one we didn't understand would become our beginning and our end, opened to a blank page, rustled by wind creeping in from the open window on the sun deck, the unseen ficus plants who, in the dark, bent their heads passively, avoiding any request for an alibi.

late. Too late. It's easy to tell a story from the beginning when the beginning is something you've devised. Harder to drop into its middle, muddle your way through tarried earth, a war, a mother's death. If he had to start from the beginning again, he would recall nothing but American Nurse's hand against his mouth. How it felt to kiss his own flesh to find hers, two bodies touching as through a pane of glass.

American Nurse's hand released, leaving behind the indentation of her sweat-shriveled fingers. She ran her fingernails down his curved spine. Sang a song he didn't know with low, dire tones belonging to thick-shouldered American farmers, to fields sinking into horizons entangled with a golden dusk. She didn't smell like Commander Deng described—no cinnamon and jasmine, but the honey-sweet pods of his hometown's soap tree, his mother's favorite. She leaned closer, hand finding his lips, fingers parting ever so slightly to probe her tongue toward his. That feeling of falling again, like a body slowly descending under water. Or a stone. Burials. She wasn't his mother, he reassured himself, while American Nurse confirmed this—she spoke in rambling, pitched syllables he didn't understand, words slipping unlike his mother tongue, traversing a map he hadn't crossed, rivers and mountains forged to reach this place so far from home. Was she drowning too? He touched the cool spot behind her ear, tracing that crescent scar he hadn't noticed until now.

She placed her hand atop his.

She shook her head: 'No.'

No, he knew. *Bu*, she said.

Bu, he said, kissing her throat, her skin salted soap.

Bu, she said, her lips curling into a child's smile, eyes cool.

Bu, he would not speak a word.

Bu, they would not speak together.

Bu: her whispers catching on the penetrating strobe of Fat Chen's flashlight.

Sirens rang, awakening Skinny Wang from a world in which he'd become Chuang Tzu's storied butterfly—he flew over the Yalu's slate gray fields alongside another blue butterfly. Overnight, Skinny Wang had become a romantic.

American Nurse was beside him, rolling in sleep above the sheets once stained by his comrades. Her hair was a swallow's nest. He closed his eyes and flew toward that dream abandoned minutes earlier. The earth, steady in the distance below, the sun a globe he could reach for with wings. But who was the butterfly? Their wings singed when they reached the heavens—unlike the famous xian immortals, he would fall...

Flashlights pulsed through the canvas, shredding what civility they attempted in sleep. Boots stamped an uneasy chorus on the Yalu's crusted banks.

"Kuai zou!"

"An air raid," Skinny Wang noted, as if the events outside their tent were still distant and he was still that wisp-winged butterfly. He stood slowly, shuffling blood into each limb, reaching confidently for his pants and fastening his belt, envisioning himself like the heroes of those Soviet films, but he wasn't playing the part well—American Nurse didn't understand. She opened her eyes and quickly stood at the next siren's wail, cupping her ears and allowing the bed sheet around her to drop, exposing her naked body, all those curves and indentations the troops loved so much, expected of her golden skin. Despite the fact Skinny Wang had been more intimate with her than this, in this instant, she looked blisteringly naked.

He gasped. She gasped, experiencing her unexpected nudity, then dashed around the tent, buttocks wiggling, searching for her old uniform, the white faded yellow. After some searching, she pulled the coat over her head, mud penned across the garment's chest. The mud was in the shape of the character:

说

To speak, to say, to tell.

What could Skinny Wang say? American Nurse, now dressed, shushed him. She crouched in the corner, arms sheltering her head. He quickly buttoned his shirt, its once-starched collar lilting. He pulled on his People's Volunteer Army jacket with its gold buttons rusted brown, readjusted the five-tipped star pin, and jogged to her side. He placed his hand atop her head, attempting a gesture of both gratitude and protection, but she shied away.

"Qilai," he instructed, softly. *Stand up.* The vocabulary of his nation's newly-penned anthem:

Qilai! Qilai! Qilai!

He gripped her elbow, but she pulled away.

"*Qilai,*" he said, this time in the tone Commander Deng used to rouse the battalion each morning. American Nurse rose reluctantly; he'd never felt more like a woman's man, as protective, despite the fact that, fully standing, her height dwarfed him, reminding him how quickly his size could suddenly be made a mockery. She pinched his side. He reached behind to feel her hand straddling his bony hip.

Shadows washed over the tent from outside. Sirens swallowed their pulsing drone. American Nurse buried her nose in his armpit and inhaled. Her arms enveloped his waist. Her chest's rise mimicked his. Suddenly, there was enough time. To listen. To wait. But to think so would be as daft as a fish attempting to fly.

"You coming?" Deng's face slipped past the tent's flap. His cigarette smoke circled upward in a slow tango with the dawn sky.

Deng.

Deng.

Deng.

Spoken in a different tone, their leader's name could mean "to wait." Realizing this, Skinny Wang laughed. Deng squinted. American Nurse, instinctively, ducked behind a Nationalist-era wooden wardrobe. She remained there, sheltered by the sturdy outline of that well-constructed Soviet furniture. How long had they been naked before this quick, instinctive dressing? An eternity, and yet like the span of an eye's wink. *To wait.* "Deng" could mean *to stare* or *to ascend.* Deng could be anything. They all could.

"Deng," Skinny Wang said, smiling. "Deng. Deng. Deng."

Deng shook his head, smiling. He was handsomer than the rest, with more highly-guarded cheekbones, fuller lips, a taller, less Southern nose.

"Thanks for taking care of my possession," he said, winking. He nodded at the rows of soldiers marching toward the barracks. "You better get in there soon. This air raid's not waiting for you, Comrade."

As he closed the flap after him, Skinny Wang was relieved Deng didn't know nor care what happened in this tent. He walked behind the wardrobe and pulled American Nurse closer to his chest, but she slipped away, found her belt and looped it into her uniform, eager to be fully dressed. Why was she acting as if she'd seen a ghost?

"Deng," Skinny Wang said, pointing at the tent's flap. He pinched his own cheek to confirm he was truly here, that he wasn't the butterfly he'd transformed into minutes earlier and looked to her strong shape outlined in the lights spearing the tent. He didn't recognize this form. They were now two different entities altogether, existing in universes so far from one another they could only examine each other through the telescopes of their own devising.

"No," she said, shaking her head. "*Bu.*"

"No Deng," he said, tapping his chest with his thumbs. This was not a Deng. He was not Deng. He was Skinny Wang. He could see across rivers, into forests. He'd found American Nurse first. With these eyes. The same eyes, he wanted to explain, which now lost focus, could only see the tip of her tall Western nose. He supposed this was what love was like but who was he to say?

"*Bu Deng,*" she repeated the Chinese, smiling timidly. A relief: language working with them for once, not laboring against them.

"No Deng," he repeated, taking her hand and leading her outside.

Above, a fading full moon struggled against dawn, its face patronizing and sullen. There weren't any planes as the sirens warned but still the blaring calls pulsed on, retiring to a place inside their heads where repeated sounds are difficult to silence. Skinny Wang's comrades filtered sleepy-eyed out of their tents, marched in line to the 40th Battalion barracks at the northern edge of the camp near the proud bronze arches of the Yalu River Bridge connecting two great empires. They'd practiced this march a thousand times.

"What's going on?" Skinny Wang asked Liu, who instructed men where to go.

Liu stood outside the barracks, feet planted, arm outstretched.

"*Qiren you tian*," Liu said, quoting the Chinese idiom about the man from the state of Qi who feared the sky would fall and crush him. "No sky falling on you tonight, Skinny Wang. It's just a drill."

"I'm taking American Nurse with me then."

Liu's eyes peeled open dimly and for once Skinny Wang saw what his young wife loved in him—his coolness, his calm wide face, his ease. His mouth rose wryly, a smile befitting only the victor: Did Liu think American Nurse would choose him? Was this what it was like to love a woman? She couldn't be anyone's but Skinny Wang's: this he'd established in the time it took for the dream of the butterfly to fade and for her to find her uniform balled beside the sputtering gas lamp. *She is mine*, he wanted to insist, but already he knew: in wanting to own her, in wanting to consume her like swallowing a pork xiaolongbao whole, he would destroy her. She could no more be his possession than she could be free to roam this frozen stretch of river, between a nation newly minted and a land filled with the sounds of fighter jets, the spitting crack of gunfire.

"You sure you can handle the bitch?" Spit lined Liu's lips. He pinched American Nurse's hip. She didn't flinch, frozen solid as the Yalu's shores.

Liu laughed then jogged to follow the last of their comrades into the barracks, breaths trailing behind.

American Nurse and Skinny Wang walked arm-in-arm, ice crunching beneath their slow, heavy feet, breath rising beneath a wanting winter moon, cranes rummaging for tubers between the pines, the river's frozen layers speaking their own language of awakening. How many years would Skinny Wang remember this moment as if it were his wedding march? As if he were returning home with his bride on his arm, his parents waiting in the narrow doorway of their cluttered pingfang, his mother's lips rising into a knowing smile: *A woman,* she would say, *someone to finally make a man of you, Wang Guanling,* using his milk name as she always did. He'd show American Nurse: Sword Temple with its stooped monks kowtowing before the golden Buddha and the gifts of oranges and dates, the Xiao's rows of fermented tofu steeping in wooden cauldrons, the river where his brother once pulled him from the weeds after he attempted to swim downstream without knowing a single stroke. And the mountain. The tall, towering mountain where his mother's body rested, peaceful, except for the occasional earthquake tremor, the mudslides arriving each May. He'd been looking for her for years. Where would he find her? The beloveds would hide behind Sword Temple, kissing, insisting she'd always stand beside him smelling like soap. Even among the ringing sirens and stomping army boots. Falling in love was easy. Digging yourself out was harder. "Bu Deng," she'd said. "Bu." She'd seen what he saw. She knew of a place beyond this place, of a world where butterflies become human and hair becomes weeds. She taught him this. She knew the human eye, when shut, witnesses more than when openly examining the green of a leaf or the trek of an ant. He knew all this because he loved her. She knew because she'd found him. *What is it about people that makes me sigh, their endless encounters with happiness and pain...*

The wide wooden doors of the barracks smacked open then shut again as soldiers streamed past. Now the pair's turn to step inside, to enter the rest of their lives alone. As if to signal this shift, the sirens ceased. In the brief silence, Skinny Wang's ears widened. Listen: American Nurse breathing, fleshy lungs expanding and contracting beneath a solid, confident breastbone. Her heart beat: strong and coarse, singing a victory song for him.

For me.   *Ta-dum.*

For me.   *Ta-dum.*

For me.   *Ta-dum.*

The sirens resumed. Deng pushed the pair into the barracks, petalled bruises of cinnamon lipstick lingering on his wide, tanned neck. He'd found his Manchurian princess after all.

"You," he said, pointing at Skinny Wang. "Get to your telescope. This isn't a fucking drill anymore. The Americans are coming."

Deng grabbed American Nurse by the shoulder and pulled her toward him. With his touch, she bared teeth.

"Stop," Skinny Wang said, but his words were made inaudible by the renewed siren drone.

As Deng dragged her away, Skinny Wang stood helplessly, hands withdrawing into fists inside the pockets of his damp, wrinkled pants. Deng's arm aggressively (or was it protectively?) around her waist, bodies side-by-side, she slowly grew smaller such that she was not the tall woman standing beside Skinny Wang, but the size of his hand. Her hair, which she'd pulled into a bun during her frantic dressing, loosened into wavy snakes that crawled over Deng's shoulder.

His arm on her back. His palm on her waist. Her hair glancing his skin. The moon swallowed by the blue-gray sky. Clouds flirting with the hillsides, tip-toeing closer. The earth, brown along the rivers, green atop the forests, swelled with lonely pride.

Skinny Wang's feet instinctively made their move, as they would always do in times of fear or anger. "Wait!" he called

Deng's name in the falling-rising tone. As he ran, he pulled his hands from his pockets and his mother's thimble tumbled down the frozen riverbank toward the mismatched shapes of Deng and American Nurse. Skinny Wang reached for it, but tripped, knees landing harshly on hard mud. White on brown could be silver on brown, could be American Nurse leaning forward, digging her hands into the earth. She could turn, reach for his hand in the distance, a hesitant last grip, but where the thimble had been was now a comb—he stretched forward, extended his arms to scoop up the fallen amber object. Why does memory play games with the objects of our lives? The teeth jabbed his fingertips. Teeth and mud and the last grip of her fingers before Deng dragged her into a boat that peeled the river's navy skin. He held the comb to his face, wondering exactly what he'd lost, what scene of the story he'd merely imagined. Had his mother left him her thimble or her comb? Such was a mind capable of resisting reality. Such was a man whose arms and legs were drawn by a distant puppeteer, the eager flicking of wrists that lifted an elbow, shrugged a shoulder, cocked a head.

Hello, Hawk Eye. Nice to meet you.

As he lay prostrate, the comb in his outstretched arm, the earth crumbled beneath him, a steady heel stomped into his back.

"Hurry your turtle feet, Hawk Eye." Fat Wang stood over Hawk Eye, the little boy from Cen Cang Yan who was once called Skinny Wang and now was mastering a new name. Fat Wang helped his fallen comrade to his feet then directed him to the line of soldiers running to shelter by the riverbanks, the telescopes with their greedy gazes. Hawk Eye shoved the comb in his coat's breast pocket where it could be warmed by the heat of his chest. He thought he glimpsed silver on the bank, but then a fellow soldier's boot stamped it away. Like awakening from that dream, he'd forgotten, momentarily, who led him here, how he had a name, several in fact, how he'd always marveled at the sound of someone calling for him, reminding him who they believed he was meant to be.

"Hawk Eye!" a voice spun in the distance, but this time he didn't turn to see who called. With his bare eyes, he scanned the horizon, but couldn't see American Nurse, or Deng, or the boat, or barely the far bank of the river shrouded in morning fog or the cranes[18] who'd since alit to some other shore, a more quiet, passive riverbank on which to make their roost. Around him, his comrades swarmed the banks of the Yalu like river rats while roving shadows blackened the hills from above.

*

They say you see them before you hear them, blue birds dampening the soil beneath your feet with wide-winged silhouettes. Fat Wang yelled for Hawk Eye to cover his head as the rising sun's rays disappeared. Black everywhere, morning blinded, and a sound like the sky being torn in two.

His comrades kneeling beside him, Hawk Eye stood, gripping the scope, his stronger eye trained on the near banks. He fixed his view on the boat cutting across the remnant ice floes, a silver army cruiser with the requisite five red stars freshly painted on its sturdy flanks. *Our boat.* The People's Republic of China's boat heading away from these western shores to the eastern forests on the opposite side of the Yalu. To a war that wasn't theirs, a war that implicated them all due to the sheer audacity of shared borders. Lines on a map so thin the boys could trace them with one long pinky nail. Lines that could be shredded, born anew. Their boat straddled that line like she owned it.

He searched for the golden head, the hair that slid from its

[18.] Cranes in Chinese poetry: symbols of the immortals. Li-Ming never spoke of cranes but Cold Mountain wrote of them. I've never seen a crane but in my research, I discovered there's a hotel at the base of what is likely Cold Mountain's home called Double Golden Crane. The hotel's website photographs advertise a bedside panel to control the room's lights and television, a haw candy left on the pillow by housekeeping each night. Where is the mountain now? I call the hotel to inquire but the receptionist laughs and says something in a local dialect I can't understand. "There was once a mountain!" I shout but she hangs up while her wisped laughter boils my ear.

bun, once beneath his nose. On the boat, a cluster of black-haired men donned mud-caked army-green helmets. So many men that looked just like them. Where was she?

"*Bu*," Hawk Eye whispered, hoping she'd hear his call down the long barrel of his telescope. "*Bu Deng*."

"What? Get down, you turtle shit!" Fat Wang huddled beneath Hawk Eye's feet within an oil drum's tin box big enough to fit two men. Behind them, their troop's Russian *pps* submachine guns trained the sky.

Someone yelled: "Hawk Eye! Did you catch that last pass?"

But he hadn't been looking up. He'd seen nothing but the winged shadow beneath the scope, heard the sound of the world being split in two, everything he'd known cut between two sides: *here* and *there*. Halfway across the river, with his good eye, he watched as the boat hit a chunk of ice and the motor spun in place, churning froth. Another screech in the sky, another damp shadow. Fat Wang screaming for him to crouch, Hawk Eye held steady the scope's lens, feet a determined tripod. He scanned the length of the river—the far bank misted white and brown, tall pines lining the shore—knowing he'd make it to the end, could add whatever what metaphorical flourishes were necessary to their love story until he found what he was looking for: *her, me, us*.

From the boat, like a white flag of surrender (or a rescue flag?), an arm poked out of a sleeve and waved above the mass of bodies. The palm flashed, five fingers, distant and white as a star. He watched as the hand became an arm, the arm a shoulder, the shoulder a hip, a femur, ankle bone, last tenuous snub of toe. He loved her because he'd made her with his thoughts, because somewhere someone decided this was the way his story would be told. He thought she was beautiful because he was told she was. He thought she was American because that was the word they'd used, nation conjured, when no other temptation, loathed and admired, would suffice.

His eyes reached the length of the scope to touch her fingers, to interlace them with his own. *There*, he thought, manipulating the glass to reflect his fingers grappling for hers.

But the arm recoiled. Silver jets sluiced the sky, spilled a black rain onto the far shore and the riverbank's ice moaned. Fat Wang dragged Hawk Eye to the ground, the telescope tilting absently on its base, its view of winter's streaked cirrus clouds above.

The boat's engine sputtered against an icy expanse of river. The only sounds were human: machinery created for war, an ever-chattering industriousness. The jets dipped beneath the horizon, trailing white ringlets.

As Hawk Eye crouched, defeated, on the ground beside his comrades, his arm remained outstretched, fingers hopelessly combing the chilled dirt. What did he hope to find? Maybe he believed there would be another day they'd wake with limbs entangled, eager to tell one another (说) the story of their own inventing. But somehow, too young for this, he knew what he gained that night was already lost, churning its wake across the angry, uprooted chunks of river ice that now flowed, untethered, downstream. How long could he await a return? He raked his fingers through the cold mud. Peeled away a layer of earth, smeared a clump across his lips, cheeks, chin, throat. He reveled in the cool touch that always supported him, relieved perhaps some things always remain. But what are they? What form do they take when we're gone? His comrades—they were silent for quite some time. They were listening for the next fall of rain.

*

After American Nurse's departure, after Deng returned from the other side of the river with information about the American advance from the peninsula's southern region and a frostbit tip of nose, there were meetings, questions behind closed doors, in no-windowed rooms clouded by cigarette smoke, sweat dripping into eyes, stinging and sour. After a week, they lined the boys on the far side of a cold gray metal table. A swinging bulb hung from the ceiling, bending light atop their heads and shoes. In the time since the air raid, they'd lost what stubble and girth made them feel like men in the months prior. Even Deng looked like a boy donning his father's too-baggy uniform, wrists swimming at the cuffs, lips and cheeks kissed by winter's bite. Despite his size, Deng killed a man once. He told the troops stories of taking down National-ists in the wetlands of Hangzhou Bay, tall-spun tales verified by the bulletins tacked on the battalion walls, by Deng's status in the troop. But standing beside him now, how could Hawk Eye name the way Deng's eyes pulled toward his cheeks—sadness? No, not sadness. Regret? Guilt? Not even this was shared among those who'd been responsible for a death. What he saw in Deng that day was actually hardness. Not a protective hardness, but the hardness befitting of calcified bones or petrified wood. This calcification clung to the creases around his lips and brow, in the dim light fluttering behind black eyes. He was much younger than these wrinkles insinuated. Did the rest of the troop also bear this look, stripped of the masks of manhood and responsible only for the sweat blinking from foreheads to eyes to chins? What did they share, after all, but the memory of a night they'd selfishly wished would never end?

Deng shuffled his feet and stood tall as they announced his sentence: for leaving American Nurse alone in his tent that night, he would be demoted from Commander to a lesser post and sent to the wind-harsh western provinces for the remainder of his service. Liu, who Fat Wang quickly pegged as the instigator of their unlawful entrance into the tent, would be sent home to Jilin without any honor and blacklisted from the Party. Fat Wang was given a promotion in Beijing for his 'heroism' in turning in Liu. As for Hawk Eye—they didn't know what to do with him. They knew he was responsible for taking American Nurse away from the tent and into the 40th battalion's barracks that morning of the air raid, but this didn't interest them. The party elders merely wanted to know how a boy from the rural outpost of Cen Cang

Yan could be given the job of surveying the border. They dismissed the rest—they wanted to talk to Hawk Eye alone about the morning of the air strike. They wanted to know about the American jets: what color were they? How many shot across the white sky above Andong? What color was the hair of the American pilots? What shape and glean of their button eyes?

One of the prosecutors, with a birthmark the silhouette of a rooster's foot on his cheek, coughed on his smoke then waved away the cloud between them. He asked, "So tell us, country boy, how many planes did you see?"

"Seven," Hawk Eye said, lying. He hadn't seen even one, only a series of shadows slipping beneath him as surreptitiously as a spider. His lie satisfied them. They passed around unfiltered Panda cigarettes and sipped tin cups of erguotou, the firewater that warmed their bellies, lubricated their throats, loosened their tongues.

"You know a shell hit just feet from your post on the river bank, Comrade Wang? You heard that from Deng, right?" The prosecutor's birthmark glistened in the cool, damp light. Everyone was telling Hawk Eye this for days. For days, they said it was a miracle Fat Wang and he survived. They said the river transport taking the prisoners back across the border was sprayed with bullets. That a few of the prisoners had been injured, maybe worse. They said Deng dropped the transport off at the other side and returned with someone else's blood dappling his uniform. They said Hawk Eye shouldn't be standing here today telling this story. They called him a Miracle Man.

You've got a spine of steel.

You must have some strong spirit sitting on your shoulders.

You're one brave son of a bitch.

Hawk Eye nodded. But what he didn't tell anyone, not even Fat Wang, was that he hadn't felt a thing. He hadn't felt the gunfire because all he'd known was the distance between what we can touch with our hands and see with our eyes.[19] He hadn't noticed the American bullets dappling the ground because he'd been stuck inside this distance, the telescope's lens flexing and narrowing as it attempted to reach that shore from where another pair of eyes once looked into his, told him to follow them to their logical conclusion: a white stretch of sky, a dead tree's gnarled branches listing in the wind, a magpie calling from the hills, beckoning— where had he seen this scene before and trusted it to be true? He knew with utter certainty he was not alone, that someone else saw this too even though his brain resisted the notion he could be nothing more than Hawk Eye. Comrade Wang. Skinny Wang. Wang Guangling. The country boy. The boy worth forgetting. Memorializing. Paying attention to—then discarding.

Forget it, a voice reprimanded from a place where the lights had been turned off. Forget you're seeing this or hearing what you hear. Pay attention and you'll find me again. Can't you hear me? I'm speaking to you with the words inside your own head, your fingernails digging into your thighs. That's me crawling an itch up your spine and into your chin. Haha! I'm writing you from the inside and you can't even see me. I hear your laughter hidden between your ears.

He tipped back his tin cup of liquor as the swinging bulb reflected shells in his palms. A moth landed on the table, flexed its indigo wings and flew upward, enticed by the light. Insects: how

---

[19.] One spring afternoon, as her breaths belabored, Li-Ming asked me to walk into the courtyard with her, eager to feel sun on her cheeks. She held my face in her hands, tilted my view to the failing aspen trees in the apartment complex's central gathering area. What had she wanted to tell me? I saw a skeletal shape, dead branches, blue sky. Was this all that was left? "Have you ever felt an earthquake?" she asked, but I was an east coaster—we didn't experience the shifting of tectonic plates but feared the rise of hurricane oceans. "No," I felt foolish and fragile. "A beautiful thing," she said but I didn't know if she meant the tree above us, the sun in its curling perch, or the earthquake she'd once felt. The afternoon sun tugged at the square danwei buildings crowding this dusty neighborhood. Neither of us knew that in less than a decade these courtyard trees would be buzz-sawed, the earth beneath them upended to make way for a parking garage, an office building with windows so shiny the gray sky looked almost infinite.

stupid yet how brave.

"I can't believe you just stood there. You should be given a medal for that kind of patriotism," the prosecutor said as the moth's wings made gauzy shadows beneath folded hands. "Seven American jets," he repeated. He shook his head. Flakes of dandruff drifted in the light. He reached below the table to scratch his crotch. "Fucking imperialists," he said under his breath, as if the curse alone would save them from another smattering of bullets on northern shores.

Above them, on the swinging light bulb, the wings of a moth sizzled and the tiny, frantic body dropped from the ceiling into his cup of erguotou, black legs thrashing aimlessly. He plucked the poor, dumb creature from the liquor, placed it on the table where it careened, wings damaged, toward the edge.

The rooster-cheeked investigator grew drunker, along with his fat-faced colleagues. Carelessly, his lips perched on words like "border" and "artillery," he flicked the moth, still teetering on the table's edge, and it skidded forward, coming to a dead rest on its side. Then Hawk Eye's comrades abandoned talk of the war, the jets, Imperialists. As if the erguotou functioned as a love potion, they wanted to know where to find the freshest female entertainment in Andong—the city known for its Russian residents remaining from the war with Japan and the Korean refugees with their high cheekbones and fuller-than-Chinese chests. They clucked as if women would appear at the door, raising their skirts for the men to see their knees, the pressed V of their inner thighs, their...

Drunkenly, Hawk Eye closed his eyes, lulled by the laughter, the eager talk of women. When he opened his eyes, he was alone in the room, voices teetering down the hallway. The tin cups were in various states of disregard, rings of erguotou penning a silver honey on the steel table. Across from him, the moth renewed its journey, plodding through an ashtray filled with smoldering gray embers. When the insect reached the tray's end, he flexed his indigo wings as if to fly but merely fell sideways again. His thin legs kicked, wildly trying to right himself, wings shivering and useless.

"You coming?" The rooster-cheeked prosecutor leaned into the doorway. Only the frame could bolster him. He scratched his crotch. That crotch of his required a lot of attention. "We'll find you a good woman tonight. To reward you for your patriotism."

Behind the prosecutor stood several shadowed figures, shifting in eager-to-leave, eager-to-fuck positions. Hawk Eye pushed back his chair and it squealed against the concrete. He didn't want a woman that night. He didn't want anything but to sleep away the last few months, to wake up somewhere other than the crowded bunks always smelling of unwashed hair, stale piss, and dried mud.

"Yeah, I'm coming." He'd already learned—there wasn't any point in fighting Party officials; questions only lead to more questions, so not asking any was the best plan.

He followed the listing shapes down the hallway, suddenly recognizing the liquor's effect on his balance, tripping over his own feet and trusting the walls to keep him from falling over altogether.

Baba

They say in the dark a twenty-year-old's eye receives sixteen times more light than an eighty-year-old's. They say an eye's lens yellows with age, like skin or a well-worn undershirt. They say by the time you realize this, by the time you know you should have worn hats, shielded your eyes from the sun, it's too late. They say all this because they know nothing about sight. Know nothing about looking directly into the light of the sun. To be blinded by all that seeing.[20]

After the interrogation, after a night stumbling Andong's crowded streets, the investigators climbing into and out of lousy, mildewed mattresses with too-tall women while Hawk Eye sat on icy stoops smoking an entire pack of filter-less Russian cigarettes, the battalion's leadership ran their usual battery of tests on the troops: Deng first, then Fat Wang, then Hawk Eye. The boys sat on metal chairs outside the barrack's infirmary, warped, crooked legs wobbling beneath them. The leadership wanted to know how the air raid, all the questioning that followed, affected their bodies; the investigators cared little about the boys' minds, hearts. They made them sprint up and down the hallways, listened with stethoscopes to the *click-click* beating within their chests. They peered down their throats, into their noses, up their assholes. With pinpricks of light, they examined their eyes. Retinas. They

---

[20.] I'd like a red bean baozi and two youtiao," she instructed. "For my final breakfast. Tomorrow we'll rise before dawn." Her words made gasping sounds we learned to ignore. She lived in the apartment's main room where we also ate our meals; she slept on the futon, wrapped in a cotton beizi. "Carry me downstairs to my wheelchair. Take me to Jishuitan and we'll ride the subway to Tiananmen. Then we'll walk to Coal Hill. Don't forget a heavy rope, thick enough to guide me home."

wanted to know if the boys were still good for the fight against the Americans, those wide-eyed imperialists. If they were still worthy of being counted as one of the comrades.

At the end of the tests, Hawk Eye was the last to stand in front of an eye chart hanging from a frayed string above the doctor's desk. He stood, as instructed by Nurse Kang, a young woman who smelled of another man's tobacco, and read the letters as he saw them. Letters that pulled their foreign sounds awkwardly across his tongue, reminding him of his primary school teacher, Feng Laoshi, and her insistence he was too stubborn and righteous to speak English's more nuanced tones—he wasn't. He was loath to let his tongue slip, to spout meaningless words. Nurse Kang nudged him, like Feng Laoshi would. He sighed, then read:

    BZFED
    OFCLTD
    TEP...

But the 'O' following that demanding 'P' was not a letter. It was a mouth, wide and gaping, waiting for him to kiss it.

O

He squeezed his lips together, incapable of making a sound. He dug his fingernails into his thighs. O. O. Ohhhhhhh.... Oh, there was the letter 'O.' A child's gaping mouth looking up from a riverbed, that muskrat body too tanned to be a rich boy now. Oh, how was he supposed to follow this O to its inevitable conclusion? Thump. There he was on the bottom, trying to say the letter always his downfall, a reminder he knew everything and nothing at all. O was a circle. O had a beginning and an end. O was a mother's hair beneath the river's surface. O was the wife he didn't yet know, circling the Zhongnanhai moat awaiting a trout's absent nip.[21]

[21.] Oh, what was there to say about Li-Ming and Baba in her final months? They were a pair of carp encircling one another in a murky pond, her colorful tail faded gray, his whiskers catching the sun's white.

Branches raked the window. Ice melted, drips collecting in buckets outside the barracks; buckets full of last month's melted snow were everywhere, saved for the leaders' nightly baths. The rest showered in the bathhouses every other Wednesday, where the steam wasn't enough to mask their flaccid privates from the view of their comrades. Heat was a luxury. They huddled together at night near the communal fires, rubbing their forearms and crowding closer.

Hawk Eye shook his head as Nurse Kang pinched his back.

"Keep reading," she said. Her breath: garlic shrouded in floral overtones of jasmine tea. Something ugly; something beautiful. Her fingers were stronger than he'd expected. She pinched him again and he winced, waiting for that O to transform into another letter altogether.

"What's wrong, Hawk Eye?" Deng stood in the doorway. Deng: leaning like a dead tree, a sullen trunk of a man, a brown cigarette sappily dripping from his lips. He hadn't yet left the camps for his new Western provinces post—a soldier's reassignment was a slow, bureaucratic task filled with stamps and paperwork. "Can't see, Hawk Eye?"

The nurse turned on the florescent bulb dangling from the ceiling and the O disappeared, all the letters melting into a mass of shapes, triangles and circles, squares and rectangles. An uneasy geometry on Feng Laoshi's chalkboard. Hawk Eye couldn't see them any more than he could see Deng's smile rising, taunting him from his slanted stance in the darkened hallway. Where had that language gone? How could words so quickly be rendered futile?

"Read again, Hawk Eye," Nurse Kang said, assuming his nickname like an old friend.

"I can't," he said. The truth: where there was once an eye chart now hung a mass of black and white etchings, none visible nor discernible to him. His pulse drummed behind his eye sockets and he mimicked the rhythm with the tap of a foot. How good to hear the beating of his own heart. Nurse Kang wasn't impressed—her job was to test men's bodies for continued military service. She was a woman who followed orders impeccably; although she smelled light as a freshly-steamed baozi, her personality was as dense as Hawk Eye's brother's. *His brother:* He hadn't spoken with the elder Wang since the night he left Shanghai and he preferred it that way. Here, he was Hawk Eye. There, his brother called him by his milk name or 'Xiao Di'—Little Brother—and thus, he was always pegged to a perpetual youth. Here, he could be whatever he wanted. Or so it seemed until this moment. He blinked again. The world crowded inward, the old frame of his vision reduced to near nothing.

"Maybe if I close my eyes for a bit," Hawk Eye said. "I think they're tired."

"Suit yourself," Deng snuffed, then sucked on his cigarette. Since the investigation, he'd been hanging about the barracks with the air of a man recently returned from battle, only his wounds were superficial, courage untested. The boys wondered when Deng would be dismissed from Andong and sent to that western post where he'd one day meet a local goat farmer's daughter, marry her, and start a roost of twelve children—all boys. Funny the way the first words at the beginning of a story can so quickly become the drone of pages, Hawk Eye thought of Deng's inevitable life to come. Down the hall, nurses in training walked in from the cold, stamping wet snow off their boots. Deng turned to watch their slow undressing—each coat, hat, scarf, glove—eager to witness slender female shapes taking form from beneath puffy winter layers.

Nurse Kang called for the doctor who was patrolling the hallways chatting up the nurses as they returned from their rounds at the front lines. The doctor, a lump of a man, stomped into the room without recognizing the obtuse slapping of his shoes, tilting his head forward such that his eyeglasses nearly careened off the tip of his nose.

"What's the problem?" he asked.

"Watch this," Nurse Kang said. She asked Hawk Eye to re-peat his reading of the letters tacked to the far wall.

Hawk Eye blinked, staring at the letters still sliding into one another. At the 'O,' everything stopped, as if life itself began and ended with that 'O,' only he hadn't yet realized how much emptiness one circle could contain. Nurse Kang pinched him, asking him to repeat what he saw. The doctor perused Hawk Eye's records, which included his first eye exam from the party headquarters in Shanghai the day he left the city.

"How odd," the doctor noted. "This soldier's near-sightedness is still perfect—in fact, it's better than perfect." He scribbled something on Hawk Eye's chart. "But his far-sightedness," the doctor remarked with slight agitation, "it's as if he's been involved in a blast, that an accident marred his view of anything farther from him than the length of a gun's barrel." The doctor penned additional notes in the record.

Together, Nurse Kang and the doctor fitted a series of lenses on Hawk Eye's face to correct the malfunction, the glass smelling like his childhood—all those Cen Cang Yan backs slouched over grinders sparking white-gold in the midnight black. He couldn't return home now. What good was he without his eyesight? *Hawk Eye.* He shook his head as the nurse and doctor spoke in technical terms about his condition. They nodded to one another then walked down the hall to find a pair of lenses they'd loaned to the microscopy department. This pair, they told him, would save his vision.

After they left, Deng said, "I have an idea." He shuffled from the doorway to Hawk Eye's side and placed his hand on Deng's shoulder like an older brother. Deng smelled like winter, having spent so much time in recent weeks standing under a cold, ambivalent sun. Both the smell and gesture made Hawk Eye's eyesight grow in focus temporarily. He wanted, more than anything, to impress his elder "brother"—he had no idea why aside from the fact there are certain people in this world who impress us despite how much we loathe them. He'd never felt like this around his own brother, or any of his other elder cousins. Something about Deng demanded greatness. Maybe that's what killing a man gave you—the ability to believe in the necessity of life, the immortality of young men.

"I know the *danwei* leader of a factory in Beijing," Deng continued. "A factory that makes lenses just like this one." He picked the latest lens from off the doctor's desk. In the dying afternoon light, the object sprayed muted flashes across the floor, all the way to the window where a descending sun pulled skeletal shadows through the river's rowed pines. The world was only light and shadow. Shadow and light. Or so it seemed from here.

"I can arrange a transfer for you to the city," Deng said. "They need someone like you there. A man with strong hands, an understanding of telescopes."

The word 'man' still ringing in his ears, Hawk Eye said, "Beijing. Okay." He inhaled the nurse's smoke-rose smell still lingering in the room despite her departure. Funny: whenever he'd think of Nurse Kang from this point onward, however distant his vision of her face, he'd only remember her smell, matched as it was to this particular afternoon, the tea-scented oils she rubbed behind her ears upon waking that left such a deep impression upon him, even after so many years. She'd age, as we all do, but his memory of her would remain fixed to a perpetual, scented youth. She'd given him this inadvertent yet indispensable gift that conquered time.[22]

[22.] "I think this is as good a spot as any for an ending," she said. She looked at a sky that hasn't been that blue in Beijing for a long time. I didn't understand: her ending or mine? A luck-filled sky, a magpie's sky, the ringing bicycle bells not reaching us, a murmuring city awakening to its global era, distant hills still swathed purple, still hemming the valley's heat. "I don't think so," I said. The courtyard was filled with pigeons as if all of Beijing's stock of mangy, claw-footed birds descended here to surround us in their filth. "This is an ugly place," I said and instantly regretted my honesty. I should've protected her. I should've done whatever she asked—but I wasn't ready yet. She had to indoctrinate me. She had to lead me to believe that in looping the final ring, in making that perfect O as the moon showed its face, I'd follow her somewhere beautiful. Was there enough to hold the two of us? Our weight: I'll never know. That's the thing about new friendships—we sacrifice so much in walking to the water's edge but when the boat drifts away... *Ye might at least have done her so much grace, Fair lord, as would have helped her from her death.* I stood on the shore, watching the boat drift aimlessly, Li-Ming's wet hair draped over the side, long as in youth, purple as in moon, lost as in the sound of a coin dropping to a river's bed, its shine muted by time.

Beijing. The word still rung as in a glittering temple bowl. The capital was always a distant locale, an unlikely destination: if Shanghai was the rooster-shaped nation's beating heart and pulse, Beijing was its colder, less civilized head. Hawk Eye was not befitting of the Capital. He was a man of emotion, action—not pensive thought and cooler minds prevailing. He shook his head.

"No," he said. *Bu.* The strength of the word rattled a row of lenses stacked on the doctor's desk and a few toppled like fragile dominoes.

Deng dug his fists into his thighs. "No? You're really going to turn down a good job? You won't be of any use here along the river without those hawk eyes of yours. You'll end up in the western provinces slugging wheat over your shoulders the rest of your life."

Footsteps: the doctor and Nurse Kang descending the dark hall to them, to the eye chart hanging limply on the wall with its faded black letters, symbols and shapes Hawk Eye couldn't make a language of. Reading was only seeing, after all.

Deng met them in the doorway. "I'll take that," he said, pointing to Hawk Eye's health report. "They'll want it in Beijing." Hawk Eye thought he saw Deng wink, his signature slyness. What happens to a man who has killed other men? What edges of his being have been irreparably notched?

"Bei*jing*?" Nurse Kang pulled on the second syllable as she fit the perfect lenses over Hawk Eye's eyes. "The nation's capital!" This was how country people spoke of cities. How Hawk Eye's mother referred to Shanghai those early years in the fields of Zhejiang. But he didn't feel any camaraderie with the nurse's country folk fascination with everything shiny and new. Instead, he pitied her naiveté.

"Beijing," he said, standing confidently, hands on hips. "Yes, I'm going to Beijing." Little did he know that from the outside, from where we stand now, he merely looked like a mouse fighting a cat. No matter how wide he puffed his chest, how tautly he pursed his lips, he was small and the world around him was much larger. Unconquerable. Impossible.

Deng adjusted the lenses on Hawk Eye's eyes. "He'll be a fat cat in Beijing," Deng asserted.

Without thinking, Hawk Eye placed his hand atop Deng's. Deng left his there, the pair staring past the walls to something neither of them had witnessed together. Maybe Deng had seen Hawk Eye with American Nurse, maybe he knew of her whereabouts. Hawk Eye didn't want to think she'd been one of the passengers injured in the transport. To him, she was only as beautiful and perfect and naked as she was when she ran around the tent, buttocks wiggling, pearled skin gleaming in the early sun. He didn't ask Deng what happened to her, what dream could be folded into a palm and blown off course into a brisk wind. He blinked wider as Nurse Kang and the doctor positioned a set of lenses atop the bridge of his nose. Deng's hand slipped, but his own hand lingered there, feeling that remnant heat. From behind the lenses, yes, Hawk Eye saw clearly—the window shade drawn enough to view the riverbank, the boats and soldiers standing guard, trucks backing up, tires spitting profanities of mud. He could see all this, and then, closer, Nurse Kang's patient smile, a large mole on the doctor's neck, a thin black hair spouting triumphantly. He could see shifting cloud shadows on the concrete floor, a fly buzzing at the window to get outside (*a grand escape!*), every letter on that hanging eye chart. But of course when we see with such clarity, we see beyond these objects too, noticing something we can't sketch with pens nor speak with words. Hawk Eye opened his mouth, wanting to say that, in actuality, he preferred to have his old vision back—the kind that blurred at the edges, couldn't distinguish between a river boat and a floe of ice. There was something comforting, serene, in blindness.

But he didn't speak. His mouth gaping, the doctor and Nurse Kang nodded to one another, pleased they'd found his vision's perfect match.

"Good then?" the doctor nodded, stray mole hair waving in response.

"I can see…" Hawk Eye waved his hands in front of his face. He opened his eyes widely then squinted, quickly rambling off the letters on the far wall's eye chart, the English not so foreign anymore, his tongue succumbing. "Glasses," he mused aloud, laughing giddily at the insanity of this scene—the boy who spent a childhood at his father's grinder now able to view the world, to live a life for that matter, merely because of a lens's shape.

The nurse and the doctor laughed too, proud of what they deemed a fitting diagnosis, not knowing what was so funny except that it was like watching a blind man coming back the dark. They wanted to believe they were capable of miracles and Hawk Eye, momentarily, wanted them to believe this too.

Three days later, Hawk Eye left at nightfall on the bed of a military truck along with a command returning to the capital for additional training. He closed his eyes, tilting his head to gulp the cool mountain air one last time. Beijing, they said, was full of dry, desert winds, the hot press of the Gobi bleeding in when March arrived. Here, there was the wetness of temperate rivers, winter's ice melting into the blooming of Dandong's famous springtime azaleas. Hawk Eye knew somewhere in the distance another pair of eyes looked westward as he looked eastward. Another pair of eyes searched the horizon for a familiar sight, or maybe those eyes had long closed, retired behind the screen of dreams. When Hawk Eye opened his eyes, all he saw was the black night. He removed his glasses. He didn't want to view the world through lenses, this forced artificiality, how distant objects seemed close, and yet, when he reached to touch them, he'd find only air. Eyes bare, the stars blinked back at him, approving his decision. From several kilometers away, fresh troop transports grumbled toward his truck, headlights honed and glimmering like hand-plucked diamonds.

So Hawk Eye can see after all. He laughed along with the mindless laughter of the latest transport to Beijing, the laughter of forgetting the distance between what's been left behind and the soul's final destination. No one knew him here. No one knew his nicknames or why he was leaving the front.

"Can you believe it?" He shouted to the wind. His comrades paid him no attention—they'd seen much worse, the breaking of men so tall, so broad-chested, they'd forever believe the world is split into two types of people: those who've seen and those who haven't. So they smoked their cigarettes between chilled fingers, watched as the forest closed in thicker around them, the mountains that once broke apart empires now sheltering them from the overwhelming blackness of what was surely a dark, unsympathetic sky.

Hawk Eye threw his glasses into the forests blanketing the hills. Did it matter anymore what he could and couldn't see? Now it was someone else's party-assigned job to stare down the barrel of a telescope, to watch the world sharpening into focus: a moth, a bullet, an arm, an eye. It didn't matter what one saw out there because objects could be replaced, refocused, renamed. All that mattered was the distance between your own eye and the observed, the lingering question plaguing your mind of whether or not that moth, that bullet, that eye, had been there at all, or if it was just light refracting off lenses, lenses warped by rain, time.

So that's it then, he said to himself and settled into his seat on the open truck bed. He pulled the issued wool blanket over his shoulders, tucked it behind his back. He was heading to the capital. *Beijing!* His heart quickened like a bird's. If only he could fly. Hawk Eye, they called him for his ability to see such distances, to perfect a lens's shape. Now he was near blind without his lenses. If he believed them, he would've been slave to those lenses the rest of his life. Instead, he fashioned himself a man of action, a man who could walk from the city streets of Shanghai to the mountains of Liaoning. A man who, when he got to Beijing, would be the director of one of the nation's most esteemed lens factories. He imagined the party banquets, the long tables covered with bowl upon bowl of chicken feet and trout heads bathed in spicy-sweet mala sauce. And then he saw her long, cold face at the end of the table: she winked, beckoned him closer with the curl of an outstretched finger, the scent of a jasmine bush passing, masquerading as perfume, as the first hint of a dream, the requiem, recalcification of closed eyes.

He laughed into the quiet night, breath briefly fogging the cold air before disappearing, a locust's blink, from view.

Letter #2

Dear Kang-Lin,

    Chronology is a farce.

    Better to be long than cold.

    Desert cliff beneath bones betrays a bitter melon sunset.

    Judge the length of mountain shadows.

    Build a home within the clouds.

    And me, here: a pinchable shape. Between two fingers.

    That book beneath my bed; no one knows. The absent glimpse at the market—no, someone else.

    If wu-ming[23] is a form, formlessness is a form.

    Words make cocoons, bind us to what isn't.

    Mother in the corner, tsk-tsking me for reading—

    Father at the danwei, bullet-making a war we fight only in our dreams.

    Your Comrade,
    Li-Ming

[23.] "Wu-ming" = darkness. Or maybe, better said: absence of light. How strong a rope would I need? And where in Xinjiekou can I find a hardware store?

    绳 ("sheng") = "rope".

    Do you see the body hanging there, dangling beneath a calligrapher's stroke? I walked into a corner store whose windows displayed every object ever needed: toilet plunger, wrench, curly-haired wig, industrial-grade bleach. And rope. Coils of it looped around a wide, silver spool, waiting to be cut.

Baba

Wang Guanmiao had forgotten how the countryside was just a collection of smells and colors—manure, moldy hay, angled evening sun cutting reddened rooftops, soil-starched faces of village girls at washboards, their limp breasts that would one day rise pert, slack-jawed mouths singing folk songs in local lilts. He'd forgotten the quiet of places like this Jiangxi village. Forgotten loud insects and silent snakes hidden in knee-high grasses. Forgotten moonlight, his full moon invisible behind a city of buildings but now, unabashed, white faced and unforgiving. *Look up*, that moon said, beginning its journey across the sky's waist. And he'd forgotten blue. A sky the color of her irises. He'd forgotten what it felt like to be in love, how there was rapture and repulsion, how he'd once held a mirror to his face and hoped to see the reflection of someone else staring back: his first and only love touched him *here*, and *here*, and *here*. Tenderness bruised his neck, cobwebbed kisses only a practiced lover could make of his boyish body. So much forgetting he didn't believe when the sun slanted just so across her back, bare shoulders revealing a Jiangxi tan and a compulsion, because there couldn't be any other word for the impulse, to wrap his arms around her, to swallow her as wholly as a cormorant to a trout—all throat, no bite. She danced beside a pile of pig manure in a stall soon-to-be cleared for slaughter, her back brushed with freckles, shoulders tinted yellow-gold in a beam of late day sunlight. Who cared that these pigs would soon be the soy-sour jinjiang rousi at the campfire or the flecks of cheek fat relished in a morning's congee? The pigs snorted and she jigged; what music accompanied her steps was hidden, silent as the city was to him now.

Wang was sent from Beijing by his superiors to take a letter to a sent-down young woman named Ms. Huang. Given her assignment, she should've been pitching hay or transporting manure to the slop bins outside. She shouldn't have been alone in the stys where he found her—most women here were solitary, their chattering birdsong catching on mountain breezes and finding any prospective suitor's eager ears. Instead, this girl danced to a rhythm she hummed loudly, arms lifting above her head, hands bursting open, palms white and wide and waving like a distant distress signal. Her knees bent and straightened, cotton skirt ballooning with each beat. Sweat stains circled her underarms, burned a damp crescent onto her lower back that smelled alive. He walked closer. He reached to span the distance between them, to touch that dark, animal moon above the waist of her skirt. He knew that place in a woman's back, didn't he? Only once did he press his palm into the dented crease between spine and bottom, those plum dimples, how they'd make her buckle. His fingers tentatively glanced the tuck of a crisply-pressed shirt, that tight elastic waistline unyielding. But this waist was thinner, hips narrower. He recoiled his hand as she sensed his presence, turning suddenly, forced pleasantry on her face.

"Oh, hello, Comrade. Can I help you?" She reached for a pitchfork atop a stack of hay, wiped sweat off her forehead.

A thick wrist. A strong wrist. He didn't know this wrist. Nor this face—it was young, relaxed, and attempting a soft, cordial smile before a stranger's gaze. Whose face was this? The face smiling at Comrade Wang was not long and thin and pink-white beneath a winter-white sky. Her eyes were not rings of ice. Him: arms slack, grimace pulling a tentative grin, mind tilted on its axle attempting to rewrite the history he thought was his. But who was he to claim a part in this story? He shook his head, blinked feverishly to wash away temporary blindness. He was standing in Jiangxi Province. He was Wang Guanmiao (now called by his given name, an adult bound to formality by all measures).

He attempted to answer her question—but no, she couldn't help him. How could she? Wang made himself helpless long ago and this girl standing before him could never understand what it was like to live one's life on the fringes, incapable of trusting the sturdiness of one's feet, the stability of one's frame. She was a city girl attempting to be rustic, have country roots. He wanted to hate her naiveté but that's exactly what made her so attractive.

"Ummmm," Wang Guanmiao sputtered. He needed to say *something*.

She waited, a patient soldier dressed not in the typical Red Guard olive army uniform, but a blue-and-white-checkered blouse clinging to her teenage figure, all jutting hips and shoulders. She bent at angles comfortable only on the young, not quite trusting her body. The hem of her navy skirt cut above slightly-knocked knees. *Knees…* the sight of bare knees made the hair on his arms stand at attention, a distant yet familiar desire to draw her closer. Since his border years, the glimpse of the back of a woman's knee was enough to send him running to the latrines to relieve himself of the nervous jitters invading his abdomen. Aside from a brief, after-hours encounter with a distributor from Heilongjiang—a lean, wide-eyed woman who walked his factory floors for a week inspecting samples as well as the men she'd take to the back office for a flurry of kisses and errant groping (twice that happened to be a flustered, yet flattered Wang)—he hadn't been in a woman's company. His days were filled with an almost religious devotion to his work in the factories such that he was regularly allotted an extra ration of beef tongue or pig hock for his better-than-expected manufacturing quantities. The beef tongue and pig hock did nothing for his frame—lanky, still hunched at the shoulders, bones on bones—and nothing to distract him from the unending day-in, day-out of life on a factory line. But now, Ms. Huang waiting his response, blood flushed his cheeks. Here she was; here he was—in some before-unknown county in a province he'd only known on maps. He looked at her looking at him and swore she winked, knowledgeable that the greatest secret passed between them in this moment—*here we are, finally.*[24]

He blinked and shook his head again. In the distance, a truck rumbled over the sole dirt road leading to this mountainous perch. If the two of them stood on tiptoes and looked outside, they would've seen the vertiginous drop into the valley that only storks could navigate without fear, a mighty bird with a wingspan to blacken a rooftop, a child's game of marbles, a riverboat drifting off-anchor down the Gan River toward the lazy shores of Lake Poyang.

"Sorry," he said—but all he could do was look at this girl's face and try to reconstruct the one he knew years earlier. Why did he think he'd see a familiar face here? What insanity existed

---

[24.] "What gauge of rope could support a fifty-five kilo woman?" I should have asked, but instead, the shop clerk, a dense man with a wrinkled forehead handed me a key to the back storage unit. "Help yourself then I'll ring you up." "I don't know what I need." "Ta ma de," he cursed and I asked, jesting, "Why do you hate me already? You don't know me." "I know your type," he said. "You'll need a stronger rope. 24mm width. American hips and all." "Thanks," I said, temporarily annoyed he thought I was inquiring for myself and he didn't care about my intention. This ending. But I didn't buy the rope that day. The day I bought the rope was a few weeks later, after we'd already gone to investigate a number of places for Li-Ming's final act: Rending Lake Park where retirees ballroom dancing inspired Li-Ming to vomit onto her lap (which I cleaned with a generous janitor's toilet mop), and then to Houhai with its arm-locked lovers (where Li-Ming elbowed one couple and glared at them; were she not in a wheelchair, they may not have forgiven her), and finally to Chaoyang ("no way, not here," she said, nodding at a rusted merry-go-round filled with Donald Duck and Minnie Mouse-faced horses). I don't know why she made me go with her to the parks, to test the sturdiness of tree limbs, when she knew all along there was only one option. As was always the case with Li-Ming, everything was a test—she wanted to know how much you'd believe her, if your fortitude in her kindness or insanity (depending on the day), was enough to gird her weight. "Fifty five kilos!" I shouted on my empty-handed way out of the hardware store that afternoon. "Do I look like I'm fucking fifty five kilos?" I wanted him to stop me. I wanted him to know this wasn't about weight but about the many ways we attempt to weigh down lightness, to fool ourselves into thinking even the most detached of us won't eventually drift away.

in going to an unknown place in order to find something you never lost? He was sent from his danwei, his assigned work unit in Beijing where he ground telescopic lenses, to this re-education camp in Jiangxi province to deliver a letter to a girl named Huang Li-Ming. He was to report back to the capital she was a model student, on her way to becoming a "barefoot doctor." She and her family had been listed "black" because her mother once signed her name to a Nationalist Youth Party list long before Li-Ming's birth—it was another member of his danwei, frown-faced Mrs. Xu, who reminded everyone of this during the Destroy the Four Olds Campaign. After Li-Ming's mother was the victim of a virulent public struggle session, Li-Ming was *sent down* to the countryside with other children of questionable backgrounds from her graduating high school class, the class his generation called the Old Threes because they hadn't studied past their third year of high school. A year later, the party elders sent him to the camp to investigate Li-Ming's progress; if she acted as a model villager, the council in Beijing would upgrade her to Class Number Five Red.

Five: the number of points in a red star.

Five: the number of days he'd stay in Jiangxi Province.

Five: the fingers on her dancing hand flashing from the dark, a hand divorced from work, from the sun's tangoing rays of affection and loathing.

Five meant nothing to this girl. She'd shoveled pig slop for more than five days, more than five months. Wang Guanmiao lowered his eyes to her knees, wishing he could trace the wrinkles in the grimy skin above her kneecaps. He didn't know in a few decades he'd hate her for those wrinkles, hate that her body became a cage, and would encage him too.

"Comrade," she cleared her throat. "You need a sip of water? The mountain air and altitude can make heads go hazy."

He shook his head. "No, thanks. I'm fine." He dug his feet into the hay-strewn earth. A pig snorted. Outside, trees rustled, nothing more. Quiet closes in on you when you haven't heard it in some time; his ears attempted to find a talon's scratch on the roof, his own heartbeat.

He cleared his throat: "So you're Huang Li-Ming?"

She nodded and stood upright, well-trained in the art of deference to officials. The earth settled at Wang's feet and he looked to her boots covered with mud and pig shit.

"I am Huang Li-Ming, of Beijing's PLA School, Zhongnanhai," she announced. He didn't welcome the formality of their exchange. But her face softened, she smiled while looking to her feet—was there something else she wanted to say?

You, he wanted to say. *Surely, you know what it's like to look up into the sky and feel both the heaviness of the earth and this lightness of living. I saw how you danced alone. Is this the beginning or the end?*[25] But how could he tell her? They were merely strangers. She peered up sheepishly, as if overtaken by reason, wiping her hands on her skirt and laughing softly to fill the space. Whatever words he formulated were lost to the silence between them. Did she know what she did to him?

He smiled, a pool of feeling at his feet. He shuffled the earth to return gravity to his limbs. The Party officials called this girl *"naoteng"* —mischievous—in her official report and he saw what they meant; there was something unnerving about her smile. This fit with her name, which meant "daybreak" because, she told him years later when there was time enough for the magic of this moment to be forgotten, she was born just before her hometown Nanjing was liberated from Nationalist rule. He later wondered: how could her stodgy mother have such a poetic heart? The girl standing before him was indeed like the early morning sun, tossing petulant light over everything around her. But she looked nothing like her father. He'd met the elder Huang just once in the

---

[25.] "I don't think two people could've been happier than we have been," wrote Virginia Woolf in her last letter to her husband before entering the River Ouse with twenty pounds of rocks jostling in her pockets. Li-Ming requested the rope, not the stones, but does it matter the method?

crowded hallway of their shared danwei, a glass-grinding factory built after Liberation. Her father was short with words, square-shouldered. He handed Wang Guanmiao the letter the young man delivered now and said: *My daughter's name is Li-Ming; tell her to serve the people well.* Wang pictured Huang's daughter as a miniature version of him: stout, stubborn, prone to tantrums and pride—naoteng. He didn't anticipate seeing someone eager to smile, light in her gestures yet harboring a buried strength, an introspective heart so different from that of her father. Hers was the strength men feared and desired to consume them with a tornado of kisses. That's the funny thing about beginnings—we don't realize we already have a sense for the ending. For Wang Guanmiao, he'd already written forward a life of loneliness: how could he predict Li-Ming was like the fledgling swift he once saved from his danwei's drainpipe? He later learned young swifts fly endlessly from the nest, never stopping for years and landing only to breed.

"Huang Li-Ming," he stammered. Her name was bright: yellow, cheery, blinding, clinging to the back of his throat like Shanghai's famed pear candies. That rescued swift's weight was imperceptible in his palms, wings shivering and purple-black. "Li-Ming, I have something from your parents."

Wang Guanmiao reached into his pocket for her letter, only his fingers slipped through. He felt his own bare thigh. A hole! The letter must've fallen from his pocket on the walk here. How hadn't he felt it? He scrambled for something to say, an appropriate excuse. How could he tell this soft-smiling girl his pockets were full of holes? That he'd been so careless with the one task he was assigned?

"There's a letter I came here to deliver to you, but I must have left it in my bunk," he lied easily. It felt good to say "bunk," meant he was sent to Jiangxi from Beijing on special assignment, his ranking high enough to warrant sending him specifically for her.

"No problem, really." She walked to a piglet in the corner, but must've breezed through a cobweb because she brushed something invisible off her shoulders, plucking threads from her ears. She picked the animal from its stall and held it against her chest. "Did you know you have to clip the teeth of newborn pigs?" The piglet squirmed and squealed, but despite its obvious discomfort, Li-Ming continued talking about a professor of veterinary medicine named Zhang who was at the re-education camp with them, how he taught her the process of birthing pigs, how he knew everything about farm animals, was the most knowledgeable, patient man she'd known. As she spoke, the pig smeared mud along her forearms, rubbed streaks onto the breast of her shirt. Calligraphy on one's body. Mud on one's skin. He saw moth's wings, felt the rustling of paper against his cheeks, the strands of that web. He should've known what this was like. But how could he? This was a girl he'd only just met. Still, he yearned for Huang Li-Ming to give him a life different from that which he'd anticipated: a man of the city living in a tall courtyard apartment bringing home eggplants and pork knuckles for dinner, enjoying long walks in the park with children skipping alongside them as sunset dampened their hair and shoulders. A strange fantasy for an unwed thirty-something year old former PLA soldier, a glass grinder who worked alone, ate alone, lived alone. He wanted to be lonely with someone else. What else was life but shared loneliness?[26]

"...don't you think?" Li-Ming's rising tones returned him to the barn, the dying sunlight. Her words reminded him of the lost letter. Of piglets. *Of naoteng.*

"Of course," he said, not knowing the question.

"*Hu shuo,*" she said—*silly talk*—slapping his arm and gingerly placing the piglet on the ground. "Don't forget, teeth clipping is

[26.] If we know the thickness, then how long should the rope be? At Jingsong Hardware, I looped the rope into wide, concentric Os on the glass countertop. The proprietor, that wrinkle-foreheaded middle-aged man who dumbly watched a staticky television set to CCTV 4, didn't pay any attention, despite my outburst weeks earlier. Could I ask him what length of rope was needed to loop 2-3 times around a neck? Was that the way this was done? I settled for three meters—surely long enough, but not too long. We could always double the loop around the tree for extra support. Funny the way the details rub clear now like a clamshell in the sun, opening in excess heat to reveal a shiny, spit-shined pearl.

the most important thing to remember. Professor Zhang said if
you don't do it, they'll rip each other to shreds, even their brothers
and sisters, fighting over food."

The piglet happily plopped into a puddle. Wang Guanmiao
resented the piglet's easy contentment with its life's lot. "I'm sorry
about the letter," he said. "I'll bring it to you tomorrow."

Li-Ming placed her hand on his forearm. "It's nothing," she
said as if they were old friends, as if the letter was indeed a trivial
matter and he entered the barn this afternoon to learn about pig
birthing, not to deliver a message so important it would change
the course of this girl's life. Li-Ming's hand released; as it did, a
tightness inside him loosened. Gravity returned, reminding him
how heavy he usually felt when standing on his own large feet.

"*Shou mang jiao luan*," Li-Ming said, using the proverb to
imply Wang's hands and feet were so busy he messed up this one
task. "Don't worry about trivial things."

"I should return to my bunk." He bowed his head—a feudal
politeness he hadn't used since before Liberation.

She bid him farewell, reaching for a pair of water buckets
she slipped over her back as easily as a farmer. She followed his
steps toward the bunks then veered down the rambling path toward the river, buckets slapping her ribs. She looked happy to be
awarded such a mundane task[27], as if life could be simpler when
filled with routine. He envied her. Maybe this is what drew him

---

[27.] The rope wouldn't fit in my backpack on the way home so I looped it over
my shoulders, draping it such that it wouldn't impede my bicycle ride. Li-Ming
instructed me to hide the rope in a storage unit they rarely used just above the
bike sheds outside their building. I unlocked the unit with the key she'd given
me and placed the coils there, content to fulfill an expected task. By this point,
I wasn't thinking about whens or whos or whys or how comes or how muchs
or so whats. Being an accomplice means losing yourself in the most mundane
details of the task, which has the unintended side effect of making life livable.
I returned the key to my back pocket, trudged upstairs, my stomach led by the
smell of sautéed scallions and ginger and peanut oil and sesame seed as if all
meaning we'd ever know was contained in the making of a stir-fry on a spring
evening in the center of a city which was the center of a country which was, according to local estimates, the center of the universe.

to her—her naiveté, the way she believed in the density of mud under her feet, the rushing river at the valley's basin.

"Li-Ming!" he shouted when her face was too far away to see in perfect detail.

She turned slowly, careful not to disrupt the balanced weight of her buckets.

"Yes, Comrade Wang?"

"I'll see you at the mess hall later?"

"We shall see!" She smiled cryptically even though everyone at the camp ate at the same tables every night and of course he'd see her there. "Now go get my letter!"

He nodded, smiling his assurance as she returned to the path. He waited until her pigtails dipped beneath the hills then walked to his bunk, his body denser than it felt in weeks. He looked to the sparse pines speckling the mountain and shielding them from the afternoon sun, shadows expanding as day descended into night. There wasn't a bird, a cicada, nor even a housefly to accompany Wang's walk to the dorms, everyone in the fields or attending to communal livestock, those feverish pigs who nibbled on Li-Ming's arms. No one witnessed him methodically retracing his steps from earlier that day. He was excused from a meeting with the camp's leaders that afternoon by employing the excuse he was sick with diarrhea—it was common for city folk to fall ill from the glutinous local millet. He checked the mess hall. Nothing. The latrines. Nothing. He perused the path back to the barn. *Nothing.*

An overwhelming sense of purpose sent his feet shuffling, scuffing earth. Her name repeated its pulse, propelling him toward that last rising note: *Li-Ming, Li-Ming, Li-Ming.* Never before had he wanted something so badly without understanding the ramifications of what he needed. As he dug at the roots beneath a tree where he watched the sunrise that morning, he thought he felt a scratch of paper, but it was just a dried-up root, already useless at nourishing the needy trunk. Assigned just one purpose, he'd failed spectacularly. If the Party leadership in his danwei knew better, they would've assigned this task to someone less likely to trip on his own feet, would've recognized his inability to control the reaches of his long frame, as if his ego, his soul, whatever it was within him that governed his movements, was merely a dwarfish resident of a vacant, drafty home.

Evening spread across the valley, darkening the stalls. Still there was no sign of Li-Ming's letter. Wang Guanmiao walked more briskly as night fell, eager to find the note before twilight swallowed the mountains. Whenever he thought he saw a speck of white, he raked his fingers through the grass—but each time, he found nothing. He convinced himself the letter was lost forever as he returned to his bunk that evening to formulate an excuse to tell his party leaders in Beijing. Could he say someone stole the letter? What if he pretended he'd given it to Li-Ming? Could he live with the guilt of that lie? Wang Guanmiao knew it wasn't about his sense of duty to the Party; he didn't want to disappoint Li-Ming. Or was that it? His mind was cluttered in a way it hadn't been in a long time. Thoughts piled atop one another, confusing him even more—if he didn't find the letter, what would happen? He could return to his solitary, well-defined existence at his grinder in Beijing and live the rest of his life in bachelorhood. But where was the boy who once walked Shanghai's dawn-swept streets with the feeling of infinite possibility, that a life could be lived and not simply prescribed by one's superiors?

As he rounded the corner to the men's dormitory, he saw a group of girls standing outside the lavatories. They clapped and sang, and in the center of the crowd someone danced.

Li-Ming stood in the middle of the circle. He recognized those pigtails, plump arms waving white beneath a dangling light, the piglet mud now caked along her forearms like a tribal marking. What did the mud tell him? He squinted to see the lines clearer in the dark, hoping to catch a glimpse of her smile. Ever since the border years, his eyesight vacillated from better than 20/20 to a dim haze, the world around him a mirage above a sweltering summer field. There was no way to know when the mirage would appear: sometimes in the morning, it would take minutes for the fog to lift and finally trust he was safely situated in his own dorm-style danwei bedroom; sometimes, when walking down Xinjiekou, the trees would briefly turn to rivers of brown and green, the bicycle traffic a long stream of red, and then, just as quickly, each object would slowly announce its outline, a verifiable presence, but there remained a lingering haze in the periphery reminding him at any moment his perception could falter, not easily trusted. Tonight was one of the better nights and he was grateful he could witness, in stark clarity, Li-Ming performing a version of the Dai peacock dance. The girls around her clapped the beat to a folk song playing scratchily over the camp's loudspeakers. Li-Ming seemed to be improvising and yet everything about her looked rehearsed. Wang wanted to join the crowd of girls and watch until the moon swelled above the mountains, but he couldn't—men and women in those days were assigned to their own camps, bunks, latrines. He wanted to watch her forever, for this dance to be the center of his existence, her swaying hips, her white palms flashing in the dusk. The clapping strengthened as the music ascended.

One of the camp leaders, Sheng Li, broke Wang Guanmiao's reverie.

"The women here make the most of it, eh?" he wrapped his arm around Wang's shoulder. Sheng had been at the camp for years and as a result of his long stay, smelled of garlic and the imbedded sweat endemic to those who worked their days (*sun up, sun down*) in the fields, but he didn't notice his own odor as he puffed happily on a cigarette, smoke clouding Wang's view of Li-Ming. Wang exhaled loudly, blinked twice to clear his eyes. There were hundreds of discarded cigarette butts at their feet in a trail like bird droppings leading from the bathrooms to the dorms and back again. Humanity's mark was everywhere at this camp—the cigarette trails, the washboards leaning on the river's edge, the bare hillsides ransacked for firewood to feed the valley's hunger, the mountain's skin eternally scarred.

Sheng coughed. "That Li-Ming—she's sweet, isn't she? They tell us not to date our comrades, but if it's in the spirit of Mao then I suppose a marriage would be appropriate. Our love for Mao triumphs all." He laughed heartily, expecting Wang to join, but Wang wanted to shake off his arm and be alone again.

Instead, Wang Guanmiao nodded and quoted a Maoism about the importance of putting Marxist thought above inter-personal relations so Sheng wouldn't think he had bad intentions with Li-Ming. The song finished and the girls dispersed, slapping Li-Ming on the back and returning to their dormitory with their arms around each other's waists, heads leaning into one another like loving swans. Wang wondered if they felt the same lightness he experienced earlier, if Li-Ming had that effect on everyone. He was suddenly, inexplicably jealous.

Wang tapped his new friend on the hand and told him it was time to retire to bed. Sheng smiled and cocked an eye, implying Wang's statement meant something else.

"No, not that," Wang reassured him, but Sheng's smile wid-ened, exposing tobacco-stained teeth—his was a countryman's mouth. He smacked Wang's back so hard it stung. Sheng laughed, muttering something about "a man's bed time" as Wang walked toward the dorms. The laughing man struck another match and the acrid smell followed Wang, seeping into his shirt.

As he walked, cockroaches skittered like wind-blown leaves across his path. Fog obscured the brightness of the moon. Outside the dorm, his boisterous comrades clustered around the doorway smoking and coughing clouds into the clear mountain air. Their breaths hovered, lingering beneath a flickering spotlight, before disappearing into the dark. He elbowed his way through them and they barely noticed; like wind cutting through a wheat field, they gave him only the slightest room to pass.

That night, he lied in bed watching halos of smoke rise above the bunks. Li-Ming, he thought. With every puff, he sung her name again:

Li-Ming.

Puff.

Li-Ming.

Puff.

Li-Ming.

Puff.

The name, the repetition, began to have a soothing effect, a prayer solely his from that day forward, a word to fill spaces without words, a poem whose silence comprised the vacuity carved around it, a man clinging to the sound of a tongue, two syllables, waiting for them to make their appearance over and over again like a child anticipating a mother's call, a bird navigating the old way home:

Li-Ming.
Li-Ming.
Li-Ming.

*

The next evening Wang Guanmiao found Li-Ming in the stalls. A pig was pregnant and she was excited by the prospect of birthing the gilt. It was finally her turn after months of watching others perform the task.

"So many piglets will soon be running around here," she said.

He sputtered proudly: "I found the letter." He didn't tell Li-Ming that after his comrades went to sleep, he spent the night with a box of matches in hand, circling his dorm, walking the path to the pig troughs, striking a match every few minutes for light and bending to run his fingers through the dirt and grass. He finally resorted to using a twig to comb the grasses in case he stumbled upon one of the many mountain snakes said to slither the fields, deadly in their venomous bite. After all that, he found the letter below his bed, brushed into a corner by a careless comrade on cleaning duty. *Cao!*, he exclaimed, banging his head against the bed frame before surfacing with the letter in hand, dust clinging to his chest.

Li-Ming smiled at him—*for him*—as she dropped her rake and reached for the letter, which he had kept, cautiously, in his breast pocket. Opening it quickly, she held the thin pages to the light of the only window, her eyes enthusiastically scanning the contents, the bleeding black ink. As she read, her face changed expressions—first her eyebrows pinched together and her lips pursed, then her mouth loosened into a frown. When she reached the end, she flipped the pages over again as if they didn't contain what she expected then dropped the letter to a hay pile at her feet.

He didn't understand—wasn't his presence here, all the effort he made to find the letter, enough? He wanted to comfort her but what could he say? He hardly knew her. He placed a hand on her shoulder; a gesture he'd seen in film and occasionally among married comrades who sat across from one another at the mess hall. To his surprise, Li-Ming didn't rebuff his gesture. Her chin dropped to her chest and a few seamless tears meandered the scope of cheek to jaw.

"I'm sorry," Wang Guanmiao said, instinctively. He was sorry, but for what, he wasn't sure.

"Did you know?"

"Know what?"

"Did you know this letter was complete turtle shit?"

Wang Guanmiao wobbled on his heels, hand slipping from Li-Ming's shoulder.

"Turtle shit?" He wasn't accustomed to speaking so crudely among comrades, let alone females.

"Yes, it's turtle shit," she said succinctly, not aware of the effect this word had on him. She raised her head, fearlessly and competently as a fighting rooster.

"I'm not sure what you mean."

"I mean you came all this way, probably spent thousands of the people's currency and ate dozens of earth-loving farmers' meals in order to give me a letter filled with useless drivel."

"I didn't eat dozens of meals," Wang Guanmiao said but it was a stupid thing to say and maybe he had eaten a dozen or so meals since he left Beijing—he started to count but before he could correct her, she interrupted his calculations.

"The exact number is not the point," she sighed dramatically, braids sliding from shoulders to back. "The point is you thought you were delivering me a letter of substance when in reality this is a declaration from my mother's struggle session. A struggle, I might add, she needn't be having in public but should be holding in private because even that is turtle shit."

"Oh, I didn't know…"

"You shouldn't have known. And that's not why I'm upset." She paused, perhaps unsure if she should continue, but her emotions were too embroiled in the present moment to stop them spilling onward. "I'm upset because this wasn't the letter I expected. Are you sure there wasn't more mail you were meant to deliver? Not a letter from Gansu?"

"I'm not a mailman," Wang said.

"No, of course not," she said. "I didn't mean to say you didn't fulfill your duties today."

"It's fine," Wang Guanmiao slipped his hand into his pocket and stepped backwards, one step closer to the door.

"And now you're leaving because I'm asking too much of you," she said.

"No, I mean, yes, I mean…"

Li-Ming walked closer. "I said too much. In truth, it doesn't matter about my mother. She'll be fine and she'll survive this struggle—what is one struggle in a life full of them? I didn't mean to sound callous or that she shouldn't be struggling alongside the great professors and minds of our nation. We must deeply consider what we're here to do, why some of us end up in positions of power and others are trampled like dust or mice. No, that's not the right metaphor but you know what I mean, right? I wasn't crying about my mother. I was crying because I've been expecting a letter for quite some time that hasn't arrived. You must know what this feels like, right? To be wanting something that never arrives?"

Wang nodded, but he couldn't explain his wanting to her. This girl who in a minute's time had turned from a sweet guardian of piglets to a petulant, selfish brat, to a competent and worldly weaver of words. There was something oddly comforting in a woman who wasn't one type of person but every measure of human ever existing, or so she seemed in this moment.

"I knew you'd understand," she said. But how could she when she hardly knew him? Before he could ask, she stood on tiptoes, placed her hands on his shoulders. They remained like that—her straining to reach him, his arms drooping listlessly, their bodies hovering dangerously close—for what felt like a very long time. Outside, the other girls returned to the dorms after their work in the fields, giggling and singing country songs off-tune. Chickens pecked at the grain piles by the latrines. Pigs squealed from the stalls, slap-happy amidst the draining sunlight. Villagers rubbed tattered, soil-heavy clothing over the ridged washboards by the river. The river rushed downstream, carrying remnant suds, discarded oil from cafeteria vats, pig shit, and moldy hay. The world outside moved on without them yet something unnamed kept Li-Ming and Wang Guanmiao standing together.

Wang was so distracted by the idea of an uncaring, ambivalent world he hardly noticed when Li-Ming wrapped her arms around his waist and buried her face in his chest, her breath wetting his shirt. He touched the top of her head like someone off stage directed his movements as he smoothed her hair, brushed off dandruff flakes that fell onto her shoulders like Beijing's first, dry December snow. Puppets—but who was the puppeteer?

"I'll see you in the mess hall tonight, Comrade Wang," she

said, pulling away just as quickly as she'd fallen into him. After collecting her buckets, she strode out of the barn to join the lines of girls giggling and slapping one another. Wang heard only snippets of their conversation—*what Mao would do, the strength of peasants, best fertilizers for green beans*—but his ears longed to overhear something else. For Li-Ming's voice saying his name again. The ability to forget, be forgotten.

That girlish laughter hugged the evening air past the empty dorms and toward the mess hall where it blossomed in a glowing chorus, echoing under the open-air rafters with their resident bats and crowded nests of barn swallows. That girlish laughter. He never wanted to join the laughter more than when he walked toward the mess hall, stomach growling. But he couldn't loosen his lips into a smile yet. Hours earlier, Li-Ming pressed her body to his then just as easily parted. Strange, he thought, the way you can momentarily be pulled into the orbit of someone else's body, only minutes later to be sent spinning on a new trajectory.

Wang retrieved his tin bowl, filled it with sticky rice and sat at a long table of long-faced comrades who discussed topics everyone before them had discussed for hours and years and decades and centuries: the weather (too cold this week), the most attractive girl at the camp (a lithe, freckle-faced student from Hangzhou with breasts like winter melons), the over-saltiness of the congee (always), who had the best chance with the Hangzhou girl (a square-faced comrade named Bing Tan), who had the least chance (the village's mute hairdresser), who would get the next bout of diarrhea. When they asked for Wang's answer on that last question, he responded "Me!" and they laughed and shook the table with laughter, slapping his back. Even their tin bowls clattered with laughter, the only sound bowls could speak.

He didn't understand what was so funny, but maybe he was the stupid one. Maybe he should be laughing. Wang Guanmiao opened his mouth and let out the heartiest, most boisterous laughter to spill from his body, water splashing from a too-full jug. This only made the table lose more control, Bing Tan's tears scrolling his cheeks, his dorm mates doubled-over, heads in hands, uncontrollably shaking and begging Wang to stop. But stop what? He'd only said one word—我—and yet it was the most humorous thing they'd ever heard. Amidst the laughter, he looked up from the table to notice Li-Ming watching them from across the mess hall, her shoulders rising, a smile expanding. *You too?* Was she as frivolous as the men surrounding him, jowls loose, bellies shaking? She shook her head and laughter rose from her unknown place, and then, in suit, the girls surrounding her, giggling at first then clutching their waists, this collective, mindless laughter ballooning in the mess hall without an understanding of what he'd said that was so funny. None of them knew. They were all equally, blissfully, stupidly silly.

Li-Ming laughed in Wang's direction. Despite how little he knew, how little he'd be able to predict of their future, of the times they'd belly laugh like this when everything in life felt too onerous to handle any other way, he laughed along, certain of only the simplest of terms: he couldn't let her go. Sometimes you know things in life, he thought, his mouth as wide as a cormorant searching the river's floor for fish, that laughter spilling from a place he didn't know existed within him, would desperately yearn for in coming years, trying to remind himself that there lies the bottom of a being, the deepest, most solid, indestructible kernel of a life.

Baba

Everywhere: *Yellow.*
 The cliffs. *(Yellow.)*
 The mud. *(Yellow.)*
 The rivers. *(Yellow.)*
 The wrinkles creasing the faces of beggars cluttering the eastward train tracks careening toward the capital. *(Yellow.)*
 Even his piss shone a deeper yellow.
 Yellow under his fingernails, in his hair, on his teeth, lining his gums.
 Yellow.
 A cruel trick: Li-Ming's surname, Huang—黄—meant 'yellow.' Ever since he said goodbye to her at the gates of the Jiangxi village where they first met, since she pinched his forearm (so tightly he bruised) and made him promise he'd send stories from the city, he'd been unable to clear her name from his mind. Now he was stationed in China's driest, most *yellow,* province, Gansu, for an indeterminate stay of re-education along with his Beijing danwei. What stories could he send to Li-Ming from Beijing when he knew nothing of the city aside from the occasional posts from the factory leaders who spoke of Mao thought and struggle sessions, but hardly the neighborhood gossip she desired?
 Wang squinted at the yellow horizon, a setting yellow-gray sun. Around him, the yellow cave walls gleamed hotly (in truth, everything there, come sunset, was infused with the chill of a moonless desert). For months, he shared this cave with his comrades and the occasional villager who made a bed in the warmest corner (everything from soap to hot water canteens to underwear was shared; the idea that any one object could be yours alone was

utterly presumptuous—yet all Wang wanted was to be alone with Li-Ming and to call her, definitively, *mine*—我的—my *Yellow* Li-Ming). Sitting beside his work-haggard colleagues beneath a wan mid-cycle moon, he pondered the proper start to his correspondence with the girl he'd barely known but couldn't wait to call his own:

Dear Comrade,

Did this letter reach you? I'm writing from Gansu Province. Here the days are short and the weather unpredictable. ~~Here, we eat only gritty corn meal bread for breakfast and dinner. Most days, there isn't lunch. Sometimes, like today, we are served noodle soup and, if we're lucky, the village leaders give us a pinch of salt each to add to the broth. Have you ever gone for weeks without salt? I'd never known what a blessing salt was until now, how much humans need flavorful food—not just any old food—to truly live. Because, as you know, there's a difference between survival and living. I would prefer the latter, if given the choice: wouldn't we all?~~

(Too much talk of food. Revise. Why can't he write what he wants to say? Though he rather liked that bit about salt and survival and living.)

Instead, he wrote:

Li-Ming, what do you think about salt? If you haven't abstained from salt, I suggest you try. The headaches are unbearable at first, but after a few days, your taste buds react with a higher efficiency. It's quite pleasant. You can sense the nuance between a bun made entirely of corn meal and one with a spoonful of oil added for moisture. It is a gift, truly, to experience this heightened ability to taste. Everything you once thought was necessary is easily discarded. All one needs is a grain or two of salt, really, to satisfy one's tongue. We've become too accustomed to anything more. Extravagance—doesn't the Chairman say something about extravagance? Doesn't he say a revolution is not writing an essay or holding a dinner party or reading books but an act, an action, of violence? I don't know how much our words can mean in the context of what's happening around them. Act!

Yours,

Comrade Wang

Li-Ming must have believed Wang's Maoist nonsense because within a month of sending the letter through the Party post, he received a reply, an exclamation of the motherland's shared affection for Chairman Mao printed in peony red along the header. He read her letter by the dinner fire—the same embers that heated the cave at night, making the men warm enough they didn't suffer frostbite in their sleep. Li-Ming wrote of the floods in Jiangxi that spring. She almost died, she explained, when the rains flushed the mountains and filled the valley with mud. She left the camp with her comrades to retrieve corn from a storage depository in the valley and, in an unexpected flash flood, their truck flipped onto its side, spilling them into the deluge. Li-Ming and her comrades clung to the truck's door, but the driver, a terrible swimmer, was swept downstream, nearly lost, save for his shirt catching on the outstretched limb of a tree. She and the other girls made a human chain to reach him. *One more life saved through the strength of Chairman Mao's thought,*[28] she wrote

---

[28.] "When words are made futile, we cannot count on poetry anymore." Li-Ming's full weight was in my arms. She couldn't walk the four floors so we took turns taking her outside, like a dog needing to pee, then carrying her back upstairs. My knees shook. I'm only 16! But who was I to interrupt this history lesson? Carrying her made me feel older. Like I was someone important. We made it to the third floor landing and I left her there while I went to ask Baba for help with the last set of stairs. "What are you doing? It's freezing out," he said from the doorway after I banged on the door's steel frame. I wore a tank top in 65-degree weather. "It's plenty warm. It's spring," I said. He said, "You'll

in her most careful calligraphy, her thick wrist flexing and twisting to craft curling strokes. She said her comrades would soon teach her how to drive a three-wheeled tractor, that in just a few months she'd be transferred to a factory in Weifang—eastern Shandong—where she'd make soap from jasmine and lily flowers. She asked him to report back who his colleagues were—*was there a girl from Beijing who'd been sent a decade earlier? A girl roughly Li-Ming's age with long, beautiful hair and double-fold eyelids? She wanted to know. She would be tall and speak of places and poets you've never know.* Do you know her? Wang shook his head when he read, as if Li-Ming could see him. He wished he knew this girl who sounded like she'd make good company among such dim-witted comrades. She concluded the letter:

That's interesting what you say about salt. Why not cry into your bowl of noodles to add spice? Maybe you aren't soft enough, Comrade Wang. Even the great poet Han Shan knows how to cry when facing his lone shadow. I suggest you try someday.

—Your Comrade Huang Li-Ming.

Wang creased the letter in half, then in half again, reveling in the soft crispness of rice paper on his calloused fingers. His Huang Li-Ming was a poet, like his own mother once dreamed to be. But what was a poet except someone who wasted time trying to fold the world into words that were never enough? Han Shan. Who was this Han Shan Li-Ming wrote of? He'd never heard of this "great poet" but made a note to ask around to see if anyone knew of him.

---

get sick and then we'll all get sick," reminding me in a Chinese family there's no individual action nor consequence—everything I would do from the moment I entered the Wang home would have an impact on everyone in the family's fates. Baba, wearing only a tank top and shorts but somehow exempt from his rules, jogged downstairs to help me. "She's freezing," he said, draping Li-Ming's arms around his shoulders so her entire body clung to his chest. "I'm not cold," she assured him, but Baba didn't hear her or maybe I'm already falsifying facts in order to make right what long ago was made wrong. Inconsequential, I hear a voice say, and if I were to follow its cue, I'd climb right back into the middle of someone else's story, snugly framed by the padded weight of a fattening fiction.

When he mentioned the poet's name over dinner that night, his comrades guffawed.

"Poetry is for capitalists," an accountant from Xi'an said, picking a maggot from his bowl and wiping a runny nose onto his shirtsleeve.

Wang sat by the fire he and his comrades built of twigs and newspapers while the locals boiled them a dinner of Lanzhou beef noodles and stir-fried leeks. This was one of those salt-less nights and, despite his diatribe, he didn't anticipate the meal.

Gansu: Too hot by day, too cold by night. Around them, the village's toddlers bent over, exposing lily-white bottoms to the whitest of moons. *Loo, Loo, Loo* their parents called to the wild desert dogs who jogged closer to lick the remnant shit off the children's naked buttocks. *Loo, Loo, Loo*... and between his ears, his thoughts echoed the call:

> *Li-Ming...*
> > *Loo...*
> *Han Shan...*
> > *Loo...*

After the villagers returned to their neighboring caves, Wang and his comrades readied for bed. Outside their rock dwelling, across the valley, an expanding cloud stamped out the earliest rising stars. The wind picked up quickly, billowing shirtsleeves, chilling spines. Bursts whistled past their perch. His colleague Xiaodong stood, abandoning his empty noodle bowl so it clattered chattily against the rock floor.

"Ai-ya!" he yelled over the valley, a view they glimpsed occasionally in the mornings when they scrambled into the fields. Walking to the perch with his colleagues, Wang noticed a brown wall slowly moving through the village in the valley, rattling windows and knocking down drying lines, heaving laundry into the air and across the fields in which they'd labored for months. This wall of dust barreled steadily toward the mountains, their caves, them.

One of the villagers, a toothless man they called "Smiley"

because of his near-constant grin, left a nearby cave and jogged over, instinctively shielding his eyes from the growing dust. Even when pummeled by wind, he smiled. The rest of them squinted, lips tightly cinched.

"Hang whatever *beizi* you have at the entrance and shield yourselves in the back corners!" he instructed. "Get ready for your first dust storm, boys!"

They did as advised, but the storm gathered energy from the earth over which it trampled, wind scrambling toward them, ensconced in increasing boils of dust. The meek cotton *beizi* they'd tucked into the rocky edges of the cave entrance was ripped from its clutch; the blanket flagged wildly as if struggling to overcome the wind's embrace but was snatched downwind where it disappeared from view. Wang's living station, just a quilt, a bamboo sleeping mat, some clothing, and what books and letters he brought from Beijing, was nearest the cave's entrance. Worried about his belongings, and specifically Li-Ming's latest letter, he ran to his station, gathering what he could with his arms.

"Are you crazy, Comrade Wang? Sit!" Smiley smiled as he talked; that dumb look: was he genuinely kind or mocking everyone around him?

"Sit!" Xiaodong echoed.

But Wang wouldn't sit until he was sure he was holding Li-Ming's letter, that it wouldn't fly away, that he wouldn't, yet again, be stripped of everything he owned so he was just himself standing there. Didn't they know? The wind demanded Wang Guanmiao stand. At times like these, the wind was all there was left to face with courage—didn't they read Chairman Mao's speech about making mountains bow to us, rivers yield to our power? Inspired by the thought a human could indeed be more powerful than all the earthly elements combined, he trudged through the heavy swirl of yellow dust, gathering all he could, but as he returned to the back corner, belongings clutched to his chest, the wind reached its long arm into the cave, stirring everything in a maelstrom of dust, gray-gold embers, loose paper. Every un-moored object sprung to life, swimming on air, impossible to catch.

"Snatch what you can!" Xiaodong shouted, suddenly worried.

Smiley didn't move; he simply laughed at the city boys who clung to their only belongings—he knew how futile objects were when compared to the might of the natural world: a villager's intelligence is, as the Chairman reassured them, greater than that of the most educated, well-read urbanite.

Smiley was right: Li-Ming's letter, all three pages of thin rice paper, along with Wang's most recent attempt at a reply, swiftly drifted toward the cliff's edge and then, just as Wang was about to snag a corner, the pages carried into the valley like seeds—look: words could fly.

Smiley pat Wang's shoulder as together they watched Li-Ming's sentences
fall and lift,
fall and lift,
fall and lift,

until finally Smiley laughed, sputtered something through his toothless mouth about how stupid urban boys are. They both stared into the distance, but Wang had a feeling they were look-ing for something entirely different. He didn't know what Smiley could possibly teach him except that all actions, contrary to The Chairman's widespread ideology, were futile.

"*Tu baozi*," Wang cursed, brushing Smiley's hand off his shoulder and returning to the cave to begin rebuilding his latest home. As he gathered what fallen objects he could, he grit his teeth, tasting the upended earth, a salt without the biting tang.

*

While rebuilding their cave, that temporary home they still called home after a full day's work in the fields, where could they live? You must start from scratch with a cave, dusting out stray rocks and bat guano and making a flat enough place for a tired, aching back to rest. While you cleaned, you must live elsewhere. Only one of the caves survived the dust storm (the villagers believed their prayers to the mountain demon Kui spared their dwelling; Wang's engineering-trained comrades said the cave's particular rock formation saved it). Whatever the reason, they were grateful something survived. They clustered in that cave for weeks, cramped and full of the sour stink of men who hadn't bathed in as long. They were only there to sleep, despite the fitful nature of the rest. Nevertheless, the cave was home—because it had to be— while they remade that which was destroyed by nature's temper.

Every morning Wang would carefully extricate himself from the tangle of sleeping bodies and scramble into the valley, past the pockmarked grasses and crags left by last year's rains. He was determined to find Li-Ming's letter before the season's weather arrived, forever dampening his chances. What had she said of Han Shan? How was he to reply? What was her new address? He'd shuffle his feet in the dust, reach between rock crevasses, turn over a boulder only to find a spider and beetle laying patiently alongside one another (what uncommon, beneficial bonds exist in nature, he thought). Was it possible to lose something never yours? He was driven by an insatiable need to see her again in that angled afternoon light, pig mud smeared on her chest, the promise of a future laid out for them like a wedding beizi on a marital bed.

He searched until one morning a spare drop of rain tapped his shoulder saying, "What's the point?" *What was the point?* Holding onto that thin rice paper, re-reading the words she'd carefully penned, was as useless as a human befriending a dog: what was in the emotional relationship for the dog? The letter didn't need me, so why did he need it? Besides, after he sent his last missive, Li-Ming never replied. Forfeiting the search, he sat on a rock outcropping, tilting his head to the bluest stretch of sky. After a few minutes, the sun was obscured by a cloud that grew from out of the earth itself, all puffy and gray and promising something much desired as of late. Finally, the villagers would get their rain. Finally, the potatoes and yams and pumpkins and squash would sprout green and brown and pregnant from the parched soil and finally, they'd remember what it was like to swallow sweetness after so much bland. Despite this, Wang knew in tasting intense flavor again, they'd only be disappointed that the dream—how they'd fantasized about stir-fried pumpkins with leek, yams candied in raw sugar!—was always greater than the experience itself.

His mouth swelled with expectant saliva while across the valley, above the slanted, hay rooftop of a villager's home, a speck of white floated in the sky. It could've been Li-Ming's last letter. Or, then again, it could have been a dove. An abandoned propaganda poster. Anything. What did this matter now? The unknown object drifted on the growing breeze ahead of the storm's brew until it melded with the flat sky and his eyes lost focus, unable to pick it out for the folds of cloud, the smoke of a chimney, the triumphantly arched wing of a bird.

Letter #3

Dear Kang-Lin,

Darkness and light: the unerring progress of days.
Months: the old apartment, our bed smelling of my mother's
unwashed bras, haw rolls cousins forgot beneath the sheets.
The only window: fly and spider carcasses collected between
dusty panes.
A new suburban life; childless aunt and belching husband,
garlic-leek, unhinged by erguotou.
Gansu: I hear it's dry, heartless, where wheat grows forehead-
high and millet bowls are filled with maggots.
Bug Eyes again today: cockroaching my library desk. Bark
fingers, seashelled nail beds.
"What you looking for, Little Sister?"
Maps and a pencil rubbed to a nub.
"You'll never find the place that has no name."
Latitude or longitude? Gravity or flight?
"Books are bourgeois. Poets the most."
Tall man in the stacks, peering above *Das Kapital*.
"You'll come with me."
His hand on my back, a familiar book in armpit—my mis-
take. The burning house, I entered:

Children I implore you
get out of the burning house now
three carts wait outside
to save you from a homeless life
relax in the village square
before the sky everything's empty

no direction is better or worse
east is just as good as west
those who know the meaning of this
are free to go where they want

Brambled night: circle of angry faces, swinging fires, black rice sack obscuring my view.

Read someone else's crimes: easier on the ear than one's own.

Baba

From his morning perch atop Gansu's yellow cliffs, the New Year arrived with the pop hiss of firecrackers set on the valley's crowded streets. Smoke rose above rooftops like flocks of startled pigeons. Following his colleagues at the camp, every morning Wang scaled the cliff to work in the terraced fields where only the mealiest of vegetables grew: potatoes, yams, squash, winter melons. Time, now, for the Spring harvest, or so said their fluttering calendar pages, the trusted tongshu with its lengthy, mis-cited almanacs (last month there wasn't the predicted pine's height of snow, but three ice storms followed by the strangest summer-like January day—villagers crawled out of caves, bare arms extended to the sun as if Heaven itself bestowed this warmth). This was the season when good children and husbands returned home to eat long-life potatoes (that hot, stringy caramel sticking to teeth) and tell long-winded stories of the year interrupted only by shared laughter and sips of hot tea.

For weeks, Wang's fellow Beijingers spoke of the New Year. How in just a few days they'd board the crowded eastbound trains to the capital. How they'd trade Gansu's dry winds for the Gobi's sandstorms. But not him. No, he sat every morning on his cliff looking east, wondering where he could possibly go for the holidays this year. The possibilities were numbered:

One: his danwei dormitory in Beijing, shared toilet smell wafting down the hallway, past the tattered underwear and darned socks hung to dry on copper wires strung between walls.

Two: a crumbling pingfang along the river in Cen Cang Yan, long assumed by neighboring villagers as the town's only granary, stuffed to the ceiling with canvas bags of wheat, rice and millet, plump rats nibbling on the grains, his father meandering between Sword Temple and Square Bridge, losing his way and then finding it again with the tap of his cane.

Three: his brother's Shanghai two-story with its dented wooden stairs, the back room where his brother and he once slept while their father and his brothers worked the grinders, those uncles long buried on Xia Gai Mountain, beaten down by the latest Revolution's thick red calligraphy.

"Little Brother Wang," a foot nudged his ribs through the cotton beizi shielding him from Gansu's icy nights, the perpetual bone-chipping chill of a cave dwelling. Of course it was his colleague Xiaodong lifting him from the reverie of a morning sunrise. Xiaodong had a wife and son waiting at home for him in Beijing, eager for the New Year visit. Xiaodong had a mustache that he meticulously shaved into an up-stretched U every morning by the breakfast fire. Xiaodong had read Sun Tzu's *Art of War* five times and now re-read Chairman Mao's *Strategic Problems of China's Revolutionary War* whenever he had a free moment between their work in the fields and their perfunctory meetings with the local villagers (where they puffed their chests and acted like knowledgeable city folk and the villagers slumped their shoulders, bowed feudally, and waited for them to stop talking so they could teach the urbanites how to milk goats). Xiaodong thought he knew everything about tactical warfare. Xiaodong didn't know anything about war. But Wang didn't have the heart to tell him. Despite the fact Wang was two years Xiaodong's elder, Wang's single status and lack of 'loud-mouthed progeny' as Xiaodong called them, made Wang a 'Little Brother.' Too much time had passed to correct him. Xiaodong poked Wang's ribs again with the rubber-capped toe of his mud-caked boot.

"C'mon, Poet," he tried. All Wang's comrades called him 'The Poet' (or 'Mr. Poet' depending on their mood) since Li-Ming's first letter arrived containing references to her favorite poet, Han Shan. They asked, "Did you find your *tangle of cliffs*? Your *bird paths* without trails?" His comrades snatched the letter from him one night and read it aloud for the entire camp, laughing at Li-Ming's careful penmanship, her love for dead poets no one cared about anymore. Or did they laugh at him?

Wang pretended not to hear Xiaodong.

"Mr. Poet, get your lazy ass up! You have to see this." It was so early Xiaodong's mustache was not yet combed into its desired shape; instead, it was bushy and morning-rustled like a wild animal. Whatever Xiaodong wanted to see must have been worth missing his grooming rituals.

Wang stood, begrudgingly, his beizi wrapped around him, an overstuffed winter kimono.

Once outside their shallow cave with its makeshift tents, Xiaodong directed Wang's attention toward a flock of red-crowned cranes[29] that had landed on an outcropping below. The villagers, likewise, amassed. As greedy as a pack of wild dogs, hunched and devout, the men and women scoured the yellow earth for small stones, for pebbles light but hard and rounded enough to spring from their slingshots.

"What are they...?" Wang asked Xiaodong, but as quickly as the words frosted the cold, the villagers raised their shots, leveling their gazes. The cranes, likely resting after a night migrating the chilled western skies, were entirely caught off-guard by this amassing human front. In martial unison, the villagers gleefully released their rubber slingshots, arching improvised bullets toward the cliffs.

The pebbles ricocheted off the rocks around Wang and Xia-

[29.] "If I could be a crane, I wouldn't have to ask for your help," she said as I uncoiled the thick rope and placed it on her lap to show her the length recommended. "Don't you think we're going to look odd bringing rope onto the subway?" She laughed: "This is China. Everything is weird. Normal is what's not." At her side: the morphine tablet Baba left each day, a pin-sized remedy for pain but not the murmur in her lungs. "Cold Mountain has so many wonders; climbers all get scared," she said, and for the first time since she launched our plan, I wanted to strangle her, to mute a mouth that proffered too much nonsense.

odong, puffing yellow dust into the morning air. The cranes re-acted slowly, flapping their heavy white wings and attempting to lift their bodies into the sky. One by one they took to the air, suc-cessfully avoiding the shots of the villagers, soaring over village streets, weaving shadows down alleyways, along the silt-heavy Wei River. Wang never realized how beautiful the scene could be from here—on most days he was preoccupied with the morn-ing's tasks (shaving his face over a pot of campfire-heated water heated, using that same pot to warm rice gruel kept overnight in a cave)—now, his gaze followed the cranes, how easily they traversed this landscape. He felt a strange expression cresting his face: a smile rising as the birds flew over the horizon, as the vil-lagers' pebbles, late to the chase, seared the wind, missing their targets. Wang's beizi loosened and the warmth of his body filled the air surrounding him. *Fly birds, fly*. His bare shoulders donned the cloaked heat of the rising sun.

飞.

Fei. To fly.[30]

Wang watched as the cranes departed, unperturbed by the pebbles, leaving white feathers drifting over rocks, evidence of an evening's roost.

But no, Wang suddenly realized. As he stepped closer to the edge, toes enjoying the warmth of sun-swept soil, he saw below, tucked beneath an overhang, a pair remained. They stood side

---

[30.] As in Han Shan:
> "I sit beneath the cliff, quiet and alone.
> Round moon in the middle of the sky's a bird
>   ablaze:
> all things are seen mere shadows in its brilliance,
> that single wheel of perfect light . . .
> Alone, its spirit naturally comes clear.
> Swallowed in emptiness in this cave of darkest
>   mystery,
> because of the finger pointing, I saw the moon.
> That moon became the pivot of my heart."
>   —Trans. Red Pine

by side, hobbling like nearly-felled trees and flapping their large, white wings unsuccessfully. Their necks careened in an unexpected dance, disbelieving this fate—how could they not summon the strength for the one instinctual motion they'd known all their lives? A bird without flight. What was a bird without flight?

"You know," Xiaodong held his fat, dry palm to Wang's face so close he could smell breakfast's wilted leeks. "A bird in your hand is worth a hundred in the forest!" He yelped, joining the whooping villagers who only now realized they'd injured at least one of the cranes. They packed their slingshots into the worn front pockets of their cotton-padded Mao jackets and climbed the cliffs to the rocks where the cranes danced the dance of the wounded: one crane's wing drooped listlessly to its side as if unhinged, the other coiled an injured leg into his body, hopped awkwardly. As the hopping crane edged closer to his partner, he nudged his long neck into his partner's wing, his crimson head growing a brighter red.

Xiaodong crouched beside Wang, searched for a rock to throw at the crane's head.

"Help me," Xiaodong pleaded without looking up, pulling on Wang's pant leg. "C'mon, we'll be able to eat bird meat for a week!" He scaled the rocks toward the cranes and the cluster of villagers.

They shouted for Wang to join. They wanted his help. But as the cranes interlocked their long black necks, as the sound of the masses burrowed through the cliff walls and to Wang, to the birds, he already knew: What use was there in helping? All this too like it happened before, was happening always—at river banks, precipices, Wang would forget his name, his tongue curling resolutely to reach for a familiar syllable, to run itself over the tip of slick teeth, searching, probing. He could be anyone.

He could be Zhang.

Or Wen.

Or Du.

Or Deng.

Or Sheng.

He could be Xiaodong with a wife at home stewing long-life potatoes in the kitchen, meticulously tending to the son's latest skinned knee, snipping the boy's overgrown hair by candlelight to save for a later date. For what?

"For what, Xiaodong?" he shouted to this man who was neither friend nor enemy but something more dangerous: the in between.

For this?

For the sound a dying bird makes?

For the sound of a villager gripping a knife, its silver reflecting the sun like a river's surface?

A knife so sharp you see the toothy-edged glint, hear pulling flesh out and away from the body in mechanical motions, frenzied stabbings that seem to say:

Shhhhhhhhh, be still, *shhhhhh, this won't hurt one bit.*

Wang Guanmiao simply stood above the strange unfolding of events, watching the world careen on with its ceaseless actions. He didn't think of his mother, or the future he would one day make with the woman he thought he'd lost to wind and Weifang, a city whose name he knew but not its springtime smells nor sunset architectures. For now, he was simply himself, or better put, he simply was. A man breathing into the cold morning a breath that would become visible and then, as if undesiring (undeserving?) of an existence in this world, would disappear. This was the most and least Wang could be in a moment when he was called to action but couldn't act. If he'd known this was a minute, more precisely, a collection of seconds upon which he would later muse, build regret, rebuild an entire story upon, a scaffolding of words forming sentences and then forming thoughts to etch into his limbs like an oracle bone's fine markings, maybe he would've acted differently. Maybe he would've said, "Cao... you fools." Maybe he would have scaled the rocks. Would have told his daughter, the one he didn't know yet: "This was my biggest failure." But was it?[31]

The sound of a wing flapping. The sound of a wing falling from its body like a leaf. Feathers clouding the sky, cirrus and cumulous. White against yellow. Or red. Or brown. He has forgotten the colors of the sunrise on a date he has mistaken for another but the sound of that wing jimmying loose is one he could recall for a thousand years. The sound of all manners of flight crashing to earth in a violent pummeling of sky and cloud.

He cupped his hands atop his ears. Closed his eyes. He saw red.

Eyes cautiously opening: Xiaodong waved to the remaining villagers watching below. This victory was his. Everyone's. He egged on the massacre like a crazed revolutionary. But isn't that what they were? What they'd signed on to become in the years leading to this? They'd agreed in the daily meetings on the factory floors with the smell of burnt metal scalding their nostrils, in the school gymnasiums crowded with the heat of bodies and boiled words, on the city streets freshly swept in preparation for the Chairman's anticipated visit, in the *danwei* mess halls where they whispered the latest 黑 gossip about Aunt Feng, Aunt Huang, Uncle Xu.

Li-Ming: you'd never believe the sight.

Li-Ming: we do horrible things when we're hungry.

Li-Ming: are we ever forgiven?

Wang's fingers pulsed, winter-thin blood rushing to warm his city skin to remind his body where it was, what was needed to survive. The wounded crane's partner, the one with the limp leg who witnessed the massacre of his mate, stood feebly, legs squeezed between the hands of the stoutest villager. Wang recognized this

---

[31.] "Seven hundred and eighty-two steps to the subway entrance." She mapped them by memory, and although she infrequently traveled by subway, I trusted her estimation. "Isn't there an elevator?" Hahahaha. Laughter above magpie song outside the window; in spring, they puff slate-blue feathers and masquerade as desirable mates.

man from his work in the fields a day earlier—the man was missing all but one of his teeth (the front one below his left nostril, but even this was rotted to a pulpy root) and his skin was puckered by a life staring into the desert sun. He might as well have been a raisin.

Yes, it was the raisin villager whose hands, chapped and purple, clung to the surviving crane's black, wiry legs—fingers blistering purple in the cold, bird legs running on air but losing the fight—as the bird flapped its giant white wings thinking this alone was the strongest motion on earth. Survival was not a gift, but an obligation. Wang Guanmiao needed this bird to fly. With his long black neck arching backward and head copper in the morning sun, the bird twisted from the grasp of the raisin villager's country-strong hands. He jabbed his beak into the man's forearm, but he barely flinched. This was a man who knew hardship, had eaten bitterness—chi ku—and even a crane's beak drawing blood couldn't cause him to retreat. The wings expanded, cloaking the raisin villager in bird shadow:

ㅏ

Xiaodong's chest was dappled in dark crane blood, his hands wrapped around the collapsed bird's limp, lifeless tube of a neck.

"Give me a knife!" he shouted. "I will slit its throat!" His fingertips were stained mustard; the cliffs that would take years to wash out of his skin. Yet Xiaodong wasn't thinking of the years ahead. His was a present goal. He looked like no one Wang had known and yet he couldn't shake the feeling Xiaodong was someone he'd always known. That this day, this death, was happening always, everywhere. How can we extricate one moment from the next, the way a word is intractably linked to that which came before and that which will follow, or a child is tied to his parents as well as his own progeny, or... we could devise a thousand similes here, but what's the point? Watching Xiaodong strangling the bird, Wang didn't move. He didn't prevent his comrade from doing that which Wang knew he himself would come to regret and therefore, he is always not moving, not following, not doing—at the same time that he is moving, and following, and doing, and dying.[32]

Indeed, if Wang knew everything of that and every moment to follow, he'd know Xiaodong would later grow old in a cramped, humid apartment in Deshengmen, would run a desperate campaign for neighborhood counsel only to lose to the defamed-then-reclaimed Mrs. Xu, then die of lung cancer at seventy-three, never to meet his first—and only—grandson.

But, Wang didn't know this and he didn't run to the rescue of the crane as it leered, flapping its last beats against the stock-strong body of the raisin villager, the newly-present strength of Xiaodong. Wang didn't tell the crane which way to fly. Didn't explain how he could escape this uncertain destiny we all face some day, some morning or afternoon or evening or midnight. We may be surrounded by others but then, we are always alone in this too.[33]

In the valley below, sunlight ricocheted off hay rooftops, off yellow-earthen walls of homes that would soon crumble, be rebuilt using the materials of the nation's newest modernity—cement blocks, copper pipes. Children sat on door stoops, dragging sticks through powdery dust that rose in dandelions above the streets. Old *taitai*, white heads shining silver-blue, teetered on too-small feet, knees bowed irrevocably, incapable of knowing a solid, foot-sure stride.

For now, the world beneath them was afire, and the tip

[32.] I think here Li-Ming is referring to this Cold Mountain poem:
"Out of work, our only joy is poetry:
Scribble, scribble, we wear out our brains.
Who will read the words of such men?
On that point you can save your sighs.
We could inscribe our poems on biscuits
And the homeless dogs wouldn't deign to nibble."
(Trans: Burton Watson)
[33.] What does loneliness feel like on another man's tongue, in another's man's mouth? *Traduttore, traditore.*

of that flame was the red rising atop the last crane's feathered head. Xiaodong crawled to the perch on which the raisin villager kneeled; he'd killed one and was hungry for another. The less-injured crane's legs struggled within the stout man's stouter hands and were slipping, ever so slightly, away from this tenuous grasp with each pump of the bird's cave-wide wings.

Xiaodong reached for the knife tucked beside the raisin villager's hip then raised his hand and directed the blade at the bird's bare, heaving chest.

Without thinking, Wang lifted his hands above his head and clapped.

The sound echoed, spilling onto the shadowed valley floor, onto children slapping sticks, old taitai teetering to the rations store, eager villagers who raised their slingshots and happily allowed red rivulets to run down their forearms, to stain their clothing in blossoming petals like the first words of a good story. How deeply and lovingly they clung to those stains, believing it would heal them of every injurious act they'd committed. Wang raised his hands and clapped again.

The sound was enough for the raisin villager to raise his eyes briefly in Wang's direction. Wang never knew if it was the unexpected vision of his razor-thin shadow blocking the sun, or his tanned, balding head haloed by a golden morning, but whatever it was—the sound, the sight, the insanity of this interruption—caused the raisin villager to lose his grip on the crane.

In one framed instant, the sky above them, above the village, above Xiaodong, the raisin villager, and all the villagers paused with their knives dug deeply into the pink-gray flesh of their only kill was white with winter morning: 飞

White with flapping wings rimmed in charcoal, black neck stretching toward the swelling sun: 飞

White as if forgotten: 飞

White, a color in a poetry book she'd one day give him, blank spaces around words falling into an abyss of silence. Wang wanted to unfurl his own feathered wings, to step onto that invisible air and remember the feeling of falling, of flight.

But it was still morning. And he was not a crane. Not even a bird. In fact, it was just another morning when a flock of migrating cranes, known only to the villagers by the red-green-gold stories painted on the walls of Yuquan Temple, found these headless yellow mountains in the deserts of Gansu, to a May 7th Camp filled with city-blooded Beijingers ravenous for the once-familiar taste of meat, charred skin and chewy tendons.

The raisin villager looked up at Wang, eyes narrowed and red, hands curled tenaciously, as if forever clinging to the crane's legs. Within the man's palms, he held only air.

"Ta ma de!" Xiaodong plunged the blade into the soft earth. "What the fuck were you thinking?"[34]

Wang's tongue slapped the roof of his mouth as slickly as a lie (*No, I didn't lead Mother to the river's edge; Yes, I saw the planes; The letter's in my room; No, I didn't kill my wife; Yes, I'll go with you to the protests; No, I don't know why Xiaofei hasn't called*). "I'd once read cranes bow at the sound of two hands clapping."

"Well, Poet," Xiaodong said, "That sounds like bullshit poetry to me. Clearly, you were wrong."

The raisin villager didn't say a thing. He wiped his hands on worn pant legs then shuffled to help his neighbors in the skinning

---

[34] He was thinking, "Maybe if I save just one, I've saved them all." Radio static of a song we've never sung and his chest to mine repeating the chorus ringing in my ears. Didn't he know that's what I needed too? To save someone in order to spare myself? "It's not going to happen," he said. Although the weather turned nearly to summer, the basement's darkroom was still cool; a chill passed between us, ruffling arm feathers, marking time and space. The photographs clinging to the line were not of me but of strange men, smug faces stuck in static smiles. "Don't," I said as his arm raised to brush a housefly off my shoulder. I wanted to believe him. Now I find myself wanting to believe history is capable of being erased, that by the simple act of translation we can rewrite entire narratives of time and injustice. As in Valéry translating Virgil: "At moments, I caught myself wanting to change something in the venerable text…'Why not?' I said to myself, returning from this short absence. Why not?"

of their only kill. Xiaodong shook his head and joined them as well, slowly slicing the long neck of the remaining crane with the care and caution of a parent. The blood slipped effortlessly to the earth, staining red what had been eternally yolk-yellow.

For years, decades perhaps, the villagers would speak wistfully of this day: The Day of Killing Cranes. On this day, the entire village roasted the black-rumped hide of this mythical creature on fire spits hand-prepared by dutiful wives and daughters. The villagers and their city comrades crowded the heat, warming their hands and drinking hot water from rusted tin mugs. They smoked cigarettes and chewed on tar, willfully spitting cud into growing flames. They told each other stories of the hunt. In these stories, they were all heroes. They fought graciously over the singed wings:

You first, Comrade…
No, you, please, Honorable Elder…
No, Uncle, take the skin.

"Are you returning home for the holidays?" Xiaodong's face removed Wang Guanmiao from the reverie of bird song in flame, of the writing forward of a history no longer his.

Wang shook his head—he didn't feel like running through the various impossible options that qualified as 'home' to him. Xiaodong wasn't the kind of man who'd understand. His home was always the same, easily contained within the courtyard walls of the birthplace of his parents and grandparents—his ancestry spoke to him from the stones.

"Smoke?" Xiaodong kicked an unwrapped pack of cigarettes across the dirt that skidded to a stop at Wang's feet. On the cover, Wang didn't believe what he saw: the Yellow Crane Tower of Wuhan, one of China's four most famous pagodas, the same tower Li Bai's poetry often mentioned. These cigarettes were Yellow Crane Tower 1916 cigarettes. They were expensive, even for an urbanite like Xiaodong. This level of cigarette was allotted from its state-owned factory in Hubei to only the highest ranked Party officials.

"Impressed?" Xiaodong winked and Wang noticed that sometime between the hunt and the following campfire, his comrade managed to find time to shave his mustache into its requisite U. Although this usually made him look more mature, now all Wang could see was a boy freshly emerged from his parent's closet, donning his father's Liberation-era PLA jacket, stuffing his pockets with army-issued condoms, pretending to be a man.

Xiaodong elaborated: "The village boss gave the cigarettes to Xu Min for feeding the entire village. That bird has enough meat on it to make Lanzhou 'bird' noodles for a week!"

"Xu Min," Wang repeated.

"Yeah, that's the man who killed the bird. The man I helped."

"Xu Min," Wang said again. So Xu Min was the name of the Raisin Villager. Xu Min: 'Small People,' or 'smaller than the people.' Wang couldn't decide which was more fitting. Nor what his mother ever thought in naming him something so diminutive.

"Yeah, so what if that's his name?" Xiaodong didn't understand Wang's confusion.

"So, nothing," Wang said, opening the cigarette box, pulling out a stick and inhaling the floral-sweet tobacco. Honey. Fields filled with flowers, women lying on their backs between tall grasses and men on their knees laughing into a forgetful white day. Laughing. He laughed. Xu Min was the name of a man in one of Lu Xun's stories Wang read in what classes his father could afford to send him to as a child. In the story, Xu Min buys his wife an expensive bar of soap so she doesn't have to wash behind her ears with honey locust pods, but the man is ridiculed by schoolboys when he wants to unwrap the soap and inhale the first whiff. Back then, Lu Xun's story was from a time of 'New Culture'— irrelevant, except in its discussion of scrubbing, how you could turn a bad woman filial by buying her some good soap. Scrubbing clean. That's what Wang could use, he thought—a proper shower, not the tossing of a bucket of cold water over his shivering, naked body as was the custom in Gansu, but a warm bath surrounded by steam and shrouded figures of one's comrades in the communal shower halls. Of course Xiaodong wouldn't know any of this. He was born in an era when students read only the Chairman's books. Xiaodong was schooled in the ways of keeping step and smoking expensive cigarettes when they were handed to you. Xu Min—the man who thought soap could cure everything. Wang wanted to tell Xiaodong and Xu Min: you need more than a box of soap. You need an understanding of objects that goes beyond the object itself. As soon as the soap performs its function, it becomes something else entirely—no longer capable of simply cleaning, but bestowing on you yesterday's filth as well. Soap can clean, but it can also cake, mold, grow foul and ugly.

Wang returned the cigarette to its roost and closed the box's top with a crisp snap, then handed it to Xiaodong.

"Not smoking, Little Brother Wang? Not even a victory smoke?"

Flames blanketed the body of the bird spinning on its spit, charred feathers dropping to the ground like wasted black snow.

"No," he said, lowering his head. 不.

"Still thinking of that woman?"

At the fire, the villagers stepped away from the crane, contemplated the best way to roast the meat evenly—the bird's head revering the sky or placating the earth?

"No," Wang repeated.

Xiaodong was undeterred. "That Li-Ming, I've been meaning to ask you: is she the same Li-Ming who went to the PLA school near Zhongnanhai?"

"Yes," Wang confirmed, confused how Xiaodong could know her.

"Then she's the same Li-Ming my wife went to school with. Said she was quite the catch then, making the boys run after her. You think you can catch her, Comrade?"

Wang's fists clenched. He stood, hovering above Xiaodong, his figure drowning his comrade's face in shadow.

"What's gotten into you, Poet?" Xiaodong nonchalantly dragged on his cigarette, exhaled smoke in a victorious puddle at Wang's feet. "First you're too weak to kill a damned bird and now you're angered at the mention of a woman who's not even yours?"

"I…" Wang wanted to strangle the words spilling from Xiaodong's ignorant mouth. He wanted to stop everything from happening as if the world had a distinct plan for him and he was to follow along, like the last bird in a flying V. His fingernails dug deeper into his palms, breaking the skin. His jaw clenched tightly around the ready muscle of his tongue. He swallowed loudly, acid settling into his gut like a stale mantou.

"Let's see what the Poet's capable of," Xiaodong egged.

Wang's nails dug deeper, clenching his own pulse, peeling himself to his stoniest core.

His comrade's eyes glistened in the firelight, nostrils flamed. The young man gripped his knees, about to stand to face Wang, but in that mocking gesture implied he didn't truly anticipate a fight. Wang raised his fists to strike his comrade, but then, in the evening shadows collecting at his feet, waltzed the body of a dancing crane. Wang blinked and dropped his hands to his thighs. The crane turned, raised its wings, and ran.

Baba

Perhaps it was the memory of a dead bird roasting on a spit, the taste of flight on one's tongue. Or perhaps it was that spirited anthem, 'The East is Red,' braying through the crackling speakers like a bird's final, raspy hoot. Or how Wang's companion Xiaodong sang along as if every time the song played publicly it was his duty to provide the harmony. Always he sang shrill and off-tune. Everything about him was unabashed, even his lyrical ineptitude.

The pair was finally heading home to Beijing after the requisite three years of reeducation in the deserts of Gansu. The villagers taught them what they needed to know—the proper height for corn stalks to grow in dry soil (*two and half meters*); how many piglets a sow births in a litter (*eight to twelve*); what to do at the first sign of frostbite (*liberally apply zi cao ointment*). The city boys left the villagers with the memory of rose-cheeked, tall-nosed northerners who daintily plucked meat off the bones of a roasting crane, goat, or pig. They'd never think of the western provinces with the spite they once had for these cold, rugged regions in their childhood years; now they knew the coldest cold, the hottest heat, the happiest Hui villagers, what it meant to be family, comrades. They'd experienced entire days (*sun up, sun down*), shoulders bathed in the heat of the desert sun without any promise of shaded respite. Heading home to expectant wives, children, and parents, these men were supposed to be exuberant. They were supposed to be thrilled at the prospect of instructing their city colleagues in the ways of country villagers. Comrades in the field. In the caves. At the communal fire.

But why wasn't Wang more excited? Li-Ming's last letter

never arrived as promised—he heard from other colleagues in his work unit she was transferred to a factory in Weifang, a city on China's eastern seaboard. More than a season passed since he wrote to her about the killing of cranes and noted the Yellow Crane cigarettes, the uncanny link to Li Bai's poetry. Had he been too presumptuous in making this intellectual leap? Or did he lack academic rigor entirely? Had he not cited Li Bai properly? Had she learned something of his uneducated background, his lack of a university degree, and his tenuous understanding of poetry?

He missed her letters' stoic introductions:

Greetings Comrade, What do you think of Chairman Mao's proclamation we cannot waste two hands lazing about the city?

He missed the way she seamlessly transitioned (and with such effortless pragmatism) into an analysis of the country's greatest poetry, how the lessons she learned from Du Fu, Li Bai, Li Shang-yin, and Han Shan could be applied to the daily life at the Jiangxi commune—she wrote once, quoting Han Shan, 'What's the use of all that noise and money?' and Wang responded by saying money and noise can be drowned out by the belief in the shadows money and noise make. She said this philosophical extension made her laugh. He missed her summation of life as a barefoot doctor, how important she made such a tiresome existence seem:

…there's no other way to put it: when you wake to the howl of a rooster and sleep to the chorus of crickets, you learn your place in this world. All the great masters—Confucius, Mencius, Chairman Mao— teach us what humans are truly capable of, but don't they also teach us humility? Today I birthed a foal. If you haven't already, you must witness this—how quickly a young thing can wobble into standing, still reeking of the womb. I envied its sure footing, its instinctive rush to stand. When did we lose our ability to live as innately as when we were first born?

He also missed her swift closings, which left him wondering

if she expected he'd know all the answers to her questions:
Your Comrade,
Li-Ming

Sitting on the train returning to Beijing, Wang tried not to think of Li-Ming. Her letters were carefully folded in his knapsack. Besides, he wasn't alone with his thoughts on this trip—Xiaodong, his companion on the twenty-five hour ride in the hard seat cabin, hammered on, one of his usual rants about the Party's new plan for Beijing, how many of the old city walls would be knocked down. Around them, Red Guards knit sweaters to send to the Chairman and gambled for pins blinding them with the Chairman's golden-cheeked face, while Xiaodong made suggestions about the shape of the Capital's new streets, the freshly-planted aspens lining the boulevards large enough for a parade of PLA officers to march down. Xiaodong's city was one of martial importance. His city represented China's destined future of greatness. In truth, Wang now found his city tiresome. He preferred the quiet of traversing a mountain path alone, bird song waking him each morning.

"Don't you care about our city's new urban planning? Aren't you interested in a capital besting all the world's capitals?" Xiaodong's questions always seemed rehearsed.

"What's so thrilling about urban planning?" Wang asked.

Xiaodong discarded Wang's ambivalence with a guttural "Ai-ya..." he continued. "Only a true country boy wouldn't care about the state of his city. Are you a country boy now or have you always been one?" His pretentious breath clouded the window beside him. Although his eyes casually glanced the platform rolling away, the desert cliffs slowly turning to flat, dry fields, he didn't see any of it. Xiaodong, Wang wanted to ask him, where are you now? Although he sat beside Wang, his body rocking forward as the train chugged away from the station, his thick thigh scraping Wang's, his dreaming mind was already stepping off the train onto Beijing's newly paved streets. But what of the scene rolling by outside their dusty window? Yellow soil exhaled beneath the train's wheels. Yellow everywhere and not a hint of the red and green turrets of Beijing. Beijing's gray. Beijing's brown. Here, the world was only soil and rock and earth. Hard. Unforgiving. Somehow more real than the ground beneath one's city feet. Barren, yes, but a barrenness to which Wang grew accustomed during the months sleeping on the cliffs of Gansu. He'd learned the strength of a man's lean legs, his wide, firm fingers. He examined the grimy crescents lining his fingernails. Maybe Wang was more a country boy than he'd known; maybe we can never fully unshackle ourselves from our birth place (a Gansu former astrologer with whom Wang once shared a corn harvest told him the entirety of one's life is governed by the position of the stars at the time of birth). But maybe Li-Ming would be impressed by Wang's new practical abilities. Her Poet could not only grind glass into the perfect shape for the army's telescopes and binoculars but also knew the exact temperature at which to plant soybeans in spring *(at least 15 degrees Celsius)*, the best soil type for a gourd's growth (*in full sun, on a raised bed*).

Xiaodong didn't look out the window but merely stared past his companion to the line of railway cabs chugging forward, all the Red Guards cluttering the floor with their eager banter and cigarette butts. "And then, in place of city walls they'll build avenues wide enough for eight lines of bicycles!"

Xiaodong. Xiaodong. Where are you buried now? When he sat next to Wang and casually allowed his breath to fog the window, his hands were more weathered and thick-fingered then than they'd ever been, would ever be again, one day receding into their original slender form. Yet he paid his appendages no attention—not once did he look to his nails as he gestured the span of Beijing's newly paved avenues. He already knew one's hands weren't much use when one's tongue can flick words into the world with such precision and ease. Wang should've known his comrade was destined for the one rung below truly great things, the constant over-striving his life's greatest hurdle.

Despite Xiaodong's drifting mind, his flap-heavy tongue, Wang wanted to grasp his comrade's hands. To tell him he'd once known hands as large as these. His mother's, his father's too— snapping corn husks to hang to dry along their pingfang's slanted doorframe. In the last letter she sent, Li-Ming asked about Wang's parents: *Where were they? What had they studied in university?* Wang casually avoided any mention of his family. His father hadn't written in years. What was the point? Strange, he thought, how we share blood and yet feel so different. What ties us is an inevitable fate: everything about his parents' lives was inexorably linked to his own—the way his inability to admit a certain truth about himself embroiled everyone around him in a tornado of likely tragedy.

Wang searched his knapsack for the last letter Li-Ming sent. In the sunlight skittishly waving through the cabin's blinds, he held the letter to his eyes, blinking away a falling dusk.

"That *wife* of yours," Xiaodong laughed. "You know what a wife is? A wife is a woman warm enough to heat the snake hidden beneath a beizi."

"Bizui," Wang said. *Shut your mouth.* "She's not my wife."

"Well, my mouth will be my old wife's in two days time. *Two days.*" Xiaodong sighed and finally turned to acknowledge the world outside his window, a world that wasn't theirs anymore— hills bathed in golden dusk, villages spilling brown-legged children along the tracks that click-clicked like the under beat to a folksong.

"In two days, Beijing will be nothing like you expect," Wang said.

"The city needs to abandon its feudal ways. Those walls are useless in the face of new technologies—nuclear warfare would grind them to dust," Xiaodong said.

"I think the city is fine as is," Wang said. "Why do we need to demolish the city walls? They're historic and make nice borders on a city map."

"Do you not believe the Chairman's proclamations about our nation's great capital?" Xiaodong's childish cheeks grew ruddy with contempt and confusion—an emotion Wang often noticed on faces of Party members, a look masking their deepest insecurity: that what the nation was embarking upon was in fact one giant ruse, the entire populace and its governing body moving as fast as they could toward a future they imagined in such glittering perfection, it could only exist within a man's foolish mind. Past, present, future. Did it matter? They were just reinventing the angle from which they viewed a world they'd never comprehend. Surely the great Chairman himself knew this—which was why, Wang believed, he sent urbanites to the countryside: to give them a taste of their own humble beginnings. Or maybe it was to shake things up. Besides, routine comes with its own perils, namely, the inability to differentiate between yesterday, today, and tomorrow. And also gossip. Frivolous talk thrives under boring circumstances. Does gossip exist in a war zone?

Xiaodong's mustache twitched uncomfortably.

"Nothing will be as you expect it," Wang said. "Uncertainty is the only certainty."

"The poet returns," Xiaodong scoffed.

"Yeah, the Poet."

Xiaodong peeled Li-Ming's letter from Wang's fingers. "Another letter? More love poems? Shit, you're one lucky husband."

"We're not married," Wang reiterated, snatching the pages before Xiaodong could read the date and mock him for clinging to an old correspondence.

"Well, Poet, given your predilection for love letters, you might as well be married." He lifted the shade just as the ancient city of Pingyao with its tall beige turrets rolled by. Wang learned about Pingyao in primary school, how it retained its city walls for thousands of years, despite the fact it was ruled by the Jin, the Zhou, the Qin, the Han, then the Ming and Qing. Even its city name had changed from 'Ancient Tao' to 'Pingtao' to 'Zhongdu' then finally to 'Pingyao.' This city, like Wang, had many nicknames, known as 'Turtle City' because its eastern and western walls have two gates each, giving the city the semblance of a turtle, four gates as legs. Their train sped past Ping Yao, once the financial hub of China's silver trade, ignoring the time and space they'd need to fully comprehend its crumbling walls, how so many wished to conquer it from the outside.

After a stretch of golden fields, the train stopped in Taiyuan. On the platform, the usual groups of Red Guards clamored to board the already too-crowded train, swelling up the stairs with forgetful laughter and red books clutched fervently to their chests. Beneath Wang's window, old ladies with marbled eyes shook wrinkled hands begging for food. Xiaodong ignored these pleas, contemplated the shape of an apple he'd pulled from his knapsack. He bit into the fruit with a loud, satisfied crunch.

Wang leaned back and held Li-Ming's letter to the late day light pooling in from outside, knowing he had only a few minutes respite from Xiaodong's pestering, only a few minutes of remaining daylight. What could he learn in this re-reading? He always sought a secret hidden behind Li-Ming's colorful stories of her new life in Weifang. If Li-Ming couldn't explain to him the truths of the world, who could?

Shangri-la, a song played over the loudspeakers in Taiyuan. *Shandong in the winter is like a silver Shangri-la.*

香
格
里
拉
！

When the train peeled away from the station (gravity-stricken old lady faces wavering good-bye in the glass; old lady faces wanting *Apples! Apples! Apples!*), Wang heard Li-Ming's voice warbling: *Shandong in winter is like a silver Shangri-la.*

The next morning, the train stopped in Shandong's provincial capital, Jinan, where the men were to change to a northern-bound train to the Capital. They waited on the station's busy platform for their next departure, breath fogging the chilled air. The eastern hills were dusted white, morning sun casting them opal. Beyond them, a silver Shangri-la.

Across the empty tracks, crowds of Red Guards milled about, dressed in Mao coats with the Chairman's face beaming from a thousand red and gold buttons. They awaited an east-bound train headed for Shandong's tip, the curved beak of their nation's map—China: the thick-headed chicken. *Chicken.* Wang heard that familiar childhood taunt ringing in his head. *Chicken.* The chant of children on the schoolyard, of Wang's sure-footed cousin as they ran clumsily down Shanghai's rain-sodden alleyways toward the Park Hotel. Chicken. Without thinking, Wang slung his knapsack over his back and jumped over the steel tracks to the train that would lead him toward a silver Shangri-la.

"Little Brother Wang!" Xiaodong called over the whistling pitch of the eastward departing train, Wang's hot water canteen still at his comrade's feet. "Where are you going, Mr. Poet? You forgot your canteen!"

But it was too late. Wang was already digging into his pockets for his last five yuan, the only cash he'd saved from a year's work in the fields. He was ignoring Xiaodong's calls, ignoring any better judgment about abandoning his work unit and potentially ruining his chances for future work, let alone inspiring the prospect for a further character examination. He pushed past the crowds of Red Guards with their eager banter and tattered Little Red Books and onto the train that was slipping away as his foot stepped up the first stair. He wanted to see that silver Shangri-la with his own eyes. Li-Ming would greet him beneath the snow. They'd share a dance. She'd smile. Icicles would melt. He'd tell her the truth: who he really was. What her Poet had seen and known. They'd understand the dripping nuance of a shared, sheltered spring: 夏.

As if approving his plan, the conductor smiled and slapped his back as he boarded the cabin for standing-room only ticket holders and found a place beside a hunched farmer, a burlap sack at the man's feet filled with bruised apples. Of course, enough apples to feed the watering mouths of an entire train: without prompting, the farmer passed his bounty to the eager Red Guards who dug their teeth into the fruits with the mindlessness of well-fed horses. Outside, the mouths of Jinan's beggars swelled with saliva, craving the sweetness the students casually discarded to the floor, browned cores rocking at their feet as the train pulled away from the station, edging its way toward the mountains, toward Weifang, Li-Ming's Shangri-la.

*

Snow alighted delicately on Wang's feet. Snow on the backs of his hands. Snow powdering his hair. Snow dripping winter tears into his eyes and down the long bridge of his nose. Snow. Weifang in winter. But Weifang in winter wasn't anything like Gansu's coldest months—the desert's cutting wind that sliced your skin like a kitchen cleaver. No, Weifang's winter melted you, softened your bones. Wang touched his cheek and laughed at the unexpected magic that brought him across the silver hills into Li-Ming's Shangri-la—a steam locomotive chugging over the Taiyi mountain range until he could see the flat marshes leading all the way to the Yellow Sea, to Li-Ming, Worker #223 of the Shandong Soap Factory.

Waist-high snowdrifts were piled at the feet of unoccupied brick buildings, beside ping-pong tables too short to fight the rising white, games abandoned to the shifting of seasons. He knew she worked on the factory line for industrial-strength soap, the type strong enough to erase the grease and dirt from even the raisin villager's hands. Sniffing at the cold air, Wang hoped to smell an undercurrent of jasmine, but all he received was the overwhelming constancy of burnt coal. From the quiet buildings beside him, smoke stacks emitted a constant plume of black snaking into the heavy white sky. Black on white.

Through this smoke, the snow continued falling. Even his footprints couldn't follow as he walked the silent streets of this unknown city. The impending sense no one knew him here made him want to shout his presence:

I am here!

I am here for Huang Li-Ming!

I am here to take her home to Beijing with me!

But his voice froze within his throat, an air bubble in ice.

Wang followed the blanketed streets from the town's central station into the city square, an empty gray expanse, toward the factories with their thin chimneys confidently spearing the sky. Wooden nianhua carvings with stories of the New Year still flapped, lonely, against the doors of two-story homes and shuttered office buildings. As Wang neared the row of factories on the southern side of the city, he passed a doorway atop which a rusted blue and white plaque announced a city office. The door was open, perhaps awaiting a visitor. He reached out to close it, keep in the warmth. But the door would not shut. A snowdrift inside held the door open. In piles, the shifting snow said: *Welcome inside, Comrade Wang.* He shoved the door wider, making enough room to enter.

"Ni hao," Wang announced to the empty, shadowed room. No one responded. There was only a wooden desk overlooking a fogged window, a three-legged stool, and a gray microphone with a wire snaking through a hole cut in the wall, likely leading to a loudspeaker system through which the city heard important propaganda announcements. Wang switched on a small lamp on the desk, golden light orbing his hands, warming them enough to move, to begin what he came here to do.

"Li-Ming, your Wang Guanmiao is here to rescue you!" he

shouted at the microphone. There wasn't a reply. Was it on? He tapped but couldn't hear the speakers reverberate outside the window. He laughed. The insanity of this journey! Was this anything but funny? But his laughter broke when it met the concrete walls of this small room, claustrophobic and kept. He pulled himself closer to the speaker system, sitting on the lone stool. A small red button beckoned. Press it, he told himself, summoning the courage to make his voice heard. Within seconds, the microphone crackled, inviting him to lean closer. His hot breath wet the metallic wiring. The wind rattled a suggestive *tap tap tap* on the wooden roof. The wind, too, wanted him to announce he'd come here to find Li-Ming, that he was ready to abandon his past and start a future with her.

"What now, Li-Ming?" he asked the wind.

A tapped reply: 说.

Shuo. To speak.

Wang pulled himself closer to the desk where a day-old People's Daily was turned to the local news: a headline praising a ten-year old girl for reporting her teacher to the local bureau; he was a suspected capitalist who once tried to retain landed plots from before the war. The girl beamed at Wang from a black and white photograph.

"Proud of yourself?" he asked and she nodded, winked, pointed at her tight-lipped traitor teacher. He held his gloved hands to his mouth, blew warmly, inhaling the damp woolen smell. At least here he could decide what he'd say to Li-Ming when he found her leaving the factory floor at dusk, skipping toward the crowded cafeteria, her hands flashing white against the whitest snow. Her dancing could clear snow off streets, make rooftops shutter icicles onto unsuspecting walkways.

Just as he removed a pencil from his front pocket to scribble a speech on the back of the schoolgirl's face, a bell rang. The chatter of a thousand voices shattered the snow's silence, sharp female tones rising like shrieking magpie calls, men's grumbling baritones.

Outside the window of his cramped perch, gray and brown clad bodies of thousands of freshly-emerged workers paraded the streets. *Lunch!* Their eager strides announced. *Lunch.* Stupid. Wang had forgotten about lunch. Without thinking, he reached for the record player next to the loudspeaker's microphone. Slapping the stylus into place, he pressed the red button again to make an announcement, to change the course of what was quickly becoming a train speeding in the wrong direction. But what could he say?[35] He didn't know—but time, he knew, was important, irreplaceable. Time was words etched into caves. Books hidden under beds. The masses plodded through the snow toward the mess halls. Famished, skinny bodies the leanness of winter aspens. Where was his Li-Ming? To his astonishment, the record clicked into place. Familiar music blasted onto the streets.

At the first trembling notes, the bodies outside the window stopped to listen to that well-known voice, despite the years that passed since they'd first heard its warbling tones. She sung, honey-sweet:

This beautiful Shangri-la, this loveable Shangri-la

[35.] Halfway through the journey isn't the place to turn back. You either set out or you don't. Cold Mountain didn't pause on his departure, turn to his wife and say, "Goodbye, my beloved." Once he took the first step he kept walking, up that mountain path and to that hidden, wind-sheltered cave. That is, if the story we've come to believe, rewritten numerous times by numerous men, is true. But I wasn't Cold Mountain. I wasn't Li-Ming. I was a 16-year-old who'd never traveled outside the U.S. but believed I was old enough to smoke cigarettes, sleep with my physics teacher, and step off the edge of my mother's roof, only to shatter a collarbone and tibia. Everyone thought China would straighten me, not bend me further. Tiananmen, my nesting ground—where I'd go when the light was shifting and the world felt too cluttered and broken—was full of life that year. The only place in the city where you could sense the enormity of a northern, desert sky. One day, this square was so silent only a gun's soft-pitched rap-tap-tap broke night's rapture. "Okay," I said, and Baba loosened his grip around my wrist. The rock music dulled to a soft coo and the night turned to something resembling day. The unraveling began then; we clung to one another for fear in its loosening, we'd both fall apart.

I deeply love this place… I love this place…

The syllables slid—*xiang ge li la, xiang ge li la*—rising, rising, then falling with the snow trapped on a swirling column of wind outside his window, incapable of touching down on the shoulders of still-warm workers.

Unexpectedly, the bodies outside formed pairs, danced a waltz Wang witnessed only once (*whose memory?*: fogged windowpanes, high-heeled shoes, bodies floating across a ballroom's waxed wooden floors, the low drone of trumpets). They leaned and swayed in the wind, puffed torsos padded by the weight of matching winter parkas. Snow lifted into swirls above their heads, drifted in waves beneath their feet. Numb toes tapped beats, heads swayed. Wang stood at the window watching, his own body inspired by the rhythm of the dancers, their lilting turns and patient, contented smiles. He traced their tree-like shapes on the frosted glass, against the fog of his breath. Their movements were rehearsed yet instinctive—Wang was reminded of his first day on the grinder, how his fingers didn't hesitate to find the shape of the lens.

He hugged the ghostly body in his arms, held it so close her breath warmed his shoulder, made his hips sway. Then, just as suddenly, he felt the cold wind of a body removed from his grip and a return to *this* body, *this* earth. A face pressed its cheek against the window. A face Wang recognized. Had been longing to see for years. Warbled glass, the blues of water-logged eyes and the blacks of eyelashes batting snowflakes. Behind this face was the tempered jaw of a face he'd known before that. And then, behind that, layer-upon-layer of faces that once stood pressed to panes of glass, masked by his own incapacity to see the borders of chins, the true shape of rouged cheeks. He saw people he hadn't yet met—Li-Ming's round-faced friends, the bicycle repairman on the corner of Jishuitan—and then, the past too: Smiley's figure on the cliff, his ragged pants slapping at thin legs, Commander Deng's shadow shrouded by a tent's khaki shield,

Uyghurs lounging outside a restaurant he didn't recognize but knew, with a strange and certain insistency, he'd one day come to pass every day on his way to an office where his work station faced a courtyard and the courtyard was filled with aspens that only in spring would drop seeds to earth like snow. Nose pressed against windowpane, Wang knew the cold winter on that tip of smudged skin, shared with it this desire to be warm, to clutch a body, be swaying along to the *xiang ge li la li la li la li la li la li la li la* of an imagined youth.

Sparks flew from beneath the glass, sprayed white piles outside the window with hot blue-silver.

"Comrade Wang," a voice said. A voice belonging to a hand that gripped his shoulder. Tightly. Fraternally. "Comrade Wang, collect your things and stop dreaming. Our dreams have come true: We're home, you ass."

His nose was pressed into the window, breath masking the familiar red-gold street lights flickering into view, bright orbs illuminating empty streets. Nearly midnight, the capital city was covered in the dry snow he'd despised, dandruff-like flakes that powder shoulders and get stuck in the creases of shirtsleeves. Wang cursed himself for what would prove to be a string of cowardice—Had he never gotten off the train? Where was his shining Shangri-la?

An announcer cleared his throat into the train's loudspeaker: "Beijing," he said. "Passengers alighting here, ready your belongings for arrival."

Wang took several minutes to pack his canteen, his Tang dynasty poetry books, two worm-ridden apples, and Li-Ming's letters, tied with a fraying hemp string, into his knapsack. But it took him much longer to feel the earth land heavily underfoot as he stamped clusters of freshly-fallen snow from his boots on the station's platform. Took him much longer to shake the feeling of his nose pressed to the glass, the strange faces he knew so well yet couldn't name, the chill on his cheeks like a once-familiar word now forgotten. It took him even longer to turn to witness his large-footed tracks disappearing with each new layer of snow, as if reminding him that by turning back to witness, he would wash away any trace, any resemblance, of the path home.

Letters #5, 6, 7

Letters addressed in your name:
An unknown location in the western hills,
piled under my bed like hungry children.
Nibble the pages, a new nutrition.
My mother's peony stamps: they'd never reach you.
Ghost girl, sitting beside Houhai, opera-faced Mandarin
ducks bobbing like puppets.
City walls are falling down now.
The only reply:
Are you sitting still?
That's all.
Greedy as a pigeon below Tiananmen's Revolutionary statues
peck peck peck at the stony feet of heroes
How many years?
Didn't you see? Of course I was sitting still.
But then: dinners to cook and husbands to placate and chil-
dren to birth and work units to report to.
Lifting box after box, dank rooms filled with stacks of letters
in wooden boxes awaiting delivery.
Eagerly awaiting:
an ear, a touch, an audience.

Baba

How many hours did Wang Guanmiao sit on that metal stool alone in the center of cavernous Factory Hall Number Five beneath the pitched, bat-laden rafters? Six? Ten? Fifteen?

He measured the passing of days at the start of the Great Unraveling[36] by observing the shifting light, the golden beam beginning as a sliver in the corner of those factory floors and sliding, searching for something lost, across the cement beneath his feet.

Then the lights would flicker on, the only song he heard during those unending, slow-minded factory days. Music: electricity jumping circuit-to-circuit above their heads. Electrons. The spinning of grinding machines, sparked glass to metal. Music was something they invented to pass the time.

One night, when Wang sat on his stool counting the hours since lunch, after his co-workers retired from their grinders and walked home, he decided it was time to find Li-Ming's father to ask for her hand in marriage. It had been months since he'd received a reply from her; he worried she might be losing interest in their correspondence, especially as he hadn't made it to her Shangri-la—or had he? Wang flicked off his station's switch, the

---

[36] "You don't understand," she said during one of the afternoon lessons, then realized this hurt my feelings so softened her tone. "The Great Unraveling was the beginning of the end. It's when we lost our way. Maybe we never should've gotten married." "You can't say that," I said. Her hair gone now; a butterfly silk scarf knotted at the nape of her neck. "And why is it a Great Unraveling? Maybe it's a raveling?" "No, that's not how it works." Why in death, or so near it, was she so stubborn? In the apartment kitchen, the wok sizzled, garlic added to peanut oil, a toss of ginger too. My stomach peaked, tongue caressing teeth. "I'm hungry," I said, ignoring the fact she couldn't rise on her own to follow the smells into the kitchen where Baba hunched over the stove, quiet, his thoughts merely his own for just a few chapters longer.

well-worn belt sighing as the spinning slowed. He was always the last one on the factory floors at night, his comrades home in their crowded apartments on the leafy factory campus. He'd see their smiling faces through the dusty windows on his midnight walks to the apartment he shared with the only other single men in his *danwei*: Pockmarked Zhang, the dormitory's most flatulent sleeper; and Wu Wei, a smooth-skinned, perfectly-built Beijing native (the girls remarked he was even better looking than the exemplary Comrade Lei Feng). But on his walks alone under an oblivious moon, in the apartment blocks beside him, families readied for bed, reading from the Little Red Book before the children dozed off and parents listened for the latest propaganda announcement on China National Radio.

Wang knew that Huang Daozhen, Li-Ming's father, regularly returned to his office at night to smoke a pack of cigarettes and play mahjong with the other factory bosses (although the game was outlawed by the Party, danwei leadership played after hours in the privacy of their offices). Click-tap. Tiles smacked against one another, slid across the table. At Huang Daozhen's office, Wang waited for a lack of sound—signifying a lull in the action—then rapped his knuckle on the slightly-ajar door. The wood reverberated, sending an unexpected chill up his spine, then the door opened wider, exposing his entire frame to the room.

"Shei-a?" It was Huang Daozhen's recognizable gruff and unforgiving baritone wanting to know who knocked. Huang was known around the factory as the 'Singer Boss' because of his gravely voice, a voice that betrayed the fact there was something unexpectedly soft in him, as if his years in Moscow studying Leninism taught him more than his comrades would ever know.

"Ah," Wang said, his tongue suffocating itself. How could he not remember his own name? He cleared his throat, reminded himself why he was here: *Huang Li-Ming*. Getting her would mean the end of a story, mean he could finally rest, would reach a certain pinnacle in his life, a cliff from which he could view the rest of the world. What he didn't know was none of this was true. The surety of ambition: one day he'd look back, rub his balding head, and muse at the stupidity of middle age.

"It's me, *uh,* your comrade Wang Guanmiao of Glass Grinding Station Number Five, Factory Five."

"Of course, Wang Guanmiao. Our most diligent worker. What are you doing here so late? And why stand in the doorway like a deeply rooted tree? Are you a mahjong fan?"

Wang didn't know which question to answer first. He chose the last.

"Mahjong is not my specialty, but I do enjoy our nation's special game." He couldn't believe how rehearsed this sounded. When had he become like his dull comrade Xiaodong? Why couldn't Huang Daozhen have been here alone? His plan was not built for success. Maybe he should try another night.

Too late: "Come in," Huang waved Wang to the table, to a mahjong game in progress, all four men, Huang included, hunched over their tiles. "Sit." He pointed to a stool nearby.

The other men didn't look up but Wang recognized them as his factory's leadership: Comrade Zhang with the scoliosis spine, Comrade Gao with the kite-shaped birthmark on his scalp, and Comrade Ting who always shook his head 'no' when he was actually saying 'yes.' These men were not truly Wang's comrades—they served in the Party prior to Liberation, some of them even participating in the Long March. They were on a first-name basis with the Chairman himself, studied Marxism in Moscow, and regularly met with the Party politburo at the CCP headquarters in Zhongnanhai. To them, Wang was just a country boy. He didn't deserve to sit at their table, so close to their hunched, important bodies.

"You know Confucius himself wrote the rules of this famous Chinese game, don't you, son?" Huang Daozhen was especially loquacious tonight, which made Wang even more uncomfortable. Zhang shifted in his seat, rubbed his back. Ting tapped his cigarette into a stuffed ashtray. Gao combed the hair above that birthmark with a sun-spotted, quivering hand. Above the table, a fan spun lazily. Blade shadows flickered like old film across the hands of the mahjong-playing party leaders, the white and black tiles, the brown table. White on brown. Wang's mind spun like that fan. His fingers tapped the rhythm on his thighs. Could he leave? From deep within his abdomen rose the unmistakable feeling of swimming, of trying to get to the other shore—the far shore where muddy reeds enclosed ankles, water traded for air. But Wang didn't know how to swim. His mouth tried to sputter a response to Boss Huang's question about mahjong, but his words were underwater: no one could hear him.

"Speaking of sons," Comrade Ting cut in, drawing a cigarette to his mouth and saving Wang from drowning. "When's that lovely Li-Ming of yours returning to Beijing to marry and give you your first son?"

Huang Daozhen leaned back, placed his hands sage-like on his lap. Lips placid, neither smiling nor frowning, his face never conveyed emotion, as if the best way to live was to remain detached, unaffected.

"My Huang Li-Ming is a funny child. She's not like her comrades in Weifang." He seemed to be searching for the right words to describe her and Wang grew elated that Huang Daozhen felt the way Wang did about his daughter, believed in the absolute uniqueness of her.

"Actually, Honorable Sir," Wang said, turning to Huang Daozhen. The stool beneath Wang wavered.

"No feudal titles needed, Comrade," Huang said, sounding more like the man Wang knew on the factory floors: distant, but kind—like the father figure portrayed in Party films, a father for the nation: he expected the most of you, if only because he knew you were capable of greatness, so much to make the Party proud.

"Yes, *Comrade Huang*," Wang corrected. The fan clicked. "Li-Ming." He said the name he'd repeated so many times, only this time the tones fell flat. Wang straightened his seat and the stool beneath him came to rest. "I came here to ask you a question about her."

All three factory bosses released their tiles to the table. Four pairs of eyes turned to Wang, so many eyes he didn't know where to direct his gaze so he dropped it to his hands, to the flickering gray shadows playing lazily over his calloused skin. Light and shadow. Everything he knew about the world could be reflected atop his hands: light, shadow, men coughing in corners, tiles sliding across tables, machines clicking on, clicking off, bicycles rumbling down frost heaven alleyways, smoke catching in his nostrils. Everything he knew yet never really understood: Now. Steady. Breathe.

"I want to ask you for Li-Ming's hand in marriage." Wang raised his eyes to meet Huang's.

Zhang shifted in his seat and slapped unkindly at his lower back. Gao's eyebrows rose, wrinkling his forehead and crumpling his birthmark. Ting choked back a cough (or was it a laugh?), ashing his cigarette in the communal silver tray. But Boss Huang didn't move. He didn't so much as lean forward. Nor blink. He was a man of patient action.

"I'm sorry, Comrade. Her marriage is already arranged," he said, unflinchingly. "Didn't your roommate tell you?"

Pockmarked Zhang, Wang thought, his stomach tightening. Everything was suddenly clear: Pockmarked Zhang with the scarred purple cheeks, the gaseous ass that shook the bunks at night. Pockmarked Zhang escorting Li-Ming down Xinjiekou, beneath draping willows. Pockmarked Zhang straddling Li-Ming's hips in a cold, stark dormitory bunk, his white backside flashing with moonlight as he thrust himself upon her, teeth flashing a smile as he witnessed Wang in the doorway. The children Pockmarked Zhang and Li-Ming would make: squatter versions of Zhang, with her soft cheeks and his wide, dense forehead. How could Pockmarked Zhang have won Li-Ming?

"That Wu Wei is quite the catch," Comrade Ting said with the exhale of a large plume of smoke that hovered above the table, the tiles, the steady bars of—
shadow-light
shadow-light
shadow-light
—*Wu Wei*. The cloud dissipated, leaving behind a viscous web. Sweat pooled beneath Wang's palms. *Wu Wei*. Of course it would be Wu Wei who'd win Li-Ming's heart. He'd won the city's Athlete of the Year award five years earlier for running the fastest 100 meter sprint, swimming the fastest 100 meters, and jumping the farthest (almost six and a half meters). He'd won a spot on the coveted glass grinder near the doorway, closest to the fresh, chilled breeze, won the top bunk in their dorm room and the most desirable cleaning duties—sweeping the hallways, not scrubbing the squat toilet stalls as Wang was assigned. Wu Wei's wide smile allowed doors to open magically, as if the wind itself believed in his powers, his moral and physical strength. Wu Wei. Wu Wei and Li-Ming. An odd pair, surely, but the more Wang thought about it, the more likely the betrothal seemed inevitable, practically heaven-ordained.

Wang stood, his thin shadow barely masking the table.

"And so the charmed suitor departs," Comrade Zhang said, laughing softly beneath his mustache.

"Gone so soon, Comrade Wang?" Huang Daozhen's words trailed Wang outside, past the slapping of the heavy metal doors, the bare aspens scratching each other, swollen moonlight suffocating the city's alleyways.

Gone so soon, said the wind.

Gone so soon, said the pigeons with whistles tacked to their wings.

Gone so soon, said the emptiness of bicycle-less streets closing in around him.

A hand gripped his shoulder. "Where are you going?" Wang

turned to see Huang Daozhen's unsmiling face, somehow patient, somehow paternal, under the omniscient moonlight. He
breathed heavily—he'd jogged to catch Wang, was fast enough
to catch him.

"I'm going home," Wang said. At least this didn't feel like a
lie.

"Can I walk with you?" Huang asked.

"I think it's too late."

"Well," Huang said, ignoring the protest. "I just wanted
you to know Wu Wei and Li-Ming were a match since primary
school. They were top athletes in their classes, companions on
school trips to the countryside. I'm sure you'll understand." His
hand was still on Wang's shoulder, but now they faced one another. Huang's face: crests of wrinkles lining his forehead, frowning eyes pulled downward by gravity, a squat Southerner's nose,
a nearly invisible neck. All the marks of age, of time, in his face
alone. What did he see in Wang? What did Wang expose in the
double-folded expressivity of his eyelids, his tall nose, his frowning, wide mouth? No matter how hard he tried, Wang couldn't
fake the confidence of a man like Wu Wei.

"Li-Ming's no prize," Wang said before he could prevent the
words from spilling off his lips.

"Perhaps you're right," Huang Daozhen said, surprisingly. "But she's my daughter... and I can only do what The Party
thinks is right for her."

"Of course, The Party," Wang said and wondered if Li-Ming's
father saw the way his eyes rolled slightly, lips quivering, eyebrows pinching. The Party. What had The Party given them? In
Andong, The Party made him lose his perfect vision. In Gansu,
The Party made him an accomplice to a crime—the killing of
a mythical creature—that his ancestors would surely haunt him
for. And now in Beijing, The Party took the love of his life from
him. The Party wasn't for the people anymore. It hardly stood for
anything but the blank stare Huang Daozhen gave him before he

shook his head and continued on his way.

"Remember what Marx and Chairman Mao say about knowledge!" Huang shouted to Wang's shadow. "True knowledge begins only with revolutionary practice! Don't forget that more than mere thought is valued here!"

Wang didn't respond. What use was there in attempting civilities with a man who would only be his factory's leader, nothing more? And he disagreed: true knowledge could never arise from the practices derived from a wrong mindset. If he lived in a world where only the Wu Weis could win, he didn't want to participate. He'd stop "practicing" all the revolutionary activities, and thus stop creating any of this false "knowledge" to which Huang Daozhen referred.

"Did you hear me, Comrade?" Huang's voice cracked.

Wang didn't respond but allowed the *click-tap* of his footsteps to reply. *Click-tap* around the abandoned factory grounds toward shuttered Rending Lake Park. *Click-tap* until the sun rose purple-pink in the eastern sky. *Click-tap* until the window shades in the apartments lifted one by one, each family awakened by the waking of their neighbor. *Click-tap* until he stood outside the danwei mess hall at breakfast, chopsticks smacking porcelain bowls of congee, a chorus of voices so loud, so intermingled, not a single word or phrase could be extracted from the cacophony. Nothing except…

"Stop daydreaming, Comrade Wang!" Wu Wei shouted from inside the mess hall. Behind panes of glass brushed yellow by the Gobi's sands, Wang could see Li-Ming's future husband— his wide, coffee-colored face, his strong jaw stretching into a proud, straight-toothed smile. A victor's smile. Wang's comrades lounged in a circle around Wu Wei, laughing for the beautiful man in a rehearsed way. They waved for Wang to join them.

"Are you coming or what, Wang?" Wu Wei's tone was unmistakable. His laugh too: pitched and frivolous, a chicken's cluck.

Wu Wei, like his fated wife Li-Ming, was always the center of every crowd while Wang stood on the outside, his lonely shape wavering like the wind now shuffling past the cracked window pane.

Wang exhaled: his breath fogged the scene. He looked at the sun's early slant for forgiveness, shoved his hands into his pockets. He wasn't the strongest man in Beijing. He wasn't the victor. But at least, he thought, walking into the mess hall to greet his comrades, he knew how to conquer distances with his hands, feet, and eyes. While most of them had yet to leave the bounds of the capital's ancient city walls, he'd gazed down the tube of a telescope and seen shores so distant, so foreign, they didn't have names. Only those who've traveled such distances can understand the simultaneous grandeur and smallness of this world.

Wang took his seat at the head of the long, wooden table. Wu Wei straddled the far end, telling a story about the first time he caught a trout in one of the aqueducts surrounding the Forbidden City. His admiring disciples looked on as he wrestled with the imaginary fish bare handed. What stories victors tell themselves, Wang thought, reaching for a bowl of tepid congee. The liquid slid down his throat and landed, lead-like, in his empty belly.

"Another Tale of Wu Wei!" one of their fresher-faced comrades shouted, a man Wang recognized from the dormitory's shared latrine whose piss smelled like burnt cinnamon.

Wu Wei obliged his hungry masses. Wu Wei's men listened, slack-jawed, the duration of the meal, nodding their heads like dogs to a pork bone. They did not speak, but smiled when directed, clapped their hands when inspired. When breakfast was finished, they followed Wu Wei outside, their shadows hovering darkly at the cafeteria windows, before dissipating into a world unseen. Wang waited at the table until their voices were overcome by the wind, trying to decide what was to be done in a world not his to conquer anymore, in a scene now brushed gray at the edges, the cafeteria's slouched janitorial aunties clearing bowls from the slop bins, making clucking sounds at the mess the men left behind, tired by the lot life handed them but still going on living this life, arms elbow-deep in vats of discarded congee.

*

The problem, Wang Guanmiao realized, was Wu Wei looked even more handsome naked. Whenever the danwei men entered the communal showers together, Wu Wei was the first to remove his towel from its tight wrap around his sculpted hips. Wu Wei's chest wasn't sunken and bony like Wang's. His limbs didn't reach toward the earth like dead twigs. His body was made in perfect precision. Even his penis seemed to retain its girth at all times of day and night, despite the lukewarm temperature of the shared showers. Yet none of the men envied him; they were more in awe the world provided them with such a beautiful sight. They wanted to believe nature was kind, not that the heavens regularly doled out cruelnesses like Pockmarked Zhang's acned skin or Xiaodong's short stature and watermelon belly. For so long, they wondered which of the five women Wu Wei regularly dangled from his bulging hipbones every night at the mess hall would eventually call him 'Lao Gong' and provide him with an equal-ly-attractive son. And so, naturally, Wu Wei would turn Wang's blade of fate upon its head while he and the others soaped them-selves in the steaming heat of the danwei's mildewed showers. Water at full blast, an opaque wall of mist, their voices carried far, echoing against the tiled floors, spilling out into the dressing room along with clouds of steam. Wang needn't be in the showers to hear the pronouncement that would eventually change his life and send Li-Ming running back into his heart with a swelling *ta-dum*.

Fate, Wang's father regularly reminded his son from a young age, throws daggers at you. Wang never understood what he meant by this seldom-used idiom. He'd tell Wang at night, before they curled onto their floor mats in the two-story Shanghai home: *You've got to grab fate by the handle, not the blade.* But what fate had Wang's father handled so successfully? His father: the farmer's son who learned a trade as best he could, who built from wide country hands a quiet empire of glass, now living alone, impoverished, in his hometown's granary, sleeping beside well-fed rats and cockroaches. Did he know how to grab the handle instead of the blade?

The winter had been Beijing's coldest—killing thousands of chickens in suburban coops and requiring the Party to declare a free run on coal—and Wang was drying off with a starched towel, enjoying the heat of the room's only radiator when he heard the news that would change his life.

"Shi Lili said Pockmarked Zhang's balls are as big as grapes!" Wu Wei's voice was unmistakable—loud, brash, and adding *'er'* sounds to the ends of *'ah'* words. His was the voice of a native Beijinger, full of the privilege of urbanity and inherited Party status.

"No way!" one of his compatriots doubted: how could Pockmarked Zhang, with those fleshy hips, have such small balls?

"Oh yes, Lili told Qinglin the other night she and Zhang had been up to their ears in a snow bank behind Factory Building Number Five. She said his balls were as big as grapes."

"As small as grapes!" someone corrected.

"As shriveled too!"

"Oh *that's* a story."

"It's no story." Wu Wei's laughter carried from within the showers, that clucking chicken pecking pointlessly at dry earth. Compared to his body, his laughter was frivolous, feminine—an anachronism. At least he was somewhat human.

"I'm telling you," Wu Wei spat into the streaming water as one-by-one the shower heads turned off, sputtered a mindless dribble. Feet splashed toward the exit, voices—still marveling over the size and shape of Zhang's unusually small testicles—drawing nearer.

The metal door to the showers flapped open, releasing into the room billowing steam. The three freshly-showered men sauntered to their belongings, which were strewn haphazardly over wooden benches. They seemed not to notice Wang standing beside the radiator in the corner in only blue underwear and socks. As they toweled their legs and asses, Wang turned away, rubbing his hands to the heat. He pulled on his pants, buckled his belt.

"What about you, Wu Wei? Which women have been naming your balls?"

"Cannonballs!" Wu Wei shouted, correcting the crowd. There was the slapping of wet skin. That tweeting Wu Wei laughter. There must have been stomach muscles contracting and Wang wondered what kind of masculine display he missed by not turning from his perch at the radiator to watch.

"What's this going around the factory about you and Boss Huang's daughter? The pretty one with plump ankles and hips wide enough to shake a bed?"

Wu Wei bellowed a quick, polite laugh. "Oh she's just one of the pack," he muttered with his trademark confidence (could Wang hear his smile?).

His cohort expressed their approval—whose pursuits could they live through if not Wu Wei's?—and dressed quickly, still speaking of the gossip, how Pockmarked Zhang made a woman of Shi Lili, a girl Wang knew only for her freckled cheeks, her dog-like obedience to her suitors, and inability to quote Chairman Mao thought.

"Shi Lili and Pockmarked Zhang. What a pair," someone remarked.

Wang leaned over to tie his shoelaces as Wu Wei swaggered toward the door.

"Who will it be tonight, Comrade Wu?" the stouter friend, the same man Wang knew as the one with cinnamon piss, looked to his leader like the sycophantic Shi Lili. Wu Wei had everyone in his grip, even Wang himself was in awe of his comrade's every motion; Wu Wei gestured with a wrist as if the latest pursuit meant nothing—was as effortless as slipping into a wide-knit sweater—then his face unexpectedly scrunched in concentration as he made his decision. When thinking, as when laughing, Wu Wei wasn't particularly attractive. His face was meant only for moments of distraction, petty talk. In pensive thought, his body betrayed him, his mind incapable of controlling the smooth, tanned muscles of his cheeks and square jaw. Perhaps the heavens are not so kind after all, Wang thought with crude satisfaction.

But what thinking on the part of Wu Wei, what internal discussion, was required to answer his comrade's question? *Li-Ming*. The answer—quickly, confidently, unabashedly—was *Li-Ming*. Wang's answer was only *Li-Ming*. It should have been Wu Wei's too. How could he take so long to reply?

"Shi Lili!" he finally announced, finishing the flick of his waiting wrist (suspended in air while his face, his mind, betrayed this grace). He confidently slapped open the door to the entryway.

"Pockmarked Zhang's girl it is!" the stout comrade shouted in astonishment. "Well done, indeed! You can show her those elephant's balls of yours!"

"Cannonballs!" Wu Wei corrected again.

Laughter, always laughter: the loud laughter of Wu Wei's men punctuated by Wu Wei's chirpy giggle as they exited, leaving the door flapping behind them, the same singing approval trailing the leader happily down the hallway and forging into the fogged autumn cold.

Wang dressed quickly, nearly forgetting to don his woolen hat and gloves to protect against the frigid chill that descended that morning from Manchuria. But he didn't feel cold as he walked from the showers to his dormitory in the purpled dusk. All he knew was the warmth that slid into Shi Lili days earlier, the same warmth that promised to slide into her tonight, was the warmth that now gave him re-inspired faith Li-Ming could one day return to Beijing for him. *For me!*[37]

At the corner of the dormitory, Wu Wei's gang, their leader in the center, chatted, slapping one another's backs, still laughing. As Wang walked past, Wu Wei called out for him.

"Roomie!" he said, speaking as if the pair had any camaraderie when, in fact, they were barely acquaintances.

"His name's Wang," one of Wu Wei's gaggle whispered.

"Come over here, Comrade Wang, my roommate! We have a question to ask you." He waved his broad white hand and the deeply embedded image of a similar hand waving made Wang's foot snag concrete. White on brown: an image stored in his brain, or, in reality, closer to his chest, hoping one day he'd wake up to find it there, a seed blossomed like a lotus in mud, its fragrance overwhelming the world with light and heat. While Wang reached to pull this flower from the surface, he fell forward, knapsack flying out of his hands and toward the pavement sprawled between him and Team Wu Wei. His knee burned. His back kinked. When he looked up, Wu Wei leaned over him, extending a hand (it was smaller than Wang imagined).

"Need help?" But behind his eyes was the glimmer Wang knew well: like the shimmer at the bottom of a pool, that vapid space where *knowledge* becomes *revolutionary practice* becomes *nothing*. Wu Wei's eyes: beautiful, if what you loved was a version of human beauty, but when you looked deeper, you'd see a pool of deep, lovely, nothingness.

[37.] In Rending Lake Park, where we went before she was too tired to walk, old men with oversized calligraphy brushes sat on wooden stools painting water-poems on stone earth. Poems whose beginnings would evaporate before the last stroke was penned. Why didn't we stop to read the words, write them down in ink on paper? I know she'd have an answer. She'd say something about the mountain being a mountain and not being a mountain. Suchness/no suchness. Form/No form. As I waited for the Route 22 bus to Tiananmen last week, I watched a grown man pluck a nose hair from his nostril, examine its slick form for a minute, then flick it to the ground. Such was the nose hair, I thought, as he must've too. Such and such not.

Hatred and love: neither really an emotion, but an action. For Wang Guanmiao, his hatred had little to do with Wu Wei, he could admit that, and, had little to do with his hunch-backed tu baozi father, his mother's final walk into the river, his temporary blindness at the front. What he hated was not himself but his body's boundaries—that he could stand now, shaking feeling into his feet and hands, and face Wu Wei, that he could cock a fist and lash it across those perfect cheekbones, shattering nose bone, eye socket, jaw. That the blood could run down his wrist but not be his own, would never match his in color or viscosity. Wu Wei could fall to the pavement, smack skull to cement, and all that laughter could spew out of his mouth, a sewer drain unplugged. But who would be the victor then?

Wang's hands pressed the pavement. No wonder everyone loved Wu Wei. No wonder everyone wanted to be him—isn't it easier to live without questioning the reason why we're living than be burdened by the weight of answers without questions?[38] His arm was still outstretched, beckoning.

Once Wang was on his knees, Wu Wei extended a hand again, this time closer to Wang's chest, too close, Wang thought, to the flower that blossomed earlier then recoiled.

"I don't need you," Wang said. "不," but when he spoke, consciously or not, he spit on Wu Wei's hand. 不.

Attached to the words clattering off his tongue (*bu bu bu*), Wang's saliva landed on Wu Wei's skin where it glistened, river slime on reeds.

"Turtle shit!" Wu Wei shouted, wiping his hand on his pant leg. "What's with the inconsiderate fool who can't walk or talk like a true Comrade?"

Behind him, the gaggle swelled, full of revolutionary talk and words without meaning or place here, but they didn't care. Their faces looked down at Wang as he struggled to his feet. Who were they? In what Party office or at what government job pushing

---

38. "His two actions are open and shut, between which we all live."

papers and stamping strokes of red did they now sit, smoking Panda cigarettes, coughing and complaining about their *lao* wives and their *zisi* children, waiting on an inevitable death that felt like the closing of a book, the final pages growing slender and so, what was the point in paying attention? The sun, most days, was shrouded not by clouds but by what weather reporters called smoke or fog: *Wu. Wu* was in the sky and wu was in their lungs. *Wu* was everywhere.

Bu bu bu.

Wu wu wu.

"I'm just trying to be a good roommate," Wu Wei said, a smiled scoff, that glimmer behind his eyes beckoning. Who was he? Wang wanted to believe in him. They all did. Because without people like Wu Wei, how could they trust the earth beneath their feet?

He gripped Wang's elbow. "Don't you know what Mao says about roommates?"

"Yes," Wang said, allowing Wu Wei to help him stand. He'd never noticed how he was actually taller than Wu Wei; despite how large the mythical man grew in their minds, he was quite average-sized.

"Yes," Wang repeated while within his mind that chorus grew:

不.不.不.

无.无.无.

Wang knew what Mao said. Who didn't? "Mao says 'roommates' are the fools of the bourgeois. Our real roommates are those who stand beside us when we fall—like the sparrows, the cranes, the river's fish. Are you calling yourself as great as a bird, as a flying fish?"

The crowd parted, water past cliffs or a bird through mist.

But what Wang really said was: "I don't know." What he really did was walk away, past Wu Wei's gaggle of faces, the faces that had been above the surface while he struggled for breath, their feet kicking him back under. He'd seen enough.

After the run in with Wu Wei, after his team dispersed to their various apartments, wisps of laughter following them home, Wang stood at the entrance to his building's stairwell, waiting for the flickering lights to flick on, fixed as they were to the sun's unacknowledged setting, knowing with just one step he'd be entering the rest of his life. With that step, he grip fate's handle tightly, a surging confidence. 'Hello dagger, meet Wang Guanmiao,' he told himself, as the Soviets did in films the Party showed on Saturday nights at Chaoyang Park, backlit screens with fluttering images of mustached generals greeting one another with head bows and handshakes. So much formality in a world so colorless and stale.

The next morning, after the gossip about Wu Wei and Shi Lili became public, Wang would walk into Huang Daozhen's office to meet the knife that splintered his own ancestral name into his daughter's—Huang Daozhen becomes Wang Guanmiao's Huang Li-Ming. That same fated knife would now cleave to their lives like the scent of the communal squat toilets at the end of the dormitory hallway, that sweet, buttery refuse rising to one's nose with added zest, reminding Wang it was time to walk upstairs, that he was, as much as he was anywhere, home.

*

Of course, fate is trickier than one can expect. Fate, like life, gives reasons to wait. Makes hours become days become weeks become months become years.

It would be nearly half a year from the day Wang grabbed fate's handle that Li-Ming returned to Beijing. Her homecoming was arranged with a Weifang native working as a porter in Beijing's Chaoyang district—those days when travel was only ordained by party affiliation. Without a proper Beijing danwei, Li-Ming was the property of Weifang's Shandong Soap Factory. Huang Daozhen requested that Wang deliver to the Weifang native a new Phoenix bicycle, purchased for the exorbitant price of 150 yuan, in exchange for the man's Beijing hukou; likewise, Li-Ming would give her Weifang resident status to him. The Weifanger (a bow-legged, freckle-cheeked man) accepted the trade begrudgingly—*Beijing's my home*, he told Wang as he examined the bike. But he had an arranged wife waiting for him in the fields outside his village. Wang wanted to say he understood better than anyone the distance that grows between spaces over time, but he simply rolled the bicycle toward the man. The Weifanger would talk to the party bosses that night and would arrange for Li-Ming's return in exchange for his departure. That was the way things were done those days, the red stamps necessary to complete a transaction, to leave factories in the fields of Shandong for factories within Beijing's now-demolished ancient city walls. Wang waited until the bow-legged man rounded the corner on his new, shining bicycle, then jogged to the danwei's dormitory, his feet finally regaining the lightness they'd felt years earlier.

A month later, the day Li-Ming arrived in Beijing, Wang waited for her at the entrance to her family's apartment building clutching a bag of guazi, the lightly-spiced sunflower seeds he knew she loved. Magpies jumped between the branches of flowering pink peach trees, children chased their shadows in the complex's courtyard, duck egg vendors bicycled the alleyways shouting for patrons to test the salinity of their once-buried product. This was the Beijing Wang loved.

Just as another magpie touched down, as the egg vendor's call was swallowed by the busy city streets, Li-Ming's voice billowed from around the corner, drawing nearer with each breath. What pleasure was this? What was the unexpected wincing pain cradled within it?

Now that Li-Ming's return was imminent, now that her voice reached Wang before the image of her smiling face stretched around the corner, he could not will himself to believe the rest of his life would unfold so blissfully.

Of course Li-Ming wouldn't see him. Instead, as Wang stood beside the entrance to her parents' apartment building, Li-Ming, freshly-butchered pig head happily stuffed into a burlap sack swinging from her wrist, bounded up the stairs without once stopping to say 'hello', not glancing in his direction. Wang remained alone clutching his guazi at the bottom of the stairwell as she hopped ebulliently upstairs.

Of course she would not see him in the shadows.

Of course he would be forgotten, the guazi bag hanging limply by his side.

She bounded to her parents' cramped apartment, her parents, who, in a year's time, would move to Nanjing, her father transferred to a higher position in another glass grinding factory and her mother's health deteriorating due to those struggle years where the label 'black' hung heavily upon her neck.

Wang tipped his head: through the column of staircase windows, he counted each of Li-Ming's steps, those light-tapping feet climbing higher, higher—

Shi-er...

Shi-san...

Shi-si...

Er-shi...

San-shi...

And finally: *si-shi-liu*. Forty six. The door slapped open, followed by the expected commotion over the pig's head.

Who would eat the roasted ear? Who would receive the fattiest piece?

The magpie perched on a branch above Wang's head, long tail flexing.

"You alone too?" Wang asked. The bird's head twisted inquisitively, but before he could speak, he stretched his neck to wrestle with a particularly stubborn berry then flew into the blue-gray sky, slowly growing smaller, as if the pair were never friends to begin with, birds alone immune to the loneliness plaguing humanity.

Wang envied his easy escape. But what had Wang expected in this waiting? He wanted his future wife to bound down those stairs to find him standing there. To throw her arms around him, tell him how much she missed him in the years that passed since their first and only meeting. To shout to the entire courtyard of homes, all the apartments with their spring-happy windows, the descending evening sun: "Comrade Wang: I'll marry you next week!"

But the sun tucked itself beneath the horizon of nameless brown buildings, leaving shadows of phone wires draped above the city in dusty, abandoned webs, humming conversations pulsing between posts, words that weren't Wang's—like all the invented dialogues he created in anticipation of this day:

Wang Guanmiao, you're taller than I remembered!

Wang Guanmiao, you're truly a poet!

Wang Guanmiao, we can begin the rest of our lives now!

Instead: steps folding behind rusted banisters. A stolen glimpse of white sock above black saddle shoe, the faintest hint of the creased back of a knee. A pig's snout pushing against the thin burlap sack, exhaling. Did he witness the animal's last, punishing breath? Who had seen the last blink of an eye closing its final cinch?

Wang waited.

He waited until the snaking wire shadows were swallowed by a navy night, until the duck egg vendors bicycled home with empty cartons rattling, until shifts ended at the factories, dinners cooked, dinners eaten, apartment lights proudly ticked off—*click tap tick*—as if they'd been waiting all day for this moment, for children slumping into sleep at the dinner table, for wives and husbands sliding wordlessly into bed.

Wang waited until waiting itself became a chore. Then, shoving his hands in his pockets, he walked slowly toward the empty courtyard, to the shared apartment in the western block, nearer the factory floors, the machinery droning until dawn. Why hadn't he called ahead to Huang Daozhen, or allowed Li-Ming a day alone with her parents to exhaust all the stories of Jiangxi and Weifang? Why hadn't Wang considered he might not be welcome here? Was there an old folk song about him? *Lo, lo, lo, you've made a fool of yourself again, old man*—but while the song droned on, families pulled chairs to tables, the moon silvered the city blocks, and even the magpies retired to crowded nests. *You're a fool to think you're anyone, the song should have sung. You're a fool to think you deserve to be loved.* Musicians would write songs about people like Wang. They'd write songs about all the times he stood beneath doorways, outside windows, beneath trees. Waiting. Waiting. Deng. Deng. Deng.

Finally, as Wang traversed a long expanse of concrete toward the alleyway leading him home, a familiar name pierced the slowly descending evening:

"Comrade Wang!"

"Wang Xiansheng!"

"The Poet!"

"Comrade Wang! Stop!"

He stopped. He was Comrade Wang. He was The Poet even though he'd never penned a verse.

When he turned, he saw Li-Ming's head poking from her apartment's sole south-facing window, hand waving. He could ascribe three wan's worth of metaphors to her hand waving because he's remembered it like this for decades, telling everyone it was like this, it *must have been, could only be* this way.[39] But Wang

---

[39]. The first time I visited Jingshan Park to scope out the tree Li-Ming mentioned, the park was surprisingly quiet—school children in early summer exams, danwei units still in session, not yet released for lunch. I read the plaque, a history lesson: from this perch, Emperor Chongzhen watched his city crumble, asked his most devoted eunuch, Wang Cheng'en, to string him from the lone tree's branches then follow with his own rope, their final glimpse of the world together, a city ablaze, an empire crumbling. A janitor shuffled down the path, glimpsing up at the foreigner sitting beneath the dead tree, then returned to his task, sweeping away Orion choco-pie wrappers, relics of a busy weekend full of sound and forgotten sweets.

didn't yet know what hope he had in Li-Ming would leave him, ultimately, an old man with the same habits and rituals ruling his youth: lifting chopsticks to mouth over a meal shared with only a bouffant-donning TV game show host who announced a new-lywed couple eager to try their hand at the Wheel of Life—*What would they win this time? A trip to Hainan Island? A Japanese-made microwave?* Old Wang would shout: *You will win a lonely death alone!* But no one would hear him, not even the host with his superfluous hairdo waving mockingly.

But that night, his would-be wife stood there waving. They would try their hand at the Wheel. What would they win?

"Where are you going, Wang Guanmiao?" Li-Ming asked, as if Wang was the one who was rude that night. Huang Daozhen stood behind her, his hands pressed firmly into her shoulders, a gesture bordering on paternal, but lingering close to condescen-sion. She was his only child—how could he do anything but love her indiscriminately?

"Why are you standing outside in the cold so late? You must come upstairs to join us!"

"Comrade Wang, please join us for a second dinner."

It was Huang Daozhen extending the offer.

It was Li-Ming laughing expectantly and raising her shoul-ders as if his question demanded no other answer than what Wang quickly responded.

"Yes, of course." Wang nodded, already playing the role of husband that would enact itself occasion after occasion in coming years: *Bicycle Xiaofei home from school, will you?* Yes. *May I meet my colleagues at the office for evening badminton?* Yes. *Can you pick up sanitary napkins from Pang's Grocery?* Yes.

Huang Daozhen's face disappeared from view, lost to the darkness of their candle-lit apartment, the scene familiar those nights, the near-daily power outages they blamed on the imperialists and their unscrupulous trade embargoes. Li-Ming smiled at Wang, made a gesture with her once-waving hand that meant 'hurry up now' and then she too was lost to the quivering golden light behind that open window.

Now it was Wang's feet bounding up four flights of stairs, the forty-six steps. Forty-six seemed an easy number to climb to reach Li-Ming. Forty-six could pass in a heartbeat. Why had he waited so long?

Letter #8

Dear friend,
Are we now both mothers-to-be?
Strained, stretched skin: an elbow, a knee, my crotch.
The train south, my husband's lao jia a dead, brown weight on his shoulders, visible on the horizon.
Vomit curds—congee or stewed egg?—crusting my lips.
Suck the last tendrils off the lychee, leave me bare, child.
I never wanted to be a mother.
It began with the Tangshan earthquake:
My mother woke us up, banging her head on the wall and begging us to crawl outside. Glittering glass underfoot, a darkened city. How many aftershocks until the neighbors stopped screaming? How long for gravity to return to our feet?
Slant of sunlight, my husband's body rocking with the train's pulse: "That crazy man's words are etched on your cheeks."
A calligrapher's sentences stroked my skin.
I laugh too, Mr. Wang, when you make a poem,
Like a blind man trying to sing of the sun.
Tick tock: the Soviet-made Pobeda, my father's.
Time on wrists, walls, school bells, train whistles.
What of this? Lin Biao's plane flattened in the Mongolian grasslands, The Gang of Four in black and white:
Mao and Yao and Chang and Wang—poetic justice?
Where is our bow-legged goose Lei Feng now?
sun-shadow-sun-shadow—
barred window frame and this body hedging me in
I need to get out
First tremorless night after the Tangshan quake, we made a

daughter.

Wang said: "Oh no, the earth would *not* move again! *It couldn't!*"

Until one day, it did.

How could we trust the earth wouldn't shake itself loose once more, casually shedding us?

This time: One last layer of skin, a pleated skirt pooled at my Lao Wang's feet.

Baba

Silver moonlight pooled at my wife's side as she nestled, too tired to resist sleep, into the mat of my family's old pingfang. We'd come to announce our betrothal to my father and show him Li-Ming's growing belly—our baby. Here I was: her husband, and a poor one at that, this lanky body willing itself to standing, waiting for the night to end—so what? So I could tell my father I was finally a man, a husband? A stupid idea. For so long I'd been Skinny Wang, Hawk Eye, Comrade Wang, Lao Wang. Who did I think I was?[40] Below me, the sleeping bodies of my pregnant wife and elderly father looked like bags of hay or millet or—what difference did it make the shape of their forms?—their bizarrely matched snores rocked the granary's maggot-ridden bags of rice, millet, flour. This was not a home. Homes are more than four walls.

"We're having a child," I wrote. Three months later, the reply: "Let me see the wife first."

When I walked outside, I tried to reconstruct a failing geography: the bamboo forest in the gardens flanking my first home,

---

[40] From the perspective of this translator, I cannot ascertain why Li-Ming's narrative shifts from third to first person—and why here, all of a sudden, we receive such intimate access to her husband's interior thoughts. Perhaps Li-Ming is taking a cue from Cold Mountain, reminding us—
"People ask the way to Cold Mountain
but roads don't reach Cold Mountain
in summer the ice doesn't melt
and the morning fog is too dense
how did someone like me arrive
our minds are not the same
if they were the same
you would be here."
                    —Trans. Red Pine
But aren't you here? Isn't your mind enough?

cobblestone streets wobbling underfoot, and over there, Mr. Li with his cotton pajamas and horn-rimmed glasses out for his midnight walk, slouched monks shuffling across Square Bridge to retire at the candlelit Sword Temple. My mind had a dangerous propensity for superimposing past upon the present.

Through the old bamboo forests, shuffling over the same path on which Mrs. Li would walk in her silk, butterfly-print night robes to retrieve her husband from his nightly escapades, I picked my way to the river's edge. I removed my shoes and wriggled my bare feet in the mud. Lazy, sewer-fed worms perused my toes. This river was my mother's last home before her brothers buried her bones atop Xiagai Mountain. But her skin had already disintegrated from the weight of water and stone, flaked into the mud in which my toes wriggle and slip. Is she here? I reached down to pluck a worm from its path, examined him in the moonlight, his wriggling, fragile body translucent. *Die!* I squeezed his body into submission but he simply encircled my finger in pointless loops. I tossed him back.

When I returned to the old pingfang, my father was still there, his snores filling the room to the web-laden rafters, but there was a gap between where I'd been and he was.

"Li-Ming," I whispered, wondering if she was sheltered beneath the blankets but there wasn't a response or a lump big enough to betray a pregnant woman's shape.

I checked the kitchen, where flies danced above rusted pots, dried zhou still clinging to the rims. Had she gone for a midnight walk as well? That wasn't like her, but in the months since we learned of her pregnancy, she'd been more distant—like the outermost planet of a galaxy just close enough to be drawn into orbit but precariously wobbling along. With just one touch, we both worried, she'd spin off kilter.

I walked outside and the moon, which I hadn't noticed before, nearly blinded me in its whiteness: *white* rooftops, *white* parched river, *white* forgotten village.

The alleyways of my old town were a labyrinth of small shop fronts, wooden doorframes unhinged, shriveled ears of corn hung to dry from eaves. Nothing new, nothing bright, nothing worth holding on to. The villagers, I knew, were a dying breed—only the sick and elderly remained here, even the local peanut crops not yielding as big a bumper as years before.[41]

I turned back to the river, following the moon's footsteps nearer the glimmer of water. That's when I saw her crouched like a wide stone.

"What are you doing?"

She didn't look up but I saw silver in her hands, mocking moon dance.

"Give me those." Wrestling the scissors from her grip, she slipped—her bare feet in the mud, top-heavy ass yielding forwards. I wanted to catch her but with the blades in my hand, any attempt at salvation would be puncturing as well.

She landed on her stomach, one cheek to the mud.

"Get up," I demanded. She rolled to her side, her knees. That's when I saw it—the bald patch on her head, the hairs she managed to cut in what reflection she could see in the moonlight.

I peeled off my nightshirt, gave it to her to wipe her face.

"What did you do," I said, but it wasn't a question as she stood looking in my direction not really seeing me.

"Let's get you home and I'll wash you off with rainwater."

I tried again: "They once brought soy sauce all the way down this river from Shanghai to Hangzhou. Qian Wanlong soy sauce. You know that kind?"

---

41. "It started in Cen Cang Yan," Li-Ming swept a sweaty lock of hair off her forehead. "You can't understand. You're still a young woman. You still believe you can do whatever you want." I couldn't disagree; as I listened, I traced the tattooed crane on my inner wrist, a gift from a tattoo artist I'd met, slept with, and received as a gift in a Beijing alley months before. "I chopped off all my hair at that damn river," she said. "You did what?" "I. Chopped. Off. All. My. Hair." Wheezes between words: I should've counted her last breaths but I didn't know how to contain them, if I could keep them in a glass jar like a firefly whose feeble light would die without the reply of a lover's pulse.

When I reached for her, she didn't budge. Forty years earlier, I'd been the one stuck in the mud, my father's grip demanding I move, Sword Temple monks shuffling over Square Bridge and the world continuing in its orbit that morning when everything around me stopped. If I can hear my heartbeat, I'm still alive, I thought, but where was that pulse behind my ears now?

"C'mon," I said, but again, she was stuck. "Do I have to carry you home? You know that'll break my back."

A joke: a softening. She yielded enough for me to pull her over the embankment and along the dirt path to my father's old home.

"Where's the trail to Cold Mountain? I saw a mountain but now it's gone," she said. The moon was setting and a blanket of dawn obscured the old skeletal shapes. "Can we go there?"

"There are heaps of mountains around here. Nothing worth throwing a stick at," I said.

My wife grimaced as her bare feet rolled over the cobblestones. "I want to go to the mountain."

"We'll clean you up and we'll leave in the morning," I said. A cuckoo babbled from a branch, too early for bird song but singing nonetheless. I led her back to the house, pants still rolled to my knees, shins stinking of fish shit and kitchen grease.

My father had set three bowls of tepid porridge on the wooden bench near the beds (the only bench awarded as dowry from my mother's family, the year of its making—*Year Three of the Republican Era*—etched into the bottom, an unalterable reminder of its place, and ours, in our republic's confused history). He didn't notice the mud smeared on Li-Ming's face or my pant legs dampened to the shins.

Dutiful husband, filial son: we spoke of the weather in spring, the inaccuracies of this year's foolhardy *Tongshu*. We spoke of what a summer's harvest could bring. But my father was not a farmer anymore. Who would tell him this? The money he saved from decades making lenses dried up, much like the soil of the once-fertile fields surrounding his village. Now my brother and I shipped him a stipend from our salaries. No one wanted glass lenses anymore—it was plastic the masses preferred, the sturdy, flexible material that wouldn't degrade. Glass had seen its day, as would soon be the case at my Beijing factory. Father moved back to Cen Cang Yan where, during the land reform campaigns of the '50s, he'd been awarded two mu of land—but the soil was thirsty and dry. Overworked, his patches produced nothing more than a few limp green beans, a thin-leaved cabbage head each fall. The sweeter produce did not grow here anymore and my father bemoaned the loss of good earth as we ate our breakfast, a pearl of white zhou dribbling down his chin. His teeth gone, he gummed his food. I didn't wipe his face clean—I wouldn't make a child of my father.[42] I owed him this much courtesy.

"You'll go with me to the mountain later," my wife whispered. Her lips synched the rim of her bowl.

"The mountain, yes," I replied but I knew: the mountains had been blasted into boulders; buried bones pulverized into dust.

My father didn't hear us—his hearing compromised by age. He slurped the last of his gruel and tipped back the bowl, rimming the surface with his tongue like a wild dog whose belly has never known fullness.

"We're leaving as soon as we're done with breakfast," I said but my father didn't reply, the bowl encompassing the entirety of his face as my wife kicked my shin under the table and I recoiled, the blanched sting, rubbing my protruding, lanky shinbone,

---

[42.] As in one of my favorites from Han Shan:
"A white crane carries a bitter flower
a thousand miles without resting
he's bound for the peaks of Penglai
with this for his provision
not yet there his feathers break off
far from the flock he sighs
returning to his old nest
his wife and children don't know him."
—Trans. Red Pine

wondering, briefly, if this was in fact the place in which I was meant to be or if there was a parallel history that could lead me to a different ending altogether. There aren't any mountains, I wanted to say, only fragments of stone where dynamite ripped open whole hillsides, granite packed onto the truck beds and transported to seaside marshes where pharmaceutical factories are built every week to cure society's headaches and toothaches and backaches and…

"I'm so damn hungry these days," my wife said.

My father, his hearing attuned only to the impoverished, nodded in agreement.

"Hunger is the fiercest of human emotions," he said as if once a scholar or a scribe. So many untruths licked clean from these bowls.

"We'll miss our train," I said. "Can Cousin Ming drive us in his fancy truck?"

My father nodded quietly and even though I could see the shape of his jawbone beneath his paper-thin skin, I didn't realize this same silhouette would be mine soon enough.

After breakfast, as we gathered our small packs and readied to leave for the station, Li-Ming stopped me at the doorway, gripped my arm. "I wanted you to take me to Cold Mountain. To show me where your mother remains."

I should've told her there was nothing left, but little untruths are somehow easier than the bigger ones. "We'll have to take the train there," I said and she nodded, hand on belly, the baby kicking inside but I'd never know that feeling—a man's creation lives and dies with his desires. Like my father, I was neither executor nor deliverer. For that, we needed our women.

*

When we boarded the train that morning, Cousin Ming was so distracted by a Shanghai peach candy vendor (seldom did the sweets come all the way to Shangyu) he forgot to show us off, so my father stood alone at the platform's edge.

The train's whistle blew, a shrill cuckoo. On the platform, slowly at first, then with a hop in his step, my father mirrored our cabin's movement, shoulders humped, a hand meekly raised, waving at us—but it wasn't clear: was he shooing us away or calling us to return?

"Say good-bye, Lao Wang," Li-Ming instructed.

I did as told, propping myself onto the seat to stretch my neck out the window.

My father smiled at this last, filial effort to show my face, his palm flashing its reply in the sun. I waved.

Li-Ming slouched into her seat, exhausted from the walk to the station. She closed her eyes. Soon, I knew, she'd sleep. Sleep was all she did these days.

But me: I kept watching and waiting, fearing that moment when my father would disappear altogether. We were two people moving in the same direction, but at a distance, like the sun and moon rising and falling from an identical eastern horizon but never catching one another. He'd returned home. Where was mine?

At the end of the platform, my father stopped, toes nudging the edge, palm still waving, wide sleeves flapping in the wind and exposing old man arms, thin and slack with blue-gray skin.

I waited, one hand on Li-Ming's distended belly, the other frivolously waving into the humid air outside our open window, until my father's figure slowly shrank, the train turned north, and he was gone.

A Buddha-like smile spread across Li-Ming's face, insinuating that for her, the journey was just beginning. Ridiculous.

"You know, there isn't any mountain," I muttered and although her eyes opened, shock-wide, that dastardly-sweet smile remained. She patted my arm, patronizing in its tenderness, then rested it there. She didn't need to say anything. Didn't need to remind me that although our train coursed north, wheels assuredly locked into the tracks, we were loosened from one another now, walking divergent paths to different mountain cliffs, unsure where, exactly, we expected to arrive in the end.

Letter #9

Dear Friend,

Old Man Lu with deer-like eyes stands half-naked from the waist up, on the corner of Xinjiekou. He should wear a warning sign around his neck: "When the words stop flowing, your heart stops beating."

Last week, my husband, like a fool, tried to chase down a flasher haunting our danwei's apartment blocks.

Naked body: schoolgirls giggling.

"Loo loo loo!" he shouted, kitchen cleaver twirling, glinting pink-gray dusk, a cow shell's sheen.

But he was a coward again: a fainter, fallen to earth, smacking head to pavement outside Lao Jiang's baozi stand.

They brought him home wrapped in shrouds, blood flower-blossoming in his palm where the knife sliced his skin.

"Silly, stupid man," Xiaofei aped and added: "Mama, I saw his penis!"

The flasher's penis. Limp or taut? I couldn't ask.

Lady Meng and her Tea of Forgetfulness:

Immortals sprouting wings, becoming cranes.[43]

That night, we landed in a dark cave.

My teeth: ridged in grooves, the reach of my tongue.

Did my arms extend into wings?

Human!

We laughed; how silly! Searching for a place we didn't know

---

43. What is the weight of a bird? Twenty years after Li-Ming's death, a flock of storks nearly took down a passenger plane heading from Istanbul to Singapore. I wonder: if Kinetic Energy is KE=1/2mV^2 and m is the bird's mass and v is the true air speed of a plane, how many red-crowned cranes does it take to kill three hundred and thirty five people?

was so deeply ordinary, full of pines and cold sea wind, rocky faces and a sun with the same insidious pull from light to dark to light again. Laughter dissipated, valley fog rose, an unexpected sunset across black chin, white chest—even though it was only morning.

I folded my wings into my hips, hopping down the rocks, ecstatic to think one day I'd bring you here.

You nodded: your husband was right, you said.

I tssskked through broken teeth and the penis that flapped for my daughter was not the last penis she'd ever see but because it was the first, we couldn't laugh just yet.

Baba

They told us the American was fragile. They used that word specifically: Fragile.

脆: Brittle as porcelain.

Principal He's voice cracked on the phone as he read the list of problems our "American daughter" had already encountered in her sixteen years in the richest nation on earth:

A parental divorce.

A suicidal mother.

A suicide attempt herself.

Too low a roof.

Broken fibula.

Cigarettes: The expensive imported kind in sleek boxes.

Alcohol.

Sex with too many boys.

I gasped, more for Principal He's sake than my own. I didn't need to see his face to know when he talked of cigarettes and teenage sex his cheeks flushed like the girls in the Shanghai Soap ads, how this made him endearing to my wife and all the Erfuzhong Middle School mothers but to us husbands he was soft and easily misled.

"Don't be fooled," Principal He cleared his throat. The connection crackled: someone was listening. What a stupid conversation to play audience to. "This girl is rich! All Americans are! And they attend top American high schools. So this girl may be fragile," the word skinned a serrated edge, my stubbled cheek against the receiver, "but she's smart. You know what they say in the 36 Stratagems? '假痴不癫'[44]—about playing the part of

---

[44] "That's me," Li-Ming said, "Fake crazy but not insane." "You're not crazy," I needed to believe. She cawed like a bird. "Not a terrible day," she tilted her

the madman? My guess is this is what she's doing. And why she's perfect for your family. You and Li-Ming will see right through her and bring her around. You know the saying: 'A long road reveals the strength of your horse, a long time reveals the heart of your friends.'" Principal He spoke tirelessly in idioms, as if being intentionally opaque made him smarter than the rest of us. I didn't know how long this road would be, or how strong our horse could become, but decided it best I not tell the girl's history to my wife.

"Thank you for the introduction to our American daughter," I said.

Behind me, Li-Ming and Xiaofei sat on stools in the kitchen making animal shapes out of floating potato skins in the sink. A horse. A dog. A snake. For only the Year of the American, and only in the fading light of an afternoon, did they share a temperament.   Three weeks later and there she was, that brittle, "fragile" girl, leaning against the coal-dusted bricks of Erfuzhong Middle School with her cargo pants, tight black tank top, white canvas sneakers, and skin that glistened in the sun like something cold needing licking. Xiaofei's shiny Mary Janes scuffed the pavement, the shoes Li-Ming read about in smuggled British children's books, paid a ridiculous sum for at the Friendship Store and forced our daughter to wear for this momentous occasion. For the past three weeks since Principal He's call, while her mother skittered about like a house cat, preparing pyramids of oranges, cleaning and ironing the bed sheets, our daughter pouted in her room, the only room in the apartment, save the bathroom, with a door. But Li-Ming wanted Xiaofei to know: maybe China wasn't the center after all, maybe nowhere was.

Her fellow Americans stepped off that rusted green bus full

---

head to the ceiling. Fake crazy. Not insane. Afternoon shifted such that what was once yellow was now gold. When the wind touched the trees on a distant hillside, it set them a-jig briefly then moved south and everything green went colorless and silent.

of winning smiles and tins of chocolates so sweet they'd burn your teeth. But Lao K scowled to the sun—it took us an hour to match the beautiful girl in the photo Principal He sent us weeks earlier to the pigeon-toed, lanky teenager near the coal pile stealing a smoke, hoping no one would notice. In the file Principal He gave us to prepare for her visit we learned she attempted to throw herself from her home's roof last year but was "reconciled" now. Yes, "reconciled" was how Principal He explained Lao K's situation. The world is always trying to find a proper place for those of us who don't fit, squeezing us into ever-smaller spaces.

She flicked her cigarette to the coal pile at her side, the dying butt rolling off the briquettes saved for the coming winter. Her figure was so much larger than ours, even from this distance, her knotted hair an auburn cape decorated with flowered pins like in the costumes of Dai dancers. She was neither girl nor woman but held the promise of both. This may explain why we loved her so much, or why this love harbored attraction and repulsion.

From where we stood across the courtyard, we weren't sure whether we should boldly approach or angle our eyes to the earth and wait for her to join us, occasionally glancing up to see if our tactic was working. A hot day: sweat crawled from our necks to the creases at our lower backs. We swatted at mosquitoes driven into the city by a drier than usual season. The other students found their parents; when there were just a few left lingering, Principal He walked to us, one hand in his pants pocket, one on his chest as if saluting a flag.

"You want to meet your American?" he directed us to the girl. She had started another cigarette and as we approached, she squelched it beneath her boot.

"No smoking," he said in Chinese.

She didn't extend a hand as we'd practiced for her arrival.

She shrugged.

We shrugged.

When she smiled, we smiled.

This pantomime continued for weeks. And for weeks after the girls left for school, Li-Ming searched the American's clothing for cigarette cartons, even a spare butt, but all she'd find was the lingering scent of rose hips and tobacco leaf on the breast and cuffs of the girl's shirts. Even her socks reeked of tobacco, but we'd never catch her smoking again—was she able to make objects disappear? That shrug. *Sure*, she seemed to say, *bring it on*. Could a scent alone implicate a greater crime? We clung to the hope she was greater than this girl who barely spoke our language, who jumped from rooftops like Fan Qiniang[45] and survived.

A girl is a girl is a girl. That should have been Principle He's idiom of our year together.

What I didn't know was how alike they'd be—the girl and my wife. How the girl, weeks later, would pull a hat from her luggage and give it to me, saying "gift," insisting I wear it. How for years I'd never go anywhere without that hat, sometimes mistaking the smell of my hair for the smell of hers and thinking, instinctively, that made us close, almost kin.

*

I couldn't have predicted the rest: the diagnosis of my wife's illness, Li-Ming shuffling the boxes under the bed, looking for that

---

[45.] "Don't you want to be like Fan Qiniang?" Li-Ming asked me. "I don't know who that is." From where I sat I saw dying light peeling off buildings, the sun's former apricity fading. Baba's ficus plants scratched our backs, requesting attention. Li-Ming said, "Fan Qiniang studied the way of the crane as a form of self-defense." "Are cranes particularly violent?" I asked. "Not at all," Li-Ming said. "They duck and avoid attacks, striking only when the perpetrator is most vulnerable." "I like that idea," I said. The cigarette I smoked that afternoon still clung to the back of my throat, making me hungry. "How do you know so much?" I asked. What I should've asked was, "Why will it one day be impossible for me to remember your face without recalling it in one particular photograph?" Li-Ming winked, raised her arms in a bird-like gesture. "Because I'm a bird too." "Funny," I said, and she laughed, patting my back, reminding me years later I'd keep a photo of her from that afternoon in a frame, her face turned, slightly in profile, her lips almost smiling, if that's what her expression could be called, was bound to be recalled.

book she'd hidden for so many years, and then, once she found it, dusting off the cover, and spending hours cloistered on the sundeck with the American, attempting to translate into her own language the words of a long dead Chinese poet-monk.

"You're teaching her drivel!" I'd shout from the kitchen—because we both knew the only thing leading to Cold Mountain is madness and the only thing driving us from Cold Mountain is the same thing that propelled us up. There are no answers in anything contained within the thin spine clasped with two hands. A book is a foolish replacement for real knowledge. Couldn't she remember? I wanted none of this anymore.

One evening after the coal fires started in the courtyards, after the heat was turned on from the Huai River northward and all Beijing became a smelting pot, I banged three times on our apartment's only bedroom door then swung it open with a thrust of shoulder (an unnecessary show of force: the door was unlocked, and easily opened).

"What are you doing?"

The women were not reading a book this evening. Instead, my wife held a rouge blush in one hand, her father's Fed Zorki camera in the other.

"Oh," I said. Oh: Always my best retort. What had I thought I'd uncover? And what would I do with the book when I found it? Burn it like the old taitais in the danweis of the '70s, that insidious language so threatening it demanded a violent reaction, or would I chuck the heavy tome out the sundeck window, leave it prey to Gobi rains that seldom kissed this dry-mouthed city?

"Oh, *what?*"

My wife. How did it take me so long to see: the problem with a marriage is you're always two individual people, so close but never close enough, and then you're standing in a doorframe panting, rubbing a bruised shoulder, and your wife is applying rouge to an American's cheeks in a photography modeling session the two of them have planned for weeks. There was no poetry.

Was there ever?[46]

My wife elbowed me. When she was strong, she was strongest. "Okay," I agreed.

Xiaofei slowly glanced up from behind her math textbook, a pencil wedged between her lips. "You're weird, Ba," she said.

I stood for only a few seconds longer in the doorway before I knew there was nothing left for me to ruin. For now, I'd let my wife play her games with her new American doll. She could think this was the way her ending would begin, the cancer we'd ignore for so long we'd lose ourselves in the dance of deceit. Was I the fool? Did my wife know I'd enter the room on this particular evening and witnessing nothing as I expected? Was I writing a story that wasn't mine to write or was everything already written somewhere I hadn't yet discovered?

Look at the wooden puppets! Worn out by their moment of play on stage....

[46.] Here's what I've learned about bird strikes during the course of translating this book: Along with the properties of kinetic energy, you must understand several other factors in assessing a bird's potential damage. How high you are, as well as what speed you're traveling, will impact the scale of force. A few years ago, after several snowy owls flew into planes, officials at JFK airport demanded the birds be shot. Angry birders protested, asking for a swift policy reversal. At Boston's Logan airport, over one hundred snowy owls were captured and released elsewhere, expected to make a home in a place they didn't know. Black vulture, cackling goose, Laysan albatross, dark-eyed junco, boat-tailed grackle, anhinga... all guilty of deaths. In 1962, a mute swan killed 17 in Ellicott City, Maryland. A speckled pigeon took out 35 in Ethiopia in 1988.

Letter #10

Maybe everything begins and ends with Coca Cola—
ke kou ke le: *thirst-quenching happiness*
quickly turning into
bitter-quenching bitterness.
"I'm dying," I told him.
Not:
I'm hungry to *death*
I'm tired to *death*
I'm bored to *death*
不可能　　　*It cannot be.*
可能　　　　*Can.*
不可能　　　*Cannot.*
可能　　　　*Can.*
He didn't believe in impossible to undos.
The day of the chandeliers: we four—a family,
even the tall American writing Chinese ideograms on
notecards,
a trip to Xinjiekou to learn the richest could buy what we
couldn't afford.
Yellow.
Why is everything in my memory yellow?
A bee on Xiaofei's back as we parked our bicycles near a
light post; gust of wind, off it flew, unsure the destination.
No, the bee is not of consequence.
What we loved: glittering chandeliers hung from rafters—
Buy me! Love me!
The brightest also the most blinding—
Sparkle, rat tap tap.

Entranced, ensconced:
heads tipped,
fish-scaled light shotgunning ceiling and skin.
His fingers kneading my hand,
bloated palms that once birthed pigs, massaging away
how many days it would take to re-write this memory
so I'm dusting dishes,
he's placing groceries in the fridge,
the duck egg vendor calls from outside,
the girls giggle in the back bedroom:
vanity, cock, hierarchy, manic.
Voracious vocabulary of early language learners.
How a city is built in layers, like a person.
How first we are organs then only our skin holds us in.
Chuang Tzu's fabled mountain tree is *not* cut down.
The cackling goose, neck sliced, song slung
from open throat *is* the choicest victim.
Always magpies on my window
—yet I've never seen a nest.

Baba

Aside from poetry, Li-Ming and our American daughter shared a new obsession: photography. For much of our married life, Li-Ming was transfixed by the focused view of the world through a camera's lens, how she could reinvent the angle, the lighting, the frame, such that the ordinary could be seen anew. When she was in Weifang sculpting soaps, Li-Ming's father returned from Russia with a gift for his youngest daughter—a Fed-Zorki camera. This possession made us feel dangerously rich.

In our early months of courtship, Li-Ming sat me on a stool for extended sessions during which she insisted I pose in several positions:

—knuckle to chin (scholastic)

—cheeks in palms (boyish)

—hands on lap, back straight, face unsmiling (my true yin nature, she mocked)

The evenings she spent in the danwei basement darkroom were a welcome respite, hours when I didn't feel the need to answer her every question, the weight of her descended underground so I was left walking a little lighter, whistling old tunes unearthed from a country boy's tongue and teeth.

I hoped after Xiaofei's birth our daughter would became my wife's newest model—but with her arrival, the camera disappeared, and with it, my evening retreats. Instead, my wife rolled Xiaofei on her tricycle in the park, absently admiring every detail around them (the draped willows caressing the glassy lake, the slumped old men on concrete benches), then escorting our daughter to the library to collect images of every bird they'd seen: azure-winged magpie, spotted dove, red-rumped swallow. Panels

of pastel illustrations were soon tacked to our bathroom wall—
"What are you studying?" I'd ask, but she'd merely cluck and say,
"This isn't a lesson. You're missing the point."

We tip-toed around Li-Ming's shifting obsessions, her attention to the most mundane details in our world—how many
worms the magpie in our courtyard could carry in its beak (three,
if they didn't wriggle too much), the exact angle of the slanted
window panes on our block's sundecks (49 degrees), and then,
with the arrival of air conditioning units, the unexpected symmetry of Freon droplets on the pavement below our feet (horizontal
lines, but only in the morning). Despite her desire to chronicle
life's regularities, she reveled in only the most chaotic forms (like
when the magpie didn't carry any worms and the Freon droplets
were as random as splattered paint). "Only one worm!" Li-Ming
would shout, and we'd nod, briefly looking up from whatever
book, newspaper, hangnail was holding our attention that day.

When the American's vocabulary turned from syncopated
words into syntactical sentences, Li-Ming and Lao K realized
they had more in common than any of us suspected. Within two
months of her arrival, the Fed-Zorki reappeared, lens dusted,
knobs greased.

Lao K played the perfect model to Li-Ming's revived obsession: my wife rouged the girl's cheeks with department store
blush, slicked her long eyelashes with mascara. Lao K's green eyes
shone translucent when blinking against the bright external flash.
Xiaofei moaned that her mother was 'nao zi feng'—muddle-
headed—with all this photography, but the American couldn't
speak enough of our language to protest. She'd sit on the sundeck
and stare at our city's fading haze, cheeks glowing, lips parted so
the slight gap in her front teeth showed (but didn't Americans
spend a Chinese's annual salary on orthodontics?). Despite this
obvious dental imperfection, Li-Ming thought our new American daughter was beautiful, that the idiosyncrasies in her face
(those teeth, the freckles, the long, thin nose and dimpled chin)

didn't just make her different, but desirable. We quickly learned how she slurped her soup (loudly), how she handled her chopsticks (like a child). Eggplants were Lao K's favorite vegetable. In fact, the American seemed an expert on all manner of vegetables. They were all she ate. She promptly informed us of this the first night we dined together over candlelight (Beijing's latest heat wave knocking out the city's electrical grid), listing the vegetables she loved and Li-Ming translated:

Tomatoes — 番茄

Carrots — 黄萝卜

Cucumbers — 黄瓜

Cabbage — 白菜

"Unfathomable," Li-Ming said in the language we shared. Unfathomable that our American, so rich her hair was the color of young ginger, would be a vegetarian, would choose not to eat meat.

As autumn descended into winter, the days growing shorter and the courtyard pigeons making feather roosts in our building's eaves, Li-Ming chronicled the American's every idiosyncrasy: how she cautiously ate moon cakes for Mid-Autumn Festival, inspecting the sweet yellow innards before biting; how she pulled the longest string of caramel off the long-life potatoes and would, as said the tradition, outlive us all. In this time, she transformed from 'The American,' to 'Menglian.' Between the months of December and January, when Beijing's pipes cracked and the Gobi spat chilled air down Chang'an Boulevard, the girl whose American name we knew began with the letter 'K,' a long, complicated name we could never pronounce, received the nickname we'd call her the rest of our lives: 'Lao K' or 'Familiar K.' Li-Ming said it first, when our daughters trod upstairs from school one afternoon, slapping open the door and leaving it swinging behind them. 'Xiaofei and Lao K are home,' Li-Ming said; just like that the name stuck, indelible as a wooden seal's red ink.

*

噢......你这就跟我走?
噢......你这就跟我走?

As winter turned to spring on an evening when Beijing's misted sky melted the horizon, a wailing saxophone called to me from the dark basement hallway of Li-Ming's danwei. The voice of the Chinese rock star Cui Jian (now familiar due to Lao K's replayings of the cassette tape in her bedroom every night) wailed its incessant, unanswered questions: *Ohhhhh…. When will you go with me? Ohhhhh…. When will you go with me?* Lyrics from a song I hadn't heard for years, when roadside stores regularly blasted it from tape players positioned proudly on stoops, but Lao K discovered the tape in a cluttered music shop in Xinjiekou specializing in rock music. She hadn't stopped listening to the album since. What could she possibly find soothing in this combination of electric guitar and thumping drum?

Ohhh… When will you go with me?
Ohhh… When will you go with me?

"Lao K?" I asked of the cavernous hallway, but my voice was weak compared with Cui Jian's throaty, scratchy vocals.

Because it was nearly midnight and Lao K still wasn't home, Li-Ming sent me to find the American, my wife's body already too tired for impulsive missions. I pushed open the door to the makeshift photography developing room where my wife once spent her evenings. A red bulb hung limply from a ceiling wire. Lao K hunched over a bucket of glossy liquid. With silver tongs, she carefully removed a photograph of two men playing mahjong on a street corner, mouths eternally frozen in laugher.

The makeshift dark room was barely big enough for two bodies—certainly not the bodies Lao K and I possessed with our too-long limbs and barrel chests. I moved cautiously into the space, my torso nearly parallel with hers, the heat of her back resonating against me. Her hair, hanging limply, brushed my collarbone and a shock rang through me, warming my abdomen and toes with a rush I hadn't experienced in years. My hands clenched at my side, but I didn't move closer—how could I? We were the closest we'd been alone, but she didn't sense my presence. I allowed my body to sway and bend in symmetry until she sniffed, hand raised to smooth hair from off her forehead and she turned—

Ohhhh... When will you go with me?

Ohhh... When will you go with me?

"Ba?" We were chest-to-chest, a red sliver between us. She wiped her top lip with the back of her hand, a wet photograph clinging limply to her tongs. "What are you doing here?"[47]

She acted as if it were natural for her body to lean into another's, as if she didn't live, like most Americans, with an invisible shield of empty space surrounding her. America: land of endless exploration, happiness. Happiness: a frivolous word in Chinese, so hopelessly American. A stupid pursuit. No one would ever be happy. Hadn't Lao K read Li-Ming's Cold Mountain enough to know there's no happiness and no unhappiness? The true path lies in between, in the space that cannot be caught with a clap of hands or a brush of wind—

"Ba, are you okay?"

I leaned back, cleared my throat: "Li-Ming was wondering where you were."

Lao K shrugged and waved her hand across the tight sweep of the room. Her fingertips graced my stomach. My insides hugged my spine.

"Clearly, she's not here." Her Chinese grew more confident by the day. Her accent barely betrayed her origins, filling me with a disconcerting parental blend of pride and fear. "Does she need me for something?"

The music's tempo increased and I recognized this section

[47.] What did Li-Ming see that we didn't? Baba's footsteps surprised me but then my body softened as I heard his breath catch up to his body. He stood in the doorway watching. When I was a teenager, I liked being watched. "Did you know he was there?" she later asked. "Yes," I affirmed, although I didn't know that our story was being rewritten from the ground up. After an earthquake can a home rebuilt look the same or will the cracks reveal its history?

of the song when the crowd is asked to sing along: during the Tiananmen days, the streets rang with this melody as we shuffled between the apartment and our danwei, hands to ears and a growing clutter of confusion in our chests.

"I think it's best you come home. It's late," I said, but Lao K simply tacked the wet photograph to a clothespin. The smiling faces of the men steadily darkened, shadows on the wall behind them echoing their shapes. Shadow on shadow—Lao K's own shadow melding with mine in a pool at our feet too perfect, a mockery of us as Cui Jian sang on:

You always laugh at me… nothing to my name…

Lao K harmonized.

"You're a better singer than Cui Jian."

"Na hai yong shuo ma?" *Is that even worth saying?* She asked and I realized she'd inherited some of Li-Ming's signature idioms, as well as her confidence, in the months Li-Ming's had waned. Strange, how we can cling to someone else's old forms even when they're barely a shadow themselves.

"It's *still* worth saying," I said.

Lao K laughed, peeling the photograph back to judge it. "I know Mama's sick," she said, but her eyes remained fixed on the now-steady image of the two men caught in the middle of a joke.

"No," I said.

Why did I say no?

"No?"

"Well, maybe."

What was I doing?

"Maybe?"

"Perhaps."

Perhaps?

"Perhaps?" she asked. Her eyes hadn't lifted from her photograph.

I looked to my feet. My shoes were worn so thin that my frayed, gray socks showed through, edges of bulged bone. I wriggled my toes and reminded myself this ground could move, like Cui Jian reminded us. The water beside us was flowing, sloshing in its buckets. I wasn't ready for another earthquake. Not yet.

"Ba, we both know Li-Ming isn't dying. Remember what Cold Mountain says about that tree older than the forest? How the world laughs at its useless exterior but when stripped of flesh and outsides, there's only the center of truth?"

I wanted to strangle the words spilling so carelessly from her tongue, how her jumbled vocabulary and grammar now reminded me she wasn't one of us, could never be; she wasn't anything more than a stranger trying to own a land that could never be hers but who thought she could simply hop on a plane, dictionary in hand, and then—

The laughing men between us unhinged, landed in the pool of their conception. She cursed in a language we didn't share.

I lost my moment, whatever could be resurrected from it: Lao K hunched over the developing buckets, attempting to save the faces who now struggled to return to their crisp, smiling forms. For years, I witnessed Li-Ming in this same light: glowing red, hands steadily washing the liquid over each frame so that the memory, as she witnessed it, would patiently rise to life. In the underground light of this developing room, nothing felt perma-nent—everything caged between dreaming and waking. *Past/ present. Here/there.* Lao K sighed as she worked to save what was already lost. Maybe she didn't want to talk about this any more than I did. Maybe she wanted to believe some long-dead poet could save her, save Li-Ming, save the rest of us whose fates would one day follow the same inevitable trajectory. We name things and then we have a place for them—put the *comb* in the *dresser.* Tack the *map* to the *wall.* Position the *futon* beside the *bed.* With names, we know where the objects of our lives belong. Only we really don't know anything, except where we stand rela-tive to our beloved objects, all the tangibles that will outlive us, the intangible as transient as dust. I stood behind Lao K, so close I could smell remnant cigarette smoke on her clothes, the sugar-sweet strawberry chewing gum she chomped on unabashedly like the American she was. Beneath my belt, a familiar stirring rose. What craving within me had never been filled? What poems hadn't been written, never would?

Ohhh... When will you go with me?

Ohhh... When will you go with me?

Lao K's hair loosened, untangling from bun to ringlets, flamed by the light crawling the width of her shoulders, her t-shirt angled diagonally. She raised the smiling men from their bucket, returning them to their clothespin, where they would dry and eventually be made whole again, or as near to it as men can be. Her t-shirt dropped lower, the whole of her shoulder and arm, even a partial glimpse of a black bra: exposed. So much skin. Sometimes it feels all we ever are is skin. And there it was—that long-buried impulse: I raised my hand to touch her hair, to run my fingers through the strands like a housewife clearing webs from window frames. What did I expect to gather in my palms? She smelled like sweat and vanilla-scented smoke and strawberry chewing gum and I wanted to tell her I'd never eaten a fresh strawberry, didn't know what she could give me that I couldn't name. How had we, speakers of wholly two languages between us, miserably failed at finding the right words?

When my fingers glanced her back, she turned and caught my wrist in mid-air.

"Ba," she said, pulling on the syllable.

The red light swung above, and beside us, still swinging, was the photograph of the men in their most skeletal shapes, their constant laughter incapable of turning to a frown. *Damn the perpetually smiling!*

"Don't," she stated, calm as a schoolteacher. She returned my hand to my hip.

My palms instinctively sprung to her cheeks, pressing them

so tightly the sharp outlines of her teeth spoke back to me.
I'm telling you, I've waited a long time
So I'm telling you my final request
I want to grab you by the hands
And then you'll go with me...
"*Ba,*" she squeezed my name between taut lips then reached for the radio and slapped the cassette to stop. Silence would have been comforting. Silence would have been far better than what followed—

The stamping of feet echoing in the basement hallway then jaunting upstairs.

My hands dropped, fists wrenching the mechanical tightness with which they gripped the American's face. They didn't regret a thing. Hands never do. Following the sound, I caught only a glimpse of a short nylon sock above a boot as it ascended up the basement stairs, the creased back of a nyloned knee flexing beneath a bobbing tattered hem of a familiar sleeping robe. Immediately, I regretted running so quickly after that knee. How much time is wasted in dark rooms. How much we wasted without ever wanting to turn on the light, alone in the artificial night, hands to faces, meeting ourselves for the first time. *To hold a face...* she had said, the pig squealing. I didn't stop her, would always think of that pig when slicing pork years later, her hands on his animal cheeks, his eyes imploring hers for an answer to a question he couldn't ask. But what was the point? Vision: useless to those who don't know how to see.

"Li-Ming," I called up the stairwell. But when I reached the top, the white of an unwelcome dawn forced tears into my eyes. I blinked incessantly. When had night turned to day? When had the page flipped to today, an 'X' on the calendar's square for *yesterday*, that calendar that was Li-Ming's favorite, "Tropical Scenes From Around the World"? A more familiar scene: the city's pigeons wobbling like old country women among day-old puddles, edges crusted with frost. Even pigeons can make puddles their homes. I'd never hated birds more.

"Li-Ming," I called again, but she wasn't here.

A panting breath laid itself upon my shoulder.

"Ba, it's okay," her voice, once singing, attempted to reassure me. "You'll understand soon. And so will she. Believe me."

When I turned, her face was white-washed, a boat on water. Outside the studio's red, she grew in intensity, developing into her final, unalterable frame. Here in the dawn she was the girl I'd seen that day across the banks—unrecognizable, blisteringly foreign with her tall nose, yellow hair, pink-flushing cheeks. She spoke words with such tenacity she believed them to be true. But she didn't know a thing.

Had I slapped her then or was it years later? Or had it been the opposite? Had her hand coolly lapped my cheek, skin-to-skin, flashing from metacarpal to jaw, the fragile, frigid flick of one to another?

What I think I remember: her green-gray eyes blinking vapidly, like Xiaofei's favorite childhood doll, that blonde head my daughter combed for years until the damned creature went bald and we had to buy a baby wig to satisfy her craving to *comb* and *comb* and *comb*. No, the American wasn't standing there before me as much as my wife hadn't been standing there in the doorframe as much as my entire history would soon be erased unless someone had the time, and the patience, to write it into being from the beginning. But what use was a pen when the world was swirling with the petulance of early spring's dust storms?[48]

That wind rolled over the outer purple hills, gaining speed in Beijing's flat valley, rushing through the city's cinderblock alleyways, pushing tender willows and early-budding lilacs into backbends, scouring the streets in a deep, howling moan. Homing

---

[49.] Cold Mountain now: "If you can stop struggling," he wrote, "I'll carve your name in stone." (Trans. Red Pine). But what use is a name? Then again, historical accounts note this poem may not have been Cold Mountain's after all. May have been his friend Pickup's. Whose name should we carve on the headstone?

pigeons and magpies hopped, branch to branch, trying to hear what was being said, to listen with the ears of birds, creatures whose lives depend on the density of air. There must be something in nature we cannot hear—that we've erased from our most innate natural abilities in a desire to *civilize*, to *construct*. There must be stories passed from leaf to leaf, whole histories of sound and knowledge we've forgotten in order to pursue other ends, to make up for unforgivable means. But for what? To what "end" exactly? The second afternoon I knew her, Li-Ming sat in the pigsty with a hand to her forehead, a piglet at her feet. *For what?* She asked me, for the first and final time. I didn't know she knew the answers. I didn't know she actually didn't know anything at all. She'd ask the masters and their books for their opinions. She'd ask colleagues. Her camera's lens. Freon droplets on alleyway cement. She'd ask verses no one spoke anymore, buried in dust and caves, beneath beds and between long-lost friends. She lost her way between the hills of Jiangxi and the concrete streets of Beijing. How quickly one was subsumed by a life that wasn't meant to be lived. The wrong paths. Lost footsteps. Everyone we knew was turning in their danwei badges for the trading of stocks, pig stomachs, ivory ashtrays, timber, petrol… so many items to be bought for a too-good-to-be-true price, sold to the highest bidder. Money! Piles of pink and blue and purple and green renminbi transferred by the bucket to the China Construction Bank on Xinjiekou. Markets unexplored: Xinjiang, Shenyang, Changchun, Changsha, and then the cities too small to be recognized on a map but with millions of potential customers. Within this all: the promise of something other than this—quiet city streets and neighbors you've known since childhood, rosy-cheeked corner store vendors who served the best dumplings in the nation for prices still reasonable, dumplings filled with the most buttery pork and chives you've tasted, not cardboard shreds dyed to resemble meat—only we didn't know this meat, the real thing, was what we'd loved all along, was as good as our lives would ever get.

The trees ached and moaned. The girl stared at me, waiting for me to tell her the rest of her story: of what future did the wind speak? What warnings did we not heed?

Lao K. I knew her name, but not her family's surname, nor her ancestral name, nor the hometown to which she would some-day return where the graves of her ancestors were buried, where she too would eternally rest and then all her progeny with their bottomless green-gray eyes. How did we get here?

Before or after the slap, she turned and walked ahead of me down the swirling columns of fallen lilac petals, Cui Jian's music pleading with me to go somewhere. Lao K hummed that incessant chorus. I looked to her for a clue as to where people like us were supposed to go, but she simply stared ahead, nose too tall, cheeks too thin, eyes too wide, and for a moment she was ugly, but I didn't want to believe this. I shook my head, blinked until my vision returned to its old habits of the autumn prior when Lao K was beautiful and my wife was a still a woman who would live forever.

The wind plucked feeble lilacs from branches, scattered a purple confetti to the street.

She stopped, bent over, ran her fingers through the petals. "It looks like snow," she said. "Only that's not what it is, is it?"

I smiled, knowing she saw what I saw—that beneath us there could have been winter snow dusting the pavement. We could have been exhaling white breath in puffs between us. It could have been winter. Maybe it still was. There was magic in believing time could move sideways, that we were nothing and everything at once.

"Did you fly from the roof or did you fall like they said?" I asked.

She stood a few seconds, blinking. The growing windstorm riled the windows of the nearby danwei, tested the integrity of city walls. What could she say?

"Can you ask me that again?"

Had she not heard me? My tongue looped my teeth. "Fly," I said, lifting my arms like a bird. "Fly—" arms raised, "or fall?" My arms fell, body tipping forward in a tight, head first dive.

Her old habits: picking at her teeth with her thumb when she didn't understand. But she didn't pick her teeth now. She knew what I'd asked. Why wouldn't she answer?

She shook her head, that reedy hair bristling her skin and mine. I thought of drawing it to my nose so I could smell it, or plucking it, strand by strand, from her scalp and collecting it in a bushel to hang from the front door. So we'd have a piece of her always.

"That's a silly question, isn't it?" she asked as she pushed open the door to the pathways snaking between the danwei and the neighboring apartment blocks, the way home. I followed her, knowing where she was leading me, what was waiting at the end of all this.

At the entryway to our apartment building's courtyard, Li-Ming stood, a collection of books at her feet.

"What are you doing?" Lao K stopped.

We were trapped between late night and early morning— early enough that the first shift at the danwei hadn't mobilized, no one jogging down stairways to rickety bicycles, no mothers walking to the dumpling vendors off Xinjiekou for the morning baozi run. The books were in a pile, not unlike a campfire's kindling, and Li-Ming crouched, as steadily as she could in her condition, but a burst of wind shifted her backwards onto her bottom.

"Shit," she said.

Lao K and I jogged over, Lao K helping Li-Ming to her feet. My wife's eyes were glazed but I couldn't tell if she'd been crying or if the wind had whipped them into something resembling sadness. She raised her arms and within her hands, she held a match.

"No!" Lao K shouted, but it was too late: Li-Ming struck the match, the small blue-orange flame rising, then dropped it to the pile. The first pages of some unknown book quickly disintegrated, turned from white to brown.

Lao K crouched, blowing the flames, using her coat sleeve to stamp them out. The first flick of flame wasn't enough, had barely fringed the edges of the pile.

My wife drew a heavy breath. "You can't always be looking for answers."

"Of course you can!" Lao K stood, the books behind her, her body framed by the first touch of a rising sun. But always in this city the sun lost the battle—whether to coal fires or clouds of factory smoke or the day's draw to night. Lao K turned toward me, reached up and touched her own cheek, insinuating the first version of the story was the one she remembered too: "And I fly," she said defiantly, forgetting to tack on the 'le' for past tense, then walked toward our apartment block, kicking the damaged books out of her way.

"I flew," my wife corrected, adding the 'le,' then crouched slowly, her body already betraying her, to gather burnt books in her arms, pleased briefly by the hint of destruction, by her ability, if she were to choose, to erase whole histories with one flick of wrist, one petulant toss—like a slap, or a kiss.

Letter #11
Wode Jiantao (My "Confession of Wrongdoing")*
Pidou Hui #102;
Dewai District, Beijing, People's Republic, Era of Mao

I am a bourgeois poet.

I read nonsense.

I was told to read this book by a friend who is not a friend anymore.

The friend who told me doesn't live in Beijing now.

I don't know where she lives.

The friend who told me to read this is bourgeois. Her thoughts are bourgeois. She has a corrupted mind.

My mind is corrupted. My mind can be rectified. Can be cleansed of bourgeois thought.

I hurt when you prick my head with pins because I am human. That is a foot in my stomach; I don't taste blood.

I am a loathsome child born to cockroaches. My mother is the biggest cockroach. She is a bourgeois poet who hides books under beds!

I hate poetry.

Poetry is written by pigs and capitalists who think art will feed people. Art cannot feed people. It will only make them starve. Poetry is art. Poetry will kill People. The People will revolt. The People will win.

I am Huang Li-Ming, named for Nanjing's liberation. I am a child of cockroaches. I am repentant. I will burn the books. I will chew the pages because this is all I will eat for weeks. I will not starve because words cannot feed me. Only the People and the Party will feed me.

I am Huang Li-Ming. I am not a poet. I am not an artist. I do not believe in Buddhist thought. I do not believe in the Four

244

Olds. I must smash the Four Olds! I believe in Mao Zedong thought. I believe in The Party. I believe in The People.

My friend is dead because words are dead because poetry is dead because art is dead because ~~believing is dead and I am dead.~~ I am dead. I will be born anew after the dark and I will look like the girl I once knew but I won't recognize her in any mirror. I will be the beneficiary of a new China and there will be food on my table and sunsets draining from window frames and I will not starve because I will till soil and believe in farmers and the People who are in the Party and I will renounce words because only Mao's words are the words we speak and Mao is the greatest poet of all.

*Because I am forced to talk. Because silence is incriminating. Because words can be made vile and murderous. Because words can be made irrelevant. Because I am talking huli-hutu. Because you won't believe me anyway.

Baba

In Beijing, we judge the seasons by the shifting of sounds: in autumn, pigeons sail over sloped roofs with whistling tail feathers trailing behind; in winter, there's the tick tick of heating furnaces clicking alive, each building's rusted pipes cracking against descending cold; in late spring, dust storms smatter the windows and raze the city in yellow haze; in early summer, we wait for cicadas to brashly announce their arrival. Vastly outnumbering the lucky magpies, our cicadas signal the arrival of real heat. As if they too are angered by the spoiling of a less-balmy spring, the insects scream their displeasure, harried bodies dropping to the streets where hard shells whip-crack under the wheels of unsuspecting bicyclists.

Beneath a canopy of cicada chorus, we rolled my ailing wife to Xiaofei's last diving meet, while my brother, who I still called Doufu, visiting from Shanghai in order to help while Li-Ming's condition deteriorated, stayed home to cook dinner. My brother, retired from his work as a ship builder, was oddly comforted by playing the role of homemaker. He didn't seem worried that his chances to explore the South China Sea like his favorite ancient Chinese naval adventurer Zheng He had long ago disappeared. Retirement cloaked him in passive contentedness.

Lao K planned to join us at Beijing Normal University's pool after her classes, promising to bring Li-Ming's Fed-Zorki to chronicle Xiaofei's assured win (most days, the device hung from a strap around Lao K's spring-tanned neck, an unlikely talisman). The heat that spring day could have felt oppressive. We could have cursed the impenetrable wall of cicada sound, but we didn't. Li-Ming's wheels rolled over the occasional flailing cicada, but she didn't flinch. She wasn't entirely with us anymore; her head lilted absently, hands flat on her thighs.

Crunch.
   Lilt.
Crunch.
   Lilt.
Crunch.

"Lili's doing an inward," Xiaofei said, distracting us from the insect massacre beneath our feet. "So I guess I should do an inward one-and-a-half somersault." Everything Lili did, Xiaofei must surpass: although our daughter only began diving lessons a year earlier, she'd already progressed to the fourth form. Her instructor, Mr. Peng, called Xiaofei a 'tenacious girl.' I didn't have the heart to inform him she was only trying to please Li-Ming, that nothing she did was for herself anymore, especially now. But when Mr. Peng named Xiaofei the 'next Fu Mingxia,' China's gold medal Olympian diver, Li-Ming didn't beam. What Li-Ming wanted was for our daughter to not be comfortable in water, but to conquer it. Meanwhile, Li-Ming herself hadn't done more than dip a toe in a body of water in decades, a holdover of her harrowing experience during the Jiangxi floods.

"You will do well," Li-Ming said through chapped lips.

I attempted reason: "Don't push yourself. You don't want to get hurt."

Xiaofei forced a frown. She never appreciated my caution.

"I'm fine. I've been on the 7.5 meter platform for three weeks now. It's easy. Just like a bird!" Our daughter skipped to the university pool's entrance as I tipped Li-Ming's wheelchair up the stairs, one by one.

"Lao Wang, I can walk," Li-Ming said, pushing herself into standing, but I forced her into her seat.

"Don't overdo it." For weeks, the radiation made her sturdy frame more fragile. Xiaofei made light of the situation, joking eventually her mother's bones would be as airy as a bird's and she could fly away to judge us from the skies. Lao K didn't like her sister's description, revised it to say Li-Ming would fly only as far as the ceiling so we'd always have a view of her wings. Both descriptions unnerved me, made me realize neither girl understood the situation. My legs shook despite my wife's lighter weight. She still weighed enough for carrying her to be a burden. After much grunting on my part to lift her chair up and over the stairs, we made it to the gymnasium's lobby.

"I'm sick of sitting," Li-Ming said. "You know it's not in my nature to be so still."

"I know."

I pushed her across the waxed floors past trophies in dusty display boxes and photographs of young, lithe athletes on the wall. A banner draped across the entrance doors to the pool announced the university swimming team's winning of the All-Beijing Championship the year prior. Everywhere one looked was evidence of accomplishment.

"Look at these proud athletes," Li-Ming said. "Didn't you say you once beat Chiang Kai-Shek's son in a track meet?"

How had she remembered that? For a moment, I thought I should let her believe this. Maybe she'd be better off reaching the end of her life thinking her husband had once been so quick-footed, so capable of crossing the line before all others. But the faces of the smiling athletes stared down at me, admonishing me for considering lying to my wife.[49]

"No, that was my cousin—not me."

"Oh," Li-Ming said, digesting the revised history as we reached the pool's entrance and I finagled her wheelchair past the doors. "Well I'm sure you could've beat the Generalissimo's son if given the chance."

[48.] Li-Ming handed me the scissors. "Start at the nape of my neck," she said. I held the blade to the thinnest hair, took a breath, then snipped in a taut, straight line. For days, I found her short, blunt hairs caught within the fabric of my sweater, the crease of my wrist, trapped within the folds of my pillow.

"You overestimate me." I rolled Li-Ming's wheelchair onto the pool platform and toward the stands where spectators sat, rows of parents awaiting their child's performance. Xiaofei had already skipped into the women's locker room to change into her bathing suit for the competition.

"I don't want to sit here," Li-Ming said. "Take off my shoes. I want to put my feet in the water."

"Really? You think that's a good idea?"

She nodded.

Despite my better judgment, I kneeled, knees sinking into a puddle, wet seeping through my cotton pants. I carefully untied my wife's shoes and placed them at the foot of the stands, bundling her socks and stuffing them into the soles. I rubbed her heels, twisted the skin atop her bloated ankles in both directions. Her body had the feel of something expired—when had she transitioned from someone wholly alive to slightly less so? Where had I gone astray in this? Before I could reach a conclusion, my wife placed her hand atop mine, rubbing the bones of my fingers as I rubbed her ankles.

"Thank you," she said, sighing slightly, then nodded for me to escort her, arm-in-arm, to the pool deck. Behind us, parents looked on, full of pity—that man, the dying wife, hobbling precariously toward the water. They probably worried we'd trip, that we'd fall into the cool water and quickly drown, our bodies floating limply to the surface, eyes staring past the arched ceiling to the sky. How much we'd be able to see, that they couldn't, with that unblinking stare.

But we didn't fall. We shuffled carefully to the edge, where chlorine burned our nostrils.

"Sit here," Li-Ming instructed, voice cracking. Once a songstress, Li-Ming's words now chafed like the ragged scrape of grasshopper wings.

I wanted to tell those sad, downward peering eyes in the stands above us Li-Ming was the best swimmer I'd ever known.

She was so strong a swimmer she'd saved a man from drowning during the famous Jiangxi floods. But what was the use? Li-Ming didn't swim anymore. The floods taught her the true power of water. I lifted her off her feet, positioning her rigid body at the pool side. Her round backside, sore from so much sitting, cushioned her landing.

I rolled up my own pant legs, removed my shoes. Our toes stretching in the water, we felt young again.

"If only your daughter had her mother's round head, she'd enter the water more smoothly," Mr. Peng's hands spread atop my wife's round head. Her head, now bald, was covered with a magenta silk handkerchief painted with blue butterflies. Mr. Peng rubbed that handkerchief as if it could bestow good fortune upon him, as if Xiaofei's only downfall was she'd inherited my large, square jaw and not Li-Ming's perfectly smooth apple head. "Ready for your daughter's debut?"

Li-Ming nodded and I didn't need to look at her face to see her smile. What pride is wasted on the dying. Our water-happy toes flexed and stretched, flexed and stretched. I couldn't remember the last time my feet felt so unencumbered, like a caged bird finally released into the expansive, airy world beyond the bars. What world is outside the one we know?

"Our debuting daughter better be safe," I muttered to my own unsteady reflection.

Mr. Peng tapped my shoulder. I looked up, recognizing those sunglasses he always wore, even on the indoor pool deck—he blamed an astigmatism but we knew he preferred the crowds not see his gaze lingering on his girls as they climbed up the board's steps, their arms and chests dripping as they pushed their slick bodies out of the water. He never touched any of the girls, but there was an uncomfortable closeness in the way he spoke of them; then again, parents are always protective of the bonds they share with their children, worried about displacement by another. I shuddered, remembering briefly my encounter with Lao K in the dark room, how a young, female body is always magnetizing: A body not yet become itself. A form before the final indelible shape. That must be it, I thought, before Mr. Peng inserted himself—

"Your daughter will do fine," he said. "And as we speak..." He nodded to the door to the women's locker room which slapped open, Xiaofei breezing past with Lili on one side and Lao K on the other, arms locked. The girls strode in unison, as if their announcement was timed to music and applause. Lao K, despite the fact she wasn't diving, wore a red swimsuit clinging snugly to her tall, shapely body. Atop her chest swung Li-Ming's camera enshrouded in plastic encasing. Xiaofei and Lili donned matching Beijing Youth Diving League suits in navy blue with angled white stripes. Their bodies paled in comparison with Lao K's womanly frame. They were all bone, hips protruding, knees knocking, reminding anyone who looked at them of the awkward, self-conscious experience of adolescence. Xiaofei didn't seem to mind we were here to watch her dive, that despite our smiles, our proud faces, we worried for her. What was it that worried us? We couldn't explain to Xiaofei that despite her eagerness to climb to the board's highest rung, we once believed we were capable of such impressive goals. How we once hoped for so much in our bodies, our ability to overcome heights, water, platforms. But we could not overcome every difficulty. That growing up—zhang da, 长大—was about this, despite the fact at a certain point we've grown as big, as tall, as we'll ever be and yet don't know any more than we did before. We're better not knowing eventually we'll stop looking upward and outward and only backward and inward, perhaps the reason the aged shrink, lose short-term memory.

My bony, calloused toes still absently flexed and stretched. Li-Ming's wide feet stopped fanning the water and for a moment, I worried I'd lost her altogether until I saw her arm lift, her hand waving at our daughters.

"Ba!...Ma!" Xiaofei waved back as Lili scanned the stands for

her parents. Upon finding their prideful faces, her parents—her father, an academic of economics at Beijing Normal, with his signature eyeglasses and bowtie; her mother, a tall, thin bookkeeper at my danwei with long, straight hair and patient eyes—smiled, nodded knowingly. Lili was the more stoic child. I didn't dare inform Xiaofei she wasn't anything like her fearlessly independent friend. That we never fully surpass the failures of our forbearers.

Xiaofei jogged to her mother, unaware of Li-Ming's bare legs and feet. "Did you see what Lao K did? She brought your camera! She's going to take my photograph from under water!" Lao K stood on the other side of Li-Ming. I avoided looking upwards at her tall body, all that skin I knew would be nakedly exposed, goose bumps lining her arms and legs, a puff of hair shielding her groin.

"Amazing," Li-Ming said. She gripped Lao K's sculpted shin, rubbing her fingers along the stubbly hairs to calm or subdue her—but who needed calming most? Either way, Lao K didn't mind. Women's intimacies were always lost on me, how they could rub one another's legs, hold hands, sleep next to one another on trains without a hint of sexual attraction. Now my wife and Lao K shared this physical relationship and although the American was supposed to be our 'daughter,' the nature of this disturbed me. Was I jealous? I dismissed the thought in time for Lao K to explain how she found a contraption capable of filming underwater scenes.

"Mr. Wang's shop has everything you could imagine," Lao K said. "I said I needed to take photographs in a pool and he found this on his shelves."

Since the day of the attempted book burning, I knew Lao K and Li-Ming took to one another even more closely than before—they left every morning for walks in the park and one day I attempted to trail them but worried they'd see me rounding the corner near Zhang's corner store, so I rushed home, readying breakfast. I wanted to know what they spoke about, how Lao K's language could improve so steadily that Li-Ming and she shared lengthy conversations, growing so close, and so quickly. Xiaofei vacillated between sulkiness and showing off—today was one of the days she expected to shine, and for her mother's attention to be directed at her. She watched her mother's hand absently stroking the American's leg. While my wife and Lao K discussed the inventory at Wang's, Xiaofei examined Lao K's rounded breasts rising with each breath, the girl's hips, then looked to her own breasts and hips, clearly comparing sizes. Her gaze descended to Lao K's thighs, how much more toned and muscular the American's were than her own, as if Lao K spent a life working in the fields, which we knew wasn't the case. Finally, Xiaofei examined the differences between their ankles and feet. Xiaofei had Li-Ming's thick ankles, her flat, wide feet. The American's were narrow, bony. When Lao K asked Xiaofei what kind of photographs she should take, my daughter shuttered into awareness.

"Whatever you want," she said.

Mr. Peng summoned Lili and Xiaofei to the base of the platform with the other competitors. There, they stretched and bended and jumped and hopped like soldiers readying for battle. How silly, it seemed, that the battleground was a diving board and the innocent bystanders were merely parents who wanted more happiness for their children than they'd experienced in their collective youth. But for what? Generation after generation played this game: more and more opportunities spoilt upon their progeny when, in the end, each generation only craved more, and—despite the money, the jobs, the education, the homes—the next generation couldn't bestow upon their children any more answers than those who came before. Wasn't it Li-Ming's poet Han Shan who told us, over a dozen centuries ago, "Go tell families with silverware and cars: what's the use of all that noise and money?" But now, thanks to Deng Xiaoping, we had *more* noise. We had *more* money. And still the diving girls threw their arms over the heads, slapped the air like tai chi practitioners. The performance was for our sake, rows of eager parents believing this was the right path for their children—the only path. The judges, two grim-looking middle-aged women with gray-streaked hair pulled into tight buns and one stout man with rosy cheeks, sat at a long table on the far side of the pool. They organized scoring placards, seemingly unaware of the gymnastics happening beneath the diving board's staircase, unapologetically preparing to disappoint most of the parents.

Lao K. What was there to say about Lao K? She slid into the pool just beside Li-Ming's feet and dunked her head as casually as a seabird, hair dampening into a seaweed's reddish brown.

What happened next surprised me: my wife slipped loose the knot of her scarf and the fabric, silk fluttering, floated to her lap. As she shook her head, the motion—my bald wife shaking a head bereft of its once long, black strands—wasn't sad, no, not even pitiful; it was a relic of an older gesture, a gesture that once meant nothing but a misplaced flirtation. I reached my fingers to comb the air above her head, that invisible, once-was hair.

Then I heard the snickers. The gasps. Hadn't the crowd seen a bald head before? *Yes*, my wife was dying. Yes, she'd lost her hair in the belated, futile batch of chemotherapy she'd only agreed to after I promised her if she went to the hospital with me, I'd stop pestering her about what she and Lao K were studying on the sundeck. Lao K re-emerged, propped herself atop the pool deck and glared into the crowd with so severe, so instinctively protective a look, she silenced their gaping; still, Li-Ming didn't notice the attention her careless exposure garnered, nor Lao K's response. My wife was too transfixed on our daughter, who now calmly climbed the stairs to the diving board's highest rung. There she was—my oval-shaped head and strong jaw, now hers, hidden beneath a black rubber cap and Li-Ming's thick calves flexing with each step. If only she'd known her true, underlying resemblance to Li-Ming. If only they could stand side-by-side to compare bodies—hairless twins. Merely the shape of their heads would betray their symmetry.

Chlorine smell: Lao K returning to the water and paddling past Li-Ming to retrieve the camera with its clear plastic shield. She winked at my wife who smiled calmly back: What had they discussed in my absence? Women—would we ever know? I thought in the time that passed since our run-in in the photography studio, since Li-Ming's attempted book burning, since the chemo treatments and Li-Ming and Lao K's late afternoon discussions, something would change. But what needed to change? My wife and I slept in the same bed but we could have been kilometers apart. Xiaofei buried herself in schoolwork. Lao K buried herself in Li-Ming's books, nights drinking at JJ's Disco.

"Tell me what you see under there," Li-Ming said, nodding at the water beneath the unsteady surface.

Lao K held the camera to her eye. "Nothing."

Xiaofei reached the end of the platform. She turned to the back wall, calves flexing, heels descending and raising, twitching slightly with each slow, cautious pump. *7.5 meters. Lili. Inward somersaults.* I thought of Li-Ming's insistent desire for our daughter to be the best at everything, how Li-Ming must have thought of herself as not measuring up to some earlier expectation when in reality we all knew we were just victims of our era. What did it mean that my wife put so much stock in the American daughter she'd barely known when her own daughter, the one who grew within her all those months and caused her a hernia post-birth, was there in front of her, struggling and trying to show her how brave she could be, how she could beat Lili, the city's best diver, and be as confident in the water as her own mother was once? My daughter stood at the edge of a board the height of a two-story building. She inhaled the breath that would keep her body buoyant underwater as Lao K inhaled as well, plunging that honeyed hair beneath the surface of the pool. They inhaled together, speaking a language I never understood. My hands raised instinctively, about to clap, to plead with Xiaofei to stop, that this spectacle would ultimately lead to failure and heartache, but Li-Ming reached back and slapped them to my lap.

Xiaofei looked to her feet.

We all held our breath as her toes lost their grip, but then, quickly, her body folded into itself, towards the board, the tip of her head just millimeters from glancing the edge, and after exactly one-and-a-half spins, her arms extended above her head and— her legs passed upright—yes, her legs continued until *flap!*—

There was no straight entry.

No arms perfectly extended (triceps firm, elbows locked).

No stomach duly pinched against an exquisitely arched back.

No legs lengthened to pointed feet, toes so curled they flicked the water like a feather.

Mr. Peng marched sternly to the pool's edge where Xiaofei surfaced. He leaned over and whispered something to her rubber-capped head, something to which she nodded dutifully. The judges frowned, holding their placards above their heads in solidarity:

4.5/10 – 4.5/10 – 4.5/10

Our daughter was less than perfect. Much, much less so.

Xiaofei climbed the silver ladder, watching as Lili ascended the platform, a soft, knowing smile painted on her friend's lips— like Chairman Mao said, *If you think just once about sinking, you'll never be able to float.* Lili wasn't a thinker and was therefore incapable of sinking. Our Xiaofei, on the other hand, seemed to have inherited her mother's impetuousness, along with my necessity to trip just when the moment called for me to stand—with that, she'd always want to jump and yet, simultaneously, fear falling, failure. She'd looked down.

Lao K surfaced, cheeks puffing with fresh inhales, oxygen flushing her cheeks pink.

"I got a good shot," she said. Water dripped down her forehead and into her fluttering eyes, but Li-Ming wasn't listening.

Li-Ming was tying her scarf back atop her bald head as if she'd suddenly experienced this odd nudity, standing on her own, a burst of energy and capability, stomping barefoot through puddles to her wheelchair beside the stands, then recklessly walking her chariot out the door while Lao K, who'd quickly climbed out of the pool, skin water-beaded, jogged beside her, telling her to *take a seat*, to *slow down*, to *be more careful*.

"Man man de, Mama," she said. "Mama, man man de." The crowd gaped: the American called the Chinese woman '*Mama*.'

I sat at the edge of the pool, knowing the crowd was waiting for my next move. Let my wife throw her tantrum, I wanted to tell them. Her own life given away in the moment she became a mother—what possibilities remained when our nation was just born; what possibilities remained when we had the rest of our lives to live. Let her make Xiaofei return to the competition for her next dive, to climb to an even higher platform and take one more spin in the air. I was done pretending. Our daughter was below average, and whatever the reason—my head, her mother's hotheadedness—it wasn't worth pushing her. What version of success had we so quickly taken to, anyhow? Dreams were for the living. Didn't Li-Ming know? We'd been writing the wrong story, the narrative faltering in the vision of our daughter's body slipping past straight, legs making a long, horizontal splash, our ability to always be on the sidelines watching, cheering her on. What we should have written was the truth, if only we'd understood what it was that brought us together all those years ago in the shadowed pigsties of Jiangxi, what made a child in the heat of summer, or made the cicadas sing, or made their bodies drop to the ground when full of too much song. *The heat? The sky?* This is what I meant about asking too many questions. I warned Xiaofei of this when she was only four years old and we were at her grandmother's funeral in Nanjing. Our daughter asked where Lao Lao had gone even though the woman's ashes were stuffed into a heavy urn at the head of the table. *She's gone to heaven*, I said, but Xiaofei was persistent. *Where's heaven?* She asked, and when I pointed toward the ceiling, she continued, *How is heaven in the sky? Can I see it? Can we get there by airplane?* That's when I said the thing about asking too many questions. Although it silenced my daughter for the remainder of the afternoon, I later regretted this lesson, worried I'd stifled some childish belief that every question has an answer, that there's someone, somewhere in this world, likely a parent or grandparent, who knows everything. For Li-Ming, that person was Han Shan. No one could compete with a long-dead poet. No one could compete with a hermit who abandoned the world in order for us to see our existence as we should: from above, from afar, both shadow and figure together, as in the sun's penumbra. All of it senseless when our lives had nothing to do with mountain perches or snow-saddled pines or years spent contemplating the distance between the horizon and the sky.

I stood slowly, feeling the heat of many eyes boring judgment into my back: *How could he let his sick wife walk away? How could he allow an American to try to help, the antithesis of what we'd been taught in our Little Red Books?* I shrugged off their gazes and followed my wife and Lao K into the gymnasium lobby, down the corridor between the entrance hall and the locker rooms, where plaques glistened golden on the walls and more eyes, these wide and unblinking, witnessed my failure to help my wife into her wheelchair. Instead, Lao K persuaded Li-Ming to sit. Our American daughter stood facing her Chinese mother with her bare arms tucked into her sides, wet body shivering. As I drew closer, I recognized the purple goose bumps raised along the flesh of her limbs. I recognized the quivering buttocks, the smell of hair and sweat and chlorine and... What use was there in recalling? I touched her shoulder and she didn't jump. I ran my fingers through her hair and she didn't flinch. I saw purple and blue, skin attempting to pulse life back into the farthest reaches of her limbs. She was looking at Li-Ming and I was looking at the girl's hair, the way I could lift it with one flick of my wrist, the weight of it damp, the density of waterless gravity, our one true curse: Time. All the spinning kept us believing the lies of our own origins. Who was this girl standing between us, who prevented us from living the lives we'd intended to live? The girl who cleaved to us both, splitting our union down the middle and making my wife's death her own entirely? I wanted to rewrite this book. I wanted to lift away the girl's skin and bones, to leave only her shadow at our feet, to resurrect the old shadows in the Jiangxi sties, the heat of the sun remnant on our forearms, the world not yet dissected into cities and countries but simple, digestible, present. I wanted, more than anything, to start over.[50]

"Lao Wang!" Li-Ming called, but we were down a deep hall where even sound was marbled, spoken in caves.

"Lao Wang! Go get your daughter."

I released Lao K's hair and when I did, the American turned, bare feet squealing against linoleum. Her entire body was at attention with the sincerity and immediacy belonging only to youth: pink-red flushed cheeks, pricked nipples pushing through her thin red bathing suit, blonde hairs standing in columned attention on her long, tanned arms. The camera straddled her breasts. The camera Li-Ming used to chronicle Xiaofei's childhood now contained within it our daughter's greatest failure: she'd tried. She'd climbed to the highest rung. She stood tall but didn't trust her feet would hold her. She spun in the air one turn too many. That camera. I reached out to remove the film canister.

"*Ba!* What are you doing?"

"Lao Wang! Stop!"

"*Ba*, give it to me!" Lao K snatched the device as I was prying it open, as the first glimpses of light spoil the edges of that final

[50.] From Baba's cluttered apartment, I stare at a Beijing sky lit afire with car exhaust, coal smoke. I close the book for the night, vowing I'll finish translating this chapter in the morning. I also want to start over, I tell her but her words can't speak back, can't assure me my ending is not contained within these pages, only hers.

259

photograph—Xiaofei's failed entrance. Lao K slapped my hand and I dropped it to my hip.

"You don't know what you're doing," she said. *She knew,* she insinuated. She knew me better than I knew myself. Was this what we loved about her, about all Americans? They always knew best, had all the answers, while we sat on the sidelines observing, forgetting to ask the questions for which the Americans had already prepared the answers. Li-Ming frowned, a tear calcifying the corner of her eye. How they knew everything and I was just the child attempting to shield us from the knowledge that this—this photograph, this moment, this daughter—will never be enough.

不

No.

Drowned legs, wasted strokes.

"Don't ruin the film," Lao K said, protectively clutching the camera to her chest. "Let's get Xiaofei and go home." She pushed my shoulders, leading me to the pool, past the flapping plastic-stripped doors, the sad-eyed spectators who grew eager with the sight of their daughters' bodies ascending the platform but looked down at us with embarrassment, as if we represented everything they wished not to acknowledge. Outside, the cicada chorus crescendoed louder, then abruptly fell to a dull hum.

Li-Ming was still behind us in the hallway in her wheelchair, unable to roll herself to the stands to watch our daughter's last dive. I didn't know how in leaving Li-Ming alone we were actually entering the rest of our lives together: me and the girl who suddenly thrust herself onto our lives with the tenacity of a sand storm funneling down Wudaokou.

If Xiaofei noticed our brief departure, it hadn't fazed her. She was due for her second redemptive dive. She climbed the stair's spokes, crested the board. Coach Peng stood cross-armed across the pool next to the judges. He still wore his sunglasses and a calm, unsmiling face. What did he see through those lenses? Although I never owned sunglasses, suddenly, I wanted more than ever to wear them, to wash the world in red and brown—to stamp out, once and for all, the unbearable honesty of sunlight peeling past the skylights to wrestle with the pool's surface, blinding us if we stared too long.

Lao K jogged on tiptoes then dipped smoothly into the pool, holding the camera to her eye and descending below the surface, beyond my reach. What she saw beneath the waves that day at the Beijing Normal University swimming pool I'd never know—if she ever developed that photograph, she never showed us. And Li-Ming was in no position to expose the film herself, her illness quickly devouring what was left of her, every bone, lymph node and organ riddled with cancer in the coming weeks. But I'll remember what I want of Lao K surfacing briefly for a breath, long enough to shout to her sister: "Don't look down!" then submerging herself as Xiaofei did exactly as Lao K reminded her not to—she looked to the water glistening meters below and as she did, her tentative toe grip on the edge of the board slipped.

The crowd behind us gasped as our daughter's body faltered, feet struggling to retain their grip on the slick board, knees bending to push herself off prematurely. It was too late: Lao K was already underwater, already snapping the photograph that would last beyond our lives, paper objects outliving the bodies they contain—this time, our daughter's body, taut and perfectly-straight, slicing the water like a knife. Like perfection alone could heal us. Or at least our belief in it.

She didn't make a splash.

*

"Did you hear that, *Ba*?" It wasn't Xiaofei's voice, but Lao K's, her proper Beijing accent with all it's rolling 'er' sounds exaggerated. We were alone—Li-Ming somehow wheeled herself home immediately following Xiaofei's redemptive dive and Xiaofei went to McDonalds for her post-meet celebration with Lili's family who were eagerly doting on their daughter who snagged first place, Xiaofei with the second place medal. Already, we'd lost our daughter to someone else. For now, this tall, slow American would have to take her place. "*Ba*, did you hear?"

"Hear what?"

"How it's so silent now."

I hadn't noticed: The cicadas were a static background noise you learned to ignore. On the walk home, I was too consumed by the events that evening—Xiaofei's poor dive and then her perfect one, a tear clinging to my wife's eye, Lao K's hair dipping beneath the water's surface. But as we left the pool, following in Li-Ming's trail, the cicadas indeed silenced their song-happy voices. Or had something else silenced them? The sky was misty with clouds and the first starlight somehow reminded me of a tropical place even though I'd never left our motherland, only seen photographs of Hawaii and the Philippines and the Caribbean in Li-Ming's favorite brightly-colored calendars. These unlikely stars winked and danced, but we didn't have time to stop and watch. Li-Ming awaited us at home, likely seething with anger: Over what? Xiaofei's terrible first dive? My inability to escort Li-Ming from the pool hall? The way I'd touched Lao K's hair? What hadn't I done?

Lao K stopped below a willow with limbs limping to the ground, exhausted by the nature of being born a tree. She tilted her head to the sky.

"What are you looking at? Hurry up, Li-Ming's waiting."

"Li-Ming can wait. Besides, haven't you noticed the stars?"

First the cicadas; now this. I reluctantly tilted my head to the cavern of black beyond the tree's limbs. Lao K was so much like Li-Ming in this way; she didn't realize that looking up would only make her trip, that a life lived so distracted by the details of the world would only make you mistrust your own form. This was a dangerous way to live.

"I haven't seen this many stars in Beijing," Lao K said.

She was right. Tonight's wind, brisk and chilled by spring,

cleared the air of any remaining dust or pollutants as it fluffed our hair. There was an entire sky above with visible, sparkling stars.

"Xiaofei will be okay," she said.

I didn't know how to respond; the willow limbs bristled at a passing breeze and the cicadas clucked, annoyed that the wind had, for a moment, stolen the stage.

"Li-Ming will be okay too." She spoke from a place she didn't quite trust, but her words were there, nonetheless, puffs of smoke rising from a valley floor. The words hovered above us before being stamped out by the sound of revived cicada chorus. The drone rose, encouraging me to speak. *What am I supposed to say?*

"Baba…"

"That's my name," I said.

She laughed softly, kicked at the earth. "She's really going." How did she not yet know the word 'to die?' Or even the softer 'to leave this world', or any other idiomatic saying we used to mask the sting of death? Her lesson books hadn't mentioned death yet—why would they?

"*Si*," I said, instructing her. "She's really going to 'si.' Like the number 'four,' but in the falling-rising tone."

死. To die. That body struggling beneath a flat, black surface, arm stretching upward. No one above reaching below, no one capable of saving that which was already lost.

"I will never say that word, Ba," Lao K said. "I like 'to go' better. It means there can be a return."

I sighed, placed my hand on the American's shoulder and for the first time, this felt right. She didn't shrug me off, her head still tipped backwards, skin resonant with chlorine.

"Where I live, there's a wide beach without any houses, no people," she said. "When I was a kid, my mother and I would go there at night to count the stars. Have you ever seen a star that falls?" I realized she meant a shooting star: *liu xing*.

"Never in the city," I said. "Only when I was a child in the countryside."

"That makes sense. You need to be paying attention in order to see falling stars and no one is ever paying attention in the city. And there's too much light."

"True," I said. I hated how she spoke as if she had the answer for everything, despite the fact I almost believed her. She still believed in something bigger than this. Yet for that ignorance, I was suddenly, unexpectedly grateful.

"Maybe if we wait, we'll see one."

"Maybe. But what about Li-Ming?"

"Maybe she's looking too," she said. "Maybe she sees them all the time."

"Did she tell you this?"

Lao K shrugged. The cicada chorus died, briefly silent, before resuming its resonant hum.

"What did she tell you?"

"We never talk of stars," she said, and although I didn't believe her, I didn't know what else to ask. Succumbing to the sky, I tilted back my head again and waited. We stayed like this for a while, all those stars staring back at us, but none able to provide what we wanted. What we needed them to tell us. I thought of all the wushu films I watched throughout my life. In every film, as in each of Li-Ming's poems, there was a categorical belief in the impossible. At just this moment in one of those films, the sky would burst with the most brilliant shooting star ever to race across the curve of earth, red-blue flame trailing. Lao K would point and I'd follow her finger's trajectory, trusting it to lead me in the right direction. But we don't live in films or poems. Lao K and I didn't see a shooting star that night, or anything as brilliant. We stood beneath the willow, peeking past its branches, hoping for many minutes the world would give us what we wanted. But what was that? Despite the changes in scenery, the walk from the country to the city to the border to the city again, the grinding of lenses, the birth of a daughter, I hadn't changed. My life was one long dead end pathway, everything I'd hungered for in vain and impossible—a bowl incapable of being filled, a burning star whose light would never reach us on earth. Did Lao K understand this? Is that why she reminded me to look upward, reminded me there was something bigger than my tall, shoulder-hunched frame?

As we walked home, I worried maybe we hadn't waited long enough, but Lao K was already ahead of me, undeterred by this failed lesson in stargazing. She skipped toward the courtyard blocks, her wet hair trailing, leaving an undecipherable script on the pavement.

"Lao K, maybe we need to be more patient," I called to her, but she slipped around the last corner, her moonlit shadow grasping for me then quickly snapping back to her body, retreating.

"We can try again tomorrow." Her words hugged the corner.

"Tomorrow," I repeated. But I didn't want to wait. I paused and tipped my head to the sky again. Thankfully, the stars were still there, blinking from their various distances. I breathed deeply and waited, but—nothing. The more I wanted, the less my life would reach its intended ending.

…Yet the longer I waited, contrarily, the less I believed this. The longer I waited, the longer the sky didn't shower me with shooting stars—or even just one—the more patient I grew. Not much had changed in the sky's map since I was the boy in Cen Cang Yan sitting by the river's edge looking at the same stars, same constellations shifting in identical patterns, same planets rising from the horizon in the same seasons as the year before. I grew taller, lankier. I watched American fighter jets peel open the sky, met a woman, made a child. All this was the way we lived a life, in one version or another, but basically holding to the same premise. What did we expect to change when above us the sky's tapestry remained essentially the same? Why, when everything around us—water, earth, sky, fire—was exactly as it had been since we'd known it, did we want more?

I remembered something Li-Ming taught me, from one of the many books she'd checked out of the National Library—that somewhere these suns we called 'stars' had burned out, that we received their light only millions of years after they died. I took comfort in this: even dead stars remain bright somewhere. Perhaps all that mattered was where we stood relative to them, that we believed their light meant something, was still here with us, after all that time.[51]

Lao K yelled for me, this time followed by Li-Ming's insistent voice. I lowered my head to my chest, but the stars still burned my retina, lingering for a few minutes until I rounded the corner and saw my American daughter and her Chinese mother, my wife, waiting in the doorway.

"Carry me upstairs," Li-Ming requested and although there was much more we needed to say, I gathered her body in my arms, worried suddenly by the lack of weight, how it was easier to lift her now than earlier that afternoon.

"Hurry," Li-Ming said, perhaps also sensing how much smaller she'd become, how now I was the one shouldering her gravity, carrying us home.

[51.] I once read a report that the biggest stars in the universe were the brightest, but these luminescent stars would also die fastest, their own fiery energy consuming them in the end. The smaller the star, the longer its life, the lesser its burn.

The Last Letter?

Can a room feel like a room when you can't see the walls?
In blackness, I stand,
brush cobwebs off shoulders, thighs,
pluck from my fingers:
the last belching operatic note sung above an empty stage.
But I cannot. See. Anything.
I see blackness.
So I suppose I see SOMETHING.[52]
But nothing and something are the same, aren't they?
Isn't no-thing a thing too?
"No one knows I'm sitting here alone," I speak Cold Mountain.
My mother and father are nowhere—I stumble forward, turn
on a light and: *aha!*
On the counter: Porcelain plates (painted blue carp alighting
edges),
catfish fried in a pan,
coveted eyes gauged with a chopstick,
smattered oil on table,
plastic chairs askew, abandoned for—where?
Warbled loudspeakers: silent;
shuffling feet: stilled;
Where am I?
Apartment windows blackened with tar,
Mocking my core: black.
How long until they forget me? Forgive?

*

[52.] Here Li-Ming used the word "wu" for "thing," or "substance," which is a hom-
onym in Chinese with the word "nothing" (also "wu," but in the rising tone).
Wu: Thing. Wu: Nothing. Rising. Falling. Going up, we are nothing. Coming
down, we have gravity, a form.

A thunderclap and the People's Daily on the kitchen table, inspired by an unhinged window, fans to a story about a boy who saved his grandmother from drowning in their farm's sinkhole. The grandmother was drowning in shit! And her grandson saved her. How utterly heartwarming.

Don't you understand? Many years ago I lost my best friend. It took me as long to read your dense, mellifluous poetry, make it comprehensible to the point it lost all meaning. We are no closer to understanding! I write letters, like this, in the hope I will thank you for handing me these words. The words survive. If you don't. If I don't. The rest have turned their backs. Over time, rain will wash away the tar and my view of the city will turn from black to gray to a yellow-tinged ecru the sheen of eggshells or abandoned bones. No one will remember my window was once black, that I lived in darkness so deep even ants and rats clung to the walls for fear they'd succumb—to what? A world without light is still a world.

Night has a way of quieting even the loudest noises—Lao Wang's cooking (slamming pots and woks and chopsticks and cleavers—does he hate to cook or just need to make shrill every undesired task?), then his nightly snores, Xiaofei chewing on her fingernails like a red squirrel, Lao K belching after a night gulping beer at Old Wu's restaurant with its infinite rows of mirrored walls. We ignored the signs because we needed to—don't we all?—but Lao K was unraveling[53]; and us: a cancerous family who'd devour any healthy specimen who entered our home.

[53.] "What was your favorite book as a young girl?" Li-Ming asked me as I continued snipping her hair, now almost complete to her forehead. Her scalp showed through in white patches, the way sunlight pours through a tree. "*Anne of Green Gables*," I answered in English, unsure how to translate the title. "I don't know this book," Li-Ming said. I said, "No, I don't think it's well-known in China." "Is it poetry?" "No," I laughed—the silly girlhood stories set on the coast of Canada would surely seem frivolous to Li-Ming and her serious life full of *ku* and *ke lian*. "Then why did you like it?" she asked. "It was from a simpler time," I said. "Before cars, television." "Ah yes, a simpler time! That's what this is about too," Li-Ming said, brushing stray hairs from off her shoulder and shaking her head,

Which meant it was time to show her your books. I brought her to Rending Lake Park. They do not practice there the way we once did beneath the Scholar Tree, but this was the closest we'd come to the patience we attempted in the back of Teacher Liang's musty classroom. We had to believe in something Great because Great had become Mundane.

Now they tell me they want to take me to the hospital; Lao Wang insists there's one more treatment. He asked my elder cousin to send funds from Meiguo because it's too expensive for my pension and Lao Wang's combined to cover.

I'm going to find you, even if it kills me (which, given my condition these days, it very well may). We'll climb the long, slow path up Cold Mountain together. We'll fingertip trace cave-drawn words, live off herbs and brush, find solace in the darkness of a place forever untouched by sunlight. I have gone completely astray in this life of motherhood and mailing box counting and cooking and cleaning and—where are you? I imagine you're there, waiting for me, watching from the cliffs with the serenity of a bird, knowing you can fly to the next crest with one lift of your wings. Soon enough, I'll take the long train south to find you on your perch. To return to the place, the time, that mountain, where we began.

---

now empty of longer locks. "That's where we're the same." Of course Li-Ming never read Anne of Green Gables, never traveled by car alone, like I did three years later, to the reddened cliffs of Prince Edward Island, and contemplated a jump. What would've been the ending to this story if an Arabian horse, meandering from its pasture, hadn't judged me with an albino eye, caused me to retreat from the edge? One of my favorite passages from that book Li-Ming never read is a scene where Anne and her friends re-enact the story of Lancelot and his lovelorn Elaine, but they don't get the color of her right. "So ridiculous to have a redheaded Elaine," Anne says.

The hair, no that wasn't right. Ridiculous!

Li-Ming would agree: when we play a role, we must get the hair right.

Baba

Time: convex and purple, the shifting of sun in the same angle morning and evening—but this is the rising sun and that's the setting sun and here's a body on its side, incapable of breathing. Breath: a poet may call it life's earliest, most impulsive art.

It's time, my brother Doufu said. He was a patient shadow in our house for weeks, watching as my wife withered into her smallest form, worried none of us sensed the inevitability destructing her. When Li-Ming reached for notebook and pen, he'd slap her wrist. "There isn't time for that," he'd say and she'd roll her eyes, take the deepest breath she could, and retort, "If there isn't *time* for this, I'd rather there's *time* for nothing." She meant: *I'd rather be dead.* But she wouldn't speak that word in our presence so we tiptoed around her; the sharpening of pencils, the chewing on pen tips. We didn't ask what she was writing; there wasn't time for questions.

On an evening when the seasons shifted from hot to hottest, I came home from work, my fingers sore and scented by sparked glass. My brother stood outside our apartment's entranceway smoking a cigarette and ashing it into our first floor neighbor's potted plants. I'd never seen him smoke, nor had he ever been so brash about where he discarded his refuse.

"You smoke? Since when?"

He ignored me, flicking the butt to the ground where he squelched it with the rubber heel of his sneaker. He cleared his throat then spit a neat globule of mucus on the cement between us. He said, "It's time."

I rolled my eyes. "Time for what? Yes, I could use a trip to the bathhouse. I stink. It's time for that." I mock whiffed my armpit.

"Fool. It's time for Li-Ming to go now."

"Go where?"

"Jishuitan."

Jishuitan: the corner of two streets that became the name of a city neighborhood that became the hospital where my wife would receive her final treatment. Funny, but it was my wife who would remind me: Naming things is what makes them tangible. Naming things makes them impossible to lose. Naming things takes an expanding pool of water at the center of the city and makes it a hospital: 积水潭.

"Come upstairs," my brother said, waving me to follow and for the first time I saw the jaundiced cheeks of a man who'd been a smoker his whole life. What else hadn't I seen until this moment? What had I missed?

I followed his oversized body as it plodded upward, marveling at how differently we were shaped. We were the last two Wang men with mismatched statures, footsteps that couldn't match a beat. Despite our shared ancestry, I should've hated him for telling me what to do, for reminding me of Jishuitan. I should've asked him to return to Shanghai on the next train. To stay out of our lives. But how could I? In truth, he filled the gap of my inabilities, aligning Li-Ming's pill bottles on the kitchen table each morning, reading the instructions and doling out her allotted dose. When the girls asked questions, he always had an answer whereas I would simply stare at them, dumbfounded by the summer red blossoming on their cheeks, how perfectly their tongues formulated language. Since I carried Li-Ming up the stairs after Xiaofei's diving meet, my head and mouth lost connectivity. Communication wasn't needed. I needed sleep. And water. And time.

My brother unlocked the apartment door and led me into my own home. He still smelled of smoke, an awkward a scent on him. He draped a cool, wet washcloth over Li-Ming's forehead; she looked like a traveler in a desert who had stopped by an oasis waiting for the sun to set.

"Li-Ming," I said, beginning my usual replaying of the day's events, a ritual we began weeks earlier when doctors required she stay inside. "I'm home from work. Did you hear what Mrs. Xu said about the neighborhood council? They want to ban automobiles from parking in the courtyard."

Li-Ming pretended to sleep, white crescents showing between eyelids. I should have slipped into bed beside her and slept away the days indefinitely, judging time's passing by the sun's shadows sliding over the canvas of our bodies. A valiance in giving up, in withdrawing from the world as it's lived, cocooning yourself in a den of your own making.

"It's time," my brother reminded me.

"Time?" I asked.

"Time for Jishuitan."

I laughed. *Time for Jishuitan* sounded like a Hong Kong movie title.

"Not funny," my brother said. Why was he always serious? Had he inherited my mother's temperament? Was she a serious person the evening I found her crouching on a corner outside Big World, waiting for us while we explored the Hall of Mirrors, licking her fingers then smoothing my hair, whistling a tune I didn't know? Was she a serious person when her head leaned into mine on the walk back from Ba Jin's film, whispering about the ways of the storks downstream, how best to avoid their clutch? When her arms waved to me from the river and I couldn't decipher if she was drawing me closer or shooing me back? I couldn't hear her voice or sketch the exact details of her face. Was she the one I needed to save at the river or someone else? Li-Ming nearly drowned. I hadn't saved her. Who was it that bore her to the air, made her whole again so this story could be constructed out of snippets of conversation and memory and photograph and one day, we would crouch beneath the futon, pulling the pages like a loose sting of yarn, eager to find the unraveling's inner core? I couldn't trust my mind any more than I could believe Mrs. Xu's gossip. Time created a tunnel and while the picture at the end was always the same, as the years progressed, the tunnel grew in scope, altering my view of the ending, making that which once seemed large and real, look distant, unreliable. My fingers, I thought, looking to my hands, were still Cen Cang Yan large, still bore the bulbous, knotted roots of a country boy.

"Tell the girls," my brother said. "I'll ready Li-Ming's things." He busied himself in the kitchen, transferring boiled water to canteens and whistling a song I didn't recognize. Maybe we were all actors in a film called *Time For Jishuitan*. What was my role?

The actor playing me nodded, but the hallway between the living room and the bedroom was longer than I remembered. Too many clothes left to dry on the wires strung between the walls: Xiaofei's starched underwear with tiny blue flowers coloring the edges, Li-Ming's abandoned padded bras, my brother's only other pair of pants frayed at the hem, Lao K's sweat-stained gym socks.

From the back bedroom, light seeped beneath the door-frame, pooling yellow. The girls whispered. I could push open the door and there they'd sit, thigh-to-thigh on the twin beds they'd pushed together, slumped over Li-Ming's camera which Lao K would explain to Xiaofei and Xiaofei would pretend to listen be-cause we were already into the long, slow progression of months during which Xiaofei stopped listening to anyone, fully recoiled into herself, like one of those fluffy rodents on the CCTV-9 pro-grams Li-Ming loved to watch. Loved. Then. There was time then for watching television programs about adorable rodents. Time to wait for the shifting evening light. Time to sit at the kitchen table undisturbed by the loudspeaker announcements or the egg vendor on the street or Xiaofei's colicky cries from the back room or—what was there was time for? Time: a slippery fish caught outside the Forbidden City's moat. We watched as she writhed in our palms, eye examining us—or pleading an unheard prayer?—while the knife pulled across the scaled, metallic skin, revealing an unexpected, thriving pink.

If only I could give that door an honest, patient push. My finger quivered.

Li-Ming's wheezing stalled me, made the girls notice my heavy breathing on the other side of the door, how it sounded like I was gasping for breath when really I was trying not to turn from the actor playing me to the man I'd always been.

"*Ba?* What do you want?"

The door nudged open and Lao K stood there in her sweat-pants from her private high school with an angry phoenix on the pant thigh. She listened to her portable cassette player. Xiaofei was at her desk, frantically scribbling the English words for:

haphazardly

profoundly

eloquence

With Lao K's presence, Xiaofei's English advanced a form, much to Li-Ming's pleasure. This also gave the girls shared words we didn't understand. On the bed where Xiaofei sat, the blankets were askew, pillows dented from the previous night's sleep—the entire room like a dormitory (books stacked, magazines splayed open on the floor, dirty socks balled beneath the bed). When had I last entered this space? Months, if not longer, and Li-Ming was bedridden for weeks. The room smelled like the only space in the apartment occupied by a human presence. Lao K tapped her foot to a beat bursting from her headphones.

"What do you want, *Ba?*"

Xiaofei still didn't look up—I'd been invisible to her for weeks.

Lao K reluctantly peeled the headphones off her ears. She looked at Xiaofei, who was still hunched over her homework.

"Give me a minute," Lao K said.

"Okay," I complied, standing in the doorway.

"No," she clarified. "One minute alone."

"Xiao-Xiao," I said, waiting for my daughter to turn. She didn't.

"One minute," Lao K said and before I could protest, she shut the door.

I didn't know what happened in that bedroom in the minute that followed, but it felt like much more time had passed when the door finally slipped open and Lao K shook her head as if she was not surprised I was still there. The kettle had cooled enough not to squeal, my brother was awake and fully dressed, and Li-Ming was not wheezing but had a look of patient certitude on her face from her beizi-laden bed.

Xiaofei was emboldened, gathering books into a bag, finding her sneakers, and a canteen bottle filled with warm water (whether this was for her benefit or her mother's, I didn't know). Lao K looked into the main room, her long bangs shielding her eyes from my view but somehow she saw everything she needed.

"You're bringing the book?" It was my wife's voice. A voice I hadn't heard so decongested for months. Who was the woman buried beneath all these layers for so long? The overstuffed beizi, the woolen shawl, the sweater vest, the long-sleeved cotton turtleneck, the first, then second, then third layer of skin subsuming further levels of fat, tissue, intestine: my wife. I knew her as my wife. And that was her voice.

The girls didn't seem startled by her voice's return, the first voice Xiaofei ever heard.

"Are you bringing the book?" Lao K asked.

Xiaofei looked up from tying her shoes. "Yeah, Ba, are you bringing the book?"

I wanted to act coy—this was my final jurisdiction as a father, the last time I'd act authoritative. I wanted to say: "the book is hu-li-hu-tu, this idea of going to Jishuitan is hu-li-hu-tu—why don't we forget everything and go to Rending Lake Park for the afternoon, and get lime icicles from the Xinjiekou stores?"

But I said: "Yes, I'm bringing the book."[54]

[54.] As Feng-kan, a friend of Han Shan, wrote: "Reality has no limit so anything real includes it all."

"Good," Lao K nodded.

My wife made a happy sound, a pigeon in a puddle.

"Now it's really time," my brother affirmed from the living room.

I joined him there.

"Your hand," Li-Ming's directorial voice scratched, returning to its more recent pitch. She reached toward the widest spot on my palm where a collection of scars crisscrossed, thin white paths across a valley landscape—like in Lu Xun's story, *My Old Home*, that ends with the thought the earth didn't have roads until men, collectively, passed along the way, leaving trails for others to follow. I wanted to know: How would we find our way home when we'd never been there together? But Li-Ming simply said, "Give me."

I gripped her warm, unscathed palm.

"Time," she said and even though it was past evening, I looked to the clock on the wall, the same clock since her parents' days in the apartment, the clock we used to judge the shifting of seasons, the raising of a daughter, the relative distance between who we were now and what we believed then. We lifted her body from its sunken shape, wrapped her in Xiaofei's childhood beizi with its white cranes alighting to distant hillsides, and carried her downstairs, as gingerly as an antique chair.

"Xiaofei, take your mother's shoulders. Lao K, hoist her legs," my brother directed. He and I took charge of Li-Ming's midsection, surely the heaviest, all that flesh and digestion and heart.

At the bottom of the staircase, we placed Li-Ming on the stoop. She slumped forward and Lao K sat beside her, propping her against her own long torso. My brother unlocked Lao K's bicycle and I readied the other bicycle with the back cart attached—the same vehicle on which we brought the American to our home two seasons earlier. We hoisted Li-Ming one last time, positioning her on the cart by leaning her against the wooden lip at the back, her daughters acting as sentries.

I only then realized I still wore my nighttime shorts.

"I need to go upstairs," I told the group.

"We have to go now," my brother insisted.

Li-Ming's chin was to her chest. For once, she wasn't spirited enough to protest.

"I forgot something," I said, ignoring the pleas of my daughters—*Ba, it's time to go... There isn't time for forgotten things....*

I jogged upstairs, jostled the key in the lock, three times to open—always the same!—and rummaged in the back bedroom for a pair of pants, retired until autumn. But who was I kidding? This wasn't about pants. This was about that book. Where had Li-Ming put it? I was suddenly inspired to burn the thing as Li-Ming had herself attempted.

I found the book tucked beneath Li-Ming's pillow. This was the first time I'd held the book in decades—not since Li-Ming first showed it to me on the train to my father's house and I traced the verses she'd copied, told her she should never write such gibberish because writing poetry was the same as telling lies.

What rubbish! I shouted to the big, empty room. My wife's life was ending because she believed in things too easily destroyed, irrelevant. But what was I to do but play along, wait for the next scene? This was always as it had been—the shadow puppet behind a screen, the voice not mine shouting "North! North!" or the hands digging in a breast pocket for a thimble I'd think was mine but would one day be burned in a courtyard fire, smelted for a fingernail of scrap metal. Whose story begins where and how are we to turn the page when we're not the ones penning the final verse? I tucked the book into the waistband of my pants and jogged downstairs.

The girls waited on the back of the bicycle cart. My brother stood astride Lao K's bike and was smoking again.

"You're smoking," I said.

"Yes. Can you pedal three women all the way to Jishuitan?"

"Sure," I said, but my legs were useless: bony and frail. Three women behind me: one old man at the helm. An illogical proposition, a challenge of strength beyond measure. I wanted to accept the trial, to prove I could pedal us the final kilometer along the uneven hutong alleyways, jangling over potholes, past frightened pigeons scuttling out of our path as fast as their stout legs allowed. I was only one man but I needed the strength to move four bodies. I stood on the pedals, pressed all my weight atop the contraption, edging the bicycle forward. We rolled backward a few centimeters.

"Ba, let me push us to start," Lao K offered.

"No need." I leaned forward again, but we rocked backward half a meter. The book, still in my waistband, jabbed my skin like the elbow of a child.

"Ba, we're not going anywhere," Xiaofei complained.

"Relax. All of you relax."

"Yeah, Ba, let me push us." Lao K's voice rose above her sister's. Together, they grew more confident than either alone, in the way many half-decent singers, when joined, comprise a pleasant choir.

"Okay," I relented. "You push us to start." She was the stronger of my daughters, and she was right—we weren't going to go anywhere without a nudge.

Lao K hopped off and Doufu joined her, the two of them rocking the cart and my bicycle back and forth while I pushed the pedals forward until I was able to gather enough speed to keep the wheels rolling.

"Jump on!" I shouted and Lao K sprinted to catch us. Xiaofei extended a hand, launching her onto the wooden platform with a thud.

"You okay?" I turned but the girls shouted: "Keep pedaling! Don't turn around!"

The book chafed my waist, sharp angles jabbing bone.

Li-Ming's noisy breathing was finally masked by the jangling of the cart's loose wheels and rusted axles, car horns honking at cluttered intersections, pigeons whistling through the air above and the sky now so black it seemed the stars had retired, retreated to their dark homes, afraid—of what? That their glimmering brightness may be seen, relied upon?

My daughters didn't know I'd once scaled mountain paths with these legs, scrambled loose rocks above a golden desert, saved a crane, rescued a prisoner of war, built an empire of glass. They didn't care. They laughed at the insanity of this scene and the laughter kept my legs moving, heart racing, my breath—that breath. What else is there to do in life but breathe? Li-Ming's head bobbed like a doll's as the cart chattered around corners and down the narrow hutongs we'd known all our lives. We couldn't stop any of this: we hurtled past the busy Deshengmen intersection—that Gate of Victorious Triumph under which so many armies claimed a win—past the lamb kabob and roasted sweet potato vendors calling from behind plumes of smoke. *Three potatoes for two kuai! The juiciest lamb in Beijing!* We encircled the old city wall aglow with green lights in celebration of the summer. Who wanted to save the city wall, Li-Ming? Was it you who taught me that lesson? Before I could ask, we rolled downhill, our city aslant, wheels gaining speed without effort, as we raced over the bridge crossing the ancient city moat on our way to Houhai Park and its metal fishing boats rocking on loose moorings, those bobbing clown-faced ducks, then turning into crowded Xinjiekou with its street-side shops shuttered after evening hours, passengers clustered around bus stops, impatiently awaiting a ride home.

"Turn right, Ba! Right!" I couldn't decipher which girl yelled, but I leaned into the brakes and maneuvered the handlebars to the hospital rising patiently on the horizon. In the last stretch, we careened around courtyard walls of siheyuan homes closing in around us as the road narrowed, a lone slivered moon struggling to be seen between tree shadows, loose strands sticking like spider webs to our hair, ears, shoulders. What were we escaping?

We pressed on. We pressed on without stopping to tilt our heads to the sky. I lied, I thought. I was wrong. Can you hear me, Old Man? The book jabbed my hip—paper spine to calcified bone. Poets will remember this. Musicians will sing of this. But my girls, 不, they were laughing the laughter of the insane, because what choice is there but to seek humor in a late night bicycle race toward a hospital named for a growing 'pool of water'?

I opened my throat, expelled a laugh that frightened a pair of doves roosting in the dragon-encrusted hutong eaves. The birds flapped vigorously to lift their heavy bodies into flight—I knew exactly how those birds felt. Even in my dreams I swam through air as if it had mass, like invisibility could buoy us. What a waste. As I laughed louder, a bicyclist attempted to pass, his stout body rocking forward, arms waving—ta ma de, I realized: my brother! For a moment, he looked like my mother—as solid and confident as the day she walked to the river's edge. He'd always be like her and I would be—who was I again?

My brother waved his hands in my face: "Slow down!"

Xiaofei, the practical daughter, brought feeling to my feet: "Ba, how will you stop?"

"Lao Wang, slower!" Li-Ming demanded, her words dense as zhou.

Why stop? I wanted to pedal and pedal, the strength of my once-young legs leading us to that destination we couldn't see but knew was there on the edge of a map, the border of a neighborhood lined in leafy trees, the far corner of a street you loved to trace its lines with a finger, a kiss.

But my body obeyed the commands, heels digging into the pedals, wheels skidding abruptly, cart leering forward then settling to earth in a heaving sigh. The girls' laughter turned into cautious, exasperated huffs. No one moved.

Finally, my brother, acting in his assigned role, offered a hand to Lao K. She stood slowly, shaking blood into her legs, then took Xiaofei's hand and the three of them then finagled arms beneath

Li-Ming's body, shimmying her to the edge of the cart.

"Brother, the wheelchair," Doufu instructed.

Although my hands steadily gripped the bicycle's handlebars, although they'd blistered from the journey, they carefully peeled away. My body took over as my mind cautiously followed. The wheelchair my brother had the foresight to load onto the cart happily snapped into form and the three of them positioned Li-Ming into its seat. As I pushed her toward the hospital, a nurse jogged from the entrance and pried my grip, wheeling my wife into the golden light of the lobby as we stood in the courtyard, our breath catching up to our lungs, eyes watching, watching and waiting, but for what exactly, we didn't know. We couldn't name this yet.

"Lao Wang," my wife turned at the doorway and the nurse slowed her wheelchair to a stop. I saw my wife's face but it was like looking at my own face atop a watery surface.

"I'm sorry," I said, because it seemed the most reasonable thing to say under such circumstances and I hadn't formally acknowledged the guilt—how I had wanted to burn the book, how I wanted to turn back time, how I didn't want to bring her to an end she couldn't rewrite.

"Don't be sorry," she said. "This isn't your fault and besides, this isn't the end."

If this wasn't the end, I didn't understand why my fingers were feeling their way to the last pages, sensing the closing of this papery clutch around me like the sun tipping over the sky's dome, bringing with it the inevitability of

dusk

/dawn

dusk

/dawn

dusk

/dawn

"Keep reading," she said, nodding at the book that nudged its way out from under my shirt.

I ran my fingers through the pages, only then realizing the core of the book was carved out, replaced with hand-written and typed papers where the words of Li-Ming's favorite poet were once bound.

"What am I supposed to do with this?" I asked, but the attending nurse, with a nod to the front door, insinuated our time had passed. There wasn't a clock on the wall to announce the turning of seconds into minutes. Not a sun in the sky to peel shadow lengths from trees and park benches. No magpies tweeting a familiar song or the smell of soap on our fingers or the remnant hot glass beneath our nails. What was I to do with the ten thousand things we'd misplaced between then and now/here and there? There was nothing by which to judge what was happening as I opened the spine and the pages tripped over one another in an ambivalent Gobi wind. From the north. In the summer.

Autumn in Beijing falls like a knife slicing a pig ear—

I distantly remembered another scene like this—how desperate I was to collect words in my palms, how deeply I believed holding on to something you once loved meant love would last forever, never spoil or turn to air or dusk or this—

I looked to my hands and saw only a broken sun, a damned, irreversible dawn.

The Last Letter

Dear friend,

I looked out the window like you reminded me before you left, before the book was lost and before I made a mess of my life on account of not being brave enough to do the opposite. I know you wanted me to see everything—the shape of aspen leaves fanning the breeze, that same breeze lifting a young girl's hairs off her sour milk forehead, a grandfather limping beside her who combed his thinning wig with camphor oil and how I remembered that tangy smell from my own grandfather, how being close to him singed my eyes and made me cry. How the buses let out the sick and elderly climbing the hospital stairs, bemoaning the state of their bodies. How time was the only thing we battled. And gravity. How I knew what it was like being in pain. How buoyant I felt when that pain subsided, if only because of an opiate drip, the slow release of a tablet a nurse placed on my tongue, how bitter it tasted, how sweet too. How life was comprised of so many equal and reverse opposites and how for every life there had to be a death. I think they call it "entropy," but I never did finish physics class, was punished for my poetry and sent down to the Jiangxi farms before I understood the physical rules governing everything we believe certain on earth.

If the girl hadn't stepped back from that roof along that Beautiful Country coast, if I hadn't tugged on her shirtsleeve and reminded her to look to the sky before the fall, would I be sitting here writing you? Would you be reading this? Does a butterfly's flexed wing cause you, three thousand kilometers away, to itch your thigh?[55] Someone set a pendulum swinging over the Japanese sand gardens Lao Wang loved to visit in People's Park—until it rained and the patterns blurred, soggy and nonsensical, a pile of mush. Nature wins. Thank the heavens: *nature will win.*

When Doctor Gang looked at me (eyes squinting, lips pursed, tongue pressing the inner cave of her cheek) and said the words I expected to hear ("three months, if you're lucky,") I already knew: Find you. You, I realized, were the only person who could save me from myself. Who could explain to everyone around me why I had to resurrect their stories to preserve my own. Why my husband's thimble turned to an amber comb turned to nothing. Why he could never tell a story the same way twice. Why I was protector and destroyer of the truth all at once. What did they call the path to Han Shan? Laughable? Haha. My underwater laugh.

But I didn't find *you.* I only found *her.*

She reminded me of you at first—even though the two of you, empirically speaking, look nothing alike (where Lao K is tall, you were short; where Lao K is broad-shouldered, you were slight; where Lao K is auburn-haired, you were black haired... and so on). But you are the same in the way two trees don't have the same height or shaped leaves but produce a pleasantly mingled scent in spring. And I love her the way I loved you those years ago, the way only women love one another: violently. When she showed up with her lanky limbs, her head in the clouds, I knew: Another one of us! Lao Wang lost his way, but he was like Lao K once. Only Xiaofei is the grounded one, born without a vision of the world within this one. Sometimes I wonder if my daughter's really mine—it's a tragedy we birth children so differ-

---

[55] This morning, from a *New York Times* report on theoretical physics: two particles separated by immense distances still feel the pulse of one other, are so entangled that the action of one instantaneously influences the other. In quantum entanglement, there's no individual body but an entire state of being whereby every object within the system is tied, energetically, to the whole. But as soon as we measure an individual particle, the entire system collapses, severing signals, disconnecting a connectivity as of yet beyond our comprehension.

ent from ourselves. I'm sure my mother would've agreed if I'd ever the courage to ask her.

But in the end, the American wasn't enough: I still needed to find you.[56]

From Jishuitan Hospital that afternoon after Doctor Gang's pronouncement, I bicycled to your family's apartment overlooking Houhai Lake, skipping a meeting with the Deshengmen Council for Preparedness during which I was to give a speech about "Postal Safety in Today's City."

I trounced up the three floors to your old sun-laden apartment, found your home smelling of freshly-sautéed jinjiang rousi as soon as I opened the door, reminding me what it was like to be a child, to crave sweet-soyed pork. All your siblings chattered in their back bedroom; your home so utterly different from my own. Mine: a quiet vestibule like a temple's inner sanctum where I tiptoed around the broken edges of my parents' unhappiness, their inability to sire a troop of children; yours, the vibrant marketplace of a village where everyone was related and spoke in the same pitched, humming accent only they together understood.

"I knew it," I imagined you said. You painted your lips for the occasion, rimming the broad outline with a deeper mulberry. And when you said, "I knew it," I knew you weren't referring to the sickness chewing holes into my breasts, but to the fact eventually I'd find a reason to climb Cold Mountain. I didn't care about the figurative. I'd spent my life scaling linguistic cliffs carved by a man long dead. I wanted to touch the cold stone walls, shuffle bare feet along dusty earth. I wanted to probe my fingers, unpeeling layers of rock, sand. Wanted to know what was behind this artifice, the hardest, yet most futile facade. I wanted you to lead me there.

---

56. In the blackness, you can't see your hands but that's of no matter—mine are blistered and raw from holding on too long, attempting to clamor my way to an ending: hers, not yet mine. An ink moon surveys the scene and although the park's peonies have faded from pink to gray, there's the faint scent of living things that reaches me on the hillside as I pick scabs from my palms, trying to find the right words to say farewell. *Hello, Moon... Good-bye.*

"How could you possibly know?" I asked my long-lost friend. You invited me to the room where we first saw butterflies burst from a chrysalis your mother cared for, the pod still tethered to a shelf on the deck. You served chrysanthemum tea in a pink porcelain mug (one you bought on the streets of Paris from a bald, toothless vendor who fell in love with you at first sight, like all men). A sunspot I hadn't noticed beckoned browner on the outer frame of your cheek, the shape of a hog's head. We're older than we realize, we said, laughing, time pulling a moat of light across the floor. I pointed out your sunspot, rubbed it like a stain on a shirt, expecting friction to erase the mark, but it wouldn't disappear. How could it? I looked up and you recognized the emergence of my elderly self. We would grow old together because that's how time works.

When did you become me and I you? Where did we lose each other?

So you'd apologize, hearing questions I hadn't asked, wiping a drip of tea from the back of my hand, shaking your head, and reminding me of the time we sat in this same room when you braided my hair, how this was the first time I understood why bodies yearn to be close, why we never fully inhabit anyone else, no matter how much we love them.

"You'll understand one day too," you said, tickling my shoulders with your fingertips as they finished the braid, causing the buds of my breasts to tick like roasted beans beneath my shirt. Your mouth was close to my ears and I wanted you to press your cheek to mine but you stood there, radiating an unfamiliar heat from my shoulders to the deepest trench between my legs, accordioning my bowels.

"We'll chase each another forever, like the sun wraps around the horizon. Always returning," you said in the book of my misremembering.

"But does it?"

A spit bubble on your lower lip reminded me we were human, unpainted and raw as the inner fruit of winter melons. I didn't understand how words could become air and then fingers typing on a typewriter, then sound (hammer slapping page!), then paper and someone else's thoughts. See! We live on typewriters like this. Pages I hammer like chiseled stone with my fingertips and leave on the windowsill beside my bed for the girl to retrieve. Pages I write with a blunted pencil, strokes trailing too early. This is how it begins, I think, but just as quickly stamp that thought below my bloated, tired feet with the advent of another thought: Maybe there *is* something more. Maybe we are too stupid to see it with our eyes.

And in that long-buried apartment not yet forced to rubble, you walked me to the edge of the sun deck where the butterfly flapped wings against pale, dusty glass. Holding out a hand, the butterfly emerged, settled on your pinky, an old friend elated by the visit.

"Before we were who we are now, we were eggplants and cauliflower our parents ate, and before that, we were rain sprinkling that field beyond the city, clouds gathering between valleys, that sun setting like a firestorm over a horizon so far and yet so near we think we can touch it."

Your slender fingers, the butterfly-less hand, kneaded my shoulders, vined words climbing these outer walls, curling between brick and glass and making ropes of strands of cells, and finally, I understood: I'll begin with this and end with it too.

I recited for you the Cold Mountain poem about living in the clouds, the one to which we turned when we teetered upon the ineffable.

You laughed, loosening your grip.

"My old friend Huang Li-Ming," you said, like we were in fact old. In truth, we were almost, we just couldn't see it yet, still believed we were as young as our girlhood bodies could ever be. "Remember the day we sat on the moat outside Zhongnanhai using fishing rods we made from string, pins, and branches, placed raisins on the hooks, and waited for hours to catch a fish?"

"Of course." There were few days I remembered so clearly. Although all I truly remembered was the exact second the bite snagged the line and we were pulled forward off our bony asses into the moat's murky, lotus-laden waters. Flailing in the shoulder-deep moat, we didn't let go of the line, pulling the struggling fish closer, arms scooping rapidly as if our lives depended on the catch, our fingers wrapping the carp's fat head, both of us kicking to shore, the fish gasping too as our mouths opened to the sky, hair slick against heads.

Here, now: the fish's scaly breast within my palms, a carbonated mouthful of the moat's warm, summer water, slippery grass between my toes as we climbed the wall, beaching ourselves like sea creatures, waiting for the sun to score us dry. We were just children, too young for our minds to wrap around our hearts like weeds to the trunk of a tree. We didn't have time to recollect the moments we'd someday remember so clearly as if they were happening all the time, even within the lives of those we loved, those we'd left behind.

But what had we remembered and what was rewritten to cord the yarn, to find seamlessness where everything is broken into shards?

Which is why I ask you now: send me away. Send me to the farthest reaches of the world, to the girl on that other shore, to the daughter who wasn't mine. Send me so that I may fly the circumference of earth, however small, however large. If I'll fit in a pineapple cookie tin (our favorite flavor!), that would be best. And please ensure the postage comes with a China Post guarantee, one of the peony stamps we loved as children. I've seen how the Post treats packages so I expect dents and bruises, but I also expect, like all shipments that passed through my offices, to make it to my final destination.[57]

[57.] I recall the first and last day of her undoing in stages:

Sweaty eggshells I rolled atop the kitchen table as Baba swept the floor, motioning for me to drop the empty carcasses so he could add them to the pile. I tossed a warm, velvety egg into my mouth, tongued the chalky yolk.

Hao ah, hao ah, he said, egging me on. *Good. Good.*

I waited at the kitchen table for Baba to leave, pretending I had a later-than-usual class that day and could stay home with Li-Ming for a few hours to read to her, make her sweet zhou for lunch.

Li-Ming pretended to sleep on the futon, the Soviet-era apartment around us hot and wet, pickling the skin behind our knees. Sun peeked past the court-yard's listless willows for a glimpse of Li-Ming's swollen, jaundiced face. To signal she was still here, she smiled. She preferred warmth to cold. I wouldn't know of her snowy soap factory days until decades later: those lemony blocks she stockpiled for the People's Revolution that never came, wouldn't know the girl who sat twelve hours a day on a wooden stool and molded her nation's most beloved soaps. That's the terribly destructive problem of meeting someone when they're an adult: you forget they were also once a child.

Chop-chop: Xiaofei on the futon, diligently wushu-hacking her blue note-books with a ruler, a study tic she devised in middle school to ace Calculus—Li-Ming's most loathed subject was of course her daughter's favorite; only years later would I understand how a mother and daughter could be so completely different, why this was a critical reversal of inheritance.

The television was on to dull the pain: a CCTV news exposé on Li Hong-zhi, Falun Gong's founder, explaining how he was responsible for the deaths of thousands of practitioners, who believed by jumping to their deaths, Li would rescue them in their afterlife.

Li-Ming awoke, gestured to turn up the volume.

Shhhhhh, she said with a dry tongue, her words cricket-cracking.

Is anyone listening?

Slip-slap: the door closing behind Baba as he left to clean the mess at his danwei work station two blocks east. The janitorial specter he left behind: broom tilted against the old Beijing-brand television with its warped, multi-colored view of a plane departing for America and the reporter's stoic voice, "Is Li Hongzhi preparing an escape?" Jet engines roared, the broadcast turned to the weather (monsoons in the south; drought in the west where Tibetans in mountainous Yunnan demanded water for fields).

Peering and peering but I can't even see the sky...

"Time for school!"

Li-Ming slapped the bed; Xiaofei readied her book bag. I held up a half-eaten baozi to examine the remainder of my breakfast. What hunger I'd dragged to China was abandoned months earlier; I knew my hipbones poked unnatu-rally through my school-issued blue and white track pants but the less I ate, the less anyone seemed to notice. I took my last bite, the sweet bean innards crawl-ing to an uncomfortable rest below my clavicle.

Xiaofei's only farewell was the clang of her bicycle slapping the stairwell walls as she dragged it down the four flights, each floor's descent a little softer. [I miss bicycle days most, riding beside the Second Ring Road's moat, hur-ried spring hair, forgetting that under this highway sat thousand-year-old walls meant to keep out people like me. In just a decade this city's bicycles were gone: Where did the wheels and ringing bells go? What sounds could replace that metallic song? Cars. Taillights as far as the eye can see.]

Lao K, are you ready?

A ticking rose in my throat as I stood to prepare a lunch of Baba's stir-fried leftovers, as Li-Ming requested weeks earlier, porting them in tin containers to take on our journey to the city's heart. We wouldn't think how foolish it was to eat leftovers for our last meal together, or how we'd look on the subway, Li-Ming in her rusted wheelchair, me pushing her through the crowds, the two of us standing outside the government's impenetrably red, gold-studded doors, stone phoenixes peering down, mocking us in this illustrious attempt to control one's fate. What songs could we sing that would finally be heard? One day, I'd learn the poems, recite them to an empty conference room:

"What's the use of all that noise and money?"

"I pity all these ordinary bones."

Nonsense! Hu-li-hu-tu. 糊里糊涂. Haha! This book of our creating is entirely nonsense.

*

An hour later, after an arduous maneuvering of Li-Ming's wheelchair down the stairs to the Jishuitan subway, after we managed to fool the ticket attendant into thinking I was Li-Ming's medical aide and could ride for free (Li-Ming's final act of frugality awarded), we stood before the gates of a nation for which Li-Ming once sang a chorus.

"This way." I pushed her rusted chariot over buckled ground to our final destination: Jingshan Park. I paid my entry fee—a foreigner's rate of two kuai; Li-Ming, a city resident, could enter for free. The park was mostly quiet save for a few old men sitting on wooden stools, practicing characters in wide, watery strokes on the pavement, first words disappearing before the poem's last verse.

Our final destination: Coal Hill. Where centuries before an empire collapsed and Emperor Chongzhen climbed this mound, a white silk belt tied around his waist. At the top, the white swatch unfurled like a bird in flight, and, with his favorite eunuch Wang Cheng'en by his side, they looped the belt around their necks and closed the Ming Dynasty's grip on the land stretching thousands of li from this central heart. A double suicide. The fall of an empire. The remaining Ming loyalists said a dragon appeared in the sky that night, the emperor's soul ascending—but to where, exactly, the Mings couldn't provide a map.

As we'd planned, I pulled Li-Ming out of her wheelchair and arranged her in my arms so I could carry her up the hill to her final resting place.

She looked up at the tree and although I wanted her to be beautiful, as young as the woman Baba met in a Jiangxi pigsty, I didn't see anything but haggard folds creasing her neck. A goose's neck is firm and taught yet hers was nothing like that—already slack and limp, anticipating the ending she desired: but no, I wanted to tell her, not quite, not yet. We were puppets controlled by a shadowed hand, Li-Ming's pen stronger than it would ever be again.

"Did you know about Chongzhen? Did you study him in your books?" Her voice, suddenly hers to claim, was crinkled, grasshopper legs rubbing within her throat.

"I didn't," I admitted. I never opened a history book that year. I thought being a foreigner in a foreign land was enough. I'd learn years later, when I was a more serious student, that the English word for "foreign" comes from the same Latin root as "forest," foris meaning "outside" or that forbidden place beyond known territories. But here, towering above the concentric walls of the Forbidden City, there weren't any forests as far as the eye could see. Li-Ming was in my arms—her head drooping to my shoulder, eyes half open and peering at a petulant sun on a day so bright and hot it was the opposite of what Chongzhen and his companion saw that night. Her hair had started to sprout in patches on her scalp, persistent weeds in dry soil. Foreign isn't on the outside, I thought. It's what we can't scrape away, can't climb within, can't carve out nor chip away. An immeasurable distance counted by the length of an arm's reach, the core of an atom where space itself comprises the center, the probability of an encounter not yet met, where absence creates matter, where what's unknown, unseen, is actually what's binding everything together, preventing the Great Unraveling.

"Let me walk," Li-Ming said. Her body's weight returned to my arms.

"You're crazy," I repeated Baba's mockery of us.

"As a magpie!" she croaked, the attempt at humor making her body so heavy I needed to place her to the earth. What did it matter if she crawled or I carried her? The old men in the distance had packed their brushes, poetic pavement wiped clean, an empty canvas awaiting words once again.

I allowed Li-Ming to scramble slowly over the rocky ground but she didn't make it more than a meter, stopping on all fours on an outcropping to catch her breath.

"That's enough," I said and she didn't protest so I heaved her body over my shoulder. How she waxed larger and I waned smaller as we trundled upwards, and then how that dead, gnarled, stupid tree could support her weight, how I would find exactly the right indentation on one of the last, stunted limbs, I couldn't imagine. An irony of fate: the heaviest burdens require the lightest spirits. I didn't know the entire story yet—would I ever?—but was naïve enough to believe a dying wish is a dying wish and a dying tree can support the weight of a dying body, no matter how broken and weak the bones.

I placed Li-Ming at the tree, leaning her against the trunk. I retrieved our last meal, Baba's congealed stir-fry, now lukewarm from the journey, and handed her a tin.

"Oh, how stupid of me. I'll feed you." With my chopsticks, I lifted a limp broccoli stem, passed it to her mouth.

Delicious, said her moan said but not her tongue.

In the distance, a car honked, a bus attendant called for willing fares, a child cried for his mother. The city was full of sound and yet here on this strange, empty hillside, we were quiet, listening only to our own swallowing throats. She chewed deliberately, careful not to choke.

"Now we wait," I said. I remembered her instructions—we'd sit here a few hours, she'd recline against the tree, meditating, and then, once night fell and the air cooled, I'd take out the rope, loop it on the sturdiest branch, and send her on her way.

Her body melted against mine, shoulder to shoulder. Where would she go from here? Where would I? As soon as one sits below the Scholar Tree and looks onto the city's hutong mazes, history itself is erased, rewritten, a palimpsest of souls buried and resurrected in this place never anyone's to own. I want to tell the girl: this is where we come to disappear, to sever a story at the very place it's meant to end.

I fell asleep with my hands still on the open tin, a slow leak of oil dappling my favorite jeans, a stain I'd never rub clean. I don't recall the dream I had that afternoon or how it felt to sleep on cool earth, but I remember peeling open my eyes to the sun sliding below the city's horizon, that maze of red and gold rooftops ablaze in the final light.

Her hand was on my shoulder.

Will you go with me?

I nodded, only she hadn't provided me the map.

*

After Emperor Chongzhen and his eunuch Wang Cheng'en's bodies were collected from Coal Hill, fed to dogs or hungry villagers, the victorious Manchu leader, Li Zecheng, entered Desheng Gate, the same wall standing outside the apartment complex Li-Ming knew as home. Passing below Desheng—Attaining Victory—Gate on a thick-legged stallion, Li rode to the city center where he launched an arrow at the Gate of Eternal Peace in a final victory gesture: the cavalry believed if his arrow reached its intended target, peace would reign across the land. But his mark fell short, landing with a dull thud in a moat.

No matter, said the new emperor's advisors, *history is ours to rewrite*.

They declared eternal peace anyway. Perhaps they already knew: The moon is within a finger's grasp, trees can build a skyline, the sky is a dragon, and this, my friend, is your mountain poem, indelible as a song sung in a cave.

Epilogue

A few months after Li-Ming was cremated, Kang-Lin sent me an envelope via my Maine address along with a handwritten letter that began: 'Mama's sarira for Menglian, as Li-Ming requested.' Li-Ming's long-lost friend wrote that she returned a season too late for the funeral. Baba had greeted her at the apartment. He handed her a box. "This is all that's left of her," he said.

Li-Ming's weight in her hands, Kang-Lin said she didn't understand how the liminal could feel so literal. She took Li-Ming's sarira from Baba, the glittering remains that could not turn to ash, insistent the bones once comprising her childhood friend's sturdy frame, her carrot legs, would turn into translucent crystals. As Li-Ming requested in her last letter, Kang-Lin shipped the sarira—Li-Ming's dust—to my hometown in Maine. It arrived on an autumn day when the sky had no end.

I pulled the package out of the mailbox; little did I know this wouldn't be the last missive I'd receive containing Li-Ming's heart, but this first delivery contained a small goldfinch-colored pineapple cookie tin, Chinese children in half-dancing, half-keeled positions. When I hinged open the top, a puff of powder rose. The dust left a crystalized, beady substance lining the golden base, resembling the silica of beach sand but rougher. There, behind the thin sheen, sat my own reflection and an unabashed sun, the strongest we'd feel until spring. Taped underneath the tin was a handwritten note whose penmanship I didn't recognize, a recitation of a Han Shan poem Li-Ming read me at Coal Hill, when the willows were heavy with rain, the scholar tree was stiff as a corpse, and Beijing was the quietest she'd ever be. Despite the fact I was alone, it felt like everyone in the world was listening as I read aloud:

Do you have the poems of Han-Shan in your house?
They're better for you than sutra-reading!
Write them out and paste them on a screen
Where you can glance them over from time to time.

*

Twenty years after Li-Ming's sarira arrived in my mailbox, and two years after receiving this book, I met Kang-Lin for the first time at a Starbucks in Beijing's crowded, neon Wangfujing. She said she shouldn't have sent me the sarira. She cried spritzing tears into her passion fruit iced tea, saying she wasn't sure Li-Ming's sarira was there after all. No, she said, correcting herself like a reformed drunk, there's no sarira in this world. *Look at this world!* She tossed back a thin arm, directing my attention to the flashing lights for a Nike store, a Popeye's Chicken, endless shoppers chatting on their iPhones, heads tilted not to the smoggy sky above but to glowing screens, faces ghoulishly and intensely distracted. What a foolish thing to believe, she said. Sarira. 舍利. Stupid. Truly stupid.

The Wangfujing Starbucks where I met Kang-Lin was the nicest in the city: wicker chairs on the concrete patio, signature green umbrellas still intact and relatively green above sturdy, wrought iron tables. Kang-Lin didn't drink coffee so she ordered iced tea, asking for a porcelain mug instead of a disposable plastic cup ("better for the environment," she'd announced to an ambivalent barista). She was nothing like the woman in Li-Ming's book; her red lipstick more *va-voom* than valiant, her breasts large, yes, but in old age they sagged. She fingered the ice cubes swirling in her cup, dabbed her eyes with the back of her hand. She hadn't taken a sip.

She leaned close enough for me to see her breasts still retained a touch of pertness. For Li-Ming's sake, I was strangely relieved.

"I never told her I was leaving," Kang-Lin said, a shrug of shoulder. "I probably should've written her to let her know but my life in Beijing felt so far away and then, eventually, like it never existed at all."

"I see," I nodded, trying to rectify a past that wasn't mine. But then I thought: if Kang-Lin had written to Li-Ming then this story would never have been written. If that brashly hot Beijing summer she'd written of their poetry outings and whatever it was she was doing in the western provinces then Li-Ming's fantasy and hope would fade into reality: the dull, mundane reality of a Beijing Starbucks on a summer afternoon when the heat of the city festered so long you couldn't see to the second story of the office building behind you, so glittering in its earthy form, so many industrious floors reaching upwards, higher still—a mountain, one may say, if only we could see its shape for the choked, touchable sky.

I thanked Kang-Lin for sharing her story, sending the tin to Maine all those years ago; despite her regret, I was grateful. Leaving behind our teas in sweaty porcelain mugs, we walked to Wangfujing station, the smog-cloaked sun drenching the city in a final blast of warmth, commuters jostling for position along the subway platform where we bid each other farewell with a chesty, hopeful hug before heading in opposite directions of the same line, looking for each other as the cars clicked forward and entered the dark, manmade tunnels illuminated with so much florescent light.

O...

So Han-shan writes you these words
These words which no one will believe.
Honey is sweet; men love the taste.
Medicine is bitter and hard to swallow.
What soothes the feelings brings contentment,
What opposes the will calls forth anger.
Yet I ask you to look at the wooden puppets,
Worn out by their moment of play on stage!
— Cold Mountain

—Lao K, Beijing, 2016

For: Mom and Dad, 妈妈和爸爸

Acknowledgments

To my earliest writing supporters, Mom, Dad, A.J., Buster, and Smokey: you read the poems about snow and spiders and the long-winded stories of bowling alley trips with love and encouragement despite how boring and awful—I suspect this time will be no different and you are now duly experienced. Auntie Grace, thank you for the whimsies of gypsies and mermaids and showing me the world is beautiful in both its smallness and grandeur. I never would've been brave enough to travel to China in 1996 and later become a writer without all your support and love.

To Baba and Chenxi, thank you for the endless bowls of 鱼香茄子, the early morning trips to the 煎饼shop, and, above all, opening your home to me and always treating me, from the moment I stepped off that bus, as family. Your generosity and support gave me a new perspective on the possibilities of not just cross-cultural communication but, more deeply, on how love, acceptance, and knowledge translates beyond language and culture.

To the Smolen family for allowing your son/brother to venture with me to China and Singapore and, despite my inability to remember a punch line or do conceptual math in my head, for encouraging me to continue the Smolen lineage.

To my earliest writing teachers—Mary Lyons, Peter Greer, Al Kildow—thank you for instilling in me a love for the written form and for encouraging my early attempts, no matter how overly wrought.

To my writing mentors, Sarah Shun-lien Bynum, Heidi Durrow, Josip Novakovich, and the kindnesses of so many writers who have read early drafts, chatted over coffee and wine, directed me to a needed book, resource, friend—writers and their craft do not exist in a vacuum and you provided me with the critical support and encouragement to stay an unlikely course.

To the communities and organizations that provided needed support, camaraderie, and on occasion, libations: School Year Abroad, the Let's Go: China team from 1999-2002 (I still need to visit "Hotan"!), the Harvard-Yenching Fellowship, the Fulbright Foundation, the Forum for Chinese-American Exchange at Stanford, Bread Loaf, Disquiet International, USC's East Asian Studies Center, UCSD's MFA program, the UCSD Muir Writing Program, the Vermont Studio Center, and the SF Writers' Grotto.

To Team Hippo: your writing insights, intelligence, and forgiveness (the late night calls with screaming baby in the background) know no bounds.

To the incredibly talented, loving friends who have always believed (even when I didn't) this work would find its final form: thank you for not losing faith and never tiring of asking, "How's the book?"

To *Anne of Green Gables, Immortality, Pilgrim at Tinker Creek, Cold Mountain, Norwegian Wood, Divisidero, Both Sides Now, Magic Mountain, Wake Up Everybody, Holocene,* and many more: thank you for existing in the world and on my shelves/in my ears/lungs.

… and to Joey and Calliope: they say "save the best for last," but I don't know who "they" are and why the best are last because in my mornings, my evenings, and my everything, you are always first and foremost. Thank you for being the first eyes I see in the morning and the last before we succumb to our dreaming selves. You remind me that while publishing this book and bringing this story to readers has been a struggle, there's so much more than literature in this world that's worth adventuring and fighting for. I can't wait for the many shared wonders and journeys to come.

11-2)-17
8-12-21
11 (LNg)